DE E

CALM

Charleston, SC
www.PalmettoPublishing.com

Deceptive Calm

First Edition

Paperback ISBN: 978-1-68515-314-4
eBook ISBN: 978-1-68515-315-1

DECEPTIVE CALM

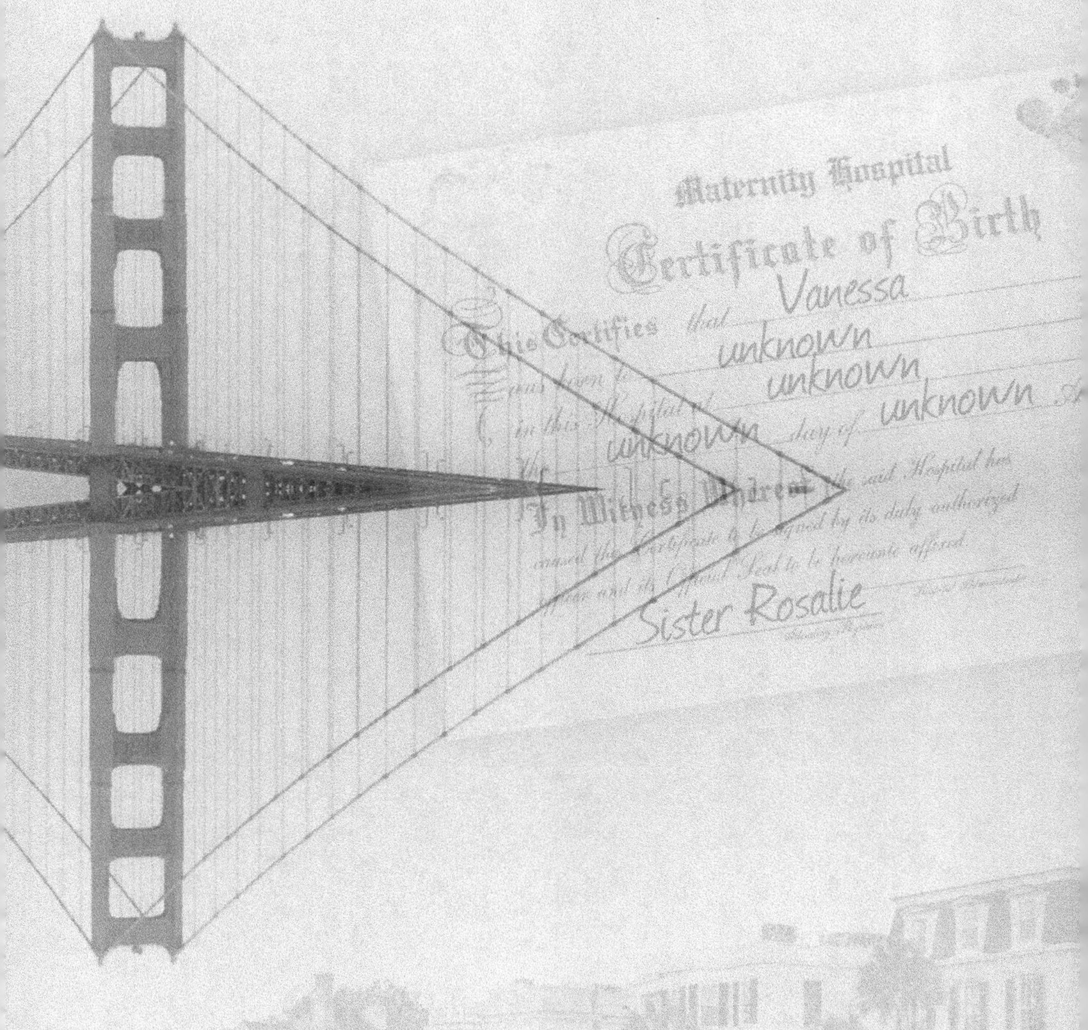

PATRICIA SKIPPER

TABLE OF CONTENTS

CHAPTER ONE

North Charleston, SC 1968

The bottlenose dolphins sailed through the air and splash-landed underneath the water of the wretchedly hot Low County marsh. If the day held any omens to come, the humidity had long since drowned them out. Echoing through the swamp, its noisy brakes brought the ancient bus to a screeching halt. Trisha hopped on, amazed to find the temperature within the bus to be higher than outside.

The eighteen-year-old driver set the brake and stood up. "Listen, you weirdos," Gordy yelled to get the attention of his fellow parochial school teenagers, who were sweltering in the Carolina heat with their green wool blazers. "Martin Luther King asked for a parade permit to march on downtown Charleston, and his request was denied. The governor of South Carolina has declared martial law and ordered the National Guard to be mobilized. Father Kelly wants all the coloreds to sit in the middle seats. Absolutely no Negroes are to sit by the windows. Got it, losers?" he asked sarcastically as he grabbed the battered handle and shut the rusty door.

The dilapidated bus left Trisha's poor, White neighborhood just outside the naval shipyard. Minutes later, they arrived at the decaying public housing projects, and a group of Negroes climbed aboard. After leaving the colored ghetto, the bus drove alongside the Ashley River. Set back along the waterway was a magnificent home with antebellum columns reminiscent of a Southern plantation. As the bus creaked to a halt, tall and handsome Barry Hale, with rich charcoal-colored skin, took the steps in one leap.

"Top of the morning," Barry tipped his green beanie while his dark-brown eyes sparkled.

"Don't sit near the window!" Trisha exclaimed.

"Why?" Barry's gorgeous, effervescent eyes glistened.

"They're expecting the rednecks to be out in full force today."

"Really, why?" Barry looked puzzled.

"I guess the city fathers did not take it too well that Martin Luther King Jr. supported the garbage men in Memphis, and it turned into a riot," Trisha explained.

"Let me get this right, you are at the most five foot four, and you are going to save me?"

"The way Gordy drives, he'll run over those guys. How's that for a plan?"

"Spoken like a true Marine's daughter." Barry glanced out the window when Gordy ran a red light, and horns honked from every direction.

The bus stopped in front of Saint Paul's Orphanage, run by the Sisters of Our Lady of Mercy, solely for colored children. One teenager, Vanessa Condon, who had never been adopted, had spent her entire life in that institution. Stunningly beautiful, she possessed a rare grace that none of her fellow students could match. As Vanessa climbed on board, Sister Rosalie, the only colored nun within the diocese, followed. The obese nun ran the orphanage and had raised Vanessa ever since she was left at Saint Paul's as an infant. Sister Rosalie spoke with a thick Charlestonian accent and claimed her family had been in Charleston for two hundred years. She loved the city's history, and as most Charlestonians, she liked to distort and twist American history and lived in a special past. She was a classic Charleston historian with her own version of events from hundreds of years ago. Though colored, her loyalty to her beloved Charleston was unconditional. Sister Rosalie's voice boomed out. "May I have the attention of the fair ladies of the South and their gentlemen, please?" Words rolled off her thick lips like dripping honey, while perspiration poured down her puggy face. Everyone listened because she was a great storyteller with a unique sense of humor, unlike the other nuns, who were humorless.

"Well, I do declare, for the safety of the passengers, I reckon not to take this bus. Goodness gracious, can you imagine giving those crackers a target this big?" She chuckled as her habit went flying backward. "Father Kelly worked himself up into a tizzy today. I tell you the truth when I say that Irishman has been out in the sun too much playing golf! Our cotton-growing heat has caused that man to forget our great city's history!" Taking her sleeve, she wiped it across her forehead before continuing in her gooey Southern drawl. "Heavens to Betsey Ross, how many of Charleston's native sons signed the United States Declaration of Independence in 1776?"

"Four!" the students yelled.

"And who was the president of the First Continental Congress?"

"Charleston's Henry Middleton for four days," the teenagers screamed.

"And what did his son Arthur Middleton sign?"

"The Declaration of Independence," they hollered in unison.

"Who was the youngest person to sign the Declaration of Independence?"

"Charleston's twenty-six-year-old Edward Rutledge!"

"With this brilliance, ladies and gents, this bus is headed for universities across this great land. We are all destined for college, aren't we, folks? Who did these Charlestonians take on without sheets over their heads?"

Giggles echoed over her thick low country accent.

"King George III of England," the teenagers roared.

"Who kicked his Royal Army out of South Carolina for their eventual defeat in Virginia?"

"Charleston's Francis Marion, the Swamp Fox."

"Where is everyone on this bus going?"

"Ivy League!"

"Now, if y'all see some uneducated coward in a sheet, what are y'all going to do?"

"Duck!" everyone screamed.

"God's speed," the plump nun bellowed as she made the sign of the cross and stumbled down the bus steps. With her powerful and amazingly professional voice, she sang, "People get ready. There's a train a-comin'. You don't need no baggage; you just get on board. All you need is faith, to hear the diesels hummin'. Don't need no ticket. You just thank the Lord!"

Gordy grabbed the handle and shut the door as her mighty voice faded away. The Negroes were sitting in the middle seats as he barreled down the road in the wrong gear.

Vanessa sat with her best friend, Trisha, and whispered, "Going to the prom?"

"Nope. No one asked me. Why?"

Vanessa put one finger over her mouth. "Hush your mouth! Barry might hear you! I desperately want to go, but I can't," the orphan whispered with disappointment. "No clothes!"

"Hold your horses! Remember my sister, the clothes horse? Yellow shoes, yellow dress, pink shoes, pink dress. The one and only fashion queen of South Carolina! She bought two different gowns with her babysitting money and never got invited to the prom! Her curse is being handed down to me, Miss Dateless. My mom will be thrilled. She has never quit complaining about how stupid my sister was to buy them before anyone asked her to go. Let's keep Barry happy so he keeps dissecting frogs for us in biology."

"Yuck!" they both squealed in unison.

"I'll bring them to school," Trisha offered.

"But Barry would see them, and that is bad juju."

"Not again with the juju, Vanessa?"

"Sister Roe said that West African slaves like her great-grandfather used certain objects ascribing supernatural powers to them concerning life and luck. Yes, it's big, bad juju."

"OK, Vanessa. I, for one, do not need a double whammy of big, bad juju."

Gordy cursed, and everyone looked up at a stalled car as he screamed, "Mayday! Mayday! Klan at three o'clock! May—" Before he got the last "day" out of "Mayday," a huge rock crashed through the front windshield, sending broken glass soaring toward him.

Flying through a passenger window, a brick struck Trisha's head as glass showered her and blood gushed down her face. A sharp pain shot through her throbbing temple as red blood flowed freely into her eyes, blinding her. The bus shook back and forth as the Klansmen sent a meteor shower of abuse at it. Rocks, bottles, bricks, and trash descended. Outside, men covered in white sheets shouted, "Listen up, you nigger-loving' fish-eaters! Hand over your niggers now!" Using baseball bats, they broke out all the windows in a vicious assault.

Blood covered her lap. "Apply pressure to stop the bleeding!" Barry yelled, while taking off his blazer and wadding it up. "Here, use this, Vanessa!" As he took off toward the front, the Klansman had gotten a pole through the door and tried to pry it open. Gordy held on to the door handle as Barry jumped into the driver's seat. "Let us get the hell out of here. Shall we, Gordy?"

"Run these sons a' bitches over." Gordy fought with the door handle, throwing his skinny frame against it as Barry revved the old decrepit engine and threw it into gear.

Trying a frontal assault on the bus, the mob screamed, "Get that nigger!"

"I'll run your asses over!" Barry yelled angrily as he rammed into the parked car in front and sent the men in their white sheets flying into the dirt. Sliding into reverse, he hit the vehicle parked behind them. As a horrible grinding noise came from the gears, the bus crashed back into the car ahead, which moved along until it slid into the next one and came to a complete stop. Barry hurled the bus back into reverse and hit the gas. It seemed free for an instant, but then the teenagers were thrown backward as the bus hit a telephone pole.

The mob flung a lit torch through the front window at Barry. "You will fry, nigger!" they screamed. "You too, nigger-lovin' fish-eaters."

Trisha had a blurred view of her friend's face close to hers, as Vanessa struggled to stop her profuse bleeding. Tears rolled down her cheeks as she whispered beneath her breath, "Come on, Barry." Another lit torch landed between Barry and Gordy, but the Negro boys jumped up in time to stomp it out. Coughing as the interior filled with fumes, the teenagers could barely breathe, overpowered by smoke. The boys got the fire out—quite an accomplishment considering how the bus kept plunging around. Jerking forward, Barry slipped quickly between gears and got up enough speed to ram the cars for a final time, which demolished the side of the 1960 white Cadillac. The

Klansmen tormented Barry as he dodged objects they hurled at him while he stayed perfectly calm. Amazingly, it was as though he had trained for this his entire life. As he applied the gas, Vanessa could hear the crunch of metal and glass as they collided with the cars.

"We're going to kill you, you crazy-ass nigger."

"Redneck, take that sheet off of your head!" Gordy yelled.

Squeezing Vanessa tighter, Trisha could hear her sobs and feel her heartbeat. "Hey, white trash!" Vanessa screamed as she stuck her head out the window, but a Negro boy pulled her back down into the seat. "Careful, Vanessa. They could have guns, so stay inside the bus," he warned as he took off his tie and wrapped it around Trisha's blood-covered blond hair.

Barry swerved into a driveway and maneuvered the bus between two houses that led to the backyard of a residential block. A circular clothesline was flattened as the pole crushed easily when the clothes-laden lines slid underneath the wheels. He made it to the next street and demolished two large trash cans before entering the pavement.

"Trisha blacked out, Barry!" Vanessa yelled, panic-stricken, as she clung to her friend. "Her blood is everywhere. Get to a hospital fast."

"We're on our way!" Barry's size fifteen foot forced the gas pedal to the floor. "To get downtown is back through the Klan or across the Ashley River. It will take us too long," Barry said calmly. "We're going to my Dad's hospital."

"We can't go to a Negro hospital. White people aren't allowed there," Gordy replied.

"My Dad is chief of staff at Cannon Street Hospital. I am what you call a preferred patient there, and that is where we are going. You got that, Gordy?"

"You cannot take Whites there," Gordy argued. "Her dad is a Marine. Go to the Charleston Naval Hospital. It's just as close."

"No, it isn't, and I'm driving," Barry replied heatedly. "The extra time could mean the difference between life and death. We are going to Cannon, period."

"Since you're in the driver's seat, I guess we're going to Cannon. But if they turn us away because our skin is White, I will personally beat your ass, Barry."

"You really think my dad would turn down a high school bus attacked by the Klan?"

"All right, all right, you win! Just haul ass," Gordy relented as his skinny frame held on.

"Besides, you probably need stitches. Wait until my dad sticks a two-foot needle in your arm. When he gets done, you might even be able to dance."

"Gee, Barry, you're a regular Nipsey Russell. You belong on the stage, and the Klan will have a stagecoach leaving in a couple of minutes." Gordy coughed while his slender frame clung to the handle with all his strength. A scary silence fell over the teenagers. No one said a word as the shock of the whole experience seized everyone. The old bus rumbled along.

As they neared the hospital, Barry shouted, "Carry Trisha off. I'll get my Dad." The only colored hospital in Charleston, Cannon Street was tiny and plain with none of the grand entrances of the local White hospitals. Admissions were through a simple double door. The emergency room's small Red Cross hung over a loading dock that resembled a factory shipping area. Surrounded by a perfectly manicured lawn, the White teenagers knew Cannon Street was a hospital, but its appearance did not instill confidence in them. The mere thought of going to a Negro hospital was scary and unfamiliar. As Barry turned into the entrance, his passengers were thrown forward when he slammed on the brakes, and the ghastly smell of metal rubbing metal filled the air. The rusty old brakes barely brought the ancient bus to a halt inches away from the loading dock. Gordy swung the door open, and Barry jumped off, not bothering to use the steps. Running inside, he grabbed Nurse Bow. "Nurse Bow, come quick. We were attacked!"

• • •

Two Negro boys carried in Trisha while her blood soaked their uniforms too. "Follow me, gentlemen." Nurse Bow led them into an examining room and pulled the curtain back. "Place her here, and then please leave immediately," she ordered.

Overhead, the paging system reverberated throughout the hospital. "Doctor Davies, Doctor Hale, ER, STAT. Doctor Davies, Doctor Hale, ER, STAT."

"Barry, I want everyone who needs medical treatment in the waiting room," Nurse Bow commanded. "The rest can stay outside on the lawn. I certainly do not need a three-ring circus in here. Now, get! You don't have your medical license yet!" The nurse quickly checked Trisha's pulse and prepared the blood pressure cuff.

Doctor Davies appeared and felt her carotid artery for a pulse. After opening her eyelids to examine her pupils, he then palpated around the head wound with his fingers. "Let's get pressure on that scalp laceration," he instructed. "What's her pressure?"

"Seventy over thirty."

"She's in shock. Get an IV started, D5 half normal saline wide open. Set up a dopamine drip. I want five units typed and crossed."

"The odds are we won't have that much blood, Doctor," Nurse Bow replied.

"Have the lab get on the phone and find some," he directed. "Surely Saint Francis or Roper has some we can borrow. Try the Trendelenburg position on her. We've got to get her pressure up, or she's not going to make it."

Quickly, they got their patient's head down and feet up to help blood flow and prevent damage to the brain. These two were quite a pair. Nurse Bow, five feet tall, barely ninety pounds, about fifty, was from the old school; she still wore her 1945 vanity (the nursing cap) and starched white uniform. In her era, physicians were gods whose orders you followed and never questioned. Doctor Davies, in contrast, only twenty-eight and two years out of medical school, stood six feet five inches. A South Carolina native, he had gone to Howard University in Washington DC, where he discovered it was best to drop the Southern accent. Now, he spoke English without a trace of his low country roots. He entered the adjoining examining room where Doctor Hale was suturing up Gordy's hand. "Considering the trauma sustained to the skull, she probably has a fracture. Why don't you let me finish here, and you go look?"

"Very well." He handed his colleague the needle. Doctor William Hale was well-respected even within the stuffy Charleston medical community. A decorated Korean War physician, he served the entire length of the action. Military doctors stationed at the Charleston Naval Hospital called him for consultation and considered him the best neurosurgeon in the state.

"So, what's the story here?" Doctor Davies asked.

"It looks like the Klan thought I had ten passengers too many. They wanted me to have them disembark near their torch rally." Gordy winced as the pain shot through his arm.

"What did you do?"

"Panicked, mostly. How many more stitches, Doctor?"

"I am not sure; it is a nasty gash. How did you get out of there?" The young resident tried to keep his patient's mind off the needle.

"The Klan is not into letting people do U-turns at their rallies. While I was trying to keep the Neanderthals at bay, Barry jumped behind the wheel and took out four cars in the process." Closing his eyes, Gordy clenched his teeth. "Wait till Father Kelly sees the bus. It looks like Atlanta after Sherman went through. I'm about to be relieved of my command."

"I wouldn't be so sure about that." The young doctor continued the suturing. "You're hurt and deserve a Purple Heart. Your command is safe."

"Where did you go to medical school?" Gordy asked, worried about his credentials.

"I didn't! I always loved my mother's sewing kit, so I thought what the hell? I'll come down here, hang out, and see if I could stitch anyone up."

"I told Barry that we should not come here." Gordy bit his lip.

"Let me tell you something, son. If you had spent the time trying to go around the river to get downtown, the young lady lying in the room next door would probably be dead right now." A chill came into his voice. "You did the right thing."

Doctor Hale came in the door. "She's B-positive, and we only have one unit."

"I finally found a woman who's my type," the resident joked as he cut the final suture.

"Draw a pint. Maybe I'll let you have the night off."

"What a deal, boss! You drain the blood out of me, and I get to go home and lie on the couch," Doctor Davies quipped while he washed his hands. "Only I don't own a couch."

"Can you do that?" Gordy asked incredulously. "Can he give Trisha blood?"

Both colored physicians turned around and answered in unison, "Yes!"

"Are you sure?" Gordy persisted.

"Son, do you think anyone in this country who gives blood knows where it is going?" Doctor Hale replied as he checked his resident's sutures.

"I don't know," Gordy responded blankly.

"Blood is typed and has nothing to do with race."

"Oh," Gordy muttered.

"Well, now you know all about blood and where it comes from. There is truly no such thing as Black blood," Doctor Davies advised as he left to give his blood to Trisha.

"I want you to come back next week and let us take out your stitches."

"Doctor Hale, I have to go to the naval hospital. My parents don't have any money."

"Son, this service is on the house, so tell your parents. You can get down now, and I want you to take one pill every four hours as needed for pain."

"Thanks a lot, Doctor Hale." Gordy slid his skinny legs off the examining table.

Nurse Bow came to the door. "Doctor Hale, there are eight police cars outside, and their sergeant is asking to speak to the chief of the medical staff."

"Tell him I'll be right out, but first I need to check on our Neuro patient again."

* * *

Outside, the students gathered under a huge magnolia tree for protection against the hot Carolina sun. Gordy announced that Trisha was so close to death that she was getting blood from a Negro doctor as he proudly showed off his stitches to his fellow students.

Doctor Hale appeared. "I'm the chief of staff here. You wanted to see me?"

"You can't treat White kids here, and you know it, boy," the sergeant announced curtly.

"Did you want me to turn them away so they could continue their journey to downtown Charleston? In my medical opinion, the vehicle was not quite up to the trip." Doctor Hale glanced over to the burned-out, windowless bus with the front bumper hanging off and the entire back end and sides demolished. Dents made by the bats had destroyed most of the yellow paint. Glass covered the entire floor and most of the seats; blood was scattered everywhere. The burned floor had ashes mixed with blood where the torch had landed. The interior's repulsive smell forced the police officers to cover their mouths with handkerchiefs to investigate the ugly sight.

"I want these White children released immediately, and we will take them to the emergency room at Roper Hospital," the police sergeant demanded.

"That would be a complete waste of time for the ER staff at Roper, sir." Doctor Hale spoke calmly, as he did not want to challenge the police even here on his own turf. "Only two children were treated. The rest are free to go to school if you can find a way to get them there. I have only one patient who is in critical condition and will need surgery."

"There's no way you are going to operate on a White here, and you know it, boy."

"She cannot be moved until her vital signs are stabilized. Your time would be better spent getting these kids to school and hauling this monstrosity back to your police station for evidence. If the young lady inside does not make it, you're going to have a homicide on your hands."

"Maybe we'll have a homicide on our hands because your son drove her to the wrong hospital, if you can call this place one."

"Sergeant, that's up to South Carolina's Medical Board." Doctor Hale tried not to lose his temper. "Only they can revoke my license since it's not within police jurisdiction. Now, if you will excuse this 'boy', the young lady needs a neurosurgeon. I appear to be the only one around here who has that title. Good day." His tall, muscular frame disappeared through the door.

Stunned, the police sergeant could not believe that a Negro had spoken to him like that. He turned to his troops. "Load them up, and get the hell out of here. I want as many kids crammed into each squad car as possible. Move it."

* * *

A 1957 Ford came roaring up the driveway. Sister Rosalie was behind the wheel of the old clunky car, the only one the orphanage had. The huge nun burst out of the car with her white habit swaying. Spotting Gordy sitting under the magnolia tree, she tried to run but had to walk. Soaking wet with perspiration beads streaming down her face, she was out of breath. "My dear, what in the name of sassafras happened?" she bellowed. "Sugar, show me your hand."

"Sister, everyone is OK except for Trisha," Gordy said defensively. "I overheard one of the doctors, and they think Trisha might not make it." Abruptly, she dropped his hand and trotted over to the emergency room.

Tripping up the stairs, she used the full force of her weight to open the door. As she barged in, she knocked into the petite nurse. "Nurse Bow, tell me, how is Trisha?" she blurted out.

"For pity's sake, calm down right now. The children have been through enough already. I will not have that in this hospital. Do you understand me?"

"Have mercy on my soul," Sister Rosalie said breathlessly. "There is no way the children should be alarmed. I'm distressed enough for the entire low country."

"No prancing around here and causing mass hysteria."

"Let me see Doctor Hale, or I'm going to start throwing my weight around."

Nurse Bow brushed off her starched hat. "No, you don't." Without looking around, she knew the nun was following her. "Get out, and get out now!"

"Ladies, ladies, ladies!" Doctor Hale appeared and smiled. "I need your help."

"Doctor Hale, say no more. What can I do?"

"Trisha Bibbs is in critical condition, and I need you to orchestrate the departure of these children from our premises. Do you want that buffoon police sergeant in charge of these minors? I give you my blessing to totally steamroll over him, as only you can do. My money is on you, Sister Rosalie! Please don't disappoint me."

"Doctor Hale, you have put your greenbacks on the right mule."

As the nun charged for the door, Nurse Bow exclaimed, "That nutcase gets on my nerves. You realize, Doctor Hale, that she needs some major sedatives."

"I don't think the drug companies have come up with one that powerful yet."

"I warned you about sending Barry to a Catholic school."

* * *

Sister Rosalie descended the steps just as the police loaded the students into their squad cars. "Who in the name of Pope Pius IX is in charge here?" she hollered. Completely ignoring the nun, the sergeant sat in the driver's seat with his legs dangling out sideways. As she stomped up, she demanded that he get off the police radio. All the kids held their breath since they knew failure to give Sister Rosalie undivided attention was deadly. "I am talking to you, Mister. I expect you to listen." She grabbed the receiver out of his hand. "It's blowing up a storm, but this is not a police state yet! These children have been traumatized enough today without you carting them off in squad cars with wire mesh. I'm madder than a wet hen!"

"Who are you?" he looked puzzled as he asked.

"Pope Pius IX," she barked as the teenagers laughed at a joke that only a Catholic high school student could get. History professors at Harvard might not know Pope Pius IX.

"I sure am glad y'all fish-eaters have a fat Negro pope now," he drawled.

"Listen to the cretinous creature in front of me. He died in 1878, so I surely cannot be him." Once she had launched into a dissertation, nothing the sergeant could do would shut her up.

Clearly annoyed, he countered, "I'm Baptist and could care less about a dead pope or the current one for that matter since you ain't one."

"The Confederacy's quest for foreign help was ingenious," she lectured. "Southern agents published a newspaper in London to solicit Confederate sympathy."

The sergeant sneered as he interrupted, "Gee, I didn't know you fish-eaters were on the right side of 'the War Of Northern Aggression'. It'll make me, and my men feel a whole lot better when we see you penguins milling around downtown Charleston, knowing you were on the right side." Turning to his men, he commanded, "Load them up, and get moving. We've got better things to do than hang around a Negro hospital with a Negro penguin."

"The papacy never supported the Confederacy, you nescient man! Y'all have to move me, and I guarantee y'all can't lift me." She crossed her hands over her immense bosom. "I demand you find a bus. These children have not committed a crime and won't be forced into police cars."

"Where exactly do you think I am going to find a bus in the middle of the day?"

"Just call up the mayor and explain to him how Charleston's finest in blue were unable to protect innocent children on their way to school. Kind sir, you can't even protect the Virgin Mary statue in front of our school. Every week someone puts rotten fish in her hands." The eccentric nun pointed at the students. "Children, let's hear the 'Georgia howl"

Howling, their voices soared together into a roar, quite a tension reliever for kids who had just experienced the worst day of their young lives.

"Shut up, shut up!" the sergeant yelled, but no one listened.

She explained the meaning of the "Georgia howl" to the stunned policemen. "Sherman's occupation of Atlanta buoyed Northern morale and helped get Lincoln reelected. Sherman marched virtually unopposed to the sea, laying waste as he went to make 'Georgia howl.'"

"All right, all right, you win, penguin. Give me my radio back, and I'll call it in. But my men and I are leaving. You are responsible for them. Understood?"

"Well, bless your heart! If the creek don't rise, that will do kindly, sir."

Informing the dispatcher not to tie up squad cars, the sergeant ordered a city bus to be routed to Charleston Heights to pick up the students. After requesting a tow truck for the demolished school bus, he left with his car in the lead as dust flew up in the air. Sister Rosalie had stared down the Charleston Police Department and won. No one was really surprised to see her get her way. She usually did.

Throwing her habit-covered head straight up in the air, she laughed. "Why, William Tecumseh Sherman, wherever you are, I'd say you heard the 'Georgia howl' all the way from Charleston today."

Unable to find an available city bus, the Charleston Police Department sent a van that was used to transport criminals to jail. Sister Rosalie raised holy hell, but the Negro driver told her either to take it or walk downtown. She decided to do the most expedient thing and took the only transportation offered. Despite the two hours' wait to move up from a squad car to a police van, she felt it would be less traumatic to keep everyone together.

CHAPTER TWO

Trisha's parents drove up and were greeted by Nurse Bow. "May we see our daughter?" Mrs. Bibbs asked.

"Let me page Doctor Hale for you. My preference is that you speak with him first," the nurse answered. "I know he will come down here momentarily." Before she began to page him, Doctor Hale appeared with Doctor Davies.

"My name is Doctor Hale, and I am a neurosurgeon, precisely what your daughter needs right now," he said in a matter-of-fact tone. "Please sit down." He motioned them into the tiny office. "Your daughter has sustained a severe trauma to the head, which has resulted in a skull fracture. This increased intracranial pressure could result in paralysis. She has lost a significant amount of blood, and we need to stabilize her vital signs. Once we have accomplished that, I would like your permission to operate."

"What kind of operation?" Mrs. Bibbs asked sadly in her thick Brooklyn accent.

"It is called a craniotomy," the surgeon replied.

"Why does she need an operation?" she questioned the surgeon as her husband sat silently.

"Trisha has a subdural hematoma, a hemorrhage that puts pressure on the brain. The blow to her head caused increased intracranial pressure. This medical condition can cause growing pressure inside your skull and injure your brain or spinal cord as blood leaks out of the vessel and the surrounding tissue. We must relieve the pressure on the brain, and I need your permission to operate. It's against my medical advice to transfer her to another facility."

"I'm a retired Marine Corps sergeant major. We have no money to pay you. You need to transfer her to the military hospital," Mr. Bibbs said with authority in his Southern accent.

"I've already called Captain Long, the chief of staff at the Naval hospital, to get it covered. I recommend that you let me operate," he stated his concern with remarkable detachment.

Sergeant Bibbs moved toward him and looked straight in his eyes. "We met in Korea, Doctor Hale. My best friend died on your operating table. I don't trust you."

"Is it the color of my skin?"

"Nope, my folks were sharecroppers right along with all the coloreds. I have been in outhouses my entire life with Negroes. Picked cotton right beside them. No difference between me, them, or you. I will never forget until the day I die, you came outside to tell me my best buddy was dead. You turned around coldly and went into the officer's tent to eat dinner. It sickened me. I do not think I can let you do it. I don't care about the color of your skin."

Doctor Hale looked down at the floor. "We lost so many men there. I was totally numb. I just wanted to get home to my wife. Being devoid of emotion was the only way to survive."

Just then, Captain Long, the head of the Naval Hospital, appeared and shook both men's hands. "I came as soon as I could, sergeant major," he said. "This is the top neurosurgeon in the state. Your daughter is in excellent hands here, and I plan to send over our staff surgeon to assist him since it is in your daughter's best interest to remain here. Please do not be concerned about the cost. I will work that out. Sergeant Bibbs, I was Doctor Hale's commander in Korea, and he was the best surgeon I had, bar none. On his operating table, the boys had a tremendously higher rate of survival. He is top notch. If it were my daughter, he'd be the one doing the craniotomy."

Mrs. Bibbs wiped away her tears. "Let a colored man save my daughter, and let those savages know that he did. How in the world did this happen?"

Doctor Davies interrupted. "Your daughter took a direct hit by an old Charleston brick. I've got it in a plastic bag just in case they can get some fingerprints off it."

"Give it to me. I'll have the military police dust it for prints," Doctor Long ordered.

"How do you relieve the pressure?" Mrs. Bibbs asked.

"Please do not be alarmed, but we use a drill," Doctor Hale answered hesitantly.

Doctor Long interrupted, "Sergeant Major, this is a common procedure for skull trauma. It sounds much worse than it really is. Besides, we have no choice here. If we do not do it, your daughter will be paralyzed and may die. We will make an incision in the skull and pump salt water into it to break the clot loose. We then drain the blood out through a rubber hose."

"A drill?" Sergeant Bibbs said. "What if you blow it and drill too deep?"

"I've done this procedure a thousand times," Doctor Hale answered. "To a layperson, it sounds bizarre to drill a hole in someone's skull, but it will save your daughter's life. Sir, you have no other option. The only decision you must make is which physician to use. I am asking you to let me be her surgeon. I want your daughter to get up, walk out of this hospital, and go on with her life, wherever it may take her."

"When will you do it?" Mrs. Bibbs asked.

"Tomorrow morning after she has been stabilized during the night."

"What if you kill her like my best friend in Korea? I can't believe you're going to use a drill on her. I use a drill to fix the airplanes I work on over at the base." He fixed his eyes on the doctor. "You better be a damn sight more accurate than an aircraft mechanic."

"I promise you, sergeant major, that she'll look as good as the day you brought her home from the hospital." Doctor Hale put a hand on his shoulder to reassure him. "She'll be fine."

"Well, I suggest you get a good night's sleep because you've got the job," Mrs. Bibbs confirmed and looked at her husband for the first time.

"Honey, I think we should discuss this privately." Mr. Bibbs motioned to his wife.

"We have nothing to discuss. Let a colored man save my baby girl, and let those barbarians know that he did save her. I am in no mood for any more war stories. Now let me see my child," she answered firmly as she stood up.

* * *

The physicians walked down the hallway with the couple. They closed the door to Trisha's hospital room and were out of earshot when Doctor Long advised his colleague, "I'm going to send David Cohen over to assist if you don't mind. If there is one thing that the Klan hates as much as Catholics and Negroes, it is Jews. So tomorrow you will have a full trifecta: a Jew and a Negro operating on a Roman Catholic. You better hope the Klan doesn't have any time bombs planned for your hospital."

"I can only hope that the Klan goes belly up during my lifetime."

"Certainly not a legacy that I want to leave to my grandchildren either," Doctor Long answered as they went up the stairs. "Did you hear that Robert Kennedy announced his candidacy for the Democratic presidential nomination?" He loosened his uniform collar.

"Yes, I heard it on the radio."

"What do you think?" Doctor Long asked.

"He has a very charismatic personality. I'm sure he will be able to forge a broad coalition that includes young people, my race, professionals, and blue-collar workers."

"Just think, Lyndon Johnson declined to choose Robert Kennedy as his 1964 running mate, and now the Kennedys must spend another fortune on a presidential election. But it beats the US Senate seat from New York. Can you imagine what a thankless job that must be?" Doctor Long sank into the couch.

"Isn't Bobby a University of Virginia alumnus like yourself?" Doctor Hale smiled.

"He's a law school grad and has done better than I on behalf of the alumni association."

"In my humble opinion, you're not doing so bad yourself," Doctor Hale commented as he sat down behind his desk. "Besides, I doubt whether Bobby could carry the South even if he had Robert E. Lee as a running mate. As attorney general, he stressed civil rights enforcement until blood ran through the streets of Birmingham. The South will never forgive him for that."

Captain Long leaned back on the couch. "Frankly, I'm shocked that the Klan would be so bold as to attack an innocent busload of parochial kids on their way to school."

"Can you imagine how I feel? My son was on that bus," he said sorrowfully. "That little girl is in bad shape. She's lucky my son came here instead of trying to make it downtown."

"She is also extremely fortunate that you are her surgeon. I plan to make sure that the Charleston 'News-less' Courier prints the fact that a Negro surgeon saved her life."

"Well, you better wait until she is out of here before that makes the paper. Our insurance policy on this place isn't that great."

"Yes, sir," Captain Long said with a mock salute. "Are you going to vote for Bobby?"

Doctor Hale immediately answered, "Let's see if he can get the nomination first."

"You know I am a staunch Republican. I never understood why your people abandoned the party when it was organized in 1854 to oppose slavery."

"I've heard your speech before, captain. Lincoln set my grandparents free! In Korea, I had it memorized. The Republican Party will have the first Negro on the national ticket."

"That's exactly right!"

Doctor Hale shook his head. "There's no way I'm going to live that long."

"Since I can't convert you to the Republican Party, I might as well get on back to the base." Doctor Long stood up and smiled at his friend as they shook hands. "Good luck tomorrow. I'm sending a superb surgeon and our best anesthesiologist over to assist."

"I'll be in touch as soon as I'm done," Doctor Hale promised.

* * *

Mrs. Bibbs spent the night on the floor beside her daughter. The next morning, the staff prepped Trisha for surgery and shaved her entire head. A naval anesthesiologist administered the anesthesia. After the operation, it took three more days to drain the blood out completely. It dripped into a sack that hung around her ear. The local newspapers ran stories about the incident. Governor McNair extended martial law because he did not want the state replacing Alabama and Mississippi on the national news. Politically astute, he managed during this tumultuous time to keep South Carolina's civil rights reputation intact.

* * *

Sister Rosalie spent every waking moment pestering Doctor Hale, wanting to see Trisha; the simple fact that she was not a family member did not matter to her. Neither side budged during the match-up of a rotund nun against a slender six-foot-two surgeon. The physician believed she was a little touched in the head and eccentric at best. As usual, however, she got her way and was the first person, other than Trisha's parents, allowed in.

"Now, Sister Rosalie, I am letting you go in, but I'm telling you to your face that I don't trust your lack of judgment," Doctor Hale said seriously. "You cannot upset her, period. If you so much as raise her blood pressure, you will have to deal with me. Understood?"

"Why, Doctor Hale, I do declare, you must have Yankee blood in you. You are most inhospitable." Smiling, the nun spoke sweetly in her deepest Southern drawl.

"You've got three minutes while Nurse Bow stands right beside you."

"Nurse Bow? Nurse Bow does not have enough meat on her bones to throw a Palmetto bug out of intensive care." The nun brushed by them both and entered the room. "Trisha, honey, it's old Sister Roe," she whispered softly. "Vanessa and I have been praying and talking about no one other than you. We love you, sweetie. Now, sugar, you have already missed five days of school. Do you remember all the valuable information Sister Roe has taught you? Trisha, child, tell me about Charles Town in 1776?"

Opening her eyes slowly, she whispered weakly, "Named after King Charles II, Charles Town made South Carolina the wealthiest colony on the eve of the American Revolution. The aggregate wealth of inventoried estates in Charles Town was more than six times that of Philadelphia." Her raspy throat crackled as she gasped for air and asked for a sip of water.

"Good day, Sister Rosalie." Doctor Hale grabbed her arm as she pulled away.

"You're a pain in the neck, but you did a superb job with this brain surgery."

"What?" Trisha asked in disbelief. "Brain surgery? What brain surgery?"

"We never touched her brain, Sister. Don't you ever tell anyone that wrong medical information." He shook his head and pulled her away from the bed.

"Never mind old Sister Roe. She's just babbling. What did the mightiest superpower on the earth write to the British earl of Dartmouth during the American Revolution?"

"Charles Town is the fountainhead from which all the violence flows. Stop that, and all the American rebellion in this part of the continent will, I trust, soon be at an end."

"Trisha, she's out of here." Doctor Hale forced the unwilling nun out the door.

"Take your mitts off me! I'm clergy, you know!" Sister Rosalie protested.

"If we had a psychiatric ward, I'd name a wing after you." Doctor Hale kept a firm grasp on her arm as he escorted her down the hall.

"Sister," Doctor Davies was across the hallway. "Too bad the Union let Alabama back in so have to put up with Roll Tide and the damn War Eagles!"

"Why, sweetheart, how old are you?" she asked in her deep drawl.

"I'm in my twenties and not married. You interested?" he joked.

"Why I am way too much for you to handle, darling." She grinned.

"Doctor Davies, go home, and get some rest," Doctor Hale ordered. "You are probably a menace to your patients at this point after four days. Go rest up and see your sweetheart. And please escort Sister Rosalie off the premises, and I do mean off! Ask her if West Point has a problem with an alumnus being the president of the confederacy?"

"Now, sweetheart, you never told old Sister Roe about another woman," the nun joked.

"I strongly suggest you stay in the convent and continue your mission to inflict your distorted version of American history on our impressionable youth," Doctor Hale interjected.

Turning around, Nurse Bow said, "Your son is as brainwashed as the rest of them." Shaking her head, the nurse headed down the hall to make her rounds.

"Both of you get going now!" Doctor Hale ordered.

* * *

"Tell me why in the year 1968, we have a state called West Virginia?" Sister Rosalie asked after they left the hospital together, and he escorted the nun to her car.

"I know this," chirped Doctor Davies, raising his hand. "The western section of Virginia seceded from that state and entered the Union during the Civil War. Haven't slept in four days. What a brain! I must be a Greek god!"

She winked. "Well, I, for one, am so glad that modern medical schools are turning out well-rounded physicians. But how do you work with that man? Doctor Hale is a pain and reminds me of our great South Carolinian Francis Marion. The Swamp Fox bogged the British down for years in our swamps, and Lord Cornwallis could never even find the elusive colonel."

"Sorry sister, history was not my thing except for Francis Marion and his uncanny ability to elude and outsmart British forces, the greatest military power in the world," he confessed.

"So, you do know British officer Tarleton burned thirty plantations to the ground to teach the locals the 'Errors of Insurrection'?" Smoke came out of her tailpipe as the car started.

"Yes, Sister, but Colonel Francis Marion got the last laugh. After the British retreated from our Low Country marshes, Cornwallis marched his army into

North Carolina and surrendered at Yorktown, Virginia. "Doctor Hale is no way near as stubborn as the Swamp Fox, I promise you." The muffler smoke got worse as the nun drove away and waved out the window.

CHAPTER THREE

After the incident that rocked Charleston, Cannon Street Hospital staff received favorable media reviews for their professionalism, and Doctor Hale became a household name. Following Trisha's release, Vanessa and Barry decided to visit her together.

A week later, Barry used his father's car and drove to Saint Paul's Orphanage to pick up Vanessa. As he entered through the main doorway, the smell of ammonia permeated the air. The aroma gave the room a very musty odor. The scent was unbearable as he glanced around the room and took it all in. The cracked linoleum floor had an awful black-and-white pattern. Beaten and worn, the shoddy wood below was mostly exposed. The furniture consisted of a worn threadbare couch accompanied by a junky pine table. As his eyes darted around the room, he felt increasingly uncomfortable. A cheap-looking picture of Saint Paul, mounted in a dull wooden frame, hung above the dilapidated couch. Barry was not sure what to do since no one came to greet him. Should he knock on the closed door? Suddenly, a terrible, dreadful feeling came over him. He could not imagine living in this institution. What if fate had placed him here? Could he cope with a life like this? When he arrived home, he was going to tell his parents he loved them. For the first time ever, he realized how lucky he was to have two parents who worked hard to give him an education and a great house to live in. His own home smelled of bread or cookies baking, which always made him feel warm, cozy, and safe. His thoughts turned to his mother, who was a college professor at South Carolina's oldest Negro college, Claflin University. She still liked to read with him before bedtime. After reciting a quote from a great philosopher, they would discuss it. She never told him his viewpoint was wrong. Instead, she nurtured his ideas by quietly listening to him. His mom loved her only child more than anything.

The inner door opened, and Vanessa peeked through. "Oh, Barry, you're here. Why didn't you ring the bell?"

Vanessa was stunningly beautiful, and he thought she was the most gorgeous creature on earth. At the sight of her, his dread quickly disappeared, and he became emotionally excited. As his heart pounded in his chest, he felt flushed with desire. "What bell?" Barry asked out loud.

"Only my most prized possession, darling!" Sister Rosalie interrupted as her huge frame moved into the room. "If I were going to sell my soul to the devil, it would be for that bell, sweetheart. Come here, honey, and ring this sacred bell for old Sister Roe." She motioned him onto the decrepit veranda. Reaching up, he rang the antiquated rusty bell to appease her. "The Confederate Naval Secretary Stephen R. Mallory was a visionary," she gushed breathlessly. "He and his officers spearheaded the sea power of the future. Their innovations included the torpedo boat, the water mine, and the first modern submarine, the *H. L. Hunley*. Sugar, you get two guesses as to which ship this replica came off?" Her massive hips swayed.

"The *H. L. Hunley*," he guessed.

"Absolutely! I can tell you are a man of great taste to have recognized such a reproduction of an historical treasure." The nun rang the bell with such fury that all the kids in the orphanage came running. Surrounded by youngsters of every conceivable age from toddlers to preteens, she yelled, "Children, tell this doctor-to-be about the *H. L. Hunley*."

In unison, the orphans screamed, "It sank itself and a US ship in the Charleston harbor in 1864." She rang the bell. The children giggled and grabbed her habit as she lovingly picked up the toddlers who delighted in ringing the bell during their turn.

"Now, Mr. Hale, I expect you to conduct yourself this afternoon like Louisiana General Beauregard, who commanded the action against Fort Sumter in the Charleston Harbor." Vanessa looked mortified. "President

Jefferson Davis's government wanted to show nonaggressive intent. I expect the same conduct out of you, kind sir."

"Yes, Sister," Barry answered, a little bit chagrined.

"Tell Trisha I'd love to visit with her today, but that atheist father of hers won't let me in his house. I'll have to move that old retired Marine myself, just like the Union did after the Civil War and moved our capitol to Columbia from Charleston."

"I'll give Trisha your regards." Barry grabbed Vanessa's hand to start down the stairs. Under his breath, he muttered, "Let's get out of here. My dad wants the car home by four." Vanessa smiled and squeezed his hand. She had never held a man's hand before. It was so large, rough, and different. As they descended the stairs, a feeling came over her that she had never experienced before. Suddenly, she felt very flushed but was unsure why. Barry escorted her to the car and opened the door. Vanessa got in and arranged her dress neatly before he entered on the driver's side. She motioned to all the children at the top of the stairs, who waved back furiously. Sister Rosalie rang the bell with one hand and held two toddlers with the other.

* * *

"I guess my family is a little bigger than yours," she said to break the silence.

"You have quite a clan! It looks like you are the oldest. Who is the second oldest?"

"He's ten," Vanessa responded nervously.

"Wow, that's quite an age difference! Why's that?" Barry asked as he backed the car out of the driveway and into the street.

"Sister Rosalie dragged a cast of thousands through Saint Paul's and was never able to talk anyone into adopting me. Believe me, it was not for a lack of trying. She usually gets what she wants from sheer determination. I've seen people come by just to get some information on adoption, and she hustles them into taking a child home for the weekend."

"She let a child go home with a complete stranger?" Barry inquired apprehensively.

"Absolutely not. I guarantee you that the FBI could never run a background check as thorough as Sister Roe's. I've been her assistant on many cases, and her research on potential parents is exhaustive. It is so comprehensive that she can tell you whether they drink R. C. Cola or not. Her record is flawless. She would never put a child in an abusive home."

"Not a surprise since she can rattle off the most intricate and arcane historical details." Barry looked over and smiled. "So, tell me why a pretty lady like you was never adopted when Sister Rosalie professes such an unblemished record?" While braking for a red light, he ran his hand down to stroke her fingers. "Please sit next to me," he whispered.

"OK," she murmured, sliding over. Her heart started to beat rapidly because she had never been in a car before without Sister Rosalie. She felt incredibly excited and uncomfortable at the same time. Vanessa had never been alone with anyone except the other kids in the orphanage. Sitting next to Barry felt completely exhilarating in a frightening sort of way.

"So, aren't you going to tell me why you're the flaw in a flawless record?"

"I've never talked to anyone about this," Vanessa said insecurely.

"If you can't tell me, who can you tell?" Barry leaned over to kiss her on the cheek.

Her heart pounded with apprehension as she answered. "As I was paraded before each prospective couple, they always looked at each other, and without speaking, I could tell it was a no go. The expression on their faces was always the same look."

"I don't get it. What look?"

Feeling uneasy, Vanessa blurted out, "They never liked the color of my skin! One couple even yelled at Sister Roe, 'My God, she's White!'"

"You're kidding!" Barry replied.

Leaning over, Vanessa felt vulnerable. "When you spend your life in an orphanage, there really isn't much to kid about."

"I'm sorry," Barry said as he turned onto the interstate. "But what you're really saying is that other colored people thought your skin was the wrong color because it was too light?"

"Let me quote Sister Roe. She always said, 'Vanessa, child, colored folk don't cotton to cotton, and your skin reminds them of cotton.'"

"But you're so beautiful!" Immediately, he felt embarrassed by his outburst.

"Oh, Barry! That is exactly what they all said. She's so beautiful."

"I'm sorry," he apologized. "I'm terribly sorry."

"You'll never be as sorry as I am for the color of my skin. Never! I spent my whole life in an orphanage because of it."

"Well, someday you too will have a home and a family," he said encouragingly.

"A home? Do you know I have never even been in a house?"

"What?" Barry asked in a startled voice.

"Never! I have never been inside a house," she commented, feeling much more at ease. "Once, I went with Sister Roe to Father Kelly's rectory. I waited in the foyer while they talked. I thought about sneaking around, but I was afraid that I would get caught. I always wanted to see a real kitchen in a real home. I am dying to see Trisha's house. I cannot wait!"

"Vanessa, this is unbelievable. I had no idea. I'll ask my Mom if you can come for dinner. Besides, I know they are dying to set eyes on the person I asked to the prom." As Barry exited the interstate, he felt very aroused, but tremendous sadness overtook him at the same time. These were powerful feelings that he had never experienced before.

"Are you serious?" Vanessa asked excitedly.

"Absolutely! It's a done deal," Barry announced enthusiastically.

"When can I come? I mean, when may I come?" She corrected her own grammar.

"I'll ask my Mom tonight."

"Do you really think she'll let me come to your house?"

"Of course! This way, she can check you out and see if you are good enough for her only child." Barry's chuckle was soft.

"Oh no! A parental inspection! I've been flunking those my whole life!" she exclaimed. "What if they don't like me? What if they don't like the color of my skin?"

"You're being silly, Vanessa. My parents will worship and adore you, just like I do! But please, whatever you do, do not mention history. My father thinks Sister Rosalie is a complete basket case and should be committed."

"She is the only mother I've ever had." Vanessa feebly attempted to defend the nun. "She loves Charleston, and let's face it: a huge part of its history involves two civil wars. Can she help it if fate put her in the wrong century?"

Amazed at his own boldness, he brought the car to a complete stop, and without hesitating, he leaned over to kiss Vanessa's lips. Shocked at his brazen behavior, she pulled away. But undeterred, Barry put his arm behind the back of her head and kissed her again. As she parted her lips, she felt his tongue inside her mouth. Vanessa was not exactly sure what he was doing, but she found it overly exciting in a dangerous sort of way. She responded by sticking her own tongue in his mouth and swirling it all around. Barry reacted by squeezing her closer until a loud horn honking from behind made them both sit up straight. He put his foot on the gas pedal and accelerated through the intersection.

Complete silence fell between them as they entered Trisha's neighborhood. Developers had built low-cost housing on drained swamps north of Charleston. Every house was a little different from the one next door but not much. Cheap and plentiful in the South, each exterior was made of old Charleston brick. Spanish moss hung from thick oak trees, while skinny pines separated each tiny home from the other.

* * *

Inside the small tract house, Trisha asked her father, "Dad, did you remember that I want to loan Vanessa Barb's prom dresses?"

"How could I possibly forget? You have reminded me every three minutes since they called and said that they were coming over. Why can't she just walk out of here with this stuff on a hanger? Why am I running around like a chicken with my head cut off trying to find something to put those darn dresses in?"

"Dad, I told you, it's bad luck for a guy to see your dress before you wear it. I've told you that a thousand times."

"Trisha, it don't matter a hoot! You young'uns don't get it. What matters is that she don't look like a sow's ear in it," he said with a loud belly laugh. "If she does, that boy will cast his net back on out and pull someone else out of the sea."

"Dad, have you ever seen Vanessa? She would look good in a burlap sack. Now quit torturing me, find something to put them in, and don't forget the matching shoes."

"Shoes? I did not see any shoes in there." Sergeant Bibbs clearly felt exasperated.

"What do you mean you never saw any shoes? Remember Barb, your daughter, who wouldn't be caught dead without matching shoes? Your daughter with the shoe fetish? The one with more inventory in her room than most shoe stores? How could you not see shoes back there? After twenty years in the Marine Corps, lavender and purple shoes should stick out, Dad."

"Look, Trisha. When they get here, I will take that boy aside. While I bore the hell out of him, you two find what you want. Put it all on the bed, and I'll get it out to the car. That is my best offer," he said emphatically.

"I'm not supposed to get out of bed," Trisha whispered softly.

"You're milking this for all it's worth. More than Carter's got little pills! It's only ten feet to your sister's room." At that moment, the doorbell rang. "I can't wait to see this goddess," he muttered as he went to open the front door.

* * *

"Hello, sir." Barry extended his right hand to shake.

"Hi Mr. Bibbs, I'm Vanessa. You know that brick was meant for me. I'm the one who should be sick and in bed," she said remorsefully.

Sgt. Bibbs was amazed at how incredibly stunning she really was as he looked into her pretty face. The old Marine found himself mesmerized by her beauty. But to him, she did not really look colored at all. *She's a mulatto,* he thought to himself. He forced himself out of his trance. "Nah, the Klan is the biggest bunch of organized morons this country has ever produced. Those idiots are not bright enough to aim. Come on in. Trisha's had a bee in her bonnet ever since y'all said y'all were coming. I'm mighty proud you came."

As she entered, Vanessa's eyes darted around the tiny foyer as she tried to take it all in. Wanting to remember everything, she felt excited to be inside a real home finally! As the two men chatted, she did not hear a word and instead focused on the living room, where a throw rug was in front of the couch. *Wonderful,* she thought. *There is not one rug in the entire orphanage. So, this is how families live, with rugs on the floor!* Surveying the furnishings, she noted that a television set was in front of two stuffed chairs. Unlike the orphanage's straight wooden chairs, these looked comfortable, and she wanted to sit in one just to see how truly luxurious it would feel. Every inch of the walls held family photographs that were mostly black and white. Mr. Bibbs looked about twenty years old in a picture with his World War II Marine Corps uniform.

"Son, your dad and I had our differences in Korea, but tell him how much I appreciate his coming to visit. That was genuinely nice. I know he is a remarkably busy man."

"We were all worried, but my dad worried the most. He said it was a great relief to see how well Trisha was doing. He just hopes that she will take it easy."

"Tell him not to worry about that, son. Trisha's wanted to hold court her entire life and has gotten her wish." Mr. Bibbs noticed that Vanessa's gorgeous face was staring into space. "Come on, kids. Let's go see the princess herself!" He motioned toward the hallway.

Vanessa lingered momentarily in the dining room to study the beautiful crystal inside the china cabinet. Above the matching table and chairs hung a portrait of the Last Supper. Reluctantly, she followed but was concerned she might have missed some detail.

"Trisha, are you decent? You've got company, and one of your visitors is a hell of a lot taller than me." Sgt. Bibbs escorted them into the bedroom. "Barry, when you've had enough of these women squawking, I want to show you my model airplane collection. It's over yonder!"

CHAPTER THREE

Vanessa rushed to hug Trisha. "How are you doing?" Nervously, she straightened the sheets as Barry towered over the tiny twin bed, which took up most of the room.

"I'd feel a lot better if my hair would grow back overnight," Trisha complained. "I still don't understand why your dad shaved my entire head to drill a couple of holes."

"He didn't. Nurse Bow did, so you'll have to take that up with her," Barry replied.

"I like your hat," Vanessa lied.

"I hate it. My mother bought it yesterday. It's an old lady's hat!"

"If I had my druthers, you won't bitch the whole time we are here."

"Barry, be nice!" Vanessa turned around, hitting him lightly on the arm.

"Bitching is a family art form passed down from generations." Trisha smirked. "Besides, you're not going to get out of this house without seeing my dad's airplane collection. You might as well get it over with right now. Let me put it to you like this, Barry. Airplanes are to my dad what American history is to Sister Rosalie." Trisha smiled.

"OK, I get the big picture." Barry then disappeared into the hallway.

* * *

Trisha flung the sheets back. "Gee, he was easy to get rid of."

"I thought you couldn't get out of bed." Vanessa watched in disbelief.

"Follow me. It's a good old-fashioned miracle." Trisha motioned with her hand. At the end of the hall, they entered a small, cheerful bedroom where family pictures graced the walls. Barb, the older sister in college, whom Vanessa had never met, looked pretty in the photographs. Trisha slid the closet door open, grabbed two long gowns, and threw them on the bed. One was a beautiful lavender, sleeveless, while the other was a deep rich purple color with long sleeves. "Hurry up. It won't be long before my dad bores Barry to death." She gasped for air.

"These are gorgeous!" Vanessa exclaimed.

"Where are those blasted shoes? Dad's right. They're not in here. But why would Barb take them? They only match these evening gowns." Trisha flung herself on the bed. "Those dresses have hung here for years. My mother complains about the waste of money every time she opens this closet. And I ask you, do I look like I can go to the prom?" She lifted her hat off and exposed her bare scalp with two burr holes drilled into her skull.

Shock at the sight of her friend's totally bald head filled Vanessa's eyes with tears. "Oh, Trisha, it's all my fault." She burst into loud weeping.

"Nonsense. This is the best thing that ever happened to me. At sweet sixteen, I made the newspapers. None of this local yokel stuff like the *Hanahan News*. My picture made the *Charleston Evening Post*, and thank God that they used one with hair! Plus, my parents are totally catering to me. They have never been nicer." Trisha stayed totally flat to breathe.

"Are you OK? Should I get your father?" Vanessa wiped away her tears.

"I'm fine, but hurry up. My father is probably driving Barry straight up the wall."

"Should I change in the bathroom?" Vanessa asked shyly.

"Absolutely not! Change right here! Hustle up!" Trisha shut her eyes to rest.

Quickly taking her clothes off, she slid the purple gown on over her shoulders. "Can you help me with this zipper? It's really long."

"Bend over because all of a sudden, I'm feeling dizzy." Vanessa put Trisha's hand on the bottom of the zipper to help her zip up the dress. As she went to the dresser mirror, she could see from the waist up and instantly loved the deep, rich purple gown. "Climb on that desk chair so you can see what it looks like," Trisha suggested.

After dragging the chair over, she lifted the skirt to step up while holding on to the back of the chair. Peering into the small glass, she loved how beautiful the dress looked. As far as she was concerned, the gown was positively heavenly! She had never worn anything nice, only hand-me-downs given to the orphanage. Even her school uniform was used, donated by a graduating senior the year before. Brand-new clothes felt different, a strange yet delightful experience! The material on her usual outfits had been worn thin. This starched material had a distinctive feel as it rubbed against her skin. "I want to wear this one!"

"Don't be ridiculous. Try them both on here so I can see." Trisha tried to open her eyes.

"Why? I love this one." Vanessa was entranced by her own image in the glass.

"It's drop-dead gorgeous, but no one ever buys the first one. They try on dozens. For Pete's sake, try on the other one and take them both." Trisha felt exhausted and weak and just wanted her best friend to leave so she could sleep.

"But I adore this dress, and I'm going to wear it. I assure you." She lifted the gown to get down, and Trisha used her last bit of strength to help Vanessa into the second dress. The sleeveless lavender gown flowed to the floor. Totally transfixed, she never looked away from the mirror. "I love this one more, but Sister Roe will never let me wear it."

"Why not? I'm glad you tried on both. I come from a long line of shoppers."

"It's too much, way too much. Sister Roe would have a coronary."

Trisha attempted to lift her head. "First of all, it is full length, which would automatically give it an A plus in any nun's book. Even the nuns would admit no boy could take a mirror and look up your dress. It is too darn dark in there for even patent leather shoes to reflect up! The only body part that shows is your shoulders. Listen up. Even my mother, who is a 'nun without a habit,' gave her stamp of virginal approval to this dress. You're nuts, completely nuts, if you think my mother would think any differently than Sister Roe."

"I have never worn a dress without sleeves in my entire life. It just seems so risqué, like a hussy. If he looks down this top, he'll see plenty." She carefully stepped down from the chair.

After a quick knock, Mr. Bibbs opened the door, "Come on, girls, and give this poor fellow a break. Quit doing whatever girl stuff y'all are doing in there. Get on out here and visit with this guy." Irritated, he slammed the door shut.

"Oh no, did Barry see me?"

"No way! Dad only opened the door two inches for a split second. I guarantee Barry saw zero. Where in the world did my sister put the matching shoes?"

"We keep shoes underneath the beds at Saint Paul's. I bet she put them there." She bent down. "Here they are." Vanessa placed the shoes on top of the bed, as Trisha swatted them away.

"Quick! Get them off! My grandmother told me it was bad luck to put shoes on the bed." Reacting instantly to the wicked premonition, Trisha knocked the high heels off the bed, and they landed on the other side of the room. One thing Southern women know a lot about is bad-luck omens. If one tells another how to avoid evil, the other will listen and follow instructions.

"Boy, that's a new one! Shoes on the bed must have slipped right on by Sister Roe. How am I ever going to get these things back to Saint Paul's?"

"That's weird. I cannot believe my sister put those shoes under her bed. It just shows you how much we dust around here! Anyhow, do not worry! Just leave everything here, and my dad will put them in the back seat of the car." Trisha got more fatigued by the minute. "Don't worry. Barry will never know a thing unless y'all decide to go parking."

"Trisha, I can't believe you said that!" Vanessa feigned shock.

"Methinks thou dost protest too much!" she quoted from her Shakespeare class. "Now help me up." She placed the hat on her bald head.

* * *

Sgt. Bibb's airplane lecture was still going on until the girls interrupted him. Barry seemed interested, but it was hard to tell because he was so polite.

"Well, ladies, I'm glad you could join us," Sgt. Bibbs said with a twinkle in his eye.

Trisha climbed into bed and got under the sheets, and the three teenagers spent the next half hour laughing about the latest school gossip. Completely bored, she did not want Vanessa to feel badly, so she put the best face on her misfortune. Finally, Sgt. Bibbs came in and told them that Trisha should get some rest and to say goodbye.

* * *

Sgt. Bibbs walked them to the car and opened the door for Vanessa. Before getting in, she turned to Mr. Bibbs and timidly stated, "Do you know that Sister Roe is dying to come visit Trisha?"

"When I get to the point where I cannot stand one more phone call, I will quit torturing the old broad and relent. Can't wait to see what weird new book she is peddling on American history. Drive carefully, and have fun at the prom."

* * *

Mrs. Bibbs drove up.and her husband came over to greet her.

"Hi, honey," she said as they hugged. "I pity the poor girls at the prom! That Barry is prettier than any girl at that high school!"

"Ain't that the damn truth

They laughed as they went through the front door.

* * *

Vanessa turned around to see the Piggly Wiggly grocery bags in the back seat. She smiled and slid across the front seat. "Barry, it will be a night you will never forget."

"It looks like it's going to be an afternoon that we'll never forget."

"What do you mean, afternoon?" Vanessa came out of her romantic trance.

"Didn't you hear? Today at school, they made an announcement that the prom is going to be at high noon instead of Saturday night. With martial law still in effect, we have to be off the streets and home by five o'clock to meet the curfew."

"Don't they make exceptions for important dances like the senior prom?"

"Apparently not! They are continuing to refuse Doctor King's request for a parade permit. The governor of South Carolina has decided to keep martial law in effect with a curfew so all citizens must be in their homes by 5:00 p.m. Since the Francis Marion Hotel will not let us cancel, Father Kelly said we will have it during the day. Everyone started booing and hissing. Raising his hand for silence, he told us to wear sunglasses and imagine that it is nighttime. Father Kelly said he would personally make sure that the hotel manager kept all the drapes closed, so we will really think it is nine o'clock at night. He was funny as all get out! Where were you anyway?" Barry accelerated onto the interstate to take Vanessa back to the orphanage.

"Sister Roe had no one to stay with the toddlers. One of the older kids was sick and needed to go to the pediatrician. I was not there so I had no idea. Is it still formal?"

"Absolutely. Father Kelly wants us to wear a tux with our sunglasses."

A strange and powerful sensation came over Vanessa as they drove along. For the first time in her life, she had been touched by someone other than Sister Roe or one of the younger orphans, and it felt incredibly wonderful.

CHAPTER FOUR

After entering the orphanage, Vanessa ran upstairs excitedly. She could barely wait to show Sister Roe the two new evening gowns. She found the nun in the nursery with all the toddlers. The youngest baby, only six months old, slept soundly in the corner. Sitting on the floor and using old broken pencils, the two and three-year-olds were drawing on scrap paper. Crayons were much too expensive, so the children used pencils confiscated from the bishop's office. "Sister Roe, I have the formals I borrowed from Trisha's sister, Barb. Want to see them?"

"Honey child, you know that I do! Don't hesitate a plum second to slip them on!"

Vanessa lifted the rich purple gown out but decided to keep the sleeveless lavender dress hidden inside the grocery bag. She imagined that the nun would not agree to let her wear it. "Hurry, child. I am absolutely dying to see them on you. I just know you will be the belle of the ball!"

Slipping on the deep purple dress, she managed the zipper without any help and leaned over to get the matching shoes. A three-year-old cooed, "You look like Cinderella!"

"Indeed, she does, child. Indeed, she does!" Sister Rosalie exclaimed.

Standing up, she slid her feet into the purple high heels. As all well-dressed Southern ladies did, Trisha's sister Barb had her shoes dyed perfectly to match the color of the dress.

"You look pretty, Nessa," a toddler muttered through her pacifier.

"I wish Robert Mills could be alive today. We sure do need him. Yes, indeed!"

"Who?" Vanessa looked puzzled. "And why do we need him?"

"Child, Robert Mills was the first professional architect in the United States, born and educated right here in Charleston! During the antebellum age, the nation's greatest architects designed buildings for Charleston. We need Mr. Mills to design a staircase worthy of your descent in that breathtaking gown. Now hurry, sugar. Let me see the other one in case Mr. Mills descends from the heavens to do the perfect blueprint of a stairwell for you."

"But, Sister Roe, the lavender dress is sleeveless."

"So?"

"Well, don't you think it's a little risqué?" Vanessa anticipated her disapproval.

"Child, lavender is my all-time favorite color. Put it on quick."

Vanessa slid the gown on.

"Turn around, child. Oh my, I see Charleston's Mrs. Charles Cotesworth Pinckney in 1797, when her husband was the American minister to France. I bet she wore a dress like this in Paris. Of course, it is your choice, but you should wear this one. You look positively marvelous in it."

Leaping forward, she threw her arms around the nun's neck. "This is the first thing I've ever worn in my life that wasn't a hand-me-down." Vanessa beamed with the nun's approval.

"Child, if I hadn't taken that blasted vow of poverty and had any money, you would never have been forced to wear those old rags. I would have dressed you in the finest silks."

"It's OK, Sister Roe. Look at me now! I really am Cinderella!"

"Honey child, watch the young'uns. I'll be right back." After lifting her huge frame off the floor, she scampered down the hall and entered the tiny space with a twin bed that the nun called a bedroom. Its only furnishings were an old Tiffany lamp that adorned a tattered desk. She put her chubby fingers around a box that was visibly battered by age and lifted out the contents. After sailing back down the hall, she was out of breath when she extended her hand to display a gold hairpin while she smiled proudly.

"Oh, Sister Roe. I cannot wear this pin! It's your mother's. It's gold!"

"Nonsense, child. If my momma were alive today, she would say, 'This isn't doing my daughter the nun any good!'"

"Are you sure? What if I lose it?"

"Well, child, I suppose you will be in trouble with my momma. God rest her soul!"

"I've never put my hair on top of my head before."

"Why, sugar, that's why we must go to visit the Heyward-Washington House. My momma spent her entire life cleaning that place from top to bottom! My momma was always proud to work there because Mr. Daniel Heyward Jr. signed the Declaration of Independence. His wife's portrait is in the foyer, and this is the hairpin she used. The Charleston Museum runs tours of the house, and they gave it to my momma upon her retirement. The curator felt certain that Mr. and Mrs. Heyward Jr. would want my momma to have it. On her deathbed, she gave it to me and said she hoped it would bring me joy. I want you to have it. That's real joy for me."

"Oh no! I cannot take this! It is yours! It's your mother's!"

"Child, she gave it to her only daughter, and now you are sweet sixteen, so I'm giving it to you. The Lord sent you to me on October 10, 1952, and you have made my life magical since the moment I set eyes on you. I am your momma, and I want you to have it. Take it, honey, and always remember from where it came." Tears swelled in their eyes as they hugged. "Let's go over and see Mrs. Hayward's hair." Sister Rosalie chuckled. "Our volunteers are here to watch the little ones. Let's scramble."

"I'd love to." Unzipping the gown, Vanessa slipped out of the high heels.

* * *

Grabbing the one ten-year-old, they all piled inside the orphanage's beaten-up Buick. They arrived just in time for the last public tour. The Heyward House staff knew Sister Rosalie and let them in but insisted that the youngster stay in the garden because of the valuable antiques inside. After entering, they stared at the portrait hanging high above the staircase. While the tour guide on the second level lectured about the early inhabitants of the house, they studied the oil painting. Without speaking, they turned around and left.

Once outside, the nun exclaimed, "If Mrs. Heyward could do that to her hair two hundred years ago, we can figure out how to do it today, child. You'll be pretty as a peach!"

"Sister Roe, it's so beautiful that no one is going to look at my hair." Vanessa beamed with pride as she spoke. "Everyone will be staring at my golden hairpin."

* * *

A week later, on the morning of the prom, Vanessa woke up early and washed her hair. Right after breakfast, Sister Rosalie started fussing with it as the orphans watched with fascination since no one had ever messed with their hair. Usually, a comb was quickly run through all the children's hair so they would not cry. There were no bows and no time to primp! Mounted over the communal sink was the only mirror in the entire orphanage. It was the size of a small puzzle. Sister Roe dragged a chair over so Vanessa could see herself in the tiny mirror. Working tirelessly, she used all three of the orphanage's combs. She was quite pleased with the results, but the nun was not so she tore the whole hairdo apart and started over again. While fumbling with Vanessa's hair, she reached into her habit and produced a brand-new tube of lipstick that she placed in the teenager's hands.

"Where in the world did you get this?" Vanessa asked in astonishment.

"Where else but my favorite store, the Woolworth Five and Dime?" she proclaimed proudly. "It was on sale, too. It is called Carolina Poppy. I do believe it's a great color to wear."

"Oh, I love it! Thank you."

"You are most welcome, my dear."

"I can't believe you are going to let me wear makeup!"

"Honey, if I weren't married to God and wearing this habit, I'd for sure be painting my lips every day of the week. Sundays, too! Lipstick must be heaven-sent!"

"Can I try it on right now?"

"Why, of course, darling! Your hair and lips must be perfect for Mr. Barry Hale. Why the poor boy won't know what hit him!" The nun giggled with the surrounding youngsters. It was a big occasion, and all the children, no matter what their ages, were excited. At eleven o'clock, Vanessa put on her gown and matching lavender high heels. A strand of curls cascaded down both checks, while the rest of her hair was piled high atop her head. Sister Roe's lipstick was a perfect complement to the lovely lavender silk formal that hugged her bare shoulders. "With this much exposed skin, child, we must find you a gold chain to wear!" Obviously delighted at her own fashion sense, the nun took off the gold chain from around her own neck. "We'll leave the Lord here with me today." She took the crucifix off the necklace and placed it in her pocket. With two hands, she gingerly arranged the gold chain around her bare neck as Vanessa started to sob. "Now, now, sweetheart! I have worked too hard today to have you go out of here with red eyes. Red clashes with lavender. No crying and no red eyes."

A loud ring of the *H. L. Hunley* replica bell diverted their attention. "He's here!" screamed the orphans as they stampeded to open the door.

"I have a surprise for you," she whispered. "Mrs. Hale called, and since martial law is still in effect, she invited you for supper and to spend the night in their guest room."

"Why didn't you tell me? He's here right now."

"Don't worry, honey. I already packed a bag with your favorite things. Look, it is right here! Check and make sure I thought of everything."

"But why didn't you tell me?"

"Because, sweetie, I didn't think you could sleep if you knew what a big day this was going to be." She opened the battered overnight case for the orphan to inspect, but Vanessa was so stunned she barely glanced inside. "I'll carry it for you, honey. We mustn't soil that beautiful silk." Holding hands, they walked slowly toward the front entrance. The children had surrounded Barry, who held one toddler in each arm while the others grabbed his thighs. The older kids stared at him because they had never seen a tuxedo before, and it looked strange to them. With a matching cummerbund, the white formal attire made Barry the most handsome man Vanessa had ever laid eyes on. She felt her heart pounding at the sight of him until Sister Roe interrupted her trance.

"Why, Mr. Hale, I do declare, you are a sight for this old lady's eyes! Son, I reckon you are taking the wrong girl to the prom! Why, with my white full-length habit and your white tux, we could cut a rug until that old nasty martial law forces us apart at five."

"Why, Mrs. Robinson, are you trying to seduce me?"

"Now, don't you go comparing me to that old Anne Bancroft in *The Graduate.* When I got done with Dustin Hoffman, there is just no way he would have gone running off with Katherine Ross. No way!"

Regaining her composure, Vanessa intervened. "Now, Sister Roe, you wouldn't want to scandalize Charleston society like Scarlett did in Atlanta, would you?"

"Oh, how could I possibly have raised such a levelheaded child?" The nun lifted her hands toward the heavens in prayer. "Child, you are right. I will just have to stay home tonight with the man that I married! Now y'all get off Mr. Hale before we must take his tux to the cleaners. Come on, children, get off him this instant." She gathered the toddlers in her arms.

"Vanessa, are you ready?" Barry asked shyly.

"Yes, I've been ready since last week." She cringed when she realized what she had just said.

"Now, children, I want to take a photograph of this most auspicious occasion." Sister Roe ushered them onto the porch and thrilled the oldest orphan by letting him take the picture. The nun stood between the two teenagers, and Barry put one arm around her. The child focused the camera and pressed the button carefully. "Mr. Hale, I'm going to ask you a question. If you get it wrong, you take me to the prom. If you get it right, you get to take the lovely Vanessa. As a South Carolinian, I hope you take the time to study this great state's history."

"Be merciful, Sister. Just remember, I could be alive when the Vatican comes around asking questions about your sainthood," Barry retorted. Vanessa could tell from the smile on Sister Roe's face that the nun loved Barry just as much as she did. She hoped for a quick question, so they could go to the prom.

"Son, if you do not know the answer, then you should not be allowed the honor of living in this extraordinary state." The nun grinned while contemplating her own sainthood. "Our eminent South Carolinian John C. Calhoun served our country as vice president under John Quincy Adams and Andrew Jackson. Why did he resign his vice presidency under Jackson to become a South Carolina senator?"

"Piece of cake, Vanessa. We are out of here!" Barry quipped confidently. "Calhoun wrote the 'South Carolina Exposition and Protest,' which our legislature adopted in 1828 as its manifesto against bad federal laws. Calhoun claimed the right of states to nullify federal laws that they deemed unconstitutional." He paused to take a deep breath. "When South Carolina declared the tariff laws null and void, President Jackson responded with the threat of force."

"Oh, child, can you imagine it?" the nun interrupted excitedly. "The president threatened military force on his own ex-vice president's state! What marvelous times these were! Unlike today, those politicians had backbone!"

Barry ignored her outburst. "Calhoun devised a theory of secession and prescribed the steps for leaving the Union. Calhoun died, but his ideas lived on, to be invoked again in 1861 when South Carolina did indeed leave the Union."

"Positively excellent, Mr. Hale!" She clapped her hands as all the children joined in a hearty round of applause. "Why, Mr. Calhoun, I pray you had no clue your ideas would destroy the Union thirty-three years later when you were dead and six feet under." She swayed her hips. "Go dance up a storm, and come back with sore feet. You do know how to dance, don't you?"

"I learned from the best: my mother!" Barry answered eagerly.

"Well, time's a-wasting! Y'all better get going. Five o'clock will be here before y'all know it." Sister Roe ushered them to the stairs. "I go to bed at midnight. Y'all call me before then."

"Yes, ma'am," Vanessa replied and descended the steps carefully in her high heels.

"Make sure you are a proper Southern gentleman, Mr. Hale." She grinned while letting all the toddlers ring the bell. He threw the tattered suitcase into the trunk and opened the car door for Vanessa. While backing out of the driveway, they both waved to the orphans on the porch, who were furiously ringing the bell. The nun laughed as she helped each one up for a turn.

* * *

When they arrived on Calhoun Street, Barry confessed, "Vanessa, you were right. It was obviously going to be Calhoun."

"She's predictable." Vanessa grabbed his hand and used him as a crutch to help her walk in the uncomfortable shoes. "Did your mother really teach you to dance?"

"My mother is as predictable as yours. She only taught me ballroom dancing."

Vanessa felt like a princess as she walked gingerly inside the stately old building that represented the grandeur of the old South. The Francis Marion Hotel boasted vaulted ceilings accented by its legendary spiral staircase. Stirring portraits lined the walls within dramatic wooden frames. A magnificent crystal chandelier, from which sublime lighting radiated, hung in the grand foyer. Reminiscent of the antebellum era, hardwood floors were exposed ever so slightly while covered with oversized antique rugs. An oil painting of Mr. Francis Marion himself was prominently displayed at the top of the stairs. After they ascended the stairs, the couple stood in front of his portrait and stared.

"He was distinguished looking," Vanessa commented as she studied his face.

"He looks good for a guy who hung out in our swamps and harassed the British for years. I wonder what he would have to say about fighting the Vietnamese in their swamps?"

"I think he'd say, 'Hey! Hey! LBJ! How many kids have you killed today?'"

"Come on, Vanessa. Give the guy a break. He says he won't run again."

"I know, I know. I heard his, 'I shall not seek nor will I accept another term' speech yesterday. Just remember March 31, 1968, another broken promise."

"Boy, you are hard on the old guy!" Barry interrupted.

"He deserves it. You know that the only ones getting killed over there are poor."

"Hey, Vanessa, don't forget that I'm getting a student deferment."

"And you're not poor, are you?"

A hand touched each of their shoulders, and Father Kelly, their principal, joked, "Well, what do we have here, Mr. and Mrs. Bishop England?"

"Wrong skin color, Father," Barry quipped.

"We are all God's children." The Irish priest winked. "I can assure you that the big fish on the high school campus today are no bigger than a minnow in a fishing pond, as you locals say!"

"We'll get to be big barracudas after high school?" Barry asked in jest.

"I expect great things from the both of you. You two are clearly our best and our brightest. Especially today since I got roped into being today's chaperone. I hope you will be on your best behavior when I skip out of here for my two o'clock tee-off time."

"Gee, Father, why didn't you ask Sister Roe to do it? She would have loved to come."

"Of course, I asked her. She was my only hope to rope into this miserable job. But she did not want to ruin your day, so she decided to ruin mine." He winked again.

"I'll make it up to you by giving you my first dance."

"That's all I need is for the Baptists who work here to see me dancing with one of my students! Guess what I did?" he asked in his thick Irish brogue.

"Played a round of golf?" Barry guessed.

"No, I actually went to the library and looked up the origins of the Klan. We don't have this lovely organization in Ireland!"

"Ireland sounds like a good place to be from."

The Irishman eagerly conveyed his newly acquired knowledge about a uniquely American phenomenon. "In 1865, veterans of the Confederate Army formed a private social club in Pulaski, Tennessee, called the Ku Klux Klan. The etymology of 'Ku Klux Klan' is not easily penetrated. The most widely accepted theory is that Ku Klux is a literate misspelling of the Greek word kuklos, meaning "ring," and Klan is the word for 'clan' spelled with a K."

"Great! They misspelled it!" Vanessa giggled.

"Father, they could have built a golf course and worried more about their slice than burning crosses. Golf pants, not white sheets, could have been their uniforms!" Barry swung an imaginary golf club. "Golf clubs and Spanish moss could have been the only things hanging from trees in the South!"

"Anger could have been directed at a little ball rather than people," the priest said. "OK, Vanessa, since you asked me to dance, then it's the good old Irish jig." He grabbed her arm as they entered the ornate ballroom. "Oh, you are out of luck! They are not playing any Irish jig music. It must not be a big seller around here. If anyone asks, tell them I'm cleaning Saint Mary's fishy hands, a dead fish in each hand." The priest quickly disappeared.

"Well, I guess you'll have to dance with me," Barry announced. They entered the empty dance floor as the band played a Drifters song, *Under the Boardwalk*. "Looks like we're the only ones who showed."

"I doubt that. You know those Charlestonian women! They make their dates wait with their folks so they can be fashionably late and appear not to be overly eager."

"I think it's kind of cool that we were here first. We can pretend that we live in this immense mansion, the kids are asleep, and we are dancing in our ballroom," Barry mused.

"I like the way you think, dreamer," she commented as he placed his arm around her back and slid his cheek directly on hers as they danced slowly to the music. Five fingers ran leisurely up and down her back as he deliberately stroked her exposed bare skin. She was nervous and horrified that she did not have on a bra. Sister Roe had tried unsuccessfully to create a strapless bra by sewing the straps down, but it would not stay up. Her mother, the nun, decided it would be better if she went without one. She felt embarrassed as he explored her naked backside.

He knew exactly what she was thinking and made her feel at ease. "I like the fact that I can feel your skin. Nothing but this beautiful dress is between us. The last time I touched you, I could not sleep the whole night. I tried to pretend you were my pillow. It sounds silly, but I kept kissing my pillow with my eyes closed while dreaming of you. I sure hope the entire class of sixty-eight does a no-show." While the slow rhythm of the music pressed their bodies closer together, they were oblivious to their fellow classmates wandering in. They stayed on the dance floor, ignoring everyone around them. Finally, they sat down at a table and ordered two RC Colas. Sliding his chair closer, he put his arm around her shoulders as he took her palm and crossed both legs so her hand could feel the sure weight of his thighs as he squeezed them tightly together. Glancing around, the couple noticed that the room was full now. The cheerleaders were bubbly even without their pom-poms, while the class officers worked the room like incumbents seeking reelection.

"Our class president never figured out he was a one-termer," Barry joked.

The senior class had decorated extensively and erected an enormous replica of their senior ring. While standing underneath the monstrosity, Barry and Vanessa had their picture taken. The students began leaving when the band quit playing at three o'clock. Barry waited outside the women's restroom and thought about Vanessa being inside with all the White girls. Ever since he could remember, drinking fountains and bathrooms had a sign overhead that read, "Colored." As a kid, he frequently asked his mother why they had to drink out of different water fountains than White people. A biologist, she explained that the people who made those laws knew nothing about science. Uneducated people enforced this code. Until this moment, he never fully understood what she meant. Vanessa was much prettier than any of those white girls, and she deserved to be in there with them.

Emerging from the ladies' room, Vanessa extended her hand, so they could walk together arm in arm. She glanced back over her shoulder and whispered, "Thank you, Mr. Marion. I had a wonderful time today in your hotel."

Barry stopped to study the incredibly old oil painting of Francis Marion. "Swamp Fox, you kicked the British out of our swamps. Because of you, our accents are worse than theirs."

* * *

Since it was only a little after three, the couple decided to visit White Point Gardens, which faced the Battery and overlooked the Atlantic Ocean. Charlestonians claimed a pirate had been hung there from every tree, and the oaks had been planted far apart, so the buccaneers could not return to the sea together. Local legend also alleged that the Ashley and Cooper Rivers met at the Battery to form the Atlantic Ocean as Fort Sumter guarded the entrance to the harbor.

As Barry parked the car, waves crashed over the railing. The choppy sea was at high tide when he opened the door for Vanessa. She adored the spray of saltwater mist on her face before the whitecaps hit the sidewalk pavement. The couple strolled along as breakers surged over the retaining wall. Cars passing by honked at the two lovers in formal attire. "Let's go somewhere more private," Barry murmured over the loud blast of car horns.

* * *

While crossing the street to the park, Barry spotted a group of huge azalea bushes that formed a complete circle. They were covered in a burst of assorted red, white, and pink blossoms, and the enormous flowers touched a Civil War cannon nearby. Their colors took over Charleston, renowned in the spring for the Azalea Festival, during March. Barry held an azalea bush back, and Vanessa entered a gloriously private place, surrounded by blooming walls.

Fragrant buds gave a pleasant aroma to the little hideaway while thick, plush grass carpeted the ground.

Her eyes studied nature's grandeur until Barry placed his hands on her bare shoulders and rubbed her skin gently. He thrust his tongue between her lips and kissed her while his right hand explored her body. Using the soft flow of silk from the gown, he slid his fingers easily over the material to probe and to circle her buttocks. Slowly and cautiously, he stopped at the fabric that clung to her breasts. Moving one hand below her bosom and running it over her stomach, he leaned his tall frame over to touch the inside of her thighs. He pulled his tongue out of her mouth and kissed her cheeks and ears. Her heart pounded much faster than when they had been together last week. She loved his caress since an orphan's life never contained much touching.

"Vanessa, I've got a hard-on," Barry whispered in her ear softly.

"A what?"

"Baby, I've got an erection," he repeated, thinking she had not heard him.

"What?"

"Sweetie, I've got an erection."

"What's that?" Vanessa asked innocently.

"You're kidding, right?" he asked in utter disbelief at her innocence.

"No, Barry, what is it? What is an erection? What is a hard-on?"

"Oh great! Of all the girls I could have asked to the prom, I go with the one who knows absolutely nothing about sex."

"Take me back to Saint Paul's now! Right now!" She started through the azalea branches, but his strong physique overpowered her.

"I'm sorry. I'm deeply sorry." Barry squeezed her arms tightly.

"I'm leaving. So, let me go. I'll walk if I have to."

"Sorry, but I didn't think it was possible at sixteen to not know what an erection was."

"OK, Barry Hale. I do not know what an erection is, but I do know that I am going back to Saint Paul's! I will not sleep in the same house with a cad. If I could figure out a way to set off this cannon, I'd turn it on you and try for a direct hit."

"Calm down!"

Vanessa tried to break free. "Let go of me. You're hurting my arm."

"You are not going anywhere until you forgive me for being such a jerk. It just dawned on me. Who is going to tell you about sex? A nun stuck in the wrong century?"

"Don't insult Sister Roe. She was quite a man's lady in her day."

Barry started laughing uncontrollably at the thought of Sister Roe ever being with a man. "That leaves quite a picture in my head." As he let go of her arms, tears filled his eyes and streamed down his cheeks. "Are you still going to blow me and these azaleas away with this rusty old cannon?"

"I'll let you live, only if you tell me what you are talking about."

"Gee, Vanessa! I have never talked to a girl about sex, only the guys in the locker room at school and the time my father asked me if I had any questions."

"It must be neat to have a doctor as a father. He must know everything there is about the subject. No one has ever even brought it up, much less told me anything!"

"I'm certainly no expert."

"Well, you probably know tons more than I do."

Barry leaned back on the grass, and his strong biceps gently lifted her body on top of his. While caressing her, he tastefully explained what was happening to him physically. Discreetly placing his hand on hers, he guided her between his legs while asking permission every step of the way. Inconspicuously directing the fondling of his private parts, he controlled every move, but he never stopped kissing Vanessa during the process. Soon his tuxedo coat was lying in a heap on the grass. Barry asked if he could take off her gown, but she declined so he did not force her to undress. Instead, he explained how intolerable it was to get excited and not to be able to release his passion. He begged her to let him have an orgasm as he carefully orchestrated each caress. Suddenly, he started moaning as she felt a wetness descend on her palm. Tears came to her eyes when he called out in what seemed like pain. Watching, she felt frightened as a clear yet creamy fluid oozed all over her hand. "Vanessa, honey, don't cry. Please." He embraced her tiny figure and fondled both breasts while her sobbing prevailed. She hugged him tightly as he licked her tears away. "I have a hankie." Tears crept down her cheeks as Barry used the little piece of cloth to wipe his sticky thighs. She loved the intimacy that exploring his body brought her. His physique was so different from the boys' at the orphanage.

"I wonder what time it is?" Barry extended his arm for her to look at his watch.

"It's a quarter to five! There is no way we can make it to your house before the curfew."

"Let's go!" Barry jumped up and managed to zip his pants while gathering everything else into his arms. Rushing through the branches of the azalea bushes, they sprinted for the car.

"You better not take the interstate. It's closed after five o'clock, and they block off all the exit ramps," Vanessa warned.

"Let's give it a shot. If we go on the city streets, it will take us forever. Maybe, they will be laxer since Martin Luther King left Charleston." Barry tried to convince himself that nothing bad would come of their breaking curfew.

* * *

Something brushed against her cheek and dropped into her lap. Her hair fell to her shoulders as she glanced down at the gold hairpin. Suddenly full of dread at the thought of losing Sister Roe's antique pin, she grabbed the jewel. Knowing that she would soon meet Barry's parents, she took out her comb to fix her hair, which was now in disarray. Vanessa desperately wanted to look her best, so they would like her. She did not want to face them looking like she had been in the bushes with their son. With no mirror, she persisted in straightening herself.

"Vanessa! You're going to have to help me get dressed while I drive."

"Why don't you let me drive?"

"I thought you didn't know how?"

"How hard could it be? Don't you just put your foot on the gas and aim?"

"Hold the steering wheel while I get dressed."

"Can you get that cummerbund on while sitting behind the wheel?"

"As long as you don't steer us into a tree, I can handle it. But I must admit, my mother basically dressed me this morning."

"Yeah, Sister Roe fussed with my hair for three solid hours. It's too bad your mom won't see it up since my hair suffered a major collapse."

"Vanessa, it looks great up. It looks great down. You have great hair."

"Great!" The orphan giggled nervously as Barry drove through red lights and referred to them as pink. He entered the completely deserted interstate and as far ahead in the distance as they could see, their car was the only one on the road. An eerie feeling crept over Vanessa when he let her take control of the steering wheel. Barry kept his foot firmly on the accelerator as the car sped along, and he fumbled with his tuxedo while imploring Vanessa to keep the car in between the white lines. Vanessa thought about how odd this day had become, and now her concern focused on meeting Barry's parents.

"Here's our exit. You've got to start driving," she cautioned, not wanting to maneuver the car off the interstate ramp.

"I'm having a big hassle with these cuff-links. You better do them."

I've never touched a pair of cufflinks in my life. I don't have a clue."

"It's weird. Put it through both sides, flip it up, and that holds it," Barry instructed.

"This sure is my day for holding stuff I've never held before."

"Vanessa!"

"Sorry, I could not resist!" She giggled as they entered Charleston's Negro section.

* * *

They knew they were safe and started to relax as they pulled into the circular driveway. Barry sweetly helped Vanessa out of the car while glancing at his reflection in the door's window. He straightened his bow tie and was startled when his mother opened the front door.

"Where in the world have you been, son? I was worried sick. It's five twenty."

"Sorry, Mom. We were talking and lost track of the time," he lied convincingly.

"You must be Vanessa." Mrs. Hale approached the top step.

"Yes, ma'am," she answered shyly. "I'm glad to meet you."

Their grand home had huge white columns reminiscent of the antebellum era. Immense bay windows adorned the double-door entrance. Mimicking old Southern architecture, the brand-new house was what wealthy people built in the suburbs. A house such as this magnificent one had never existed in Charleston's Negro neighborhood until the Hales had it custom built. These two highly educated professionals could easily afford this ostentatious display of wealth.

His mother immediately noticed that the entire backside of her son's white tuxedo was stained green. "What happened, Barry?"

"Is it OK if I tell your mom?" Vanessa looked at his perplexed face.

"Go ahead," Barry muttered in amazement.

"Well, Mrs. Hale, we decided to drive by the Battery to watch the ocean for a while when these awful redneck men came by to cause trouble."

"What did they do, honey?" his concerned mother asked.

Vanessa took a deep breath to be convincing. "I was scared! They said they didn't like Barry wearing white. They were going to make it black, a more appropriate color." She looked at the floor for dramatic effect, unable to think of anything else.

"Of course, you were, honey," she agreed, encouraging Vanessa to continue.

"I'm so grateful that you are both home, safe and sound."

"It's OK, Mom. No big deal," he mumbled as she embraced him. He rolled his eyes at Vanessa while returning his mother's hug. "I just want to go change before Dad gets home."

"You're absolutely right. There is no reason for these idiots who are roaming around Charleston causing chaos to ruin our night. I'll show Vanessa to her room."

"Thanks, Mom," Barry muttered.

"My dear, I adore your gown; it's positively lovely. Would you like to change into something more comfortable? Don't think you have to stay in formal attire for supper."

"Well, Mrs. Hale, if Barry is going to change, I think I will too," Vanessa answered sweetly although she really wanted to stay in the gown.

* * *

They slowly ascended the spiral staircase together as Mrs. Hale chatted while the orphan absorbed the surroundings. Overhead, a huge crystal chandelier sparkled brightly. It was suspended from the ceiling above the second level. Vanessa glanced back at the formal living room below, which was tastefully furnished and exquisite to view. Yet, it felt both warm and cozy. The highly polished hardwood floor boasted plush white carpet in front of the luxurious sofa and grand piano. A genteel roll-top antique desk located in front of a tall bookcase was completely full of artfully arranged books. Vanessa had never seen such opulence before as Mrs. Hale showed her to the guest room. Upon entering, she felt completely overwhelmed by the bedroom's elegance. To her amazement, the bed was covered by a spread made from the same material used to make the curtains. At the orphanage, bed covers were old, tattered gray blankets. Vanessa could not believe this bedroom was used only occasionally for company. To her astonishment, the adjoining bathroom contained a wonderful bathtub. Saint Paul's only had showers, so she had never actually taken a bath before.

Mrs. Hale made small talk while Vanessa remained engrossed by the furnishings. Until this moment, she had thought Trisha's house was fantastic, but now it seemed cheap and tacky. The difference between the two was unbelievable. It was her first realization that the United States had a class difference based solely on the house one lived in. Mrs. Hale left the room to get towels. Sitting down on the big post, Vanessa felt her body sink into its softness. Lots of extra pillows on top matched the bedspread. Suddenly, she wondered why Barry was going out with her. Wouldn't he want to go out with a girl who had a similar upbringing and shared the same experiences?

Not someone like herself, who grew up sleeping on a cot in a room with thirty other kids. Sister Roe asked for donations once a year. Around the holidays, clothes came in brown shopping bags, which she sorted through. Many were torn, so she would either patch or sew them under the nun's guidance.

When nothing came in her size, she had to wait until the next year and made do with what she had. She loved her uniform, even though hers were always used. Since everyone looked exactly alike at school, she never felt inferior. Vanessa jumped off the bed when Mrs. Hale returned. "Would you mind if I took a bath, ma'am?"

"Certainly, I'm sure you want to freshen up, so feel free and make yourself right at home. Is there anything else you need? I'm planning supper for seven o'clock."

"No, ma'am."

"Well, take your time then. Would you like a drink?"

"No, ma'am. Thank you." Vanessa shut the door softly and could hear footsteps when Mrs. Hale descended the stairs. She went over to the window and looked outside. Below was their perfectly landscaped backyard garden. Huge magnolia trees were covered with gorgeous white blossoms, and immense oak trees draped with moss lined the white picket fence. Hanging down to the ground, the Spanish moss waved slightly in the afternoon breeze. Numerous azaleas, as big as the ones at White Point Gardens, were planted together in a row and created a dramatic effect. The grounds were consumed with red azalea blossoms. Her imagination started to run wild, and she envisioned herself as the lady of this house. Barry would be a surgeon like his father, and they would have lots of children. Smiling, Vanessa created a picture in her mind of living happily ever after. Turning back around, she was drawn to a portrait of Frederick Douglass and a framed copy from the cover of *North Star*, the abolitionist newspaper he cofounded. Next to the painting was a matted newspaper article about his escape from slavery.

Leaning over, she read the small print. Frederick Douglass, an American abolitionist and journalist, became an influential lecturer in the North and abroad and wrote the *Narrative of the Life of Frederick Douglass*. Mesmerized,

Vanessa studied his picture carefully until a sudden knock at the door startled her. Quickly, she opened it, and Barry stood before her holding a glass in his hand. With wet hair, he was wearing blue jeans with a white T-shirt.

"Hi. My mom made you iced tea. If it tastes strange, it's because she always puts mint in it. What have you been doing in there?"

"Oh, I kind of got involved with Frederick Douglass." She pointed to the portrait.

"That's my grandmother's. She taught history for fifty years at Claflin University."

"It's really fantastic and lends such an air of class to the room. It's light-years ahead of those awful pictures of cowboys that people buy at Woolworth's."

"My mom hates Woolworth's."

"Really? Woolworth's is Sister Roe's favorite store."

"Well, here's your iced tea." Barry handed her the glass

"You took a bath too?"

"I felt kind of sticky if you know what I mean."

"Hush up! Hush up! Your mom might hear you." She put her fingers to her lips.

"No way. She's downstairs."

"Well, I'm going to take a bath too."

"OK, hurry. I miss you." He kissed her hard on the lips.

Vanessa shut the door with one hand and held the glass in the other. Leaning back and looking up at the ceiling, she felt totally and hopelessly in love. Once inside the bathroom, she noticed a bottle of bubble bath from France and decided to pour some into the running water. As the powder hit the stream, it created a mass of bubbles. Satisfied, she opened her battered cardboard suitcase. *God bless Sister Roe. She thought of everything*, Vanessa reflected. The nun had packed two casual outfits. For tomorrow's Mass, she picked her favorite dress and hat. It was very impressive that she had been able to get all this inside such a tiny space. Sister Roe had obviously spent hours on the project. Vanessa decided to wear a dress, even though Barry had jeans on. She wanted to look nice for him and particularly for his parents.

CHAPTER FOUR

After carefully placing the silk gown on the bed, she tested the water's temperature by putting her big toe in. Believing it was perfect, she slipped in and sank backward against the side. Feeling luxurious, she submerged into the warm sea of bubbles and stayed until a knock at the door made her leap out of the bathtub. Quickly, she wrapped a towel around herself while dripping water on the carpet and opened the door slightly.

"Vanessa, it's a quarter to seven. My dad's home from the hospital. We are eating at seven o'clock. You better step on it."

"I'm so sorry. I lost track of the time since I don't own a watch. Tell your mom I will be right down." After shutting the door, she raced to get dressed and then stuffed her bag in the closet. Frantically, she brushed her hair in front of the mirror and decided against lipstick just in case Barry's parents didn't approve of makeup.

* * *

Still perspiring from the hot bath, she ran downstairs and wasn't sure which way to go until she heard laughter and followed the sound into the extensive kitchen, where Mrs. Hale was stirring a dish on the stove. Polished pots and pans hung down from the lower ceiling above her head.

"Vanessa, we're having black beans and rice, fried okra, and ham hocks. It's my husband's favorite, so I hope you like it. How was the iced tea?"

"Oh gee, I forgot to bring my glass. I'll run up and get it."

"Don't be silly. Barry, go upstairs, dear, and get Vanessa's glass," Mrs. Hale ordered her son with a smile. He immediately hopped up off the couch in the adjoining room and breezed by them. Within seconds, he was back.

"Well, isn't anyone going to introduce me? I've been standing here a half hour," Doctor Hale quipped as he entered the room. "Supper smells great!"

"Dad, this is Vanessa," Barry introduced her tentatively.

Doctor Hale warmly extended his hand. "I hope today's incident didn't frighten you, my dear. I trained Barry to be a sprinter; he's supposed to outrun trouble."

"Her high heels slowed us down, Dad," Barry lied.

"I'm very glad to meet you, Doctor Hale." Vanessa wanted to stop all the lying. "Thank you for saving Trisha's life. That brick was meant for me."

"No, dear, it was not meant for you. It's a remarkably simple procedure." He kissed his wife and then asked, "What time do we eat?"

"Seven o'clock. What's with this group? I have been telling everyone since this morning that we were going to eat at seven."

"Good, I want to go change." He had on a physician's white coat over his suit.

"Be back here in ten minutes or else," Mrs. Hale ordered.

"Or else what?"

"Or else I'll start looking for husband number two," she joked.

"That's my mom's famous last line," Barry interrupted to explain.

"Keep the man in your life on notice till the cows come home," she advised.

"May I help you, Mrs. Hale?" She realized that she should have been downstairs to help.

"No, dear. You are a guest in my house. I don't want you to lift a finger. Please go sit down. Barry, please make the drinks."

After getting ice trays out of the refrigerator, he poured tea into four glasses and set them on the table. When Doctor Hale reappeared, they all sat down for dinner. Lit candles shone from the beautiful sterling silver candelabra in the middle of the table as Barry said grace.

While Mrs. Hale orchestrated the passing around of the serving trays, she admonished Vanessa. "Dear, if you have a son, please, whatever you do, don't wait on him. You see this man here." She pointed at her husband with a serving spoon. "He is helpless. His mother waited on him hand and foot. She did everything but put the food in his mouth. He could not survive on this planet without twenty maids picking up behind him."

"I'll have you know that when I went to Korea, the US Navy would not let me take my mommy," Doctor Hale interrupted. "It was the most traumatic experience of my life."

"And we were married at the time," Mrs. Hale chimed in.

"Don't pay any attention to them, Vanessa, they are always like this."

"So, how was going to the dance at high noon?" Doctor Hale inquired, taking a bite.

"We were the first ones there and had the dance floor all to ourselves," Vanessa answered but immediately decided it was a dumb thing to say. She felt ill at ease because she had never sat at a table with adults before.

"At least no one but Barry could step on your feet," the surgeon wisecracked.

"Hey, Dad, I thought the Hale men descended from a long line of great dancers?"

"Hardly, honey, it's more likely that you descended from great female dancers on my side of the genetic tree." Mrs. Hale interrupted. "Now, Vanessa, tell us about yourself."

"Mom!" Barry exclaimed in horror.

"Well, I've been living at Saint Paul's since October of 1952. It's an orphanage, you know." She thought that she had embarrassed herself in front of them again.

"Oh, honey, I didn't mean that. I meant what are your interests?"

"Well, I like to read, and I want to be a journalist." Vanessa shocked herself by finally admitting her goal, out loud, to strangers.

"Really?" Mrs. Hale seemed suddenly extremely interested.

"Journalists seem pretty powerful to me. I pray that a female Negro will be able to get a job. If not, maybe I can start my own newspaper like Frederick Douglass did."

"I'd be happy to be your first subscriber. Barry can be your paperboy!"

"Thanks a lot, Dad." Barry shook his head between bites as he chewed his food. It was a wonderful meal with delicious food, and Vanessa was fascinated to see the Hale family banter back and forth. They found humor in everything and were so intelligent, yet warm. Vanessa had never spent a romantic evening like this before, where the glow of candlelight sent a sparkle throughout the room. She wondered if they ate like this every night. For her, dinner was usually at five o'clock with toddlers climbing all over her lap. Suppertime was spent feeding the younger children, cleaning up their spills, and trying to get herself something to eat.

"So, what do you think about Barry becoming a Harvard man?" Doctor Hale asked.

"What are you talking about?" The radiance and luster of the moment instantly vanished.

"Dad!" Barry yelled frantically. "I haven't told Vanessa yet!"

"William, I'd venture to say that you're in trouble." Mrs. Hale assessed the situation and came to her son's rescue. "Why don't you two go outside in the garden and relax?" She graciously refused their offer to do the dishes.

As soon as the door shut behind them, she exclaimed, "My God, William, she's White!"

"I don't see how that's possible. She's spent her entire life in an orphanage run exclusively for and by Negroes."

"William, did you see her hair? I've spent my entire life in the field of biology and no member of our race has ever had silky hair like that!"

"I knew it! The first girl Barry brought home would get cut to shreds by you. Your son could have brought home Lena Horne, and you would have said she had a crummy voice."

"William, that girl is White!"

"Any member of our race whose family has been here for two hundred years in all probability has significant White ancestry. With all the interbreeding forced on slaves, the odds point highly in that direction. We do too, honey. It's just that her genes seem to dominate."

"Well, William," his wife said indignantly, "I predict that she is 100 percent Caucasian with not even a trace of Negro in her. Poor White trash left her on Saint Paul's doorstep by mistake. Besides, judging by the look on her face, she's furious. I hope my son isn't being a cad and using a trailer trash girl for kicks before he is off to Harvard!"

"Well, 'I S'wanee' Doris, you are as racist as any Klan member!"

"I certainly am not, and I resent you saying so."

"Besides, every man in the US would love to marry an orphan."

"How's that, William?"

"He would never have a mother-in-law! A marriage made in heaven!"

"Oh, I guarantee you that old nun would be meddling and interfering. Wonder why he didn't tell her about entering Harvard as a premed student in the fall?"

"He was waiting for his old man to totally ruin everything by blurting it out. Besides, Doris, your only son is madly in love. Look at his face. He never looks away from her, ever! Not for a second. Barry is completely fixated on her every second, and I don't blame him. She's lovely and smart. This isn't puppy love. He is passionately in lust, in love, and all the rest of it."

* * *

Outside, tears streamed down Vanessa's face, so she did not even notice the moonlit sky. Barry kissed her lips and stopped intermittently to explain that he had just made up his mind. Yesterday, when his parents mailed all the forms, along with the check, it finally became real to him. He did not want to hurt her, and he had planned on telling her about his decision after the prom. Slowly, they strolled toward a wooden bench underneath a gigantic oak tree and sat down. Covered in Spanish moss, and its immense limbs hanging down under their own weight, the tree created a wall of privacy. The breeze coming from the river caused the moss to swing slightly as Vanessa sobbed uncontrollably, and Barry reassured her that they would always be together. He promised to come home for the holidays, and he also offered to have her come up and visit the Harvard campus.

She was too distraught to protest when she felt Barry's hand go up and down her back. He thrust his tongue into her mouth and unzipped the back of her dress. He clumsily unlatched her bra after numerous attempts. While gently slipping the top of her dress down, he kissed her mouth and massaged her back. He caressed her breasts softly with one hand and felt her nipples harden as his fingers rolled lightly over them. He squeezed her breasts as he bent down to take one in his mouth. Alternating between the two, he sucked one with his lips while fondling the other with his hand. Her weeping did not subside as he slid his hand in between her skin and the elastic waist of the underpants. Slowly, he explored the very top of her moist pubic hair with his fingers. Avoiding the vagina, he reached through the leg of her panties to grope her inner thighs.

As the top of her dress fell, she could feel the warm March air blow against her skin. His stroking examination went on, until suddenly, he let his index finger touch her clitoris. Effortlessly, he dangled his fingers back and forth while Vanessa breathed heavily against his chest. Ever so lightly, he brushed over her clitoris. Then abruptly, he took his other hand off her breast and shoved one finger into her vagina. It felt warm and sticky, which made him impulsively plunge and curl around as Vanessa became aroused. He momentarily pulled out but quickly returned with both fingers and gyrated the passage leading to the cervix. While he twisted and twirled as deeply as he could, her body squirmed. Breathing heavily as her body swayed against him, she started to moan as her head tossed back, and she let out a soft wail. Although it lasted only seconds, her groaning seemed like an eternity to Barry. When he slowly yanked his fingers out, she tilted back and let out a small whimper. While circling her vagina one final time, he leisurely pulled her panties back up and deliberately rotated his hands around her breasts. Barry reattached her bra and idly brought the dress around her shoulders while kissing her deeply on the mouth. He fondled her chest one more time before zipping up her dress.

"Where in the world did you learn to do that?" Vanessa asked eagerly.

"Do what, baby?"

"Barry!"

"*Playboy* magazine. My dad has a subscription that comes to his hospital. He keeps it hidden in the bottom left-hand drawer of his desk. When he gets paged, I go directly there. No one would ever dare to enter his office without knocking."

"You mean you've never gotten caught?"

"Not yet anyway. How did it feel?"

"Oh, Barry, it was incredible. This wonderful rushing sensation turned into an explosion that I had never experienced before. The emotion I felt was unreal. It was like my body was possessed. Can I go to Harvard with you?"

"What about your last two years of high school?"

"I bet Massachusetts has a high school."

"That would really go over big around here."

"Can you imagine Sister Roe? She'd have every state trooper headed North on the Interstate. But you'll let me dream about being with you, right?"

"I'm the one who dreams of you. You'll have half of the football team after you."

"Only half?"

"Listen, I don't want anyone touching you ever. Never ever! You are mine forever."

"Since I live with a nun, you have a definite advantage."

"After my parents go to sleep, may I come to your room?"

"Are you nuts? If we get caught, I will spend the rest of my life in a convent, and Sister Roe, she'll find a monastery where you sleep on the floor, take a vow of silence, wear a robe that rubs your skin raw, and has lousy food, too!"

"I already have it all arranged."

"How?"

"'How?' you ask. You're talking to a Harvard man. I took the screens off the windows both in your room and mine since they are right next to each other."

"Couldn't you possibly kill yourself doing this 'Dirty Dozen' routine?" Vanessa glanced up at the roof and decided that Barry had lost his mind.

* * *

His mother opened the door to the garden. "Would you like to come in to play cards?"

Spades was their family's favorite game, and they spent the rest of the evening playing with partners. At midnight, Doctor Hale got an emergency call from the hospital. After he left the house, everyone went to bed. Around one thirty in the morning, Barry heard his father come up the stairs. After his parents stopped whispering, he waited to make certain they were asleep. Then, he climbed through the window and found Vanessa sleeping soundly when he entered her room. As he sat on the bed, he stared at her through the moonlight that flooded the room. As it glowed through the window, the moon glistened on Vanessa's gorgeously beautiful face. After a while, he quietly slid back the sheets. Now, only a cotton nightgown covered her firm body as he stayed up all night and never looked away from her. As the sun started to come up and peek through the bedroom windows, Barry softly kissed her on the lips. Quietly, he climbed out the window and back into his bedroom as his heart continued to beat at the fastest pace he had ever felt in his chest. Barry knew as he climbed into his own bed that his love for Vanessa was destined to last a lifetime.

CHAPTER FIVE

"Sister Roe! Sister Roe!" Vanessa screamed in sheer panic. "The Reverend King has been shot! He was in Memphis, and someone's shot him!" She ran to the nun, who was cleaning the altar of the tiny chapel where the orphans attended Mass.

With the broom still in her hands, Sister Roe turned around with a flushed face. "Oh, child, I beg of you. Please tell me it's not true! I'm begging you, sugarplum."

"I just heard it on the radio. The reverend was on the balcony of a motel, and someone shot him!" Vanessa burst into tears and grabbed the nun around the waist. The teenager cried uncontrollably as she sank her face into the nun's ample bosom. Collapsing on the floor together, they sobbed and wailed loudly while holding each other tightly in a powerful grip.

"Oh, child, we must pray for this great man's soul," she gasped as they both wept.

The orphans began to wander in since they never let the two women go extremely far from their sight. Puzzled by their intense sobbing, the youngsters gathered around. "What's the matter? Why you are crying, Nessa?" asked three-year-old Lucas.

Sister Roe finally got up and tried to compose herself because she did not want to upset them. With tears streaming down her face, she softly stated, "Children, we must pray on this sad day of April third in the year of our Lord 1968. We shall offer prayers for this great man, the leader of our people. May Doctor King find the eternal peace in heaven that he could never find on this earth." Completely choked up, she could not speak so Vanessa began to recite the rosary, and this pleased the children since they had been taught to count Hail Marys on their fingers.

* * *

After putting all the young orphans to bed, they turned on the radio. "Martin Luther King Jr., whose eloquence and commitment to nonviolent tactics had won the 1964 Nobel Peace Prize, is dead. With his sudden death, one quotation of his seems to resound in the American Black psyche: 'Discrimination is a hell-hound that gnaws at Negroes in every waking moment of their lives to remind them that the lie of their inferiority is accepted as truth in the society dominating them. A nation that continues year after year to spend more money on military defense than on programs of social uplift is approaching spiritual death.'"

"I'm scared, Sister Roe," Vanessa confided.

"Me too, darlin'. I'm scared for the entire country. Let's turn this off." The nun reached over and unplugged the radio. "Child, he only wanted a change in our priorities."

Two months later, on June 6, 1968, Barry left for Harvard. That same day, Robert Francis ("Bobby") Kennedy was fatally shot in Los Angeles after his victory in the California primary.

* * *

Now summer, Trisha had fully recovered from her operation and wanted to get a job. She talked Vanessa into working at the tomato sheds on James Island to earn money. Migrant workers labored their way up the Atlantic coast as they toiled from harvest to harvest. Tomato crops came on big trucks, and the itinerants stood at the conveyor belts until the entire shipment was sorted. A typical workday consisted of sixteen hours straight with breaks given only between truck arrivals. Mistakes on grading tomatoes were not tolerated by the overseer, who watched the produce roll by. Everyone was expected to keep up with the pace of the back-breaking work. Looking away for even a second and getting caught put a worker's job in jeopardy. The low country temperatures were in the high nineties with the humidity hovering around 100 percent. Migrant children old enough to work labored the same hours as their parents.

CHAPTER FIVE

During their first day, Vanessa and Trisha witnessed the most repulsive scene in the horrendous heat. Locked in old cars all day with the car windows down for air, the youngsters cried and moaned as terrifying boredom consumed them. Since the overseer would not permit children around the dangerous machinery, the only choice these poor parents had was to put their offspring inside of their filthy cars. After watching this ghastly and revolting sight of tiny toddlers being placed inside of such horrible, junky cars, the girls were never the same. The abused, defenseless young victims remained in their thoughts permanently.

For lack of other gainful employment, Trisha and Vanessa muddled through their summer at the tomato sheds. The overseer was a drunken gambler, a couple of steps lower than poor White trash. He paid the teenagers promptly, unlike the migrant workers, whom he paid at the end of the harvest. Finally, the last day of the crop season arrived, and the desperate migrants eagerly got into the pay line.

While he counted his money, a man of Hispanic origin approached Trisha. "Please. Look. Right? No right?" he asked in broken English.

Trisha knew exactly how much money she had made to the penny during this unbearably hot summer and quickly counted his pay. Shocked at the small amount, she added it up again and discovered he had been paid exactly half. Using her high school Spanish, she mimicked the accents that she had listened to for months. "Senor, *esto no es correcto.*"

He became incredibly angry when the other agitated migrants gathered around and handed Trisha their money. She gladly counted it since math and multiplication eluded them entirely. She told them not to worry and went straight to the overseer, who was handing out the last dollar. When he ran out of money, two people who were left in line got nothing. It was obvious that he had been drinking as he stood outside his tiny ramshackle trailer.

"Sir, may I speak to you?" Trisha asked timidly.

"Sweetheart, why don't you come into my private office?" he asked in a drunken slur.

"OK," Trisha answered, feeling brave because hostile people were behind her.

"Want a beer, sweetheart?" the overseer asked as they entered his dirty trailer.

"No, thanks." She glanced around his living conditions, which were just as appalling as the migrants'. "I'm curious. Why are you paying these illiterate people half of what they earned?"

"Simple, sweetheart. I lost the dough in an all-night poker game. I was up until around four. Then, I got a couple of lousy deuces. Too bad, the owner was happy with their output this year," he answered while opening a can of beer.

"What are you going to do?" Trisha asked naively.

"Simple, sweetheart, I'm going to tell them to hightail it upstate. There's plenty of work. The crops are coming in early this year." He grabbed her around the waist to kiss her while exposing his grimy black teeth. Absolutely repulsed, she pushed him away, and he fell backward, collapsing into a shabby, dilapidated chair.

"Look, mister. There are a couple of hundred of us and only one of you. You better find some more money," Trisha asked angrily, while backing away.

"Dumb bitch, get off this property now!" In his belligerent, drunken fury, he jumped up and put his hands around her throat.

Trisha screamed, "Ayuda!" Her Spanish brought a Hispanic man to the door. He quickly gripped her waist and yanked her down. The overseer yelled at them to leave, or he was going to call the police, while she told the migrants in Spanish what he had done. Turning violent, the cheated workers started to destroy the sheds by smashing the neatly stacked crates, crushing the sorted tomatoes, and viciously assaulting the machinery. While the overseer sneaked by and escaped with his truck, she climbed on top of a conveyor belt and calmed down the mob. She told them that she would go to the police, but the Hispanic crowd approached her and explained that they had no papers, so she couldn't go to the police. Trisha didn't understand and asked what papers he was talking about. *Illegal alien* was a term she had never heard before.

Desperate and frightened, these migrants needed the money to survive and feed their families. Trisha had no idea until this encounter that people needed permission to be in this country. It was a new concept for her and her first experience with true hunger and utter poverty.

A vehicle rumbled in the distance, and as it approached, dust from the dirt road kicked up, creating a foul cloud. The migrant workers scattered when the brakes of the fourteen-wheeler squealed, and a big, burly guy jumped out. "What in tar nation happened here?" he asked as he surveyed the damage. "Where's my load?"

"The overseer lost the payroll in a poker game last night," Trisha replied.

"I'll be damned."

"Can you help us?"

"Damn it! I'm supposed to be in Jersey with this load tonight."

"Please help us."

"Where is the asshole?"

"He took off."

"For the cops, probably."

"I beg you to help us. They worked here most of the summer and got nothing."

"OK. Get them to start loading up my truck with whatever can be salvaged, and I'll deal with the cops when they get here."

Trisha turned to the migrants. In Spanish, she convinced them that the trucker would get their money, so they reluctantly followed her to the sheds. When the police arrived with the proprietor, everything was peaceful. The workers lifted the cargo while the sirens blared against the flashing lights. Trisha stood next to the truck driver as he negotiated with the owner as he had promised. The proprietor acknowledged that he had hired a total loser to run the sheds. Obviously, both his money and the overseer were long gone, but he agreed to pay them if they would clean up the mess. Trisha asked the crowd if that was acceptable.

"*Claro que sí*," they quickly answered.

The policeman shook his head in total disbelief. "Sho Nuff, y'all gals have no right here, and don't let me see y'all around these here parts again. Next time y'all try to organize these migrants, I'll arrest y'all myself."

Quickly, they left the premises as dust sprayed into the air. Trisha sped along the dirt road to create a big space between them and the police. Relieved when they entered a paved road, she asked, "What exactly is an illegal alien?"

"Can you get the car tomorrow so we can go to the library?" Vanessa said excitedly.

"My parents will never believe I'm going to the library."

"I always thought it was like Ellis Island. If you want to come to this country, show up at immigration, fill out papers, and you're in," Vanessa pondered out loud.

"That's what I thought, too," Trisha replied. "I know what we'll do. If we check out some books on the subject, my parents will have to believe we really went."

"Great idea." Vanessa felt relieved as they entered the small bridge to leave the island.

* * *

The next day at the Charleston County Library, the two teenagers were surprised to find a wealth of information on the subject. A tremendous help, a knowledgeable librarian explained countless ways to cross-reference the topic, and for the first time, the girls realized the true value of librarians. Astutely, she found an obscure article from the *Los Angeles Times* that had been published years earlier. After reading it, they both were skeptical about the validity of the details it contained. After approaching the insightful woman once more, she confirmed that the information was true and shrewdly explained to the astonished teenagers how to do it. Unknowingly, this wise and talented lady was about to change both their lives.

Late in the afternoon, the second floor of the downtown Charleston library was deserted. Only a few people were milling around as Trisha whispered, "Are you thinking what I am?"

"I just find it hard to believe that our government could be that stupid."

"Me, too. But let's try it anyway."

"Try what?"

"Vanessa, you aren't getting it."

"Getting what?"

"Negroes and Whites seen socializing together in the South always get harassed, but we never do! People automatically assume that we are both White. This educated librarian just gave you a ticket to the 'White race' on a silver platter."

"I always go along with your crazy brainstorms like working at the tomato sheds. But..."

"But why not? Police in Alabama turned fire hoses on Negros. Churches were bombed, and innocent Negro children died. The National Guard was called in so Blacks could attend colleges in Arkansas, Alabama, and Mississippi. George Wallace is running for president! Remember his 1963, 'Segregation today, segregation tomorrow, segregation forever' speech?"

"We've never had that kind of trouble here in South Carolina."

"Vanessa, would you volunteer to be a Jew in Nazi Germany?"

"That's different."

"What's different about it? There is not a lot of enlightenment in this country concerning your race. Everyone who called for civil rights has been assassinated, Martin Luther King, Malcolm X, John and Bobby Kennedy, to name a few. You told me that when the orphans were adopted, no one could write to or see them again. In fact, Sister Roe never told you where they went. You have no family and no one to answer to. You can become anyone!"

"I wouldn't trade Sister Roe for 99 percent of the mothers in this country! Besides, I don't really believe that you can pull this off. If she found out that I obtained a birth certificate from a dead White baby, I'd join that infant. My mother, the nun, would kill me. Instead, why don't we get you a Negro birth certificate?"

"Just in case you haven't noticed, I have blue eyes and blond hair! I couldn't change my identity if I wanted to. Let's see if we can pull it off. You'll never really use these documents."

"I hate to admit this because you're so stubborn, but I'm curious too. Since we're going to Carolina, let's give it the old college try before we get there!"

"Great! I love it when you cave!" Trisha beamed.

Buried on page twenty-eight of the *Los Angeles Times*, they found a small article that caused them to embark on an impetuous high school prank. California had illegal aliens flooding across the border near San Diego, and men called "coyotes" escorted them for an outrageous price. Many hopeful South and Central Americans died during the journey in rat-filled sewer pipes or swollen rivers. They climbed over barbed-wire fences and ran across freeways to reach the land of gold. The newspaper reporter had discovered a new phenomenon concerning death and birth certificates. Bound in large books for the public record, these documents were easily accessible in the county hall of records. Illegal aliens would go through the death certificates of babies under the age of five, which contained the maiden name of the mother, the father's name, and the location. Afterward, they wrote a letter to the county hall of records, stating they were born at this hospital to this mother and father on this date. Receiving the request, the county dutifully sent the birth certificate of the dead child. California did not cross-reference birth and death certificates on applications for driver's licenses or Social Security numbers. Obviously, dead babies never applied for either one! Successfully obtaining legal documentation in the United States was conveniently achieved by assuming the identity of a dead child under the age of five. The reporter was urging the state to start cross-referencing birth and death certificates.

* * *

The next day, the girls went to the Charleston County Hall of Records. Extremely dusty bound books were unopened for decades. Hours later, Trisha breathlessly read out loud, "Vanessa Vaughn, born October 10, 1952, to Doris and Lowell Vaughn at Roper Hospital in Charleston. Six pounds, six ounces. She died on February 6, 1953, from viral meningitis."

"This is giving me the creeps!"

"She's perfect! I love the name Vanessa Vaughn. It sounds like a movie star!"

"This is really getting weird. Not to mention the fact that we are breaking the law." Vanessa anxiously studied the death certificate.

"Consider this our first foray into our chosen field, our first journalistic endeavor."

"So, when we get caught and arrested, we claim to be amateur journalistic sleuths?"

"Exactly! In our zeal to study illegal immigration, we uncovered a major flaw in our system. We'll be famous! Our country will be incredibly grateful to us for the discovery."

"I have this overwhelming feeling of being infamous and asking for amnesty."

"You are by nature more cautious than I am so that's why we will make such a great team of reporters. I'm unscrupulous, and you're ethical. Together, we'll raise the press in America to a whole new level. And don't forget our aptitude test the nuns gave us where we both scored highest in plumbing, and journalism came in second. Imagine us as plumbers. Now that's chaos!"

* * *

A week later, Trisha wrote a letter to the Charleston County Hall of Records explaining that her name was Vanessa Vaughn, her parents were Lowell and Doris Vaughn, and she was born on October 10, 1952, at Roper Hospital. She requested the birth certificate with the excuse that she needed to obtain a passport for a trip to Europe. Using Saint Paul's as the return address, she told Vanessa to be the first one to check the mail every day. Shocked, Vanessa said if they got caught, she could prove it wasn't her handwriting, but Trisha retorted that a high school prank should not concern the busy Federal Bureau of Investigation.

Weeks later, a letter arrived at Saint Paul's from the Charleston County Hall of Records. Ironically, the poor baby had been dead for sixteen years. Totally fascinated with the eerie document, Vanessa found herself studying every inch of the paper when Sister Roe wasn't around. She imagined the pain of the parents while remembering every tiny newborn orphan over the years. Creating the infant's face in her mind and visualizing the adults, she fantasized about their love for each other. Dreaming about them often, they were never far from her consciousness as she kept the birth certificate hidden underneath her mattress.

* * *

Sister Rosalie procured a used black-and-white television set, and Vanessa watched television for the first time. The nun turned on the local newscast, and the orphan sat riveted to her seat in a daze as they witnessed Jacqueline Lee Bouvier Kennedy marry Aristotle Onassis, a Greek shipping magnate. The television footage of Caroline and John Junior dressed in wedding garb paralyzed Vanessa. Sister Rosalie flipped off the set and said, "Child, this year has managed to get even worse. Now our country has been robbed of her queen!"

"Sister Roe, do I have a birth certificate?"

"No, darlin', but let me tell you about the night you came to Saint Paul's. During the 1952 holidays, as a young novice, I was assigned temporarily to help. A few days before Christmas, at three o'clock in the morning, a horrible banging at the door awoke all the orphans. The knocking became louder and louder, but I was all alone, afraid, and unsure of what to do. The children started to cry and created total chaos during my very first night on the job. As I opened the front door, the person ringing the bell was in a state of total panic and ran away in the dark night. But in the distance, I recognized the shape of a woman wearing a long woolen scarf to cover her face. I only caught a glimpse in the pitch-black night as the front gate slammed shut, and I could hear footsteps running down the street. *How strange*, I thought, as I started to close the door but then heard a whimper. Glancing down, the most incredibly beautiful baby was inside the cardboard box. Bending over, I picked the infant up and brought her inside. As I spent the entire night holding the tiny newborn tightly, the baby girl never cried once. By the next morning, I had fallen in love for the first time, and the emotion I felt for the little tot was like an all-night party. Every minuscule movement she made fascinated me because it was a new and tender experience. When the sun came up, my direction in life changed drastically. My master's degree was overshadowed by the little bundle, whom I wanted to nurture and never leave. I asked Mother Superior if I could stay at the orphanage, instead of finishing my American history doctorate."

"Sister Roe, do you ever regret your decision to abandon history?" Vanessa asked.

A glow of happiness spread across the nun's face. "Oh, child, my decision is remarkably like the one Robert E. Lee made in 1861 when President Lincoln asked him to assume command of the federal forces. A week later, Virginia seceded, but Lee was unable to turn against his beloved home state. That's what I did, darlin'! Instead of attending Catholic University, I chose to remain in my native South Carolina. Child, I love you with all my heart and with all my soul."

"But you gave up your dream for me!"

"Oh, child, you have given me more joy than I ever thought possible in one lifetime."

"I love you more!"

"Until this moment, no one has ever accused me of deserting American history."

"Shoot, you know more than any history professor ever did!"

"I sure would like to think so!"

"Sister Roe, without a birth certificate, how will I get a Social Security number?"

"Darling, aren't you precious! South Carolina is very aware that you are on this planet and will be honored to give you a Social Security number. Absolutely honored!"

"Trisha's sister Barb is away at college and told her that you need a Social Security number. She said to memorize it since they ask for it a lot."

"This Barb, with a superb taste in gowns, is absolutely correct and incredibly wise. Honey, you already have a Social Security card!" Vanessa smiled as they hugged each other.

* * *

Weeks later, the teenagers went to Charleston's social security office and a little old lady with gray hair graciously helped them. Waiting nervously, they sat in the lobby for her to reappear with Trisha's official one and Vanessa's fraudulent one, under the name of Vanessa Vaughn. Finally, the white-haired lady appeared and gave them their new Social Security cards encased in plastic with nine numbers printed in red. Relieved to get out of the building without getting caught, they rode the city bus home while intently studying their cards.

As the bus bumped along, Trisha bragged, "Well, we pulled it off"

"Yes, when I'm a convicted felon, I'll be the only person in the South Carolina State Women's Penitentiary with two Social Security cards. And you're my accomplice, so let's hope we will get to be cell mates."

"Look, Vanessa, for the one-thousandth time, South Carolina does not cross-reference birth and death certificates. My plan is foolproof. Positively foolproof!"

CHAPTER SIX

Two years later, Vanessa and Trisha received acceptance letters from the University of South Carolina. They both immediately declared journalism as their major. Each prospective student received a brochure outlining the different disciplines, but the college-bound teenagers never bothered to read the pamphlet. While they simply browsed through the color photographs, Mrs. Bibbs and Sister Rosalie read it over from cover to cover. Unheard of in their day, both women were ecstatic about their daughters pursuing a career in journalism.

When the big day came, against Sgt. Bibbs's wishes, he was forced to pick up Sister Rosalie and Vanessa since the orphanage's old car would never make it up to Columbia and back. Trisha snuggled up to her father as he drove along while Vanessa sat quietly beside her. Very uncharacteristic of both women, Sister Rosalie and Mrs. Bibbs sat silently in the back seat.

"I'm scared, Dad," Trisha said nervously. "I don't think I am smart enough to go. You and Mom never went to college."

"Nonsense, at your age, I was on a beach in Guam getting shot at by the Japanese."

"But, Dad, even your first name is misspelled. Tell Vanessa."

"I'm the youngest of eleven kids on an Alabama farm. My oldest brother served under General Pershing in Europe during World War I and returned home in 1919. After listening to his tales, my mom decided to name me after 'Blackjack Pershing' and spelled it 'Pursia,' big deal!"

"But I had to play on a different playground than the officers' kids."

"Holy moly, because of my rank, my misspelled name, and an enlisted playground, you think you are not smart enough? That is plain old horse manure! Your excuse is like trying to teach a pig to dance. It doesn't work, and it annoys the pig, and I'm the pig!"

"I hope you girls can eat the food. It's not homemade. Y'all be sure and eat y'all's vegetables," Mrs. Bibbs cautioned, obviously not listening to the conversation.

"Mom, don't worry! We won't starve to death!"

"I hope y'all can eat the cafeteria food. Y'all don't eat, y'all lose weight."

"Feel free to send me a care package, Mrs. Bibbs," Vanessa said. "Now I'm worried I'm not smart enough either."

"You girls are making me madder than a wet hen! I was against Catholic school. We scraped the money together for a superior education. Right, Sister?"

Deep in thought, the nun was oblivious and didn't answer. Oddly, she had not heard a word.

"Sorry, Dad," Trisha whispered in his ear. "I'm just really scared."

"Me too," Vanessa added. "I'm petrified."

"Being scared is fine. Just study! I bet some of the dumbest people are college grads."

"Columbia, there is a sign for our capital city." Sister Rosalie pointed out the window."

"Oh no, here we go!" Sgt. Bibbs sighed.

"Near Columbia is Cowpens, one of the most significant battles of the Revolution, along with Kings Mountain. Tarleton's brigade was wiped out as an effective fighting force by the South Carolina guerrilla militia, which forced the British to retreat into North Carolina, which caused Cornwallis's eventual defeat at Yorktown."

"It's blowin' up a storm in the back seat!" He banged his hands on the steering wheel.

"At our border during his 'march to the sea,' Sherman told General Halleck, 'The truth is the whole army is burning with an insatiable desire to wreak vengeance upon South Carolina. I tremble for her fate but feel that she deserves all that seems in store for her. Here is where treason began, and by God, here is where it shall end!'"

"Even I know Sherman burned Columbia to the ground, Sister," Mr. Bibbs blurted out.

"Lincoln's new Republican Party was organized to oppose slavery. The 1860 Democratic national convention was held in our beloved Charleston! So splintered were the Democrats, Lincoln captured the election with 180 electoral votes, but he lost by a million popular votes. A Negro Republican win spread rapidly. South Carolina adopted an ordinance of secession."

"And away we go, fast-forwarding into another century!"

"Confederate President Jefferson Davis was a West Point graduate who served long and ably in the United States Senate and as secretary of war in Franklin Pierce's cabinet. In 1861, he ranked among the most influential politicians of the country."

"Please, no! Not now." Mr. Bibbs turned up the radio.

"Not an extremist on the slave issue, Davis was nonetheless a defender of the Southern 'way of life,' and his respected reputation lent stature to the new nation. Never wanting the presidency, he accepted duty's summons and sought peaceful relations with Lincoln. Charleston was a key international port, so the Confederacy could scarcely claim sovereignty without it."

"OK, girls! It's only twenty more miles. We'll be there soon unless the good sister wants to drive up to West Point and see Davis's old school desk," Sgt. Bibbs uttered.

Trisha giggled and knew she would miss her daddy and his great sense of humor. She was so lucky.

"Jefferson Davis was captured by Union soldiers and imprisoned for two years."

"We're here! Look! The University of South Carolina, next exit." Mr. Bibbs pointed as all four women burst into tears and started bawling and sobbing hysterically. "Come on, ladies! Two years in prison is nothing to cry over when you pick the wrong side." He blew his horn loudly.

* * *

Orientation for the University of South Carolina's College of Journalism was held in a large auditorium. A hippie with shoulder-length hair sat down next to them as a lanky man appeared on stage. "I'm Doctor Ash. All print-editorial majors please report to room 201."

"What's he talking about?" Trisha leaned over anxiously as one-third of the room left.

"I have a feeling that we should have read the brochure," Vanessa said remorsefully.

"I could never get it away from my mother. She kept saying, 'My daughter, the reporter!'"

The next professor entered. "Hello, my name is Doctor Land. All advertising majors please report to room 202." Once again, one-third of the audience left.

Panicking, Trisha asked the hippie next to her, "What are they talking about?"

Totally stoned, he answered, "Like, wow, got me, babe!"

The microphone echoed throughout the auditorium with this booming male voice. "Welcome to the University of South Carolina, broadcasting majors!"

"Like, wow, we are radio jocks! Cool!"

"Great," Trisha quipped. "These are all the people who didn't read the brochure."

"No doubt," Vanessa replied. "These are the broadcasters. God help our country!"

After accidentally becoming broadcasting majors, they were considered unique, which impressed their fellow dorm mates, freshmen women majoring in either education or nursing, products of their 1950s parents, who instilled in their daughters that an education was an asset to fall back on. College was where you got a degree and found a husband who would take care of you. An instant bond formed between all the eighteen-year-olds in their Carolina dorm.

CHAPTER SIX

* * *

The big fad at Carolina was "streaking," where naked bodies ran by an established finish line. College campuses across the nation tried to outdo each other in sheer numbers for a national streakers' record. It was a remarkable sight as hundreds of nude shapes jogged by. That night, Sister Rosalie called Vanessa long distance. "Child, have you seen a naked man?"

"No, Sister Roe, I have not seen a naked man but three hundred naked men!"

"Have mercy on me, child! I sure hope you saw those men in a college biology book!"

"Guess what. Last night, we had a panty raid. Chanting boys stood outside our dorm until we threw underwear out the windows. Girls kissed theirs with red lipstick before tossing them!"

"Oh, child! Have mercy on my soul!"

"Don't worry. Trisha and I are working at the campus radio station. It's required of all broadcasting majors. Betty Friedan was on the campus, and we interviewed her. She wrote *The Feminine Mystique* and started the National Organization for Women in 1966. It was so exciting, except our clumsy recording was so scratchy that it was barely audible over the air!"

"You must be so proud, child! Your first professional broadcast!"

"Our photography professor gave us an Alka-Seltzer to photograph as it dissolved. We noticed a gorilla running by but kept right on photographing the dissolving tablet. Our professor said we completely missed the man in the gorilla suit and the point of the test."

"Oh, child, I miss you so much." Sister Rosalie starting crying.

"Don't cry! The National Organization for Women filed a petition with the FCC for affirmative action in employment and ownership against every station in the country because women only worked in secretarial positions. The CBS affiliate in Columbia WNOK-TV-AM-FM's manager called our broadcasting dean to see if he had any females to send over. Trisha and I got jobs, but I'm not allowed to talk over the air. I play records and punch in a tape that gives the listeners the news and exact time. A male jockey on the prior shift records it for me."

"Well, I do declare. Till the cows come home, why can't you talk on the radio?"

"The program director said a woman's voice over the air turns off the listeners."

"Heavens to Betsey, that is ridiculous and absurd! You have a lovely voice."

"At least I don't get screamed at by the salesmen like Trisha does."

"Till the cows come home, why?"

"They trained her as an on-air switcher running the commercial breaks. She loads reel-to-reel machines with the local spots while the national ones came in on film. Using a hot splicer to splice them together, she runs them on a projector. The minute the advertisements broadcast, she takes them down and loads up the next break. With barely enough time to get it all together, her mistakes result in screams from the salesmen. If their spots don't run, they don't get paid. They treat Trisha like dirt when she blows a commercial break."

"Those salesmen are no bigger than a minnow in a fishing pond!"

"Get this: one salesman thought the day was coming when stations would be forced to let women sell airtime. He claims the first competent woman could make a lot of money."

"Money doesn't amount to a hill of beans, but Trisha should be the first one because she could sell air conditioning to Eskimos. She's got gumption that Trisha!"

CHAPTER SEVEN

During their sophomore year, Vanessa received an emergency telephone call from Sister Roe. Mrs. Hale had suffered a massive heart attack and died instantly. After looking at the bulletin board, she got a ride home for one dollar by sharing a car with seven other students.

Instead of the orphanage, Vanessa went straight to the Hales' house. Barry opened the front door, and his face was swollen while his eyes were bloodshot from crying. Neither said a word as they embraced and held each other tightly. As he stroked her hair, they slid onto the couch and cuddled for a very long time. Softly, he kissed her as he unbuttoned her blouse and unzipped her jeans. He plunged his fingers inside her vagina and looked into her eyes. "I want to make real love to you. I fell in love with you the moment I saw you. I love you so much. No one will ever love you more. Let me inside you. It will complete us and bond us together forever."

"I don't have any birth control, and I thought we decided to wait."

"Wait for what? We could both be dead tomorrow, just like my mom. If you really love me, you'll do this for me. You're the only woman I have left. If you want me to beg, I will."

"I don't know."

"Don't worry; I'll pull out right before. You won't get pregnant. I promise."

Barry stripped and knelt on the thick white carpet in front of the fireplace. He got on top of her and licked her body all over as he slowly took off her clothes. His hands caressed her lower body gently. Tears streamed down Vanessa's face as Barry breathed heavily while tears filled his eyes. For a long time, he fondled and kissed her body everywhere. Slowly and gently, he entered her, asking permission along the way. When he cried out that he was coming, she could feel a gush of liquid enter her vagina as he pulled out his penis. Barry collapsed on top of her, and they lay there on the rug in a deep embrace.

Fear crept over Vanessa. Unless Barry knew exactly what to do inherently, he must have been with someone else. Finally, he went upstairs to put on a coat and tie, so she went into the bathroom to put on a black dress she had borrowed from her roommate. When he came downstairs, he looked gorgeous in his dark suit. Silently, they rode in his mother's car to the downtown Charleston funeral home. Feeling strange as they drove along, she knew something was off.

* * *

At the mortuary, Doctor Hale sat between Vanessa and Barry. Mrs. Hale never wore makeup, but the mortician painted her face so much it didn't look like her. When mourners said she had never looked prettier, Vanessa knew they were all lying except Sister Roe, who frowned.

After the viewing, everyone left except the threesome who held hands on the silk-lined bench next to the coffin. The door burst open, and a woman in high heels, a fur draped over her shoulders, and a lot of makeup on rushed in. She was the most made-up Black woman Vanessa had ever seen, and her fur was quite odd for this time of year. "Barry, you said not to come, but I just couldn't stay away," she gushed in a thick Bostonian accent as she grabbed him around the neck and kissed him hard on his lips. "You need me, my love, so I caught the first plane out."

Paralyzed and unable to move, Vanessa clung to the surgeon and stared at the woman in utter horror. "You have my deepest condolences, Doctor Hale. My parents send their best." Incapacitated as her heart pounded, the woman took Vanessa's hand into her palms. "Hello, I'm Michelle, Barry's girlfriend. We're in medical school together. Who are you?" She plopped down on the bench and kissed him again on the lips. Vanessa's body went limp at this nightmare of epic proportions.

* * *

C H A P T E R   S E V E N

Feeling physically sick, she ran out the door to escape into the humid night air. Falling on her knees, she vomited on the sidewalk. Doctor Hale had followed her and knelt beside her, using his white linen handkerchief to wipe her mouth. She sweated profusely as the surgeon used his shirt sleeve to dry her face. Without speaking, she got up from the curb and started walking down Calhoun Street. She hiked as fast as she could, relishing the ocean breeze as it dampened her flushed face. But she could not outpace Doctor Hale. His long legs easily kept up as they wandered in silence, passing old Charleston mansions along the way. Their race stopped at the Battery as waves crashed against the sea wall. Standing there, they watched the turbulent water.

"What does Mrs. Hale think?"

"She's laughing down from the clouds at this ludicrous situation my son has put me in."

"I'm sorry, Doctor Hale. It was just such a shock. I never ever looked at another guy."

"I'm worried about you, and for that momentary relief from this intense pain, I thank you."

"Did you know he was seeing her?"

"Yes, but these questions are for Barry, not me." He put a reassuring hand on her shoulder. "Come on; let me take you home." Silently, they walked back across town.

* * *

The next day at the graveyard, Vanessa stood in the back when Mrs. Hale's casket was lowered into the ground. After giving her condolences, she urged Sister Roe to leave immediately since Michelle from Boston was still at his side. He motioned that he would call her. She wanted to scream, but she controlled herself. There was no point in making a scene.

On the way back to the orphanage, she blurted out, "Barry said he would call me with an imaginary phone in his hand. What did Boston do to him?"

"You know why Northerners called it Bull Run and Southerners called it Manassas?"

"The North named battles after close-by bodies of water, and the South used places."

"This battle for Mr. Barry Hale, a classic case of the North pitted against the South."

"Sister Roe, I want to crawl under a rock and disappear!"

"With your permission, honey, I'll represent the Northern contingency and pick a good old Yankee river." She laughed, while steering the old Buick across a bumpy cobblestone street.

"I pick West of the Ashley River after Scarlett's lame Ashley," Vanessa sobbed.

Sister Rosalie took one hand off the wheel. "That Yankee woman is a fox, about to burrow. I declare graceful Ashley versus downright awful Foxboro and the Charles River."

"I'm a pitiful college sophomore. I've only gone out with one guy in my entire life."

"Now, child, feeling sorry for yourself is as useless as the Confederate dollar."

"How useless?"

"Why, child, the Confederate dollar was worth only 1.5 cents in Union money by 1865. You could cast your net back out into the sea to find another catch like my grandaddy used to say. Sugar, there might be bigger fish to fry." As she turned into the driveway, she tickled Vanessa, whose tears turned into hysterical laughter.

* * *

The next day, Vanessa went back to college and wrote Doctor Hale a long letter about the time his wife had her over for dinner. As an orphan, it was the most wonderful night of her life. The physician cherished the eloquent note. He kept it in the top drawer of his hospital desk and read it repeatedly for comfort.

Barry phoned constantly, but she refused his calls. Finally, Trisha grabbed her friend and pushed her to the dorm's phone, where he was patiently holding.

"I love you, Vanessa, and no one else. The first moment I saw you, it was you and only you. No one matters to me but you. Every minute away from you hurts. I only want you."

"The minute Foxboro got here; I was forgotten."

"Who? Foxboro who?"

"Ms. Michelle that wears way too much war paint."

"I met her the first day at Widener Library. She's very clingy and hard to get rid of."

"Oh me, oh my! What a twisted tale we tell when we practice to deceive."

"It's true. She is the aggressor."

"Ever heard the word no?"

"I've told her 'no' a hundred times. She just keeps badgering me all the time. She's a pest."

"It's such a betrayal. You made me swear that I would never touch another man. Not only did I never touch another, but I also never even looked at one."

"I'm sorry, deeply sorry. Please forgive me." Barry choked back tears. "I love you. Only you. You are my one and only! You are my soul mate."

"I have a hole in my heart that can never be repaired. I hurt. I can't sleep. You destroyed me; you broke my heart into a billion pieces. I've gotten blows my entire life because no one wanted to adopt me. Bye, Barry." She slammed down the phone as tears streamed down her face.

* * *

Their sophomore year ended, and Trisha got them jobs at Sam's Seafood Restaurant, which sat right next to the bridge at the entrance to Folly, the first barrier island south of Charleston. Her parents protested because only poor white trash worked there, but she had dutifully researched the differences in pay. Waitresses got fifty cents per hour plus tips, easily exceeding a cashier's wage of $1.35. Sister Roe knew the main cook at Sam's, so Trisha's parents relented.

During the day, they worked at the Boardwalk hot dog stand. Trisha was an expert swimmer, and neither the powerful nor fearsome barrier waves deterred her from buying a badly beaten-up surfboard for five dollars. In between their shifts, she taught herself to surf.

At night, they worked alongside Sam's fifty-year-old waitresses in their navy-blue sailor tops, which barely came to the top of their thighs. Sam's owner thought miniskirts were good for business, but his staff were too old to wear them gracefully. These crusty women smoked and drank heavily, but they readily taught the two young girls their trade. Remove someone's plate, and serve from the correct side. "Follow these rules, and get better tips," the gruff women said.

* * *

Sister Rosalie's friend, Mr. Maniqault, the old cook at Sam's, spoke Gullah. The Gullahs of African ancestry inhabited the Sea Islands and coastal areas of South Carolina. Their creolized language was based on English but included vocabulary from several African languages. Spoken only in isolated communities, Gullah was the only language Mr. Maniqault knew.

One night, after the restaurant closed, they sat on the back porch, which faced the adjoining marshland. Eleven o'clock at night, still a blistering ninety-five degrees, the mesmerized girls watched the five-foot-two, barely one-hundred-pound cook with his weathered jet-black skin, which matched his eyes. A mass of wrinkles made his bald head indistinguishable from his ebony face. His smile revealed a mouth with only one front tooth amid massive red gums that surrounded it. Inside a cloth bag were his perfectly smooth Juju stones that his great-grandfather brought from West Africa, where they were used as a fetish, a charm, or an amulet for Juju. He rolled them around his hands and through his fingers before spreading them out on the wooden floor. Waving his hands over the stones, he silently observed their formations as he spoke Gullah about the supernatural powers these stones held. Sweat poured off his brow, and perspiration beads flowed down his chest as crickets chirped in the distance and sounds of the marsh forced Vanessa to move closer, so she could hear his Gullah.

"Soon, you lose two in your heart. They leave this life quickly, never to return." Mr. Maniqault rubbed his left breast.

"Me? You mean me?" Vanessa questioned her translation of the dialect.

"One come from body; one is close. They move to the next life."

"Who?" She shifted on the hard floor and suddenly felt very scared.

"Strong, or no survive." He waved his hands over the stones and wiped the sweat from his brow. "Juju entering bad time for twenty years. Ends, light comes with your soul mate."

"Wow!" Trisha exclaimed. "I don't want to know what my future holds. Let's get going." A shrimp boat blew its horn as it approached the dock. Spooked, they both jumped forward.

"You mean, I'm going to be miserable until I'm forty?" Vanessa asked.

He swayed his hands over the Juju stones again and looked directly at Vanessa. "You happy during bad black times. Depends on you want to be."

"Let him tell your future. Maybe you're going to be the first lady."

"No way. I don't want to know. Remember, this was your idea to have Mr. Maniqault predict your future. He warned us Juju is scary."

"Take." He offered one of his Juju stones. "Keep. Protect you until soul mate comes back. Bring it back here to me." He rose from his battered rocking chair just as a shrimp boat arrived.

"What about Trisha? Aren't you going to tell her future?"

"Her no believes Juju." Abruptly, he disappeared into the pitch-black night.

"You were right! This stuff is spooky."

"Forget it. Cursed for twenty years, but you can be happy. He's hedging his bets."

"The low country swears by Juju. Don't you want to know your future?"

"After listening to yours, I guarantee I'd marry a pipe fitter at the shipyard who runs around on me. We'd live in a tacky trailer park; he'd have a beer belly from drinking beer all day while watching football with a lot of tattoos. Come on. Let's go," Trisha uttered as she got up off the floor. "Besides, there's no point in worrying about the future until it actually happens."

"But according to his predictions, I'm in my bad black period now," Vanessa worried.

"Exactly!" Trisha answered. "How could that possibly be true?"

CHAPTER EIGHT

Sister Rosalie made pancakes every Sunday morning after Mass. The orphans loved "Pancake Sunday." This August morning was swelteringly hot as they bustled around the kitchen. "My new book is about George Pickett, who led fifteen thousand men on Cemetery Ridge, and six thousand were killed or wounded in the repulse."

"Oh goodness, six thousand men!" Vanessa poured more milk into the bowl.

"Child, it gets worse indeed." Sister Roe tasted the dough. Violently, the nun collapsed backward with great force and landed on the kitchen floor. Vanessa rushed to lift her head surrounded by the heavy habit. Her face was terribly pale and profusely dotted with heavy sweat. She ran to phone the operator and yelled for them to send an ambulance. "It's urgent!" she screamed. She ran back to the kitchen where the pancakes were burning, and the room had filled with smoke. She turned off the gas stove and threw the scalding pans into the sink, which sent steam soaring into the air. Rushing back to the nun's side, she bent down to unfasten her habit so she could breathe easier. Feeling angry and helpless, she said to the orphans, "Why do they have to wear these stupid things in the middle of the scorching summer? It's no wonder that Sister Roe keeled over in this awful heat."

After wiping the perspiration off the nun's face, she held her tightly in her arms and could hear the faint sounds of a siren in the distance. "They sure are taking their time. It's my fault because I didn't make it sound like it was a severe emergency. If anything bad happens, I'll never forgive myself." The siren's roar became very loud as the ambulance entered the driveway. Leaving Sister Rosalie lying on the floor, she ran to meet the two paramedics. They followed her to the kitchen with a stretcher. Neighborhood volunteers heard the sirens and gathered to help with the orphans.

"I'm not getting a pulse," the paramedic said as he checked her vital signs.

* * *

Vanessa rode in the ambulance and after arriving at the emergency room entrance, Doctor Davies pronounced Sister Rosalie dead on arrival, August 3, 1972.

Nurse Bow tried to dislodge Vanessa from around the nun's neck, but she clung tightly. Using sheer force, Doctor Davies released her embrace from the dead woman's body and took her into an adjoining room. Short of breath, she barely made it to the sink before vomiting. She splashed water on her face. "Doctor Hale, Sister Roe cannot be dead. Please check her again."

In an exceedingly kind and gentle way, the surgeon explained, "She died from complete heart failure, just like my wife. Maybe genetic and exacerbated by her weight." Patiently, he wiped her pale face with his own handkerchief as Nurse Bow brought some RC Cola. Doctor Hale sat beside Vanessa until members of the clergy arrived. Mother Superior and her entire order surrounded the nineteen-year-old. Father Kelly spoke privately with Doctor Hale about his concern. Sister Roe was the only person the orphan had in the whole world, so he suggested that she not go back to the orphanage. Trisha's parents came down quickly and told Vanessa she would stay with them until college resumed. She was given a sedative as the nun's body was taken to a funeral home in downtown Charleston.

* * *

Outside her wake, a line formed on Calhoun Street, a tremendous outpouring of love for the eccentric nun. Vanessa sat right beside her casket as parishioners, clergy, friends, and orphans who were now adults offered their condolences. Overwhelmed with grief, she wept as each person offered his or her favorite Sister Rosalie story.

Doctor Hale explained, “Barry went to the dean, but he denied the request since Sister Rosalie was not a blood relative.” She nodded as the physician continued, “My son is very upset that he could not be here with you at this sad time.”

Discreetly, Mrs. Bibbs told Doctor Hale that she was worried because Vanessa was constantly vomiting. He assured her that after the funeral, he would give her a complete physical. The trauma of witnessing the death, coupled with the grief of losing her parental figure, could manifest into physical ailments. Mrs. Bibbs smiled. She knew Vanessa was in the best possible medical hands with the handsome surgeon who had saved her own daughter’s life.

* * *

On Wednesday morning, a High Mass was held for Sister Rosalie at Saint Mary’s Cathedral, the mother church of the Carolinas and Georgia. A grandiose example of early Charleston architecture, it looked even more impressive today because the huge altar was blanketed in countless floral arrangements. The archbishop of the diocese officiated, assisted by twelve priests including Father Kelly. Every pew was cramped with people, while others stood in the back vestibule. The organ’s melody resonated from the loft, and Vanessa had handpicked the stirring music. The service opened with Sister Rosalie’s favorite, “The Battle Hymn of the Republic.” With an even mix of male and female voices, the lead soprano performed a heart-wrenching rendition. She sobbed as the choir’s regal voices lowered and faded away in unison. Next they performed Ave Maria as weeping was heard throughout the cathedral. After the archbishop finished his eulogy, he sat down in a huge satin-covered chair in the center of all the other priests.

Slowly, Vanessa rose and walked up to the podium. Father Kelly adjusted the microphone and handed her his handkerchief. She wiped her tear-stained cheeks as she glanced around the church and focused on the familiar faces that made her feel safe. Her silence seemed like an eternity to the congregation.

Vanessa’s voice cracked. “Fate brought me to the steps of Saint Paul’s in October of 1952. I was a tiny, abandoned infant, and a young novice answered the bell. Her name was Sister Rosalie; she's right there." She pointed to the casket. "She was on her way to Washington DC to pursue her first love, American history. But just like all parents, once she laid eyes on her baby girl, she fell hopelessly in love. Even though she had to leave me now, she will always be my mother, and I will always be her daughter." She paused as tears ran down her face. "Such a great lady who was more entertaining than a cast of a thousand actors. Sister Roe lived every day like it was her last. Full of fun, she created magic for everyone around her!"

"Her greatest legacy, of course, was her complete obsession with American history that involved South Carolina. The minute she arrived at the 'pearly gates' on Sunday, she asked Saint Peter to direct her immediately to William Tecumseh Sherman. Sister Roe believed that 'Old Tecumseh' was insane when he burned Atlanta. His insanity led to his destructive 'March to the Sea,' which destroyed the South. 'Old Tecumseh' might make it to heaven if heaven recognized an insanity plea." Laughter rang out through the crowed church.

"Can't you see her now? Pointing her finger right at Old Tecumseh's face. Why, she would be his worst nightmare for all eternity. If he truly weren't insane, as she thought, I'm sure after a couple of weeks with Sister Roe, he would be. Old Tecumseh would be subjected to the Rosalie trials and held accountable for all the destruction he inflicted, particularly on South Carolina." Sporadic giggles spread over the pews. "My mother thought that heaven would mean the opportunity to sit down and have jasmine tea with heroes like Marin Luther King and Rosa Parks. She could grill them for hours. It would be Rosalie heaven, Rosalie style." The solemn row of priests grinned as they listened and even the stern archbishop smiled.

"My mother taught me that despite emancipation, Blacks were lasting casualties of the war as was the Declaration of Independence. In the long after-wash of war, few Southerners, White or Black, could pursue much happiness. One hundred years later, the South is still recovering. Moreover, those many Northerners, who themselves blinked at racial equality, could only be uncertain of their virtue in victory. A brilliant historian, my mom gave us a unique slant to our own precious history. Her greatest fear was our mistakes.

If we did not learn from them, we were doomed to repeat them. I want my mother to be remembered as the lady who gave up her life so that children could have theirs. She gave up her dream for me. For that, I shall always love and cherish her. Please join me now for another favorite song: 'America, The Beautiful.'"

As the mourners filed by the nun's casket to pay their last respects, everyone either kissed the coffin or genuflected as they touched it. Vanessa watched hundreds of people pay homage to her mother. After the service, the pallbearers placed the casket into the back of the hearse for the trip to the nun's final resting place. A line of cars followed the hearse to the grave site.

* * *

As they passed construction workers in a ditch, Vanessa noticed that they stopped their work, took their hardhats off, and placed them on their chests in tribute to the funeral procession passing by. Sister Roe would love this display of respect, especially since it was reminiscent of a bygone era.

The hearse arrived at the cemetery where Sister Rosalie's mother was buried. The nun would be placed next to her grave. Using Father Kelly's arm for support, Vanessa walked slowly to the space that had been dug in the ground. The priest stepped forward to recite the Prayer of Saint Francis of Assisi but could barely do so, as he was choked with emotion. Vanessa reached down and took some dirt in her hand to toss it on top of the casket. When she could no longer bear to be there, she turned and headed briskly toward the limousine with Father Kelly.

A short Black man quietly walked along beside them and touched her arm. "Excuse me, Miss Condon. My name is Mr. Peter Whalen, and I am the attorney for the estate of the late Mary McQueeney, Sister Rosalie's mother. At your earliest convenience, would you be so kind as to come by my office on Tradd Street?" He presented his business card. She had never seen one before as she took it from him. She glanced at the impeccably dressed attorney attired in his three-piece suit with a gold antique watch hanging around his waist. He spoke clearly and distinctly. "You must be curious as to what this is all about, but this is not the time nor the place to discuss this matter. Come by to see me next week, if possible, and I will answer all your questions then. I am deeply sorry for the tremendous loss you have sustained at such a tender age in your young life." He tipped his hat and disappeared into the crowd as she stuffed his card into her pocket. Father Kelly opened the limousine door and Vanessa climbed in.

* * *

The chauffeur took her to the hospital, and Vanessa was quite surprised since no one had told her she was going there. Nurse Bow greeted her and immediately apologized for not making the service, explaining that she had to work her shift. She told her Doctor Davies would conduct a complete physical. She nodded, but her mom had died here, and she wanted to leave.

As she sat on the examining table, he asked, "Why do you think you are throwing up?"

"Who on earth told you I was throwing up, Doctor Davies?"

"I'm going to do a blood test," Doctor Davies answered nonchalantly.

"Why? What will that show?"

"It will confirm whether you are pregnant or not, which is usually the reason why a woman your age is inexplicably nauseous."

"That's impossible!"

"So, you've never had intercourse?" he clinically asked.

"It would be the Immaculate Conception. Why are you doing this to me?"

"I'll eliminate the obvious with a simple blood test, and if it is negative, we'll do more sophisticated tests." He inserted the needle and drew blood. "I got a kick out of Sister Rosalie. They don't make women like her anymore! I'll call you personally with the results."

"Doctor Davies." She slid down from the examining table. "Mrs. Hale was thin, and Sister Roe was heavy. Why are so many women dying from heart attacks?"

"Heart disease is a major killer among our race. We suffer a higher incidence due to genetics, and some scientists believe it's our diet. My theory is that these two women worked full-time, and that stress creates an inordinate amount of female heart disease." He dried his hands.

"I want a career. Will I die from heart disease?"

"If I knew the answer, I would be an extraordinarily rich, famous, world-renowned physician." He chuckled slightly. "Besides, it's just a theory of mine. Good day, Vanessa."

* * *

The next day, she took the city bus to downtown. At the corner of Tradd and King Streets, she turned and walked down Tradd until arriving at a small sign printed in Old English type: "Peter J. Whalen, Attorney at Law." The quaint, two-story row house was typical of the many buildings preserved by the Charleston Historic Society. After slowly opening the white picket gate, she walked up the steps as the wood creaked beneath her feet. She banged on the brass knocker, and an elderly Black lady opened the door and escorted her to Mr. Whalen's office. Peeking around, she noticed everything, including the furniture, was incredibly old and had a musty smell.

"Hello, Miss Condon. I am delighted that you were able to come. Please." He motioned to the chair in front of his desk as she read his diplomas, which hung behind him. "I represent the estate of Mary McQueeney, the mother of Sister Rosalie. Upon her death, she left her entire holdings to her only child, Rosalie. Never pleased about her only daughter depriving her of grandchildren when she entered the convent, her will states none of the money can go to the Catholic Church. Since Rosalie took a vow of poverty, she was unable to keep the money, nor could she give it to the church. After her mother's passing, she held her inheritance in a trust for you. Unfortunately, Rosalie's sudden demise came before your twenty-first birthday." Mr. Whalen opened a folder. "Mrs. McQueeney owned a house, which I sold for a profit of six thousand dollars. She also had three-thousand dollars in savings. Not believing in the stock market, she kept all her money in federally insured banks, which generated an incredibly low interest rate. For that reason, I asked Sister Rosalie if I could be a little bit more aggressive to achieve a higher return. A smart lady, she agreed with my request. I am happy to report that the total sum of your inheritance is now worth sixteen thousand dollars. I invested it the safest way that I could under the circumstances." Stunned, she followed his words carefully. "This is a substantial amount to come into at such a young age without any parental guidance. Please, use this money judiciously. Mrs. McQueeney spent her entire life cleaning the Hayward-Washington House. It was back-breaking work she did even in her old age. I implore you not to squander this fortune because it represents a lifetime of hard labor. Do you have any questions?"

Vanessa shook her head no.

"Here is a check for the sum of sixteen thousand dollars. I suggest that you open a bank account this afternoon and deposit the check immediately. You certainly should not walk around with such a large amount of money on your person."

"Life is delivering one shock after the other."

"I have some corny, old-fashioned advice." He looked directly into her sad eyes. "Money never buys happiness. It only comes from inside your heart. Sister Rosalie never cared about money, while her mother worked her whole life to save it for her only child. Now it is all yours." The attorney stood up. "Feel free to call me at any time day or night if you need me. Mrs. McQueeney was a dear and valued client."

Vanessa followed him to the door and went outside into the sticky August air. Without thinking, she headed for the Battery. Spanish moss hung from the oak trees and swung softly in the breeze. For the rest of the day, she watched waves crash over the railing. Fort Sumter stood in the distance, a memory of all the times she and Sister Rosalie had gone there on outings and how happy they had always been together.

CHAPTER NINE

Doctor Davies entered the exam room. "Your test was positive, Vanessa."

"What does that mean?" she asked incredulously.

"My suspicions were correct. You are pregnant."

"That's impossible. I only had sex once."

"Unfortunately, that's all it takes."

"Barry told me not to worry. He pulled out!"

"Pulling out is the biggest misconception. There is a pre-ejaculation that comes before total orgasm. It is very deadly and can easily cause conception."

"What in the world am I going to do?"

"You are going to have a baby," Doctor Davies said reassuringly.

"I can't have a baby," she replied in desperation.

"There is no other option. Abortion is illegal in this state. You could go to New York."

"New York? Why can't I have an abortion right here?"

"It's against the law. Any physician who performs an abortion will lose his license and face a jail term. South Carolina law is clear on this issue."

"Can't you do it just this once?" she pleaded.

"It's hard enough for a Black man to make it through medical school. I can't afford to take that risk. They would throw the book at me, particularly a licensed physician."

"Please, just this once. No one would ever know. It would just be between you and me."

"I don't agree with this archaic law. I've see grown women come here that we cannot save. Some die, and others live permanently infertile. It's a major health problem in our country."

"Please help me." Vanessa's eyes filled with tears.

"Morally, I have no problem with abortion. It's against state law, as simple as that."

"Where can I go to get one? You must know."

"I beg you, don't go to one of these butchers. They can kill you. Have the baby."

"What about Doctor Hale? Will he help me?" Vanessa whined.

"Seriously, no way. Talk it over with Barry. You'll feel totally different afterward."

"Beside the fact I never want to see him again, I don't see what good calling him will do. He's got plenty of women in his life. That's for sure."

"I'm sorry. I truly am."

"Isn't there a way you can make it look like something else that I needed to have done?"

"It all boils down to the same thing, breaking the law. It's a crime that has harsh penalties for physicians." He was paged overhead. "I have to go. Please don't do anything foolish."

* * *

After he disappeared through the door, she slid down and found herself climbing the stairs to Doctor Hale's office in a trance. The door was open so she sat down on his couch as her eyes studied the family pictures on the credenza behind his desk. Photographs of Barry at various ages decorated the room. A two-year-old Barry in a cute swimsuit hung between his Harvard graduation picture and a pose taken in front of his medical school cadaver. A beautiful, young bridal pose of Mrs. Hale also adorned the collection.

"To what do I owe the pleasure of this visit?" Doctor Hale interrupted her spell.

"I'm pregnant!" she blurted out.

At a complete loss for words, the surgeon hesitated before speaking. "I always dreamed of being a grandfather and envisioned this wonderful news. What did Barry say?"

"He doesn't know, and I don't want to tell him. I was hoping that you would help me."

"Absolutely, you have my complete and utter support. I will be happy to help you financially so that you can finish college." His tone was very decisive as he paced the room.

"I don't want to have the baby, Doctor Hale. I want you to give me an abortion."

Her reply startled him. "I can't do that, Vanessa. This is my flesh and blood."

"Remember Miss Michelle from Boston? I can't have this baby, and you know it!"

"I will not help you abort a fetus that happens to be my grandchild," he answered firmly.

"I guess I'll have to find someone who will." She blushed at her own curtness.

"I promise, if you'll have this baby, I will raise it." He was calm and spoke in a concise, clear-cut manner. "The child can live with me. I have excellent fatherly credentials."

She glared at the surgeon. "I'm sorry you won't help me. You, more than anyone else, know the repercussions of what I am about to do illegally."

"I implore you to reconsider and call Barry. My son will be as excited as I am for this great news," Doctor Hale said as she brushed by him and slammed the door.

* * *

She left the hospital and took the city bus to Trisha's house, where her friend was in the backyard sunbathing. Vanessa sat down on the edge of the lounge chair and startled her.

"I'm pregnant."

"No way on God's green earth!" Dumbfounded, she sat up instantly.

"You heard me." Vanessa snapped, obviously very annoyed.

"How can I help?"

"Dr. Davies and Doctor Hale both said that I should have the baby." She burst into tears. Trisha tenderly hugged her while Vanessa buried her face into her sweaty chest and cried even harder. "I can't have a baby, particularly right now."

"Don't worry. I'll think of something, like I always do," Trisha reassured her. "Let's go in the house. It's too hot out here anyway. I need to brainstorm for a possible option."

* * *

Trisha took the family car with Vanessa crying hysterically and headed for Sam's. Those crusty old waitresses with their miserable lives had to know. Sure enough, the first one wrote down a number on her waitress pad, and she stuffed it into her pocket. They headed home.

* * *

Once inside her house, Trisha went into the kitchen and called the number. The phone rang and rang. After fifteen rings, someone picked up the receiver but said nothing on the other end. Nervously, she inquired if this was the correct number to call when you were in trouble. Quite hesitant, the male voice replied that it depended upon what kind of trouble. She explained she was pregnant and needed help. He asked for her name and number and said he would be back in touch. She asked how much money it would cost, but he didn't answer and hung up. She walked down the hall to her bedroom to reassure her best friend it would all be fine.

Afraid her parents might answer the phone, they never left the house. Five tortuous days passed before he called with the address and said to come with six hundred dollars in cash.

* * *

The next morning, they both got up early and arrived near the main gate of the Charleston Naval Base. The surrounding blocks were full of raunchy strip joints with hookers on the seedy streets trying to woo potential clients.

CHAPTER NINE

As they walked by, the teenagers clutched each other tightly until they found themselves in front of a dingy stairwell. Paint was peeling off the filthy walls, and the unwashed stairs smelled of urine. The intense heat made the disgustingly foul odor permeate their nostrils as they climbed the unlit, squalid stairs.

Halfway up, Trisha stopped abruptly. "Maybe you should have this baby!"

"I'm begging. Don't make me feel worse. Barry doesn't love me. No turning back now."

At the top of the shabby stairs, Trisha tried to open the grimy locked door. Knocking lightly, she brushed off her knuckles as it squeaked open. A nasty-looking man wore filthy jeans and a grubby T-shirt. Lewd tattoos covered his skinny arms, featuring naked women surrounded by obscene expressions. The disgusting man asked for the money, and she instantly recognized his voice from the phone call. Fumbling through her pocket, she handed him the six hundred dollars. After quickly counting the crumpled bills, he disappeared behind another door.

They glanced around the barren room packed with visibly poor women wearing tattered clothing with young children in tow. No one uttered a sound. Prostitutes wore lots of gaudy makeup and skirts that barely covered their crotches. Their bodies reeked of stale perfume, and the foul room smelled worse than the stairway.

Trisha felt an overwhelming urge to bolt out the door and to run when she saw a blindfolded woman emerge from the adjoining room. Blood ran down her legs into her shoes, which were stuffed with newspapers. Her bloodstained clothing had rips and tears all over it, and she could barely walk. The skinny man with tattoos took off her blindfold and advised the woman not to remove the catheter. Opening the outer door, she clumsily made her way outside as her small child followed behind. Horrified and scared, she clung tightly to Vanessa and held her in a tense embrace.

"Let's call Barry at Harvard," she whispered.

Several more women went in vulgarly blindfolded and came out bleeding profusely.

"Please call Barry!"

The slender man put one on Vanessa and crudely pushed Trisha away. "No way, man. Give me my money back."

He relented and blindfolded both girls. The brutally hot alcove had no windows or any type of ventilation. The temperature was unbearable inside the empty chamber, where only dirty newspapers lined the floor. She was told to take off all her clothes below the waist and to lie down. He gave her a piece of stained newspaper to cover herself. Trisha moved her own blindfold up a little so that she could see what transpired. A fat man with a thick mustache approached and separated Vanessa's legs while the tattooed one held her thighs firmly in place. The abortionist pulled red plastic tubing out of his pocket that Trisha recognized as a Foley catheter from her own stay in the hospital. Both the catheter and his hands were unwashed as he inserted it into her vagina. She screamed out in pain as tears flowed down Trisha's cheeks while she held her frightened friend and watched him ram the crude tube further inside her uterus. Ten fingernails dug into her arms as Vanessa's body twisted under the weight of the man holding her down while she wrenched in pain. The abortionist never spoke during the procedure, and less than a minute after the catheter was inserted, the skinny man let go and crassly told her to get up. The messy affair was finished, and he insisted they leave immediately. No waiting around.

Intense vaginal pain made her barely able to stand up, much less walk. Trisha put her friend's clothes back on, and as they entered the outer room, the skinny guy took off their blindfolds. Unable to descend the steps, she felt a searing pain shoot through her pelvis and painfully stumbled forward with the support of her buddy.

* * *

Experiencing terrible chills, her entire body twitched and vibrated as she retched on the sidewalk. They headed for the Esso gas station across the street and entered a grotesque, filthy bathroom. As the contractions got worse, she screamed as sweat soaked through her clothes on the gross toilet seat. They heard sudden sounds of split, splash, and plop as red body waste poured out between her legs. The catheter hung partway out, into the toilet bowl water. Vanessa continued to bleed profusely for hours at the Esso Station. Finally, Trisha managed to get her into the car, and they headed back to her house.

* * *

Her parents were away visiting relatives so she nursed Vanessa night and day, but her sick friend just got worse. On the third day, she passed out and could not be revived. Trisha dragged her to the car by holding onto her feet, as the pavement severely bruised and scraped her limp body. She managed to lift her into the automobile, which took every ounce of strength she possessed.

* * *

She drove as fast as her dad's car would go and headed straight for the hospital. Upon arriving at the emergency room entrance, she rushed in and breathlessly told Nurse Bow that she needed help fast. Calmly, the nurse instructed an orderly to get Vanessa out of the vehicle. Overhead, the pager system echoed, "Doctor Davies to ER, STAT. Doctor Davies to ER, STAT." His strong arms hoisted her out of the car as the plastic tubing swung between her blood-covered legs, and red stains completely covered her dress, legs, and arms.

Doctor Davies appeared and gave orders in a calm voice, and no one asked her anything. The orderly motioned for her to sit in the waiting room. She sat down and watched as Black people came in with various illnesses. No one really acknowledged her existence or even cared that she was the only White person. She felt horrible, and if her best friend died, she hoped to die, too.

Nurse Bow approached. "Doctor Hale wants to see you in his office immediately."

* * *

Slowly, she followed her up the stairs, the longest climb of her life. Doctor Hale motioned for Nurse Bow to shut the door. "Who is this coat-hanger butcher?"

"I really don't know."

"I will absolutely not tolerate any non-answers. Is that understood, young lady?" His eyebrows arched as he glared in complete disgust. "Do you have any idea how many women I see in this hospital month after month, year after year, who die from these illegal abortions? They just don't make it. Now, your friend is in critical condition."

"No, sir. I had no idea."

"These women are among the sickest people I have ever seen. Sicker than hell! With extremely high fevers, they have bad infections. Some respond to antibiotic therapy and pull through. Others are not so lucky and die. A high percentage become permanently sterile."

"I did not know anything bad would happen."

"Some take only hours to die if they are pretty far gone. Others hang on for days."

"Why do they die?"

"Septicemia is a condition in which infection is so advanced that bacteria or their toxins invade the bloodstream and circulate throughout the body. Septic shock occurs when the body is so overwhelmed by infection, there is general circulatory collapse. Often there is kidney or liver failure and a massive shutdown of the body."

"Will she be OK?"

"She has peritonitis. Her abdomen is tender, and she jumps even when only gentle pressure is applied. There is tissue in her uterus that is infected. Her temperature is 103 degrees, and we have been unable to lower it. Unfortunately, this is a condition that I have seen too many times in my career. The pelvis can withstand some infection, but, in her case, there was a serious degree of contamination when the procedure was done to create such a massive sepsis."

"This is all my fault. There is no way she could ever have tolerated that place on her own."

"I called the police, and you are going to tell them every detail. Understood?"

"Yes, sir. But they blindfolded us. I didn't get a good look at the fat guy who did it. But I could definitely recognize his assistant."

"All they need is the address. No more, no less."

"She came to you first for help. You can perform a safe abortion. You refused her. Why?"

"To lose my medical license and suffer the humiliation of a jail term is simply a greater price than I am prepared to pay."

"You would rather have mangled and dying patients than to risk your own comfort?"

"It is against the law. I will not break the law. This is an enormous public health problem for which I take no responsibility. I am not a politician."

"That's convenient. But someone should care about these women and their orphans."

"Wait in my office until the police get here."

"It was your grandchild, you know," she blurted out.

"I am painfully aware of that fact, young lady." He opened the door and slammed it against the wall, the only time she had ever seen him show any emotion.

The police arrived, and Doctor Hale sat stoically throughout Trisha's interrogation and never said a word. After the police left, she timidly asked for permission to spend the night in the hospital room with Vanessa, but he refused to grant her request. Coldly, he told her to come during visitor hours, just like everyone else. She feebly attempted to argue with him, but he held firm. Hospital rules allowed her to stay only five minutes.

* * *

When Vanessa felt physically strong enough to resume her classes, Doctor Hale personally drove her back to Columbia. Neither one uttered a single word during the most unpleasant two-hour car ride. Complete silence permeated until they arrived at the campus, and Doctor Hale asked, "Are you going to call Barry and finally tell him? It was his baby too."

Vanessa glared straight at him. “Doctor Hale, I will never tell him. Nor will I ever see him again. Your son has inflicted enough pain on me for one lifetime.”

“He cares about you and is madly in love with you. I saw it in his eyes that first night.”

“Your son cares about too many women.”

“Michelle will never last. It’s you, only you. It’s so obvious. He’s young. Forgive him.”

“Not in this lifetime.” Grabbing her tiny bag, she said, “Thank you for saving my life.”

The sad surgeon nodded. “I deeply regret that I was not able to save the life of my own grandchild—a wound which will haunt me until the end of my days.”

CHAPTER TEN

Vanessa and Trisha spent the next two years overwhelmed with their course load and working at WNOK-TV-AM-FM. Emotionally, Vanessa never recovered from her abortion and the death of Sister Rosalie. Charleston held too many detestable feelings, so she never went back. The orphan thought often about her fake Social Security card and became obsessed with it. Wanting to change her entire life, she formulated a plan and told no one about her scheme. For the first time ever, she decided not to confide in Trisha for fear that she would talk her out of it.

Her fellow dorm mate worked in the University Transcript Department so Vanessa revealed for the first time that she was an orphan and had just received her real birth certificate. Connie disclosed they changed the surnames of women all the time when they got married, but she had never changed a Social Security number. Her supervisor informed her it was highly unusual and requested all the documents.

She nervously divulged her plan to Trisha. "Are you nuts? That was a high school prank. You can't be serious about using that phony Social Security number."

"Why not? It was your idea to start with," she quickly reminded her best friend.

"Wait a minute! I'm not smart enough to think that up, and you know it. That helpful, computer brain librarian told us exactly how to do it. Besides, what if you get caught?"

"I have no intention of getting caught."

"I bet that's what Al Capone said on his way to Alcatraz for tax fraud."

"I have an appointment with the head of the transcript department, and I have every intention of changing my records. I want to transfer out and intend never to be found again. I'm starting over, plain and simple, with a new life. I've thought about it since I lay down on those filthy newspapers. Nothing you can say will change my mind, so save your breath."

"It's a very stupid idea, and you can't possibly pull it off."

* * *

The next day, Vanessa went to the transcript department to present her documents to an elderly woman who listened quietly while her pale-blue eyes fixated on Vanessa. "I've been with the university for thirty years and never encountered such a request. Changing your name is easy; we do that all the time. But in three decades, I have never changed a Social Security number. I'm not sure that it's even possible."

Nervously, she shifted in her seat. "My name was given to me by the state of South Carolina. It's only fair to change to my legal name, which includes a Social Security number."

Her wrinkled hands fingered the document on her desk. "I understand your concern about your given name, but I cannot follow what possible difference your Social Security makes?"

"It is my right under the laws of the United States of America. I can't help being raised in an orphanage," she uttered forlornly to elicit sympathy for her plight.

"I'll take this matter up with Mr. Graves, so we make sure we are not in violation of any federal law." She rose from her chair. "We'll contact you after a decision is made."

"Who is Mr. Graves?"

"The chairman of the Administration Department. Only he can decide on this matter."

Walking slowly out of the building, unable to bluff her way past a career bureaucrat, she was alarmed about their discovery of her stolen identity and the consequences.

* * *

Rushing back to the dorm, she shouted out every detail while Trisha was in the shower. She pulled the curtain back and stuck her wet head out. "This is as stupid as the stunt I pulled yesterday when I flipped on the mike at the radio station to announce that Vice President Spiro Agnew resigned amid charges of illegal financial dealings."

"You should have listened to the program director, who warned you repeatedly that the audience would tune out if they heard a woman announcer. How long are you on probation?"

"Who knows? Hand me a towel. My broadcasting career and Spiro Agnew were disgraced on the same day, October 10, 1973, the famous date of your birth!" She grabbed the towel and dried her body. "You can never escape your past."

"It was really a dumb thing to do. I wish I could go back and undo it."

"Go back over there! Tell her that you changed your mind and want to be Vanessa Condon just like the state wanted you to be." She stepped out of the shower.

"Come with me?"

"Being your friend is a big pain," she moaned. "Prison blue might actually flatter you!"

"Funny, except you're going with me, as my accomplice in crime."

"Blue is not my color," she cracked as they started down the stairs.

The transcript department was locked as they peered through the clear window. No one was inside as they put their noses to the glass pane. So Trisha went to Don's for cheap beer.

* * *

The next morning, Trisha was nursing a terrible hangover when the transcript department called. Her head ached as she struggled to get dressed. "Hurry up." Vanessa was scared. "Let's go now."

They walked over and went straight into the lady's office. "Mr. Graves rendered a decision. This is completely out of the realm of our jurisdiction. We have no authority to change a Social Security number. Mr. Graves and

I both agree that you need to take this matter up with the Social Security Administration. In the meantime, I will change your transcript to Vanessa Vaughn, since you have provided me with your birth certificate." Completely stunned, neither of them moved as she shuffled the papers. "I'll personally see to everything."

Vanessa slowly rose from the chair. "Thank you for all your efforts on my behalf."

* * *

Outside, Trisha yelled, "What the hell you are going to do with this stupid name change?"

"I'm transferring to the University of California at Berkeley on the West Coast."

"Wait a minute! Isn't Berkeley where all the radicals are?"

"I guess, but I'm beginning my life over."

"Three thousand miles! My head is killing me, and you're not helping."

"I want to go far away. I've thought about this for a long time. An awfully long time!"

"This is the first I've heard of it. Why didn't you tell me?"

"You would talk me out of it. I figured I'd better not tell you."

"You're moving to the land of fruits and nuts, where everything that rattles rolls West."

"I received the transfer application last week."

"There's no guarantee that you will be accepted. My head is banging! You are doing this just to get away from Barry, but there are such things as telephones, which are a lot less dramatic."

* * *

Later that day, Connie knocked on her dorm door. "I heard they denied your request. That stinks!" She flung herself on the bed. "Wait a couple of weeks after everything dies down. I'll change your transcript. That place is a mountain of paperwork, so no one will ever know."

"Don't risk getting into trouble for me. You might get fired if they catch you!"

"Those odds are zero. They are old and rule bound. I don't see why they won't do it in the first place. I am alone during the lunch shift. I'll do it when the coast is clear. Give me your card, and I'll let you know when it's changed." Connie waved the card in the air as she left.

After she left, Vanessa realized she was trying to get even with Barry by disappearing. But there was no turning back now since Connie was determined to help her succeed.

* * *

Weeks later, Connie dropped in with a copy of Vanessa's changed record. She sank down on the bed and stared at the ceiling as a very strange feeling came over her. Later that day, she went to the campus post office and dropped the falsified transcript and application in the slot. When she let go of the handle, the metal banged shut.

The remainder of the semester was uneventful until a letter arrived from the University of California. Trisha's worst fears were now realized. Her best friend had been accepted as a transfer student and decided to move during Christmas break of their senior year. With Sister Roe gone and Barry out of her life, she wanted a new beginning. Devastated, Trisha spent every waking hour trying to talk her out of going, but Vanessa could not be deterred.

In the cafeteria, she munched on a pecan pie. "You are on a full scholarship that Sister Roe worked hard to get you. Don't throw her money away. Stay here and finish using it."

"It's my inheritance."

"Why spend money on school if you don't have to? Use it when you really need it."

"Why is this such a hard concept for you to grasp? A brand-new me avoids bad Juju."

"I knew it. That crazy old man Maniqault with no teeth scared you. Don't blow your inheritance by running away to nowhere. It won't solve anything.

A real Juju believer knows there is no running away from it. You won't escape it, and you are just fleeing from Barry."

"Barry is not even part of this equation."

"Liar, liar pants on fire! You love him and always will. If you split without resolving your love for Barry, you'll always regret it, and it will haunt you for the rest of your life."

"Promise me one thing. Swear you will never tell Barry or anyone else where I went."

"What? I can't do that! No way!"

"A brand-new start means you must be silent about my whereabouts."

"I get to lie to Barry and the rest of the world. What about your best and only friend?"

"We'll always be together and there for one another. I just want a new life."

"What am I supposed to tell Barry?"

"Whatever you like!"

"What about my parents, Doctor Hale, Father Kelly, and all the nuns in Sister Roe's order? You want too much. You are asking me to lie to people who love you, really love you."

"Don't you get it? I'm changing my race. You can't create a new identity if you have a past. You alone will be the key holder to my prior life, which means no one ever gets by you."

"This disappearing act won't work. They can simply call to see where you transferred."

"My records are confidential and cannot be released without my consent. I want everyone to think I just dropped out of sight. It's up to you to convince them that I split and quit school."

"You sure aren't asking for much. Lie to the entire population of western civilization. I'm a lousy liar, and there is no guarantee that anyone, including those senile nuns, will believe me."

"I expect you to use your best broadcasting skills to convince them."

"I can't even talk on the air because I am a woman, some broadcaster I am!"

"We always will be best friends and will stay in touch forever."

"Or until all these people figure out what a terrible liar I am."

"You must be absolutely convincing if I'm going to have a chance for a new life."

* * *

At Christmas break, Vanessa took a Greyhound bus to Atlanta. It was a brand-new bustling, modern city without the old Southern charm of Charleston. She wondered what it would look like today if "Old Tecumseh" hadn't burned it down. After leaving the terminal, she traveled through the Deep South. Closing her eyes, she fell soundly asleep, and Sister Rosalie's voice was clear and strong. "Child, the Rebels still held a sufficient stretch of the Mississippi even though the mouth of the river was now in Union hands. Vicksburg was the key. Sugar, daring tactics enabled Grant to cross the river south."

Cuddling against the window, she again heard the story that she had been told so many times. It felt so comforting to hear the nun: "Grant initiated a siege that starved the citizens and they ate rats to survive. The city fell on July 4, 1863, and to this day, some people in Vicksburg, Mississippi, do not celebrate July 4."

When the bus driver blew his horn, she awoke from her trance, and Sister Roe was gone. She opened her eyes to a "You are leaving Mississippi" sign. She cried all the way through Louisiana but finally dozed off in Texas as they took on more passengers. New Mexico's terrain intrigued her, but she could not stay awake and slept through most of Arizona.

She stepped off the bus in the California desert and was unprepared for the intense, dry heat that hit her face as she viewed her newly adopted state. Go west, young man, she thought as the bus entered the glittering lights of Los Angeles. Palm-tree-lined boulevards riveted her to the window with the hope of spotting a movie star. As they traveled north, the scenery became increasingly spectacular as houses appeared to hang from cliffs. Her first glimpse of the majestic Pacific Ocean's steep and rocky shoreline kept her face inches from the window. Ten hours later, Vanessa reached the fabled hills of San Francisco and her destiny.

* * *

Back in South Carolina, Trisha faced a constant bombardment of questions about Vanessa's whereabouts. Home from Harvard Medical School for Christmas, Barry was adamant that she tell him the truth. They went to their old high school hangout. He knew that after a couple of drinks, Trisha would regain her lapse of memory.

After entering the smoky, dimly lit dive bar, they waited until their eyes adjusted to the lighting before proceeding to the bar. Barry pulled up an empty stool, and Trisha sat down on the torn vinyl as he ordered two draft beers.

"Where is she? A lot of people are very worried. You are not being fair to them or me."

The bartender shoved the beer mug across the sticky counter.

"Fair to you? You were hardly around when she needed you." She took a swig of beer.

"What are you talking about?" Barry watched her swallow.

"Nothing! Nothing," she pleaded in a feeble attempt to change the subject.

"What were you alluding to?" He towered over her as he stood stiffly by her side.

"Didn't your dad tell you?"

"Tell me what?"

"If you really don't know, it's not my place to tell you. Ask your dad about last summer."

"What the hell are you talking about?" He squeezed her arm. "You know I love her. I think about her every minute of each day and night. I can never get her out of my mind. Ever."

"I'm dead if I tell you."

"Bartender, another round. The twenty-ounce please." He put more money on the counter.

After two beers, tipsy Trisha blurted out the whole story. "Vanessa was pregnant, and your dad refused to give her an abortion. He even offered to raise the baby himself. A butcher abortionist almost killed her. She got an infection, and your dad saved her life. He even drove her back to Carolina. I can't believe he didn't tell you."

The bartender brought another round, and she continued, "Vanessa flipped out after seeing you with that girl at your mother's funeral. She thought you two had a monogamous relationship. Except for you, she never looked at another guy in her entire life. You were the only man she had ever been with, and at Carolina, she never went out on a single date the entire time."

Barry sipped his beer as tears clouded his chocolate-colored eyes. "I called her every day after my mom died, but she refused to speak with me. My passion for her is real; my love is true." He reached into his pocket and threw money on the bar. "Let's go!"

Awkward silence fell over the car as they rode back to Trisha's house. The uncomfortable quiet was interrupted when Barry pulled into her driveway. He went around to open the car door. As she stepped out, she spun around. "It figures he never told you. Vanessa was never good enough for his precious son. Wrong skin color, right, Barry?" She ran into her home as Barry stood frozen.

CHAPTER ELEVEN

Trisha reached over to turn off the alarm as the announcer said, "James Earl Carter Junior was elected the thirty-ninth president of the United States. *Gee, my vote must have been the kiss of death for Gerald Ford*, she thought as she struggled out of bed. She couldn't be late for her first real broadcasting job at WDCA-TV in Washington DC. Behind the wheel of her beloved "Sherry Chevrolet," a 1974 Malibu, she pushed radio buttons, but on this November morning, there was only news about the 1976 election. She had never gotten up this early in graduate school.

* * *

When she arrived promptly at eight thirty, the television station's front door was locked. She rang the delivery bell until a voice crackled over the speaker: "I can't believe it. They really did go out and actually hired a woman!"

"Nice to meet you, too!" she yelled back into the box.

A broadcast engineer with an ample belly unlocked the door. "Go see Merl the Pearl."

"Who's that?"

"You'll find out soon enough," he said as she followed him to the sales department.

A voice came from an inner office. "I'm Merl, the national sales manager. You're late!"

She entered hastily.

"Listen up, yahoo. The FCC is now requiring women in nontraditional jobs. Apparently, you're the best we could do, a master's from the University of Southern Mississippi. So how much for a spot in Hattiesburg?"

"A dollar a holler." She laughed.

"Cute, yahoo, now listen up. You're the only broad we could find that had any sales experience, and you are going to help us keep our license with the FCC. Don't even think about stealing any national accounts from our rep RKO. I'll fire you in a second. Here, you southern bumpkin." He handed her a phone book. "Your account list."

Her rude indoctrination was abruptly interrupted when a silver-haired man appeared at the doorway. "My dear, you're here. I'm Mr. Brant, the general manager. We're delighted to have the very first saleswoman in the market on our staff. Welcome to WDCA-TV, and good luck!"

* * *

The entire sales staff consisted of men in their fifties. At lunchtime, one yelled, "Hey, kid! Come on. We're going to eat. It's quitting time." She followed them to a bar on Wisconsin Avenue, where the only food served was beer nuts. Drinking martinis, the salesmen took turns using the public phone outside the bathrooms. She spent the entire afternoon getting intoxicated.

"Hey, kid, don't go back in that condition," the same man warned.

She ignored him and in her drunken state went to the station. Appalled, Merl made her life miserable. The salesmen deliberately set her up and sabotaged her whenever the opportunity arose.

* * *

She became less naive and quickly was wise to their games. Arriving early every morning, she stayed until Merl arrived. After he made his appearance, she hit the road in Sherry Chevrolet, her lonely office on wheels. *My journalism diploma could hang from the rearview mirror*, she thought as she covered an entire block before moving Sherry to start the process all over again. She went into S & K Meats to use the restroom and unknowingly walked into the president's office with walls covered with hockey memorabilia.

From behind his desk, he asked, "Are you a fan?"

"I work at WDCA, and we carry the Capitals hockey team," she replied.

"I played in the pros until I got hurt. Could I afford to advertise?"

She focused on his trophy-mounted wall and didn't answer. When he finally got her attention, she walked out of his office with a one-hundred-thousand dollar sponsorship.

* * *

The next day, she attended a tour of the Kennedy Center. When the guide wasn't looking, she stepped into the general manager's office and handed him her business card.

"I can't afford television," he stated while she looked at all the newspaper ads on his wall.

"If you can afford the *Washington Post*, you can be on our air. You are the most prestigious theater in the country. Showcase your plays on live television."

"I'll try it, but it better work. I just started today as the advertising manager."

The Kennedy Center's first television campaign was a winner. So the managers of Arena Stage, Ford's Theater, and the Capitol Centre quickly became steady advertisers. With beginner's luck, she became the resident performing arts expert and rapidly realized that scouring the newspaper for advertisers was a lot easier than wandering around the streets of DC. When she switched advertisers to television, the most powerful medium ever invented, anything advertised on the air increased their sales.

* * *

To the chagrin of her male colleagues, she landed another big account. Sight and Sound spent ten thousand dollars, the largest monthly expenditure, on the station. It was run by a Bible-quoting, born-again Christian who sleazily preyed on the poor by renting appliances to people with no credit. A three-hundred-dollar television eventually cost thousands, while unsuspecting victims paid monthly for years. She called daily with exact commercial times, but one day, a recorded message blared in her ear: "This line has been disconnected!" Not bothering to redial, she headed straight for the tiny strip mall in suburban Virginia.

As she drove up in Sherry Chevrolet, she saw the store was completely empty, and even the front sign was gone. She had been scammed. He owed over thirty-thousand dollars, an enormous amount of money, and she knew her fate.

* * *

Merl reversed all the commission out of her paycheck, which resulted in zero income for months. "Yahoo, you're making too much damn money anyway!" Merl yelled.

"You have the stomach of a horse," the unpleasant comptroller lectured in a thick German accent. "Your handcuffs are golden." As they berated her, she hated every second of sales but was completely hooked on the money. She was making four times as much as Vanessa, who worked as a glorified secretary in a San Francisco news department.

Working hard to replace her lost income, she convinced a quirky owner of electric beds that contorted into different positions that television was the perfect visual medium to reach the elderly and infirmed. His results were staggering, a 300 percent increase in sales!

* * *

Norton's Department Store catered exclusively to Blacks. After an excruciating negotiation, the owner agreed to buy the spots for half the price listed. That afternoon, Merl the Pearl lambasted her and adamantly refused the order. So Trisha went to the owner, the most politically inept move. Mr. Brant had signed on the air in an old Texaco gas station and managed the operation on a shoestring budget. The studio, along with the television cameras, was where broken cars were fixed on racks. In severe financial trouble with the syndicators supplying his programming, Mr. Brant could barely make payroll, and knowing nothing about sales, he left that up to his sleazy salesmen. He had no choice but to keep his bunch of losers. Other stations were run by top-notch broadcasters with prestigious companies behind them. Impeccably dressed, he answered the door. His walls displayed awards from his heyday as an announcer in the 1950s. "My dear, to what do I owe the honor of your presence?" he said in his engaging broadcast performing voice.

"Please intercede with Merl, and put Norton's on the air on a trial basis. They get hooked and become a regular advertiser at the real rate."

"My dear, you are so persuasive. You can easily convince your supervisor."

"He hates me because I am a woman." Instantly, she regretted the statement, but there was no way to retract it. "He discriminates against me."

His facial expression changed immediately, and Mr. Brant curtly dismissed her.

"You'll never work in broadcasting as long as I'm alive," Merl ranted after finding out she went above him. "You'll be lucky to sell gum at the local 7-Eleven."

She listened nervously to his tirade, and when she emerged, her fellow eavesdropping salesmen greeted her with smirks.

Things got worse when Mr. Norton paid the real rate but arrived with hairless grotesque mannequins. Too cheap to hire live models, he put clothes on bald, faceless plastic bodies. Furious, the production crew were forced to film one tacky ad after another. The station became known for its bizarre spots that sold everything from smokeless ashtrays to the Vegematic, a miracle blender. Trisha had the dubious distinction of bringing in every oddball account, and WDCA's commercials became the laughingstock of the nation's capital. The blame fell squarely on Trisha as the station became the butt of jokes from late-night comedians.

* * *

Luckily, her college friend worked for Representative John Jenrette from South Carolina. "After work, meet me on Capitol Hill. We'll crash the nightly cocktail parties," Gus said eagerly.

She met him at the Capitol Building, and he explained that senators and congressmen had index cards with the room number on them. That evening, she and Gus followed Senator Hollings around as he met with the South Carolina Pork Producers at six, South Carolina Electric and Gas at six thirty, and South Carolina Peach Growers at seven. "When in session, this pace of cocktail parties continues every half hour until nine o'clock." Gus pointed down the grand hallway. "These meetings hold the most important people and consequently have the best hors d'oeuvres. Learn your way around the Hill, and you'll never buy groceries again," Gus said.

Beowulf's was owned by a Washington Redskins tackle, and every night was a party. Canoeing on the Potomac River, Jimmy Carter was captured on film beating a poor, defenseless rabbit with his oar, and he claimed he was attacked by a "killer rabbit." Beowulf's owner covered his six-six frame in a white rabbit costume with ears and poured fake blood over the bandages. A gigantic rabbit carried a State of Georgia–shaped cake and threw whole peanuts on the floor.

* * *

Carrie who lived in her apartment building was promiscuous and talked openly about intercourse. The South's convoluted morality code, coupled with twelve years of Catholic school, made Carrie seem positively risqué.

"I'm taking a cab means that I'm going home with a guy. Got it?" Carrie laughed. "Tall, skinny guys always have the biggest ones! I can spot them a mile away or until I unzip their pants! I'm in a slump with a string of small penises!"

Trisha got a hysterical call at the station. "What's wrong?" she whispered.

"I've got this horrible herpes outbreak," Carrie sobbed.

"What's that?"

"You hayseed, even below the Mason-Dixon Line, it's a venereal disease."

"How do you get it?"

"How do you think, hillbilly? I have to soak in an oatmeal bath until this outbreak is over. You Southerners aren't speedy, but hurry up and buy oatmeal."

* * *

She left the station immediately. In Carrie's apartment, she encountered herpes. Red sores covered her skin down to her knees while her inner thighs were blanketed in swollen lesions. "I'll miss a week of work. It's too painful to walk. This bathtub is my bed. Crabs are easier."

"Crabs! They crawl on South Carolina beaches?"

"You Southerners are positively Neanderthals. Too much inbreeding! Listen up, you country bumpkin; it takes a prescription shampoo to get rid of crabs! Got it, hick?"

* * *

That night as Trisha left the station, Merl's two Chicago P & G clients asked, "Know a bar?"

"I know just the place."

They followed her as she drove to Beowulf's, her home away from home. Inside the front door, the two married guys said, "May we buy you dinner and abuse our expense accounts?"

She looked down at both men's wedding rings. "Let's have a drink first."

As she woke up, the heavy scent of men's cologne made her sink down in her pillow to take a deep breath. She remembered the same smell from last night. Her eyes opened slowly as she glanced around, but the aroma lingered. Her mouth felt dry, and her head ached as she took another sniff of the strong fragrant odor. Mortified, she threw clothes on and drove straight to the station to call Vanessa in San Francisco.

* * *

"Did I wake you up?" She sounded like her own mother, who always called at ungodly hours and invariably said the exact same thing.

"What's wrong? It's 3:00 a.m.!"

"I slept with two guys last night."

Vanessa sat straight up in bed. "How could you possibly do that in one night?"

"At the same time. I did it at the same time."

"Even Ian Fleming doesn't have James Bond sleep with two women at once!"

"Don't make me feel worse. I'm so ashamed, and they're Merl's clients, too!"

"For heaven's sake, Merl hates you. What if he finds out?"

"Probably move out west under an assumed name! Sound familiar?"

"Merl would find you, no matter what corner of the earth you hide in."

"Tell me that I'm not a whore."

"You're not a whore." Vanessa pulled up her sheet.

"I called for moral support, and I'm not getting it!"

"Moral, you want moral support after sleeping with two men?"

"Moral support was a poor choice of words. Would Sister Rosalie think I was a whore?"

"You better hope Sister Roe was arguing with Old Tecumseh last night when you had your 'ménage à trois. Stop drinking, and this kind of stuff would never happen," Vanessa lectured.

"I never even knew their names. I never asked!"

"Go see *Looking for Mr. Goodbar*. Be careful. You could wind up like Diane Keaton. Her killer was a total creep. I can't believe that she ever slept with him."

"He was gorgeous. I stayed for the credits to find out his name. He's Richard Gere."

"Never heard of him."

"I got the article your mom sent about Barry's wedding."

"It's not malicious. Quit pining over him. He married that Yankee. Not one date since you graduated from the University of California Berkeley six years ago. It's time to forget him!"

"I wish I could." Vanessa started to cry.

"Hey, I'd better go. It's eight thirty. All the guys will be here any second. I hate my job! Why did I listen to that radio salesman about going into ad sales? Well, we set another record, two hours on the station's phone bill. They might go broke any minute!"

* * *

CHAPTER ELEVEN

In the shadow of the White House and Capitol Hill existed the country's worst ghettos. Once fashionable, now downtrodden Logan Circle was a gentrifying area of Victorian houses, just eight blocks northeast of the White House. Trisha bought a tiny row house, the only property she could afford. Now she was the only blond-haired, blue-eyed person within a ten-block radius, except for President and Mrs. Carter at 1600 Pennsylvania Avenue.

Her suburban friends were petrified by the inner city and warned against living in this ghetto, but she brushed off their warnings. One night, when she was stopped in Sherry Chevrolet at a light, a little boy crashed his bike, and blood flowed profusely down his face and stained his shirt. She pulled over and rushed to his side. "Where's your mommy?"

"On Fourteenth and Q," he cried.

She threw his bike into the trunk and wrapped her coat around him. She drove to that corner packed with prostitutes. "I don't see my momma. She ain't here." Blood gushed from the large cut on his cheek. "She works this corner."

She tried to comfort the little boy as she sped to Howard University Hospital. The emergency room evoked memories of Charleston's hospital since the staff and patients were mostly Black. No one was concerned that a Black kid had a blond mother as they entered.

"At least six stitches," a young intern announced. "Tell admissions how you'll pay."

A Marine Corps brat, her military ID had paid everything. She searched her wallet and glanced up. "I have thirty dollars."

"We'll take it." The clerk laughed. "The charge is twenty-eight dollars."

"Take it easy the rest of the night." The tired intern yawned. "His regular doctor can take the stitches out next week," he instructed.

She carried the tiny child to her car after buying him a Coke and candy bar. As he munched on the chocolate, he directed her to a public housing project just one block away from her own Vermont Avenue row house. She stopped, yanked his bent bike out of the trunk, and carried both inside. Peeling paint surrounded cracked windows while overgrown weeds covered broken glass.

He disappeared into the dilapidated building, and she felt ashamed that she did not escort him inside. *I'm the worst person ever*, she thought as she drove the one block to home.

* * *

That night, Trisha awoke to loud banging on her front door. She knew absolutely no one, but without thinking, she flung the door open. A prostitute in tight red hot pants with heavy makeup and false eyelashes stood in front of her, exposing all her body parts as her massive breasts hung out of her ruffled top. "You done nice thing for my boy. You need bucks for sewing my baby up?" the hooker asked in almost illiterate speech.

"No," Trisha muttered.

"Jimmy say nobody bother you, you hear. Jimmy put word out." The streetwalker motioned to her pimp sitting in a vintage 1965 Oldsmobile with big fins and then disappeared. After that night, she enjoyed a previously unheard-of freedom as an untouchable. As a White woman in Logan Circle, she was never hassled and felt safe in her tiny ghetto row house.

* * *

A month later, the entire staff was paged over the loudspeaker to the studio, and all employees crowded around the cameras. "I'm Ro Grigg, president of Taft Broadcasting, and we purchased this station. Meet the new general manager, Mark Smith. Return to your desks now."

Men in polyester blue suits from Taft's headquarters in Cincinnati, Ohio, had taken over the sales department. Gone was Merl the Pearl, and behind his desk, the new manager barked, "You get five minutes to interview for your old job and five minutes to clean out your desk."

Trisha watched each salesman stream in, clean out his desk, and promptly leave. *I can't pay the mortgage if I get the ax*, she thought as he called her into Merl's old office last.

"Taft Broadcasting needs its first female to run one of our stations. All our general managers come from sales. You are the top billing salesperson on the lowest commission. You are perfect."

She burst out laughing. "You fired all my male torturers?"

"Merl's lousy records show your sales dwarf the men's, and it's all new business."

Trisha chuckled. "Merl berated me daily saying I was the worst salesman he had."

"He's a moron! 1980 starts a brand-new decade, and we need women in management. Our goal is a girl running a station, the last male bastion of power unobtainable for a lady." Mr. Grigg looked directly at her. "Let's be blunt. An independent UHF is like having a venereal disease. You need a real station, a network affiliate." She felt flattered and intrigued until his next sentence. "You are going to our strongest ABC affiliate, WBRC·TV in Birmingham, Alabama. It's the only VHF in a market with two high-band UHF stations. Gold bullion comes straight out of that station. The Alabama Auburn Game got an eighty-six rating."

"I've never heard of an eighty-six rating. Is that even possible?"

"Exactly, Miss Bibbs. You will sell a real television station and make a fortune doing it. And you will be our first woman general manager at Taft Broadcasting."

* * *

Weeks later, Trisha drove across the Potomac River as tears streamed down her cheeks. As she passed the Pentagon, the Washington Monument receded into Sherry Chevrolet's rearview mirror. *Here comes another brick at my head.* She thought of the Birmingham police spraying Blacks with fire hoses in the 1960s. On the radio, a bunch of college hockey kids amazed the country by beating the powerful and professional Russians.

"Do you believe in miracles?" Al Michaels said as the buzzer sounded and the young Americans captured the Olympic gold medal.

"No!" Trisha yelled at the car radio. "No, Al, I don't believe in miracles!"

CHAPTER TWELVE

After graduating from the University of California at Berkeley in 1974 in journalism, Vanessa got a job as a production assistant, a glorified secretarial position at KPIX-TV in San Francisco. The newsroom's explosive setting along with the excitement of major market television made her a workaholic. Her long hours were noticed by the news director, Mr. Fellows, who issued her a press badge and shifted more responsibility her way. Her impressive dedication made him rely on her to follow through on grunt work that everyone else avoided. She typed scripts, delivered them to the on-air talent, fed them into the teleprompter, cut up daily papers for the assignment desk, and viewed tapes. Constantly, orders were shouted at her, but she was calm and professional. The news staff worked to live; like all San Franciscans, they revered leisure time as a precious right not to be wasted. Her colleagues didn't spend one extra minute at the station, so Vanessa found them to be lazy as they dumped their assignments on her.

A reporter named Mackenzie threw scribbled notes at her and rudely ordered, "The trolley war was started in 1904 by Patrick Calhoun, so find out who in the hell he is."

"Patrick's father was John Caldwell Calhoun, vice president under John Quincy Adams and Andrew Jackson. He maintained states had the right to nullify federal legislation that they deemed unconstitutional," Vanessa answered.

"Is that so?" Mackenzie banged on her desk. "I said check it out. Got it?"

Mr. Fellows interrupted, "Mackenzie, I'm assigning this to Vanessa. Got it?"

* * *

After three years, this was her first big break. It was unheard of for a production assistant to write a feature story, and it came at the expense of the most obnoxious news reporter on the staff. She spent countless hours on research, and not one pertinent fact escaped her attention, as she was determined to make this news segment fascinating. "The trolley war was started by Patrick Calhoun, grandson of the famed South Carolina secessionist, John Caldwell Calhoun. As the owner of United Railroads, he saw an advantage to overhead electric lines, thus doing away with the tangle of horse and cable systems on many San Francisco streets. Patrick Calhoun promised improved service, while his screaming opponents saw a new and incredibly ugly city, choked with wires. After the earthquake, he wanted to electrify Sutter Street first."

Mr. Fellows glanced up. "This angle is excellent work, Vanessa."

"May I narrate?" she asked boldly but instantly regretted it when he got on the phone.

Weeks later, he decided to let her do the narration, but she could not appear on the air. At the San Francisco Archives, she found early photographs of the trolley system, along with fabulous portraits of Patrick and his grandfather. Featuring the annual cable car bell ringing contest for sound, she used dazzling views of the San Francisco Bay from the city's fabled hills.

"It's mesmerizing so stop already," Trisha said as Vanessa kept reading it over and over.

"Are you sure?"

"It's airing during the November rating period, the most important sweep for Nielsen and Arbitron audience measurement. That book determines the rates charged. You are on your way!"

Trisha was right when Vanessa won best feature story at the Northern California Broadcast News Awards. Mr. Fellows quickly promoted her to assignment editor, and during her reign, KPIX won more awards than any other San Francisco station.

* * *

Vanessa lived in a dilapidated flat in Haight-Ashbury with five women, and they brought home a steady stream of one-night stands. As one male stranger after another greeted her in the bathroom, she vowed to move out. It was an expensive city, and she lived as modestly as possible until she found a Nob Hill studio. More than she wanted to spend, it was right on the Hyde Street cable car line. Now her commute down steep California Street afforded a dazzling view of the San Francisco Bay, one of the world's most beautiful natural harbors. South Carolina's flat swamps of her youth were replaced by the spectacular views from San Francisco's forty-three hills.

At her new apartment, she could hear the noisy cable cars as they rattled along the rail lines, and their brakes squeaked on the sheer vertical route. The brakemen rang their bells loudly as she tried to sleep, but she loved her freedom. Her inner peace was only broken by a brakeman's racket as he maneuvered the trolley below her window and fog horns as they guided ships through the Golden Gate's narrow channel. Rain or shine, Vanessa took the cable car past Chinatown as small children scurried past the fresh fish stands. In the distance stood the island prison of Alcatraz as she got off in the financial district and walked the rest of the way to work. Her only exercise was to explore the beguiling hills as she strolled past every race and nationality. She loved her adopted home as much as Charleston, and she cherished the freedom that most San Francisco inhabitants took for granted. Every possible nationality coexisted with an ease unknown in the South. Tolerance for different races and lifestyles seemed effortless.

* * *

By 1980, Vanessa became the first woman to ever produce the late news. The devastating 1982 winter brought horrific mud slides that wreaked havoc as houses slid down the collapsing hills and left residents homeless. As the CBS affiliate in San Francisco, KPIX fed the network for their national broadcast and quickly hired talent away for CBS Network, New York.

Once the storms subsided, she became a full-time reporter. She was thirty-one. It had taken nine years to become a television reporter and fulfill her dream. Prostitution that plagued the Tenderloin and threatened the merchants' tourist trade was her first assignment. Pressure from the mayor caused the police to round them up, but night after night, the hookers reappeared to ply their trade. Her lead story must hold the viewers' interest on such a dismal topic.

As she rode the last cable car home for the evening, she saw a Marine in his dress blues escorting a woman whose mini skirt barely covered her crotch. She closed her eyes and could hear the nun's voice clearly as if she were sitting beside her on the trolley. "Why, child, the men under Hooker's command during the Civil War were a particularly wild bunch, and when on leave, his troops spent much of their time in brothels. In Washington, a large red light district became known as Hooker's Division in tribute to the proclivities of General Joseph Hooker. A theory originated that prostitutes were known as 'hookers.' Hooker's men were at times ill-disciplined but, child, liquor, not women, was the main source of their difficulties with the provost marshal. But the name hooker has stuck ever since." The warmth of Sister Roe's voice was abruptly interrupted by the brakeman yelling. She hopped off but knew her mother had given her the lead story.

* * *

The next morning, Vanessa was at the main San Francisco library as the security guard unlocked the door. While at the card catalog, she remembered Sister Roe had read Ulysses S. Grant's memoirs, and he made a derogatory statement about Hooker. Within Grant's memoirs, she found a fascinating reference where he described Hooker as a "dangerous man, does not subordinate to his superiors." She located an intriguing photograph of the actual Washington red light district that the Union soldiers used during the Civil War and found a bewitching portrait of General Joseph Hooker. "Fighting Joe" looked drunk, as he stood beside a sexy and glamorous lady. With these two photographs, she had a riveting lead story.

She handed in the final version of the script. "I have a suggestion," Mr. Fellows offered. "Here in California we have Union and Confederate uniformed soldiers, along with vintage arms reenacting battles as living history. See if they would reenact Chancellorsville for your story."

"Chancellorsville, where Hooker was defeated at the hands of Lee!" Vanessa interrupted. "Why didn't I think of that? What a fantastic idea! Do you think they will do it?"

"Grown men parading around in hot wool uniforms would die for a chance to be on the air. Emphasize that every name will appear in the credits. They'll love that!" Never wasting a second, he picked up the phone, which meant she was dismissed.

* * *

She met with the head of the Civil War Reenactment Society, who happened to be a Stanford University history professor. He constantly reassured her that he was not a crackpot, nor were his men, who were dedicated to living history. He was charismatic until she noticed his wedding band. While driving back to work, she tried to analyze why he affected her. She was a history buff, but even Sister Roe wouldn't go around on weekends in a hot uniform at her own expense. She turned up the radio volume in the news car just as the Fifth Dimension song 'Marry Me Bill' played over the speakers.

* * *

The feature ran during the 1984 May sweeps in prime time and shocked the entire sales department when it obtained an outstanding rating. The overnight metered ratings came in the next morning and Mr. Fellows invited the staff upstairs to celebrate in Mr. Collins's suite. She had never been inside the general manager's office in her ten years at the station. Superbly decorated, his massive office adjoined a gigantic conference room. Overwhelmed by exquisite furniture, she felt just like when she first went inside Barry's house.

A mirrored wet bar was surrounded by expensive crystal. After working over a decade, she had nothing to compare with this richness in her own personal belongings. Nervously, she sipped from a goblet. Afraid to spill on the plush white carpet, she wished to be back at her newsroom desk.

Mr. Collins gushed, "I'm delighted! Vanessa, you will easily win another Northern California Broadcasting Award. Mr. Fellows and I would like you to have dinner with us at the Olympic Club." Shocked by the unexpected invitation, she nodded. "Good, seven o'clock."

As he abruptly disappeared, she felt puzzled by the request since she had never eaten with Mr. Fellows, who was all business and didn't fraternize with subordinates. At her desk, she stared into space, wondering what to wear to an old-line, prestigious private club.

* * *

Promptly, they met in the lobby and were hit by a blast of cold air from heavy fog rolling in off the Pacific as they entered Battery Street. San Francisco's streets were blanketed in a thick, chilly cloud as Mr. Collins opened the door to his brand-new silver-blue Mercedes. She felt awkward sitting in the front seat because her boss was alone in the back. All three listened attentively to news radio and didn't talk, for which she was grateful. The aroma of pristine leather seats hit her nostrils as her shoes sank into the plush carpet. If not relaxing, the drive turned out to be quite pleasant. Out-of-town tourists unaware of the weather were freezing in shorts and covered their heads since they thought fog was rain.

"Do you know what Mark Twain said was the coldest winter he ever spent?"

"No," she lied graciously.

"A summer in San Francisco!" Mr. Collins laughed heartily.

At the gated entrance to the luxurious Olympic Club, security waved them in. Located between Lake Merced and the Pacific Ocean, the membership consisted of old-line San Francisco families and was so exclusive that outsiders rarely gained admittance. Suddenly, she felt scared entering a lily-White private club where Negroes worked in the kitchen or on the golf course. She felt her heart beating wildly inside her chest as they passed tall Eucalyptus trees.

* * *

CHAPTER TWELVE

When they entered the ornate restaurant, the maître d' escorted them to their table and pulled out Vanessa's chair as the two men immediately ordered cocktails. Waiters were dressed in black tuxedos as she glanced around the stately room. Elaborate windows were outlined by the dark redwood walls while plush drapes hung from the ceiling to the floor. Elegant white linen and opulent crystal adorned their candlelit table. Mr. Collins looked directly across the table. "Let's cut to the chase, Vanessa. I have an offer tonight that I hope you will accept."

Mr. Fellows interjected. "Our female anchor is leaving for LA. As a CBS owned and operated station, it's an excellent opportunity to make her way to the network. After an exhaustive national search, we looked in our own backyard, and we're looking at you, Vanessa."

Mr. Collins interrupted his news director. "We've been number two in the early and late news ratings for almost five years. Local news costs a lot of money to produce, but it generates a significant amount of revenue. A money maker, our news department's gross cash potential is watched closely at corporate in New York. It not only affects our annual budget, but it controls my own personal income. It's concerning to me and our Westinghouse stockholders."

She hadn't even glanced at the menu when Mr. Collins cavalierly ordered for them all and gave specific instructions on what appetizers and main courses to bring.

After the waiter left, Mr. Fellows said, "We've been neglectful financially, but your hard work has always been appreciated. We are in a position now to reward you monetarily."

Mr. Collins shook his finger and rudely interrupted. "Now, Vanessa, there is a caveat. If you accept our offer, I expect you to be different from your predecessor. She was a nightmare. I have no intention of making a counteroffer to keep her. She was a pain in my ass!"

"Why was she a problem?" She spoke for the first time.

"Please, call me Ian."

"OK, Ian, what can I do differently?"

"Take public appearances for instance. Station parties for our important clients. She would either no-show or come but not speak to anyone. She was too good to talk to the media buyers at the big agencies, like J. Walter Thompson and McCann Erickson. These women spend over millions in the market annually. Her rudeness made sales go ballistic. Our job is to make money for Westinghouse Broadcasting, period. I don't care if one of these media buyers is chewing food with her mouth open and spraying it in your face. Be nice! Be delightful! In other words, don't be a bitch! Keeping sales contented makes me happy. I came up through the sales ranks, and I'm bottom-line oriented. I live to see the sales figures."

"You've never worked in a news department?" she asked in disbelief.

"Ninety-nine percent of the television stations have men running them who, in their youth, were out on the streets selling spots. Broadcast companies groom salesmen and promote them through the ranks to run a station. I started out in Philly, and this is my first general manager's shot, so I want this to be Westinghouse's flagship station. I intend to be so profitable that armored cars loaded with gold bullion will head for New York. I can write my own ticket."

"You've never worked in a news department?" she repeated the question.

"The only reason to produce a local newscast is to do it cheaply, make it number one, jack the rates up, and keep it sold out. My intention is to overtake the ABC owned and operated station and kick their late news in the dirt. ABC is delivering a great prime-time lead-in audience. We must think faster and smarter to get back into the race. If we can capture the number-one position at eleven o'clock, the early news will follow. San Franciscans are creatures of habit. Once we get them at eleven, we'll easily convert them to our early news. My goal is to make this station the top biller in the market. Anyone who gets in my way is history around here."

The general manager stopped his tirade to approve a second bottle of expensive merlot. She never drank alcohol and felt the tiny amount she had consumed going straight to her head. Trisha had already told her the same thing. Sales was where the money and power lay.

"I know we are the city's most decorated news department, but broadcasting awards mean nothing unless we reign supreme in the ratings. A metered market, we get our report card every morning. I expect you and Bob to worry about overnight ratings as much as I do. Understood?"

She nodded as she remembered Trisha saying salesmen who become general managers were pond scum horror stories. *Pond scum, pond scum!* she thought as she sipped her wine.

"I expect you to live and breathe ratings. If you need to work every day, so be it."

Mr. Fellows interrupted. "I can assure you for the past decade, she has worked seven days a week. She's an unsung heroine of news." His praise was completely ignored by Mr. Collins.

"To launch your debut, I want a series of intimate dinners with San Francisco's buying community. You can dine with those old broads and charm the hell out of them. Have them eating right out of your hands, so they'll start putting more money into our news to create a false sense of tightness. This will give sales leverage over the rates. Bob, I could care less about all these awards you keep winning. I want ratings. Get out and find stories to attract an audience. A kid playing on a railroad track who gets his penis severed! Whatever! Just do it!"

Mr. Collins was incredibly rude, and she felt his hardworking news director didn't deserve this treatment. *If Sister Roe was here, he wouldn't know what hit him*, she thought.

"I'm prepared to quadruple your salary." She focused back on the conversation. "The station hasn't been overly generous compensating you, but now we can reward your hard work."

The waiter arrived with fried calamari. "My predecessor was making five hundred thousand dollars," she boldly mentioned as she took a bite of the battered squid.

"Now, Vanessa, where in the world did you hear that?" he asked, feigning shock.

"I read it in the Chronicle when Westinghouse first hired her out of Chicago."

"The most I'm ready to offer at this time is two hundred thousand."

She put a piece of sour dough bread in her mouth and thought, *Gee, I'm getting an extra fifty-grand just for reading the paper.*

"Now, Vanessa, I will throw in a brand-new car, which we can trade out and a clothing allowance too," he retorted, while leaning even farther across the table.

Tipsy, she didn't realize there was an awkward silence, which Mr. Collins couldn't stand.

"Now, Vanessa, we will reimburse you for any expenses that you incur in this position." He waved his fork for emphasis. "Corporate will supply you with a credit card."

She took another bite of Calamari and wished Trisha was here to do the negotiations.

"Now, Vanessa, you can be quite generous with yourself when using the corporate card."

Feeling intoxicated, she wondered, *Why he didn't realize that I would do it for free? Mr. Fellows knows I would.* Suddenly, it dawned on her why the news director had not said a word. *These two are incompatible.* Mr. Fellows could have negotiated a much better deal, but he was on her side and let this buffoon give away the store while enjoying every minute of it. *I'm not doing too bad myself, even though Trisha could have done better. I'm enjoying a fantastic dinner, and I just got a car. I've never owned one, and Mr. Fellows knows that I am Miss Mass Transit.*

"Do you know where the term calamari came from to mean squid prepared as food?"

The men nodded negatively, so she launched into a dissertation. "It's the Italian plural of *calamaro*, from Late Latin *calamarium*, 'pen case.' From Latin comes *calamarius*, relating to a reed pen perhaps from the 'ink' the squid secretes."

"Did you take Latin?" Mr. Fellows spoke for the first time in a long while.

"I was taught Latin at the same time that I learned English."

"I thought Latin was a dead language." Mr. Collins showed his ignorance.

"To my mother, it was very much alive, Mr. Collins. I mean, Ian."

"I thought you were raised in an orphanage," Mr. Fellows replied.

"I was," she answered curtly, and silence ensued.

Sautéed abalone, San Francisco style, arrived. She thoroughly enjoyed this meal because she ate at her desk or on the run. The job offer, the alcohol, and the ambiance of the exclusive surroundings were intoxicating. *I wonder if I should tell old Ian here that he is putting the first Black anchor on the air in San Francisco? And glory be, she be a woman!* She smiled.

She extended her hand. "You have a deal, Ian. Don't worry about our clients. I'll do everything I can to assist the sales department. My best friend is in sales back east. I learned from her how important sales are, and I will help our salespeople any way that I can."

"Fantastic! I want a press release to go out to all the local radio and television stations, as well as the newspapers. Have it on my desk by eight thirty, Bob." He reached into his briefcase and resurfaced with a typed contract and a pen. He crossed out the salary, inserting the correct amount with all the perks offered. Instinctively, she knew she should talk to an attorney. But the only one she knew was in Charleston and elderly, so he could be dead by now.

"I'm delighted. You are a tremendous asset. I couldn't be happier," Mr. Fellows said.

Mr. Collins interrupted. "I think the orphan angle is a sure seller."

"I don't," Mr. Fellows replied. "We will start with her graduation from Berkeley."

* * *

After they dropped her off on Nob Hill, she immediately called Trisha in Birmingham and breathlessly told her every minute detail of the evening. "You did an incredibly competent job of negotiating your contract. If you talk too much, you blow it. By continuing to eat while he gave away the farm, you were perfect," Trisha assured her friend.

"He was too stupid to know that I would have done it for nothing."

"Figures! He's a man, isn't he? Guess what? I got permission to attend the American Women in Radio and Television convention."

"It's in San Francisco!" Vanessa screamed into the phone.

"Right-O! And none too soon because I need to get out there before you are hounded by all your fans!" Trisha yelled back into the receiver. "I want you to be an unknown, so that we can wander the streets till the wee hours. Oh, and I want to leave my heart in San Francisco because it is breaking here in beautiful downtown Bama, honey child!"

"I can't wait! Get here as soon as you can."

Vanessa burst into tears. Her dream of becoming a television anchor was finally coming true, and after twelve long years, she was going to see her best friend again.

CHAPTER THIRTEEN

Excited, she watched the deplaning passengers emerge from the hallway. When Trisha appeared, they both screamed as they hugged and kissed each other. When they arrived at Vanessa's studio, they stood by the tracks, waiting for a cable car. Her friend marveled at the spectacular city as they hopped on the last run of the night and went down a steep hill that took her breath away. As the chilly fog drenched their clothes, they returned home and crawled into bed. They talked until the sun came up and then fell into a deep sleep. Late in the afternoon, they took showers and got ready for a night on the town. After jumping onto a cable car, they headed down the hill to Maxwell's Plum, which overlooked the Golden Gate Bridge and Alcatraz.

As the fog lifted, the sapphire waters of the bay sparkled before the restaurant's floor-to-ceiling glass windows. Ships sailed serenely past them as an absolutely enthralled Trisha fell completely in love with San Francisco and its endless beauty and charm. After dinner, they went to an outdoor North Beach café in the city's Italian section. They sat at a front sidewalk on Broadway and ordered two cappuccinos. Enrico's produced strange sights, as transvestites walked by on their way to Finocchio's, San Francisco's landmark nightclub since 1936, which featured world-renowned female impersonators.

"I was hoping to meet a man, but this isn't exactly what I had in mind," Trisha said as a six-foot man walked by in four-inch heels and their white jacketed waiter with a beret arrived.

"Do you know the history of the word *cappuccino*?"

"No, but I have a feeling I'm going to find out." She loaded her espresso with sugar.

"In Italian, cappuccino resembled the color of the Capuchin friar habit."

"Sure do. I remember those monks," Trisha replied sarcastically.

"Their order played a big role in bringing Catholicism back to Reformation Europe."

"Where in the world did you learn that?"

"Wait! The first use of cappuccino in English is recorded in a 1948 San Francisco work."

"OK, daughter of Sister Roe, where do you find this stuff?"

"I read it on the back of the menu." Vanessa laughed as Trisha shook her head. There was never a lull in the conversation; they talked nonstop, just like in high school.

"I've never taken a one-week vacation so Mr. Fellows was happy I had a friend coming."

"You're nuts! Completely certifiable! I use every vacation day and beg for more."

"Westinghouse decided my debut will be during the July sweeps. Corporate hired a speech coach to remove my trace of a Southern accent. The professor says it's not extraordinarily strong but subtle enough to come across over the air."

"I don't hear it, but I'm no expert." She winked at the waiter.

"She's British and hates the Southern dialect."

"Tell her to get in line with the rest of the country."

"She has an inordinate amount of patience and is totally dedicated to removing the flaw from my speech." Vanessa rolled her tongue off the roof of her mouth to demonstrate her vocal exercises. As Trisha watched her, she knew she would be captivating on the air. A dazzling beauty possessing an old-world charm, she would be a dynamic anchor.

"My boss thinks I'm attending the American Women in Radio and Television convention at the Moscone Center. I need wander over and get some brochures to prove to him I attended it."

"Get a job here."

'I'm giving Taft Broadcasting a short lease to fulfill their management promise to me."

On the way to the airport, she broached the subject. "What's the latest on Barry?"

"No offense but you are thirty-two years old and had sex once. Even Sister Roe would tell you that twelve years of penitence is enough, even by the Catholic Church's standards. Don't go overboard and become a slut like me, but you could date. Look at it as a free dinner, as you suffer through a boring evening with some man." As they passed Candlestick Park, she pointed. "How about a jock? That place must be crawling with them."

"You're stalling. Get back to Barry."

"He graduated and stayed to do his internship and residency at Mass General."

"I know all that. When you visit your folks, so you see him?"

"I've been here for a week. Why ask these questions now?"

"Have you seen him?"

"Last time I was home, the class of 1968 invited all alumni to the Holiday Inn with Ashley River views. I crashed the cocktail party, and the first person I ran into was Barry."

"Did he have a date?"

"If you call your wife a date. He married that Yankee woman from Boston. She's a pathologist at Saint Francis and abhors living in the South. Feel better? She's stuck in Charleston, and you're not. She's miserable, and you're not. If it's any consolation, those two look perfectly pathetic. Positively pathetic, they barely spoke to each other."

"How does he look?"

"I can't lie. He's drop-dead gorgeous! Always was and always will be. He runs every day and is in great shape. So is that body of his."

"You really think he's unhappy?"

"He went back to Charleston because his dad never remarried and is alone at his advancing age. Barry's the dutiful son, but he didn't seem too thrilled to be living there."

"Does he have kids?"

"One boy, and stop torturing yourself? He had sex once with her and once with you."

"Hilarious! Did he ask about me?"

"I'm going to burn in hell unless Sister Roe pulls some strings with Saint Peter for me!"

"What did he say?"

"He called me a liar like always and said to tell you he never stopped loving you. I can tell you this: you are one thousand times more beautiful than his Yankee wife."

"But she's a physician."

"And you're a famous anchorwoman in San Francisco!" Trisha screamed out the window. "I'd bet my crummy sales job on Barry regretting not being with you."

"All I have now is you and my memories."

"Yes, your memories, your talent, your new anchor job in the fifth-largest broadcasting market in the country. Am I forgetting something?" Trisha knocked on the dashboard and yelled, "A brand-new BMW convertible, compliments of Westinghouse."

* * *

During the July sweeps, KPIX-TV spent $100,000 promoting the debut of their new anchor Vanessa Vaughn. Billboards, coinciding with an extensive radio and newspaper campaign, featured the Eyewitness News coanchors, Dave and Vanessa. July was considered a throwaway book because by the time it came out, advertisers worried about the fall premiere ratings. But Mr. Collins was determined to succeed and become the top news station as he bombarded Vanessa's picture into the market. A series of luncheons supplemented the hype as she went to meet with national companies headquartered in the Bay Area like Chevron and Levi's. She attended the mayor's dinner with the San Francisco Board of Supervisors, addressed the San Francisco Police and Fire Departments, and met with countless nonprofit groups. As the whirlwind tour unfolded, she followed management's orders exactly, and Mr. Collins loved having a talent that he could totally control.

After the July sweep ended, Mr. Collins called the news department into his office to congratulate them. They had overtaken KGO-TV in the overnight ratings, beating them in the four-week sweep average of household ratings. A catered breakfast awaited them in the conference room as he raised his glass. "We won't have the demographics until the book comes out, but the overnights have been fantastic. We are back on top so keep this momentum up. That November book is the one we need to win, but I feel confident that we will."

Uncharacteristically, Mr. Fellows proposed a toast. "Ms. Vaughn, you are a natural on-air talent, and I'm pleased to have you on my team." A man of few words, his tribute spoke volumes.

* * *

The fall premiere party was held at the San Francisco Palace of Fine Arts, and no expense was spared. Dutifully, Vanessa worked the room with sales and met all their major clients. Finally, she was given her cue to go up to the microphone and introduce the fall premiere video, which showed excerpts from all the new CBS Network shows. The lights dimmed except for a spotlight on her. "My name is Vanessa Vaughn, and on behalf of KPIX and its staff, I would like to welcome you to our 1984–85 CBS Network Premiere. NBC had Bill Cosby at KRON's fall party at the Opera Center. As you can see, CBS spared no expense for our fall party, which is why I'm introducing the tape."

The drunken audience roared with laughter and gave her a thunderous round of applause. She paused until they calmed down. "NBC has the number-one show with Mr. Cosby, but we have better salespeople! Without a doubt, everyone in this room will be buying more spots from us than from our competition." The inebriated clients clapped loudly. "Now, one more thing before we roll the tape: will you please throw some spots in our newscast? I love San Francisco, and I'd really like to stay on the air here. I need your support to do that." Catcalls and whistles resounded throughout the hall enthusiastically as she quickly left the podium.

The CBS premiere started with clips from Dallas, Falcon Crest, 60 minutes and Murder She Wrote.

"You were great!" The sales manager beamed. "We had no stars, and you had the old bags at Menopause Marketing eating out of your hands."

The lights came up after the film. "So, pretty lady, what do you think of CBS's fall schedule?" The tall, ivory-haired man's piercing crystal-blue eyes were fixed firmly on her.

"We're hoping for the best."

"My name is Tod Von Westerkamp. I've been a fan since your cable car story. My grandfather knew Patrick Calhoun."

"Really?" Her interest was immediately piqued.

"Yes, apparently he had business dealings with him."

"I'd love to talk to your grandfather. That's amazing!"

"He's dead."

She turned scarlet red. "I'm so sorry."

"Don't be. He's been dead a long time."

"Are you a client of the station?"

"Yes, my family owns the *San Francisco Chronicle.*"

"Oh, so you're the son of the Von Westerkamp family." Immediately, she realized how ridiculous that sounded, but it was a party atmosphere, and she wasn't thinking like a reporter. Tod Von Westerkamp was the only heir to one of California's biggest fortunes. His family either controlled or sat on the board of most of San Francisco's international companies and were the most powerful and wealthiest of San Francisco's elite. Their only child was a sought-after eligible bachelor with a reputation for being a womanizer.

"What do you say? Let's get out of here." His penetrating sapphire eyes fixed on her.

"I can't leave. I'm the fill-in for Mike Wallace, *60 Minutes*; he canceled last night."

"Your job is done here, Miss Vaughn. Let's go out to the Cliff House and have a drink."

"I'm kind of boring. I don't drink alcohol."

"In that case, let's go out to the Cliff House and have dessert."

"I couldn't possibly eat anything else," she answered, not wanting to go. He was extremely handsome, but she felt absolutely no attraction for men who had pale White skin. Tod Von Westerkamp got his way with women so he persisted until she agreed to go. As the room emptied out, the sales manager complimented her on a job well done and bid her good night.

* * *

Reluctantly, she entered his Bentley but had no idea why she agreed to get in a car with a perfect stranger for whom she felt no attraction. But the night was young, and she relished the idea of heading to her beloved ocean.

The Cliff House had unforgettable views from high above the sea. Established in 1850, it was where San Franciscans said San Francisco began. Tod escorted her into the cozy, dimly lit room as the roaring fireplace sent a glow onto the glass windows that exposed the Pacific Ocean. Contented, she sank into the soft cushions of the overstuffed sofa in front of the crackling flame as Tod ordered two Irish coffees, one sans liquor. She sat quietly, savoring the warmth of the popping fire.

After last call, they descended the old stone steps to the rocky beach below. Once on the shoreline, she took off her heels, and Tod wrapped his tuxedo jacket around her. Holding hands, they strolled in the bright moonlight past the breaking waves as the cold sand beneath her feet squashed in between her toes. The colliding water created whitecaps lit by the awesome night. They explored Seal Rocks at Point Lobos, which opened the Golden Gate to the Pacific Ocean. Huge boulders positioned below the cliffs withstood the constant bombardment of crashing waves. At low tide, California seals sunned themselves on them, thus the name Seal Rocks. They watched seals dive for fish and were thrilled when one seal surfaced from the dark, wine-colored sea holding a catch in its mouth. When it was too cold for them to withstand the chilly evening air any longer, they quickly walked back to Tod's Bentley. Once inside, he turned the heat on high, and the opulent car made her feel very snug and cozy.

"I live in Seacliff. Let's stop by, and wash your feet off."

"Oh, Tod, I can't. What time is it anyway?"

"It's three thirty. Are you hungry? Would you like breakfast?"

"Oh no! I really should be getting home."

"Can I talk you into a nightcap at my place?"

"I'm sorry, but I've got work tomorrow. I should get some sleep." She declined the invitation graciously but did want to see Seacliff, one of the most exclusive neighborhoods, where mansion estates overlooked the entrance to the San Francisco Bay with stunning views of the Golden Gate Bridge. Old-line, wealthy San Francisco families lived there.

"Your amazing hair is as silky now as it was on the podium. Salty air didn't faze it."

She giggled. "You are too kind. I'm sure it's a wreck."

"May I call you?"

"That would be nice," she answered softly.

"I'm headed for Europe, so I'll get in touch upon my return. I'm golfing in Scotland and touring different courses. Do you play?"

"I'm afraid not," she replied as she cranked her car and drove away. She didn't care if she ever saw him again. He was too blond and much too pale for her taste. "Got to keep those clients happy," she could hear Trisha saying, as she waved goodbye.

CHAPTER FOURTEEN

With Vanessa as coanchor at six and eleven, *Eyewitness News* easily won the 1985 October and November sweeps and handily defeated the competition. The CBS Evening News with Dan Rather delivered the number one rated network newscast. Vanessa became the darling of sales since she gladly tagged along to meet their clients. Trisha advised her that the ultimate job security is to have sales on your side, and she gratefully heeded her friend's advice.

In her personal life, Tod relentlessly pursued her, and the more she turned down his advances, the more determined he became. Women did not refuse him, including the married ones. He even called from Europe to say he looked forward to seeing her upon his return.

After she discussed Tod with Trisha, her Alabama love consultant thought that she should remain the only blonde in her life, and she planned to follow her advice. Even though she never dated, she was only attracted to Black men and always resurrected Barry in her mind as being the perfect man.

* * *

But it was no coincidence when she was asked to emcee the San Francisco Ballet's fundraiser. The Von Westerkamp family had given $4 million to help build the new Opera Center, and she knew Tod was behind the solicitation letter.

"What do you think about this ceremony?" she asked Mr Fellows.

"It would be bad form to turn down this particular charity event. San Francisco's true money people support it, so there is nothing to be gained from alienating them. Besides, it can't hurt to be visible inside this elite community." Following his advice, she typed an acceptance letter to the non-profit group.

* * *

That night, she called Trisha and woke her up. "This guy is going to incredible lengths just to get me to go out with him," she excitedly blurted out to her groggy friend. "Normally, you turn down a man twice, he gives up. He is a different two-legged animal. What should I do?"

"You haven't been out on a date in thirteen years." She yawned. "How bad could it be to go out with one of the richest bachelors in California?"

"He's so lily White. You just wouldn't believe it."

"It's your call. I gave up on you and men years ago."

"Come on! Tell me whether I should go out with him or not."

"I already told you. Cross blondes off your list."

"Tell me what you really think. Should I go out with him?"

"Only you can answer that. Barry is very married with a kid and a wife. He's as married as you can get, and you're running around like a nun without a habit. Stop punishing yourself for that abortion. It could have happened to anyone. I was lucky, and you weren't. Simple as that!"

"So, you're saying that I should go out with him?"

"I didn't say that. Ask the million-dollar question, what if he found out you're Black?"

"No clue, but I'd assume he would flip out. His family has serious wealth. Not like Charleston where the old-line families only have their lineage and no money. Great-great-grandfathers signed the Declaration of Independence, and the Civil War left them as poor as church mice. It's different out here. They are affluent even on a national level!"

"Let me go out with him? He seems like my kind of guy—tall, handsome, and has major bucks. My three requirements for a husband. I would even skip the first two if he has the latter."

"You are absolutely no help at all."

"I know exactly what you want me to say, and I won't do it. The bottom line is that if you get involved with a White man, you have to tell him you're Black. If you don't, the repercussions could be horrendous. It doesn't matter if you marry a Black guy, and he thinks you're White. But doing the reverse could be catastrophic." She yawned again. "It's a miracle orchestrated by Sister Roe that you haven't gotten caught. Looking from the Pearly Gates, she's protecting you."

"You wrote to the hall of records and obtained that dead baby's birth certificate."

"Never in a million years did I think you would really use it. But admit it: Vanessa Vaughn is a fabulous on-air name."

"Should I go out with him or not?"

"If you are celibate for another thirteen years, you might as well join a convent. I'm sure Sister Roe's order, the Daughters of Mercy, would take you."

"Very funny!"

"This might come as a big shock to you, but women and men date people that they have absolutely no intention of marrying. Besides, this guy is a big-time confirmed bachelor. Once he gets laid, he'll be long gone. All men want to marry you until they come. Once they come, you're a whore."

"I love your distorted view of dating in the USA."

"Go out with him, and spend the entire evening talking about your terrific friend marooned in Alabama trying to get into broadcast management. I'd spend his money!"

"That's why I love you. You're so practical."

"Quit torturing the poor soul, and go out with him."

"I have been playing White so long that I'm actually starting to believe it myself."

"Remember the Baltimore Catechism? Adam and Eve were White. You might be too!"

"Get back to sleep. That brain of yours needs a rest."

"Just call me in time so I can buy a new dress for the wedding. Night. Night."

* * *

Vanessa graciously donated her time as emcee and wooed the crowd of old, wealthy codgers. She became the toast of their town. Everyone fawned all over her, except Tod Von Westerkamp, who had an unexpected, breathtakingly beautiful date. She felt sad but decided to enjoy this gala event despite Tod's latest conquest. At the end of the evening, Vanessa thanked the chairman and his staff and headed to the elevator.

"I thought you left," she blurted out as he stepped out in front of her as the doors opened.

"You didn't have a date, so I decided to get rid of mine."

"Please tell me you didn't do that."

"I didn't do that," he replied sarcastically. "Now, where shall we go to reward you for being such a charming mistress of ceremonies?"

"You are too much! Where could we possibly go dressed like this?"

"To the beach, of course! You told me that you love the ocean, so it's off to the Pacific!"

* * *

As the valet opened the door to the Bentley, Vanessa felt happy and excited that Tod had returned for her. But momentarily she felt remorse for the jilted woman as they drove to China Beach. Her pity faded completely when the Golden Gate protruded out in the distance with its lights glimmering against the water. He wrapped his tuxedo jacket around her while they walked along holding hands. *He remembered how much I love the ocean*, she fondly thought to herself as the sand crunched beneath her feet. They watched the waves crash against the shore until Vanessa became too cold, and they returned to the car.

"My Seacliff house is just a few blocks away. Would you like to see it?" he asked.

She softly nodded in agreement. Her curiosity turned into complete astonishment when Tod pressed a button in his Bentley and a towering iron gate opened. A high brick wall encircled the compound, offering formidable seclusion. As he maneuvered by the exclusive entrance, her childhood feelings flooded through her body and brought back vivid memories of her first visit to Barry's home. The rose-colored glasses of the young orphan still existed.

* * *

Her heart pounded rapidly as he proceeded along the extensive circular driveway and pushed a button that opened the enormous door, exposing a fleet of cars inside. He turned off the engine and went around to open her car door. "Welcome to my bachelor pad," he uttered as he took her hand.

Silently, they walked inside a kitchen that was twice as big as her studio. She meant to get a bigger place but never had time to look. Her first thought was that Tod should never see where she lived. They entered an immense room, where solid glass floor-to-ceiling windows revealed an amazing array of lights, which illuminated the Golden Gate Bridge.

"I feel like Sir Francis Drake is about to sail by," Vanessa commented.

"If he does, we need to get rid of that bridge." Tod laughed. "I'm sure he would say that we ruined one of the most beautiful straits in the world. What would you like to drink?"

"If it's not too much trouble, I'd love some hot tea. I can help you boil the water."

"I'm not the greatest cook in the world, but even I can boil water."

"Are you sure? Let me help you."

"Sit down, relax, enjoy the view. Pretend it's 1579, and Drake finds this channel."

"If you insist. I'm great at pretending that I'm in another century." She sat down.

"You like history?"

"Actually, only American history."

"Really? It's such a short period of time."

"I know, but it's a very bloody, fascinating one."

"I guess we have given the world cowboy and Indian movies, probably our greatest international export. Let me get your tea." He disappeared into the kitchen.

The spectacular scenery mesmerized her, but she forced herself to look at the room's plush furnishings. Quickly captivated by the exquisite artwork, she studied the bookshelves, complete with a built-in ladder that slid the entire length of the room.

He reappeared carrying a tray. "I zapped it in the microwave. Is that OK?"

"Don't be silly. Hot water is hot water." He set the tray down with a uniquely wrapped gift box. "I bought it in Scotland, but since you have steadfastly refused to go out with me, I was never able to give it to you."

"I was sitting here feeling guilty about you making me tea. Now, I really feel guilty."

"You should only feel guilty about not going out with me," he joked and sat down next to her. "Open it up. I want to know if you like it."

She unwrapped the box and lifted out a gorgeous, hand-woven woolen hood cape with a beautiful mix of dark blues and purples that had been tightly woven together. "I love it." Her fingers ran across it. "It's so wonderfully warm. It's magnificent."

"You like to walk on the beach so this should be perfect for our cold, foggy summers."

At that moment, she realized she had never gotten a present from a man during her thirty-four years on planet Earth. *Pitiful!* she thought.

"There is one caveat," he interrupted her thoughts.

"What's that?"

"You can only wear this wrap when you walk with me."

"How about when I walk by myself?"

"Only when you're alone, that's the deal!" He leaned over to kiss her, but she promptly grabbed the tea to take a sip. He rubbed her back, and his hand slid down to her bra strap.

"I work tomorrow. It's late. I think I should go."

"Why don't you spend the night?" She met his question with total silence. Sensing her displeasure, he suggested, "You can have your own bedroom. There are ten. Take your pick."

"I can call a cab. You don't have to drive me."

"Don't be ridiculous. I will take you home."

"That's too much trouble. I can take a cab," Vanessa responded coldly.

"Look, you've made it quite clear that we will not be spending the night together. You don't have to rub my face in it." Getting up, Tod held his hand out to help her off the couch.

* * *

The ride back to Nob Hill seemed very long. When they arrived, he went around to open the car door. Always the perfect gentleman, he politely extended his hand.

"I put all potential relationships on hold for my career. Don't take it personally."

"There is no other way to take it, Vanessa."

"You snap your fingers, and any woman in this town will go out with you. Correct?"

"I've been snapping my fingers since August and getting nowhere with you."

"The wrap from Scotland was a nice touch."

"Yes, the wrap and I have been waiting for you, but you never came."

"Good night." She put the key in her door. "I had a wonderful time. The gift is lovely."

"Next time we go for a walk on the beach, I won't have to give you my jacket. Right?"

"Absolutely!" She started up the staircase and didn't dare to look back.

Once inside, she examined the vivid colors of the wrap and ran her fingers over the exquisite wool. She decided against calling Trisha. "She's right. Put him out of my mind. I can't get involved with a White man without him knowing the truth about my race." At that moment, Vanessa resolved never to see Tod again.

* * *

During the May sweeps, she worked diligently seven days a week. Not to be deterred, Tod believed that once the rating period was over, she would see him again. He called the station daily to find out the overnight ratings and feigned interest in them. Growing accustomed to his calls, she felt disappointed on the few days he didn't phone.

After the ratings ended, Eyewitness News won in the overnights. With Vanessa at the helm for an entire year, the news was in first place. The news department celebrated after the eleven o'clock newscast. Even Mr. Fellows, who never fraternized with his employees, agreed to come. The staff met at Perry's on trendy Union Street, a legendary singles pickup bar.

She absolutely beamed when Mr. Fellows walked in since he rarely showed up at these affairs. Her smile quickly faded when Tod Von Westerkamp, accompanied by a striking blonde, followed him in. Nervously, she knocked over her Virgin Mary, which spilled on her. Tomato juice soaked through her pale-green dress and covered it in stains. The bartender rushed over with a towel, but the extremely embarrassed Vanessa wiped herself off and declined his help.

Tod approached. "It's a good thing you didn't come here before tonight's broadcast. The audience would stare at your dress and not at you." He winked as he held the woman's arm tightly. "Vanessa, this is Melissa."

Vanessa felt her own heart beating rapidly. "How do you do?" she muttered.

The golden-haired beauty babbled on, which gave her time to recuperate from emotions she thought were long dead inside. Her face blushed a ruby red with her own jealousy and astonishing sensations that had not surfaced since she caught Barry with another woman. Like Barry, Tod wasn't exactly sitting home pining away for her. She had to confront the fact that he wasn't going to chase her forever. At this moment, she felt a lingering, almost nostalgic desire for him, but her own feelings bewildered her. She was never physically attracted to Tod before this encounter when he pranced in unannounced with a gorgeous woman.

Melissa excused herself and went to the bathroom. "Should I get rid of my date?"

"Tod, you're incorrigible."

"No, you are. I've never seen you wearing my Scottish gift. Here you are partying, and I'd like to be part of that celebration."

"When it comes to women, you are irredeemable."

"So, what do you say? Melissa's not going to stay in the lady's room forever."

"If I were your date, would you dump me and take me home to be with another woman?"

"We're approaching our anniversary." He completely ignored her question.

"How's that, Tod?"

"It's been one year since you started your litany of excuses as to why you can't go out with me. That's probably the only anniversary we'll ever have!"

"Here she comes. She got out of a restroom fast. She must be psychic!" She grinned.

"What's your answer?"

"Our department never celebrates. I'm here for the duration on this one."

"Rain check." He put his arm around her, and his galling behavior shocked Vanessa.

When he left, she felt more comfortable and started to enjoy herself. Her coworkers consumed large amounts of alcohol and got totally smashed. Sober, she laughed along with them. She adored the news staff and felt like they were the only family she had, even though they didn't know how she felt. The bartender announced last call, so everyone ordered another round and stayed until the bar closed. She motioned to the bartender to call her a cab.

* * *

Waiting outside, she watched the late-night crowd on Union Street roam by. Unexpectedly, Tod drove up and rolled down the electric window. "My date suddenly felt very ill, so I took her home." His eyes twinkled. "How about a ride to the marina, and if you're up to it, we could try to make it all the way to Fort Point."

"Oh, Tod, I can tell you one thing. I'd never want to be married to you!"

"You said I was the best catch in San Francisco. Are you are reneging on that statement?"

"Quite frankly, I'm starting to weaken," she replied as he opened the car door for her.

At the Marina, he parked at his club, the Saint Francis Yacht Club. It offered a spectacular view of Alcatraz as boat lights glistened in the distance. They held hands as the clear night enchanted Vanessa, and she decided to listen to her heart, instead of her mind. She would date Tod Von Westerkamp, and she hoped he wouldn't take her home to be with another woman.

CHAPTER FIFTEEN

After twelve years of working killer hours, Vanessa no longer went in on weekends. Instead, she spent them with Tod at his Seacliff estate. Her uncharacteristic absence was automatically noticed by her fellow news colleagues, and word spread rapidly around the station that she was seeing Tod Von Westerkamp. His legendary female exploits were well known, and her coworkers knew the odds were against her not getting hurt.

She took her time getting to know Tod and steadfastly refused to sleep with him. An inordinate fear of pregnancy was the reason she never dated. Fourteen years had passed since she last saw Barry, but if she closed her eyes, his smell and taste came flooding back with memories of him. For her relationship with Tod to work out, she had to forget about Barry.

One year after they met, Vanessa succumbed to Tod's advances. He was very quizzical about her sexual past when she confided in him that she only had sex once at twenty. Incredulous, he laughed, but her anger flared, and he agreed never to bring it up again. His sources at the station said she never dated, which flabbergasted him, but he loved the idea of Vanessa being an "almost virgin." He assured her their relationship would give her complete ecstasy, her own private Eden. She soon discovered that Tod Von Westerkamp did indeed know how to make love to his women. A gentle lover, his patience for her lack of experience helped teach her the art of lovemaking, and she was very committed to pleasing him. Nirvana came at the end of their sessions when she felt that she had satisfied him. Methodically, he caused her to fall in love with him, and his affection became a drug, one she could no longer live without. Only two people, Sister Roe and Barry, had ever touched her. Now, she craved his caresses daily.

* * *

On Valentine's Day 1987, Tod invited his parents to join them for dinner at Ernie's, one of the city's most expensive and famous restaurants. Understandably nervous, she wanted their approval so she opted to wear a conservative black silk suit with her hair up. A chauffeur-driven Rolls Royce pulled up on Montgomery Street, and a uniformed driver opened the rear door. She instantly recognized Mr. and Mrs. Alexander Von Westerkamp from the newspaper society page. His mother wore a floor-length, solid-white fur, and his parents went inside immediately, not waiting for them. As they entered the ritzy establishment, their eyes had to adjust to the lighting as Ernie's interior was quite dark in the old San Francisco tradition. The maître d' greeted Tod by name and ushered them to their regular private corner table. Vanessa was always amazed at the treatment the Von Westerkamp name generated.

"Mother, this is Vanessa Vaughn," Tod said flatly.

"I'm so happy to meet you, Mrs. Von Westerkamp," she said warmly and extended her hand. His mother nodded but did not speak, so she turned her attention to Alexander as he rose and shook her hand. "I'm very glad to meet you," she gushed, but he also did not speak, and she was completely taken aback by their rudeness.

"Now that the pleasantries are over, let's drink," Tod cracked as he pulled the chair out.

Alexander snapped his fingers, and two waiters in white tuxedos immediately appeared. "What are you having, son? Vanessa? Scotch on the rocks," he barked.

"Iced tea, please."

"Vanessa doesn't drink," Tod announced.

"How charming!" Suzanne responded coldly.

Vanessa was so shaken and thought, *I'm on the air live in a major television market with over five million people, and these two are rattling me.* Plus, Tod seemed completely oblivious to their ill-mannered behavior. As they talked about golf, she and his mother were excluded from the conversation. The waiter came with hot water, an assortment of tea bags, and a glass of ice.

"Mrs. Von Westerkamp, where did you grow up?" Vanessa asked after.

"I'm a fifth-generation San Franciscan," she proclaimed curtly.

"How fascinating! You must have wonderful stories about the city."

"I can't think of one," Suzanne answered flippantly.

Ignoring the sarcasm, Vanessa tried to build rapport. "I fell in love with this city the minute I laid eyes on it. It's the most beautiful one in the United States."

"Is that so? Exactly how many cities in this nation have you visited?"

She blushed an embarrassing bright red since she had only been to Los Angeles and Sacramento. "You're right. I haven't traveled extensively enough to judge its beauty."

She sipped her iced tea, the worst she had ever had, and endured an eternity of frigid silence. Tod raised his glass of scotch. "A toast to the first meeting of the Vaughn family."

"What in the hell does that mean, son?" Alexander inquired with a scowl on his face.

"Simple, Dad. Vanessa was raised in an orphanage, so she represents her entire family, and we embody ours." Reluctantly, Alexander lifted his scotch to clink glasses, and Suzanne banged into his scotch, causing it to spill. "Good move, Mother! You've managed to soak the white linen tablecloth with my scotch and not with your red wine. Excellent move."

She sipped her merlot and ignored her son's verbal jab. The minutes passed slowly, and the excruciating dinner turned into a complete nightmare as Tod seemed unfazed by their atrocious conduct. An hour went by, and no food was ordered as his parents consumed more cocktails, which didn't mellow them. Excusing herself, she escaped into the powder room, slid into a chair, slipped her shoes off to relax, and gave the Hispanic bathroom attendant a tip.

* * *

Meanwhile, back at the table, Tod spoke loudly. "I have an announcement to make."

"What's that, dear?" His drunken mother sluggishly slurred her words.

"I'm going to ask Vanessa to marry me."

"What? That showgirl!" Suzanne exclaimed as her hand gesture knocked her wine over. The waiter quickly descended to clean it up and pour more out of the bottle into a new glass.

"She is hardly on the strip in Las Vegas! She is an anchor of the top-rated newscast and received the California Woman Broadcaster of the Year Award. It's very prestigious."

"She's a starlet, son. I don't care if she is on *60 Minutes*!"

"Quite frankly, son, I am speechless. You have never hinted about marrying anyone, much less this one." Alexander gulped down his scotch.

"Well, I've decided to start a family. I did hit the big four-oh last year. It's time."

"Frankly, son, I don't like this orphan story business. Scum of the earth come out of those institutions."

"Your father is right." Suzanne slurred her words. "You don't know what her lineage is. For all you know, she's descended from a long line of prostitutes."

"You two are unbelievable. She isn't good enough? I don't get it!"

"We're concerned. You've had a lot of gold diggers in your past who were after our fortune, and she could be too." His father slid an ice cube into his mouth.

"It took me over a year to get her to go out with me. Except for the international models, she's the highest-paid woman I've dated. Ironically, she is totally disinterested in money. It means nothing to her. You should see where she lives. The almighty dollar means zero to her."

"Or so she would have you believe," his mother maliciously added.

"The way I see it, you can continue your appalling treatment or welcome her into your family. I never cared about the insensitivity all the women I've dated received from you both, but this one is different. I intend to marry her, and out of respect, I told you first. I expect a change starting right now. Tonight! Understand?"

"In my defense, your cast of a thousand bimbos has been hard to take over the years."

"Mother, Vanessa is an outstanding news talent and happens to be very bright as well. She is not in the same league, and you know it. So stop it."

"What happened to her? Did she fall in?" his sloshed mother asked.

"She's probably recuperating from round one of the verbal abuses you two inflicted."

"Alexander, I think your son wants us to bring on the charm."

"As endearing as we are when we have lunch with the mayor?" he joked.

"Yes, Father, pretend she's one of your politicians."

"So, when is this blessed event taking place?" Alexander inquired sarcastically.

"There's always the possibility that she might turn me down."

"I doubt that," Suzanne interjected. "Not my son!"

* * *

"Not your son? Are you disowning him?" Vanessa inquired as she approached the table.

"Welcome back." Tod jumped up to help with her chair.

The waiters appeared with the appetizers. "Here we have the tartar de salmon, a mixture of fresh ground salmon, roasted bell peppers, red onions, capers, and lemon, served with toast points," he announced with great flare. "Brie in chimise, a phyllo-wrapped baked brie cheese with grilled squash in a roasted bell pepper sauce." Another server put the second dish down neatly. "Our traditional Burgundy escargot served in shell with garlic butter. Poireaux vinaigrette, cold, fresh leeks in vinaigrette sauce. May I get anyone another beverage?"

Alexander ordered a two-hundred-dollar bottle of Cabernet Sauvignon as she stared at the dishes and quickly realized there was nothing she wanted to try. She felt tremendous sorrow at the incredible amount of wasted money.

Sister Roe could have fed the orphanage for a year! The evening dragged on as his parents drank more and became somewhat tolerable. She no longer desperately wanted them to like her because she knew they never would. History was repeating itself. She wasn't good enough for Barry and certainly not for this rich couple.

In the limousine, Tod asked, "Understand why I'm unmarried at forty?"

"Is tonight's conduct pretty typical?"

"They have been horses' asses to every woman I have ever introduced them to."

"They didn't make any exceptions for me so at least they're consistent. Clearly, this is about money, and I resent their attitude," she blurted out bluntly. "I don't need their wealth."

* * *

After that ghastly dinner, Tod told Vanessa to pack for a warm weather mini-vacation. The destination was to be a surprise, but her first clue came as they boarded a private plane and landed in San Diego. A red Ferrari convertible was waiting, and they headed north. The sun blazed down, and hot air relentlessly whipped her hair against her face. They passed the breathtaking mountains and entered La Costa Spa and Resort.

"Isn't this an exclusively expensive, hedonistic fat farm? Trying to tell me something?"

"Here's the plan. You spend the morning in the spa getting facials, massages, manicures, whatever you want, and I spend it playing golf. We will meet for lunch, relax on the beach, take a nap in the afternoon, and dine in La Jolla during the evenings. How does that sound?"

"Perfect!"

"Try every spa treatment they offer." Tod laughed.

"You are a man after my own heart."

Their spectacular suite overlooked the remarkably groomed golf course. The living room featured polished marble with a white couch and overstuffed chairs that sat atop a thick, plush carpet. Even the bedroom was larger than

Vanessa's studio. The couple took long, romantic strolls on the beach, and Tod played eighteen holes while she worked her way through the spa.

Instead of venturing into La Jolla their last night, they walked over to the resort's main restaurant. They were seated outdoors, and the clear April night was warm as she glanced around at the beautifully landscaped grounds. Two iced teas arrived since Tod never consumed alcohol when they were alone. He had never had iced tea before, but now he considered himself a connoisseur.

The maître d' appeared, holding a small silver tray with a rounded top, and placed it in front of Vanessa.

"We haven't ordered yet. You must have the wrong table," she said innocently.

"I assure you, madame. I have the right table," he responded. "Madame, may I?"

She slightly nodded as he lifted the silver top, revealing a Tiffany's box.

"Gee, I thought I was getting the crab cakes!"

The maître d' replied, "I'm sure this is far superior to our crab cakes."

She opened the golden box. Inside was a five-caret marquise-shaped diamond. Not in a setting, the stone stood alone in the velvet lining. Gingerly, she picked it up and burst into tears.

"I hate it when you cry. Do you at least like it?" He worried.

"It's like a stone from mythology; it's mythical. Unbelievable!"

"Shall we put it in a setting and get engaged?"

"I think we shall." She leaned over and kissed him. "I think we shall!"

"I know women want to pick out their wedding rings, so I selected the diamond, and you can choose the setting. I love marquises, and I had it appraised independently to ensure quality. Besides, if anyone knows diamonds, it's the son of Suzanne Von Westerkamp."

"I have no doubt about that." She rotated the stone with her fingers.

"So, do you like it?"

"Like is the wrong word. I'm so overwhelmed. You never cease to amaze me. Never!"

"That's good. I like to keep my women guessing."

"Honey, I think it's traditional for you to give up all your women now!"

"If you insist!"

"I insist."

"I think I can live with that." Tod grinned.

"You'd better. Monogamy is especially important to me. Particularly crucial."

"Why?"

"The only man I had ever been with, his main squeeze showed up at his mom's funeral."

"You've never told me about that."

"I can finally talk about it without lunging into a full-blown depression."

"Why are you still upset all these years later?"

"It was total and complete betrayal, one you never forgive or forget. Never be disloyal."

"I've waited a long time, so I'll take my vows seriously. How old were you?"

"Twenty."

"Fifteen years is a long time to hold onto anger inside. Forget it! It's history."

"If you don't remember history, you are doomed to repeat it. Like the Nazi regime."

"Let's not throw my German ancestry into this," Tod answered in jest. "I will be as true blue as can be. Now enough of this, let's not ruin an evening I've been planning for months." After dinner, they took a moonlit stroll and made love all night long.

* * *

Vanessa worked endless hours during the May 1987 sweeps to maintain the news' number-one position in the ratings. Tod became extremely upset because she was completely exhausted and only wanted to sleep. They never saw each other, so she encouraged her fiancé to join his parents in Europe until the rating period ended. So Tod went to France and played golf every day with his father while his mother shopped. Suzanne Von Westerkamp was totally opposed to her son's engagement, so on his first night in Paris, she arranged a dinner party with his old girlfriend. At the restaurant, his mother had never acted so charming before, speaking to Antoinette in fluent French, which she had never done. Before, she used English to make Antoinette feel uncomfortable and told Tod she didn't want to waste her French. Now, his mother rattled away like Antoinette was her long-lost friend, and he found her performance to be absolutely nauseating. Educated at the French American school, he spent every summer on the French Riviera with his mother. Now, he listened to her flawless French accent against Antoinette's, a native of Paris, as the model explained how her career had really taken off. Her face currently graced fifteen different European magazine covers, and she had filmed Nestle television commercials in London. He couldn't think of two women who could talk more about themselves than this duo. Unlike them, Vanessa was always more interested in the people around her.

Antoinette squeezed his thighs underneath the table as he watched the candlelight glow on her stunning features. As she rubbed his thighs more aggressively, she occasionally touched his crotch and lingered on his zipper. After giving his penis a gentle caress, she returned her fingers to his thighs. He could cross his legs and end her little game, except he found himself enjoying this flirtation because it had been a while since he had been with another woman. He remembered Vanessa's sweet, naive speech on monogamy, which was a foreign concept to him. He had a lifetime of examples from his father, who had more women than most single men.

"Did Mother tell you that I've gotten engaged?" he asked boldly in fluent French. She quickly withdrew her hand from his leg, and her face reddened. "Yes, last week in fact."

"Oh, don't worry. This is just a passing fantasy. It will be over by the time we get back."

"Or maybe he won't go back," his father agreed in barely audible French.

"As you can see, I'm not getting much support on my entrance into the sacred vows."

She looked with a stony stare, and the evening turned into a dreadfully dull one. Suzanne turned off the charm, his parents got smashed, and Antoinette caught a taxi.

* * *

At breakfast, his mother rehashed last night's entire scenario and berated his marriage announcement in front of Antoinette. Tod jested. "So no engagement party for us, Mother!"

"It's hardly at the top of my list," Suzanne answered snidely.

"Son, are you really going to marry that woman?" He glanced up, looking perplexed from his newspaper. "If you are hell-bent on marrying her, let's check her out," Alexander ordered. "If we find her parents living in a Southern trailer park, you won't be in such a rush to the altar. After the nuptials, they will come rushing forward to cash in, like a new gold rush!"

"Antoinette is from a wealthy, old-line French family. You hated her too. Mother, your maneuvering last night was despicable."

"Son, your father is right. Hire a private investigator, and do a little prior discovery."

"You're both too late," Tod replied. "Her parents were investigated. I hired a private detective who flew into Charleston and went through the county records."

"Don't leave us in suspense," Suzanne gushed.

"Doris Vaughn died from breast cancer in 1954 at Roper Hospital in Charleston, South Carolina. Lowell Vaughn was in the Marine Corps and died in Korea in 1953. Why their only child was put up for adoption is uncertain. The private investigator told me that Catholic Charities' records are sealed up tighter than a drum. He couldn't bribe the nuns or the priests. They were unapproachable, so he never found out why she was put up for adoption. At the highest levels, he confirmed that Vanessa doesn't know who her parents were. I know more about her background than she does."

"You are your father's son." Suzanne took a bite from her croissant.

"Good work, son. I'm overly impressed. What rank was he?"

"Sorry, pops. He was enlisted and died at a Yalu River engagement."

"How dreadful," Suzanne interjected.

"Yes, a waste of American blood."

"I wasn't talking about him. I was merely observing his rank. We've never had enlisted men in our family."

"Families with Third Reich generals don't brag about it unless they live in Hamburg."

"Tod, I won't tolerate that kind of talk from you," Alexander reprimanded his son.

"Well, give him a break. He bred a beautiful and talented daughter," Tod retorted. "The consequences would be catastrophic if Vanessa knew. This shall remain our little family secret."

"When did you do this, honey?" Suzanne asked gleefully.

"After the Valentine's dinner. I wanted you two to get off my back about her."

"Personally, son, I am relieved. If you are really going to go through with this, it's best that the skeletons come out of the closet before the children arrive and complicate things."

"I figured that out on my own." Tod sipped his juice.

"Suzanne, it looks like you've got a wedding to plan. Since she's a legitimate orphan, it looks like we will be picking up the tab for the blessed event."

"I must say that when you passed on Antoinette last night, I knew you must be in lust."

"Mother, I was not going to torture Antoinette any more than I have in the past. I did not want her getting her hopes up, and then six months later, she finds out that I'm married."

Ignoring him, Suzanne declared, "I think we should cut our trip short so that I can start planning the wedding. It must be the West Coast gala event of the year."

"Only the West, Suzanne? That doesn't sound like you, limiting yourself to one coast."

"Quite right, dear. I'll make my New York and international friends insanely jealous."

"Mother, is Vanessa going to have any say concerning her own wedding?"

"She can pick out her dress, if she goes to my designer," Suzanne said snobbishly.

"Let's hit the links! The day is wasting away."

"I'll be right there, son," Alexander replied as he threw francs on the table.

"Mother, I do not want you to treat Vanessa like the help."

"What on earth do you mean by that, son?"

"Try to be decent and treat her like the daughter you never had."

CHAPTER SIXTEEN

On a nonstop flight from Paris, Tod decided he didn't want to prolong the entire process with a long engagement and decided to set a date soon. His society-page mother was the only caveat. He missed Vanessa, and his strong feelings made him confront the fact that he must really be in love when she greeted him at the airport.

KPIX-TV continued to reign number one in the news race after the May sweeps ended. Vanessa informed her husband-to-be that she absolutely would not quit her job. She saw no reason to give up her broadcasting career that she had fought so hard for and had worked a lifetime to achieve, just to follow him from golf course to golf course. Tod could not change her mind, even though he knew that his parents would be opposed to his wife continuing to anchor the news after they were married. Von Westerkamp women simply did not work and were steadfast in their charity functions and social events.

Suzanne Von Westerkamp was quite adamant that she could not organize a proper society wedding in less than four months. As he had done his entire life, Tod relented and let his mother set the wedding date. October offered San Francisco's best weather, and she chose the spectacular Mark Hopkins for its view, as well as its location atop Nob Hill. Only a Westerkamp could get the "Top of the Mark" closed on a Saturday night for a private wedding reception. Her iron control enforced every little detail. Vanessa thought it was ludicrous when Suzanne insisted on eight bridesmaids she had never met. But she didn't budge on Trisha as the maiden of honor.

Suzanne demanded that the wedding take place at Saint Mark's, the oldest Lutheran church in the West. As a parishioner at Saint Mary's, the old cathedral on California Street, Vanessa knew all the Paulist fathers and helped them raise money. She was adamant that she was going to be married by a priest, but Von Westerkamps simply did not get married in the Catholic Church. When the two women reached an impasse, Tod and his father were designated to reason with the bride.

* * *

During lunch at the Waterfront Restaurant on the Embarcadero, the two men urged her to reconsider. She listened quietly as they presented their arguments.

"I was raised by a Roman Catholic nun. Her spirit is up above, but her body is here on earth. She would roll over in her grave if I got married in a Lutheran church. She would take the news better if I went to an Elvis impersonator at a Las Vegas drive-through chapel."

"Elvis is starting to sound better all the time," Tod responded.

"I have given in on every minute detail. Your mother picked out the bridesmaids, their gowns, my wedding dress and veil. She stipulated every facet from the printed invitations to the engraved napkins. You never go to church, but this is important to me. If we are to be married, it will be in the Catholic Church or not at all. Gentlemen, this is final."

"Let's have our pastor from Saint Mark's help perform the ceremony."

"Mr. Von Westerkamp, I would love that. It's a wonderful idea," Vanessa agreed. "A Lutheran minister would be perfect, along with a Catholic priest."

"It should appease Mother," Tod interjected.

"At least," Alexander mumbled as he sipped his scotch.

"I need to get back to the station."

"Want a ride? It's supposed to rain."

"Don't be silly. I can walk back before the valet can bring your car around."

"All right, I'll see you later." Tod kissed her on the cheek, and she left quickly.

* * *

"Son, I don't think this one is a gold digger. She's spiritual, and her two stipulations were her friend and religion. She prevails over your mother, so I have to applaud her for that."

"Religion and friendship, two things that were never high on our list, especially mother's. Tell me the truth about you two," Tod asked.

"What exactly do you want to know?"

"The truth because I am about to enter into the blessed state of matrimony."

"Your mother was dazzlingly beautiful, charming, and very cunning. She was very seductive and made me feel like I was the only man on the planet. She insisted that we have a child immediately, and after your arrival, things were never the same."

"How so?"

"I can't believe that I am telling you about this buried past. It's completely inappropriate."

"Go on! I'm totally fascinated. I've always wanted to ask you about the obvious."

"Are you sure you can handle it?"

"I'm a big boy."

"After you were born, her merger into our fortune was complete. With access to money and position, I quickly became a mere inconvenience. We went our separate ways except for public appearances. It's forty-two years later, and I'm an old man."

"Why didn't you split up?"

"Better the devil you know!"

"So, living happily ever after is a farce? It doesn't really exist, does it?"

"Women are expendable, and personally, I'd rather be on the golf course. Son, there are always plenty of women to be had. It's impressive that you checked her out. I wish I had."

"No wonder I'm an only child!" Tod said as he got up and left the restaurant.

* * *

Trisha had blown all her vacation time but managed to con her boss out of two extra days and arrived Wednesday night. "I can't believe you're getting married. I'm depressed. No one is ever going to ask me. I'm thirty-five and headed to desperate."

"Don't be ridiculous. You just haven't met Mr. Right."

"I haven't even met Mr. Right Now. I'm headed for Old Maid-dom. My entire body is starting to fall a couple of feet."

"Stop it. You look great, and you know it."

"So, when do I get to meet the mother-in-law from hell?"

"You won't be subjected to her until the rehearsal dinner."

"It's on a yacht, which means we can't jump ship. Not a good sign."

"I have no say or any control over the unfolding events. I plan to sit back and enjoy."

"Sounds like a good plan. Any men there for me?"

"Who knows? I haven't even been privileged to see my own announcement list. She's invited five hundred people. For all I know, there could be only old men coming."

"Let me remind you that I was the one who was supposed to marry a rich man, not you You want to work. That nasty four-letter word. I'm doomed to sell reruns the rest of my life."

"I've got to tell him the truth."

"Two days before the wedding? I don't think so! Not a good plan."

"I feel like the tar baby who is stuck in the tar."

"The truth is that Sister Rosalie would never have lied to you. She didn't know who your parents were. The only thing that you haven't disclosed is the Black orphanage. You're on the air in a broadcast market with a population that's over five million, and no one thinks you're Black. Hello. You're on billboards and station promos during prime time, and no one, including the Westinghouse management back in New York, thinks you are Black. You've passed the toughest test of all, the Charleston bluebloods with skin so White their veins look blue. For all you know, the reality is you are White. People just naturally assume that you are White. Is it incumbent on you to run around and proclaim your alleged race? You have never misrepresented yourself. The truth is you may never know the truth. Enjoy your wedding day without the Catholic guilt we grew up with. Let happiness rule your life."

"You always make everything sound so simple."

"That's me, a true simpleton!"

"Are you really sure?"

"Let me get this through that thick skull of yours. There is nothing factual to tell him. Believe me, forty-eight hours before the wedding, it will go over like a lead balloon."

"You should have gone to law school. I love the way you phrase, 'Did I mention it'?"

"Hollywood actors change their names. You're on the air. You had the right!"

"That poor White baby!"

"That poor White baby is incredibly lucky. You have distinguished her name."

"Oh, what a web we do weave."

"When we practice to deceive," she finished the saying. "In the name of old Tecumseh himself, stop torturing yourself?"

"Any news about Barry?"

"You are not going to make it down the aisle because I am going to strangle you!"

"Does your mom have some new scoop? I don't care. I'm simply curious."

"Curious, my ass! You are in love with him and will be until the day you die. Sick! You are extremely sick!"

"So, what's the latest?" She ignored her friend's disdain.

"He's got a big promotion. The *Charleston News and Courier* article is my purse."

She opened the refrigerator as Vanessa read the article and reread it again. Studying every inch of his face, she thought he looked marvelous and had aged beautifully. She hadn't seen a current picture of him in a long time and studied it for clues about his happiness.

"Can't you keep beer around for your alcoholic friend? I'm going out to get some. I won't sit here while you drool. Pretty big article for the business page, don't you think? Even for Charleston's *News-less Courier* that's quite a write-up. Too bad there isn't a picture of his wife in there. I'm sure we both would like to see how she's aged. A pregnancy means no waistline." Vanessa still didn't look up. "Plus, she's working as a full-time pathologist. That can't be any picnic, having a full-time, super-stressful job and a kid."

* * *

Trisha returned later to see Vanessa still looking at the article as she took a swig of beer and put the rest in the refrigerator. "I hate to bring this up, but by any chance do you remember that in less than seventy-two hours from now, you will be winging your way down the aisle of a Catholic church in a very white wedding dress? Isn't it a tad tasteless to be slobbering over a married man's picture?"

"I am not slobbering nor drooling. I am simply interested in a friend from my past and how he's doing."

"Oh brother!" She guzzled the last bit of beer in the can. "It's bad Juju. Particularly right before the wedding."

"You've always been more of a believer in Juju than I have," she declared.

"Well, if that is so, where is the stone that Mr. Maniqault gave you?" She threw the empty can at the garbage pail and missed.

"I don't know," she mumbled softly.

"It's me, remember? The queen of bull manure! You know exactly where that stone is because you have been carrying it around for fifteen years." She picked up the can. "When you walk down that aisle on Saturday, you have to put Barry Hale finally behind you. He certainly has done that with you, don't forget."

"I know you're right, but it's hard and exceedingly difficult to forget him."

"You are a truly hopeless romantic. They don't make people like you anymore!" Trisha opened another beer. "You must do it. Put him back into your past forever. If marriage is the sacred union everyone runs around saying it is, Barry Hale cannot be part of the equation. Are you listening to me for once?"

"I always have," she answered as she focused on his picture.

"I am dead serious. You landed the catch of the century. Barry is someone else's husband and not the prize that Tod Von Westerkamp is. Got it?"

"It always comes down to money with you, doesn't it?"

"I haven't spent my entire working life on straight commission for nothing. You know that I'm materialistic. So what?"

"Intellectually, I know you're right, but it's hard for me. I've tried and tried to forget him, but I've never been successful."

"Before Saturday at four o'clock, you'd better get amnesia about Doctor Barry Hale, MD," Trisha warned. "Put him in the rearview mirror, for heaven's sake!"

CHAPTER SEVENTEEN

The rehearsal dinner was held on *The Spirit of San Francisco* yacht moored at Pier 39, right off the Embarcadero. The bride requested that the attendance be limited to the wedding party and the immediate family. When she and Trisha boarded the gangplank, they were greeted by over three hundred people. Suzanne described it as an intimate dinner on the bay, so she took a deep breath to calm herself as she entered the exquisite vessel's stately interior. The water glistened through the immense windows, and elegantly decorated tables surrounded the dance floor. The ballroom contained Suzanne's phenomenal choices as an excessive number of waiters dressed in white tuxedos poured champagne and others offered deluxe platters of exotic hors d'oeuvres. A musician played show tunes on the grand piano, alongside instruments set up for a band to perform.

"I need a beer. This is way beyond my wildest expectations," Trisha whispered.

"This is not a Carolina keg party, girlfriend. The only way Suzanne would allow beer is if it is imported especially for the occasion. Forget Bud or whatever that guy is that you drink."

"Gosh, network television premiere functions aren't this palatial," she mumbled.

Quickly, the future bride was surrounded, so Trisha decided to work the room as any good television salesperson would. Mr. Right Now was not on this ship; the demographics were too old! At the bar, she sat next to an older, distinguished gentleman. Handsome with a thick mane of silver-gray hair, his stately presence dignified his age.

"How are you related to this sacred event? I'm Trisha!"

"Ian Von Westerkamp, Alexander's brother," he pompously replied.

"You must be the new uncle-in-law," she joked.

"I never quite thought of it, but I guess it's accurate," Ian said in his accentuated, sophisticated speech.

It's going to be a long night when a sixty-year-old guy won't talk to me, she thought. At least his scotch is keeping him anchored to the bar.

"Where did you go to school?" She immediately realized it was incredibly stupid to ask.

"West Point."

"Are you a general?" She flattered him to force him to engage in conversation.

"No, I'm not."

"West Point has a corner on the generals market." He didn't answer, nor did he leave.

What a cold family Vanessa is marrying into, she thought as she gulped her beer.

"So, you've met my uncle Ian." Tod approached and ordered two drinks.

"We're discussing the 1846 West Point graduating class," Trisha lied.

"I can assure you Uncle Ian is not quite that old."

"What could you possibly know about the 1846 class?" He conveyed disdain.

"Everything!" she laughed.

"Let me warn you, Uncle Ian, if she is anything like my future wife, you will be at a distinct disadvantage when it comes to American history." Tod gathered the drinks and left.

"I'm waiting with bated breath," Ian indicated as his lips touched his glass.

"What would you like to know?" Trisha teased.

"Everything," Ian declared, mimicking her prior statement.

"One peculiar distinction is they spent five years trying to kill each other. Eighteen forty-six produced the generals who found themselves on opposite sides of the Civil War. Cadet friends later became mortal enemies. Adversaries who began to size up each other's qualities at the Point."

"Like whom?"

"George B. McClellan, Stonewall Jackson, A. P. Hill, and George Pickett for starters."

"Hum." Ian polished off his scotch and ordered another.

"McClellan graduated number two. As the commander of the Union Army, his overcautious tactics prompted Abraham Lincoln to relieve him of duty."

"Who else?" he asked impatiently as the bartender placed his drink down.

"Thomas Jonathan Jackson, known as 'Stonewall,' graduated seventeenth."

"So, why was he called Stonewall? Barkeep, give the lady another beer."

"South Carolina General Barnard E. Bee rallied his men during the Battle of Bull Run and cried, 'There is Jackson standing like a stone wall. Let us determine to die here, and we will conquer.' Stonewall Jackson became an internationally known hero in the wake of that rebel victory. Unfortunately, he was accidentally killed by his own troops at Chancellorsville."

"How in the world do you know this?" he uttered in sheer amazement.

Feeling a little tipsy, she decided to dazzle him. "Who graduated last out of fifty-nine members?"

"No clue."

"None other than George Edward Pickett, known for leading the disastrous Pickett's Charge at Gettysburg in which three-fourths of his troops were lost."

"You must be a history major specializing in Civil War battles. Quite impressive."

"No, sir, not me! I have absolutely no interest in history."

What does A. P. stand for?"

"Ambrose Powell." Her grasp of the facts started slipping away because of the beer.

"And what did he do?"

"Hill's charge began the Battle of Gettysburg."

"And where did he finish in his class?" he asked with obvious curiosity.

"Not important. The top cadet never made it to the rank of general during the Civil War."

"So, educate me, how do you know Miss Vanessa?"

"We both work in the television business, on opposite sides of the fence. I'm in the sales, and she's on the air."

Throughout the entire evening that was the only time Ian asked her anything about Vanessa. While consuming an ample amount of scotch, he never left her side and even invited her to sit with him. She was delighted to have won his interest and attention. Ian even made Suzanne move her nameplate to his table. Most of the guests came up to Ian, and he introduced all of them, which made Trisha feel like part of the in crowd. He never volunteered information unless she questioned him directly, so she had no idea she was meeting the West Coast's heavy-hitters. When the band started to play, Ian refused to dance, but he did agree to go outside. As the ship sailed underneath the Golden Gate, they entered the crisp night air and the evening sky. Too chilled to stay on the outside deck, they returned to the warmth inside and sounds of the band.

* * *

Forced to greet every guest and engage in polite small talk, Vanessa had not eaten. When the ship docked at the pier, she realized she never glanced out the windows to enjoy the cruise. Suzanne had turned it into an epic society event, and most guests were there to check out the bride and not offend the Von Westerkamps by not attending. She snubbed those in her disfavor by not inviting them. When the doors of the luxurious ocean liner opened and exposed the gangplank, very few people left. Vanessa just wanted to go home, eat a sandwich from her own refrigerator, and go to sleep. After midnight, the guests started to leave. Trisha and Vanessa departed in a limo and ate peanut-butter-and-jelly sandwiches in Vanessa's bed. Inebriated, Trisha fell asleep quickly while the bride stayed awake wondering if her wedding day would be an even worse affair.

* * *

The wedding was at 4:00 p.m., and Suzanne still had not arrived. Saint Mary's Cathedral had their regularly scheduled Mass at five thirty on Saturdays. Father Gotley paced impatiently in front. "I doubt whether I will be able to say Mass as planned."

"I insist that Mass be said, even if it means no pictures."

"I'll hurry," the priest agreed nervously.

At four twenty with no sign of Suzanne, Trisha consoled the bride. "Look, Mass or no Mass, you'll be married once it's over. It will be cozy when all the people show up for five thirty Mass, and they must sit in people's laps. The Lutherans will have to bond with us fish-eaters."

"I'm not amused."

"I am! This is probably the closest I'm ever going to get to the altar with a man!"

Suzanne arrived at four thirty, so Vanessa sent instructions for the orchestra to start the prelude to the wedding march immediately. It forced her mother-in-law to go straight to her seat with a groomsman. Moving up the pace, the bridesmaids no longer sauntered down the aisle and moved quickly. Trisha kissed her friend and started down the main aisle in a rich burgundy velvet formal that flowed to the floor effortlessly. She grinned for the photographer as she arrived at the altar. The wedding march started with a blast through the air since Suzanne had hired members of the San Francisco Symphony instead of using the church's choir, which Vanessa wanted.

The bride entered and proceeded gingerly down the center aisle in an original by designer Diane Von Furstenberg, a friend of Suzanne's. It was a high-waisted formal gown with puffed shoulders and hand-sewn lace. Pearls adorned the entire bodice, giving way to a wide and exceptionally long train that trailed behind her tiny waist. The antique lace veil with matching pearl tiara imported from Germany made her shiny chestnut hair sparkle while her petite body complemented the exquisite gown. Vanessa felt anxious when she arrived at the altar. Tod took her jittery hands into his, and she felt very relieved to be standing beside him.

Father Gotley officiated, along with Suzanne's Lutheran pastor. The priest flew through the liturgy to appease the bride and only paused once to glance at the congregation. "I must say this to you, my brethren. Lutherans make the best Catholics!" Laughter vibrated throughout the congregation at the priest's only joke.

Vanessa turned, glanced at the filled dark oak pews, and peeked up at the choir loft. The professional singer Suzanne had flown in from Los Angeles performed the "Ave Maria" solo. Admittedly, it was indeed the most sensational music to ever grace a wedding ceremony. Sunlight streamed through the stained-glass windows, and the church felt both warm and cozy. She loved this holy place and felt at peace as she focused her attention on her dashing groom.

The couple faced each other and recited traditional vows, and the priest solemnly announced, "For better or for worse, for richer and for poorer, in sickness and in health, until death do us part." Her hands trembled as Tod placed the gold band next to her five-caret diamond engagement ring. "You may now kiss the bride!"

Vanessa's heart pounded as Tod kissed her gently on the lips. The groom took her hand and escorted her down the aisle. As the newlyweds passed their invited guests, the bride looked to find her friends from the station. She beamed as she strolled by pew after pew filled with familiar faces. Outside on California Street, they ducked back inside for the photographer.

"Don't worry, Vanessa; no one will care if Mother is late for the reception at the Mark Hopkins," Tod whispered in her ear. "Now that this ordeal is over with, we can enjoy ourselves."

As the couple approached the altar, Father Gotley urged them to hurry since he would start the five thirty Mass promptly for his parishioners. The photographer shouted at them that the priest had given him a strict deadline of exactly ten minutes to get off the altar. Suzanne made no attempt to hurry through the picture taking. Father Gotley paced back and forth as parish members started to arrive. "You have exactly eight more minutes," the priest warned.

The photographer started to argue, but the bride cut him off. "You're wasting precious time." She had no intention of upsetting her pastor any more than they already had. Promptly at five twenty-five, she announced to her attendants that they should immediately make their way to the Mark Hopkins. Suzanne objected in a very vocal way, but the wedding party ignored her.

* * *

They followed the bride out of the side door of the church, where a fleet of limousines awaited them. Vanessa turned to Tod. "This is absurd. It's only two blocks. I want to walk."

"Honey, you really want to walk up one of this city's steepest hills in a twenty-thousand-dollar wedding dress and drag the train behind you?"

"Your point?" Vanessa smirked.

"Get in the limo, and make my mother happy," he implored.

"No, let's walk," Vanessa answered defiantly.

"Mother will not be pleased," the groom cautioned.

"I wasn't pleased either when she showed up thirty-five minutes late."

"Please don't do this. You'll get nowhere crossing my mother."

"I'm not crossing her. I'm crossing the street!" She lifted her bridal gown and sauntered across the cable car line as Tod took off after her. The newlyweds walked slowly up the incredibly difficult sheer hill until they heard the rattle of the California Street Line. "You're right, Tod. Too vertical to maneuver in these heels. Let's catch the cable car." The bride hopped onto the same cable car that she took to work. "Hi, Dennis," she said to the brakeman, whom she had known for years. "How about a kiss for the bride?"

"Oh mon, never expected to see you today on my route." He kissed her cheek. "Times must be tough for the Von Westerkamps."

"Dennis, can you wait a second for my groom?"

"You are what we call a preferred customer on the California Street Line. You want me to wait for your mon; I'll wait for your mon!" He answered in his thick Jamaican accent as his hair woven in dreadlocks shook in the light breeze coming off the bay. Reluctantly, Tod hopped on with his long black tails flapping in the wind. The brakeman rang the cable car bell in a very rhythmic, soulful way. Dennis had won the San Francisco Cable Car Bell Ringing Competition three years in a row now, and he was quite well known, having been featured in several papers.

"Oh mon, Vanessa, sorry I can't make the festivities. I got to work till midnight."

"Oh mon, Dennis!" She mimicked his Jamaican accent. "Come by after you get off, mon."

"Oh mon! Good thinking! Next stop, Number One Nob Hill, the Mark!"

"Now, this is traveling!" She laughed as he furiously rang the cable car bell.

The cable car arrived at the entrance to the Mark Hopkins, which occupied the site of one of the most ornate and extravagant homes built by railroad tycoons in the 1870s, the gabled and turreted Mark Hopkins mansion. It survived the 1906 earthquake but burned to the ground three days later in the fire that consumed the city. In a century of operation, the Mark was headquarters for distinguished visitors and celebrities from Prince Philip to Frank Sinatra.

"If that Black man shows up in his dreadlocks, my mother will have heart failure."

"Good, I mean that we can have tests run to make sure she never has heart trouble."

* * *

The tuxedo-clad doorman opened the huge front door with its shiny brass handles, and the newlyweds went through the doorway arch as a stately voice announced, "Welcome to the Mark Hopkins, Mr. and Mrs. Tod Von Westerkamp." This proclamation sounded very odd to her. Yet the sound was wonderful, and she was excited to leave the fake Vaughn name behind.

"Just think, you and my mother have the same name!" His teasing interrupted her thoughts. "Not so sure the world is ready for two Mrs. Von Westerkamps."

* * *

CHAPTER SEVENTEEN

The elevator opened, revealing a smashing view of the bay and sparkling city lights. At its most elegant best, the Top of the Mark's glass-walled sky room offered a panoramic view. Most of the guests had already arrived, and several waiters were serving champagne and hors d'oeuvres. With only a second to peek around, they were mobbed by the well-wishers. They greeted each person politely and warmly. Tod had attended formal affairs since he was a child, so it was second nature to him.

After they finished, the sit-down dinner began, and she sunk into her chair at the head table before slipping off her shoes. The bride wiggled her toes while surveying the room. Indeed, Suzanne's choices were outstanding, and her attention to detail was extraordinary as Vanessa sat back to take it all in. Each place setting had an engraved brass name plate intended as the wedding favor for each invited guest, a dazzling gift at a phenomenal cost. Suzanne had turned her son's wedding into one of San Francisco's must-attend social events, and high society responded, in turn, to the powerful Von Westerkamp name. An appetizer of sautéed frogs' legs with fresh watercress puree in white wine butter arrived.

Tod had barely said a word. "Is anything wrong, honey?" she asked in a worried voice as a cream of artichoke soup with hazelnut was followed by a bay shrimp in sour cream dish.

"I hate it when my mother makes me sit through endless courses with petite servings. At the end, I'm still hungry. Did you have any say in this?" Tod asked as he pushed away the dish.

"Hardly. This entire menu is news to me."

"Too bad your parents aren't alive. If they had paid, Mother wouldn't have had any say."

"Sweetheart, that's really a strange thing to say to a bride on her wedding day." She grabbed his hand to finger his new gold wedding band. "You know I have no idea who they are."

"I'm sorry, darling," he apologized as he kissed her to divert her attention away from his careless statement that referred to her background check.

Puzzled, his bride pulled away. "Why do you think my parents are dead?"

"I'm stressed out. My mother has turned this into a royal coronation worthy of Prince Charles. It was a thoughtless thing to say, and I'm sorry. Don't make me grovel," Tod pleaded. "It's not easy getting married at my age."

"It just sounded so strange to me since I've always thought that my parents were alive. You sounded so positive when you spoke about them being dead." She expressed concern.

"Too much champagne talking, darling. That's all." He kissed her hand as the waiter placed boned stuffed chicken with veal in green peppercorn sauce in front of him. "Let's stop this bickering and enjoy what's left of our wedding."

She glanced down at truly the smallest portion she had ever seen. In Suzanne's tradition, it was merely another appetizer: cauliflower timbale in curry sauce with broccoli and carrots. Silently, she sat during the never-ending courses and contemplated what Tod meant by his bizarre statement. Alexander sat down next to the bride seconds before the main course arrived. He engaged in some polite small talk while the scrumptious rack of lamb, marinated in olive oil and herbs and baked in a puff pastry, was served. He quickly devoured his portion.

"I told you. My father hates sitting through my mother's insufferable, unending courses. He's been at the bar the whole time."

"Wrong, son, I was not at this bar. I was one block away at the Big Four. I've spent many nights there and consumed large amounts of scotch." Alexander beckoned the waiter over.

"Champagne, sir?"

"Absolutely not! I want a real drink," he barked, slurring his words. "Scotch."

"Yes, sir." The waiter quickly disappeared.

"Amazing, isn't it, Vanessa?"

"What's that?"

"The service you get when they know you're the one picking up the tab," he commented sarcastically.

His present alcoholic blur annoyed Vanessa, so she took a deep, calming breath. Her belligerent father-in-law remarked, "Is this wedding regal enough for you, my dear?"

"A mammoth affair like this? My choice would have invited only family and friends."

"But you don't have any family, remember? Who would you have asked?" He was nasty.

She had learned not to confront him when he was drinking, so she got up hastily and listened for Trisha's laughter. Suzanne had deliberately separated the bride from her maiden of honor. While she was stuck next to his parents, the wedding party at another table were all laughing.

"Forget getting me that television job here," Trisha whispered. "If things go right, I'm headed for Boston Square." The band played a few chords. "That's your cue. It's the first dance. Who did you choose?"

"I didn't. Suzanne has Alexander dancing with me in lieu of my father."

"Lovely." Trisha grabbed her Boston groomsman to give him a hug.

"Save me a dance," he murmured to the bride in his thick Bostonian accent.

After she began dancing with Alexander, Tod joined in with his mother. Later, he switched to dance with his bride. All the bride's musical selections were vetoed, so a traditional German waltz played. The lead singer's incredible voice belted out Vanessa's only request, "I Left My Heart in San Francisco."

Trisha entered the dance floor with the best man and the rest of the wedding party.

"Where little cable cars climb halfway to the stars," he sang to Vanessa.

The bride took a much-needed rest and sat down with Trisha. "I have to give your new mother-in-law credit. The only downer has been suffering through the endless courses of weird food. The band is terrific, and so is the view."

"Three guesses on who picked it out."

"No mother-in-law is perfect; that's for sure. This guy is a living doll. How in the world did I miss Mr. Right Now last night?"

"Behave yourself. No sleeping with anyone," the bride ordered. "That's all I need."

"Gee whiz, you're making some tough standards for this evening." She laughed. "I could definitely get lucky with this guy."

"Down girl! Down!"

"Easy for happily married ladies to throw dispersions at us pitiful, perpetual single gals."

"For once in your life, would you play hard to get?"

"I've never tried that before. It's never been my style."

"It's an order. Got it? Or should I get your Marine Corps father on the phone?"

"You are no fun! I'm never going to wear white to my wedding." Trisha winked.

Her friend skipped over to the groomsman. She hoped she didn't wind up in bed with him at her place. That would just be too weird! She never had any control over her. They were complete opposites, and that was why the chemistry between them was so strong. The band came back, and she danced with one stranger after the other. Around eleven o'clock, they cut the humongous wedding cake with its ten layers, each featuring a different flavor.

She tossed her bouquet at the last second, straight to Trisha, who barely caught it. "Fixed!" all the single woman yelled.

Ironically, Trisha's Boston groom made the catch when Tod threw the garter. The bride and maid of honor laughed hysterically while the photographer attempted to get a picture of the four of them with the garter and bouquet. Tod and his groomsman didn't get the humor involved and looked quite puzzled. It was the only enjoyment she had gotten out of her entire wedding day.

The band played until one thirty in the morning when last call was announced. Vanessa asked Tod if they could go to their honeymoon suite, but he felt like he should hang around. Sheer exhaustion from the last two days crept over her, and she felt lightheaded.

"Come on," Trisha ordered. "You're going to your room. You look faint! Hey, you want me to carry you over the threshold? That's traditional, you know."

"You're crazy enough to do it. Aren't you?" Vanessa kept a tight grip on her friend's arm.

"I've got to get my kicks somehow since you cloistered me for the evening," she joked.

* * *

A bellman escorted them to the top floor and into Mark Hopkins's most grandiose honeymoon suite. After the bellman opened the door, Trisha marveled at the impeccable furnishings and the spectacular view. She brought Vanessa some ice water with lemon on a silver tray and helped her take off her hot wedding gown. After assisting the bride into bed, she opened all the windows to let in some fresh air and watched her friend fall soundly asleep. Then, she turned her attention to the cargo ships passing by in the distant bay. Lights shimmering across the water were amazing as the city glittered in the foreground. *How lucky Vanessa is to live here and to be married to Tod!* Trisha thought as San Francisco gleamed through the window. She walked over to the wet bar, opened a beer, and took a swig as her mind visualized Mr. Manigault's Juju prediction of twenty years of bad fortune. *If this is bad,* Trisha contemplated as she glanced around the posh suite, *I'd love to see the good times.*

CHAPTER EIGHTEEN

Vanessa had never been out of the country, so Tod took her to his favorite place in all of Europe, Zermatt, a village nestled in the Pennine Alps of southern Switzerland. As they approached by train, a dazzling white blanket of snow covered the peaks surrounding the lovely hamlet. This romantic resort did not allow cars, so it had a sparkling clean yet isolated feeling. Vanessa's nose stayed pressed against the windowpane as she marveled at the spectacular mountains. The massive and enthralling Matterhorn completely mesmerized her, and when the train stopped, she descended the steps and kept her spellbound eyes riveted to the majestic views. A horse-drawn carriage waited to transport them to their hotel as Tod took her hand. The driver helped her up the steps and wrapped a warm blanket around them. He took the reins into his hands, and the team of horses jerked forward.

Leisurely, the newlyweds proceeded through the charming Swiss village as her head bobbed from left to right since she simply did not know where to look. Every building seemed so strange yet exquisitely beautiful, and she loved every detail of the stunning Swiss architecture and the citizens who lived in it.

The driver halted the horses in front of a small hotel Tod had chosen. It was a quaint place, run by an elderly Swiss couple who greeted them. The proprietors stared at Vanessa since Tod had brought a steady stream of glamorous women to romance at their establishment. He spoke to them fluently in French for a few minutes and then turned to his bride to translate. "These locals say that you are incredibly lucky since the weather is clear today for your arrival. During the winter, months go by without seeing the top of the Matterhorn. They hope this deceptive calm will endure for your entire visit so your memories will last a lifetime. Today, the Matterhorn is sensational from every mountaintop in Switzerland!"

She smiled sweetly as the stocky woman with silver hair took her hand and escorted her into their tiny establishment. *What a strange way to put it,* Vanessa thought as she walked beside the pudgy lady.

While Tod skied, she explored the delightful village and loved everything about Switzerland: the people, the food, and its wondrous natural beauty. She felt tremendous excitement on her walks through Zermatt, and her childlike awe awakened a never-ending wonderment. Every afternoon, the honeymooners napped and then made love. Tod brought an entire satchel filled with creams, lotions, and other assorted paraphernalia for lovemaking. Daily, he returned from skiing with gifts of new, sexy lingerie elaborately wrapped in silky white paper with big black bows encircling the boxes. The contents consisted of a few strings to strategically place around pubic hair and breasts, and he expected his bride to model her exposed body as he waited patiently. Wanting to please her new husband, she followed his instructions precisely as he directed her in the art of lovemaking. Extremely inexperienced at thirty-five, she appreciated his guidelines for intimacy. Without phones, family, or her job, the newlyweds concentrated on sex, and if his bride failed to satisfy him, Tod would sharply critique her and give her a new sexual assignment.

A leisurely walk after dinner in the crisp mountain air was followed by another lovemaking session to enhance their earlier movements. Once techniques were mastered, Tod changed the rules again, and when she reached her highest point of sexual excitement, sometimes Tod would stop right before her climax. He gave her incredibly strong feelings of pleasure repeatedly until she begged him to stop because her emotional intensity was overwhelming. After unrelenting sex, she felt stimulated whenever he appeared.

During a candlelight dinner at a five-star restaurant, Tod informed her that he no longer wanted her to wear underwear, and she was forbidden to wear anything but dresses. He wanted complete and utter access to her vagina. Their stay involved unrestrained sexual indulgence, which Vanessa had never experienced. As days went by, she realized Tod had spent a great deal of his life, an inordinate amount of time, making love to women. He wished her to become his ultimate desired sexual encounter, an aspiration Vanessa knew she could never fulfill.

* * *

On their last day in Zermatt, the newlyweds took a train and transferred to the cable car to reach the top of the Matterhorn. After lunch, she walked around the surrounding grounds in a special dress and coat Tod had bought for the occasion. Unknown to her, Tod was not bewitched by the dramatic view of the alluring mountain and was simply scouting for a place to have sex. They strolled by a fence made of stones piled strategically on top of each other. Tod helped her down the precarious path and stopped next to a rocky wall.

It was the coldest day yet, but he still instructed his new bride to unbutton her coat, and when she protested, he placed his fingers over her mouth. He ordered her to lift her dress so he could see her vagina as he separated her legs, wanting them further apart. Her dress was now above her breasts, and freezing air hit her nipples and exposed clitoris. His weird game scared her as her body turned pink from the cold. Tod pushed her against the rocks, unzipped his pants, and brutally forced his penis into her vagina. The ferocity with which he entered brought tears to her eyes and crushing pain between her legs. The frenzy of his actions shocked Vanessa. Thankfully, his orgasm came quickly as he screamed upon ejaculation. Absolutely oblivious to her feelings, Tod sucked on her nipples and then pulled out his penis. Crying uncontrollably, Vanessa felt the warm semen running down her inner thighs after the strange assault. Without speaking, he slowly lowered her dress and began caressing her breasts through the silk material. He gave her chest a final squeeze.

"Suck them, baby!" he said, placing his fingers in her mouth to clean them off.

* * *

They walked back to the cable car and held hands in silence. Upon entering the tram, Tod leaned against the window and placed his hands around Vanessa's waist. Trapping her arms, he pulled her backside tightly to him, as she stared blankly, and people looked away when she made eye contact with them. He kept a firm grip on her body during the descent as the motion swayed back and forth. Tears flowed down her cheeks. In her distraught state, the liquid ran down her legs, and she was unaware of the dynamic scenery whizzing by as the tram plunged downward. His tight grip felt like a stranger's while her mind was on top with her body trapped below.

When they reached the platform, Tod released her, and they walked to the train station. Once on board, she composed herself as passengers glanced at her with concern. The Swiss train left promptly on its way to the heart of Zermatt as his right hand slipped inside her coat and rested on top of her pubic hair. Running his fingers back and forth, Tod probed her vagina and touched her clitoris for a second and then fondled her breasts. Vanessa pulled away and slid next to the window. "OK, baby, I'll give you a rest." Tod leaned against her and fell soundly asleep.

Vanessa took his hand out of her coat and wiped the tears from her cheeks. Glancing out the window, she saw it had snowed, and the tree branches bore a milky coat that glimmered in the sun. The Alps sparkled with a majestic quality as she took long, deep breaths to calm down. Watching the scenery made her feel more serene, and as the whistle blew, a groggy Tod strolled by her side. At the Hotel Matterhorn, Tod wanted her warm body next to him while he took his nap. She declined and went to the lobby to enjoy hot tea. Slowly, she sipped her tea as she stared out a window. When she had calmed down, she went back to their room, and Tod did not stir as she collapsed in front of the crackling fire. She picked up a log and threw it into the fireplace as Tod slept peacefully. She mulled over her earlier horror but decided not to ruin the last night. Instead, she remembered what Trisha always said, "Men want to marry virgins and have them act like whores in bed." She wished she could call Trisha.

* * *

It was dark outside when Tod woke up, and they went to his favorite restaurant. The maître d' seated them in front of the fireplace. Tod was very charming throughout the evening so Vanessa decided to forgive him for his earlier indiscretion.

The waiter brought cognac and asked, "When are you going home?"

Tod replied, "In the morning."

After he left, Vanessa innocently commented, "I hate to leave such a wonderful place."

"Sweetheart, if you don't want to leave, we can easily extend our stay."

"No, we can't," Vanessa answered bluntly. "I promised the station I'd be back for the sweeps. It was genuinely nice of them to let me get married in the middle of a ratings book."

"Listen to yourself! They need you. You don't need them."

"What are you saying?"

"You no longer need to work." He cavalierly sipped his cognac. "That's all!"

"We have been through this before." She was agitated. "I plan to continue on the air until we have a baby. You agreed when your family's attorney drew up that silly legal agreement concerning my impending motherhood. I signed that ridiculous document that stated I agreed not to return to any form of employment after the delivery of our baby. You demanded that it be a condition of my future pregnancy."

"Actually, I forced you to sign it instead of a prenup since money means nothing to you. I've suffered through your endless work hours, but I have never in my life gone to Europe for two weeks. I feel just like a couple from Des Moines, Iowa, who have only two weeks to see ten countries, and then it's back to the meatpacking plant for another year. They don't own you!"

"And you think you do?" Her anger rose.

"Don't be silly. All I am saying is that you can quit right now, and we can travel around Europe so I can show you more of the continent. That certainly should be more appealing than sitting behind a camera waiting for a red light to go off."

"This is my career and chosen profession, so don't belittle it. I don't consider it work."

"Von Westerkamps don't do nine to five. My life will not be confined by your workaholism. If I must sire an heir to get you out of there, so be it." He drank his cognac.

* * *

After an utterly exhausting flight from Geneva, the Von Westerkamp chauffeur picked them up. The newlyweds relaxed inside the Rolls Royce, where an assortment of snacks and drinks were elaborately arranged next to a newspaper published on their wedding day. She shoved it aside as the car phone rang. "Three guesses who that is!"

Tod explained that he had not seen the front page yet and gestured toward the paper. The front page was devoted to a color picture of them with Dennis, the brakeman. Tod looked quite dashing, and her gown had photographed beautifully. Smiling from ear to ear was Dennis with his dreadlocks flowing down to his shoulders. She loved the photo as a fantastic wedding souvenir. Tod motioned for the paper as he told his mother that he would talk to his wife about the matter. Tod took a deep breath and pushed the button to disconnect the call.

"What did your mother say?" she asked quizzically.

"You won't like it, and it will start a fight."

"Now I'm really curious."

"You let that Black man maul you and humiliated the entire Von Westerkamp family."

"What?" Vanessa's face reddened.

"I told you that you wouldn't like what she said."

"I don't get the 'maul' part. What does his race have to do with anything? He's a friend!"

"Mother rented a fleet, and you had to prance down California Street in your wedding gown. I told you to get in the limo." Tod glared down at the paper.

"Explain the 'maul' part to me, please?"

"His hand was strategically placed. It went over like a lead balloon with her friends. I can't say that I disagree with them."

"Oh, please! Tell me you don't mean this."

"I am not being contrary. I simply agree with my mother, and I forgive your indiscretion," Tod said with a yawn.

"My indiscretion?"

"I find that cable car brakeman to be one step above a street person. I certainly don't want his hands on my wife. Understood? I'm the only man who touches you. Be really clear on this."

Tod closed his eyes and nodded off. Vanessa had seen two sides of her new husband that she would never have agreed to marry. She cried as the driver looked with pity at her in the rearview mirror. As their chauffeur for thirty years, he instinctively knew that the new bride had been exposed to the real Tod Von Westerkamp.

* * *

The next day, Vanessa left Tod asleep in their mansion and drove to work. The newsroom staff had decorated her office to welcome her, and she was relieved to be among her genuinely kind colleagues. She knew her marriage was a big mistake but decided to put it out of her mind.

Throughout the sweeps, Tod complained endlessly about her heavy work schedule. He didn't like having sex after the late newscast, but this was never a problem prior to the wedding.

Tod went to Pebble Beach, followed by Lake Tahoe to golf until the end of the sweeps. Relieved, she proceeded to work fourteen hours a day without guilt and totally focused on her job. But Tod called daily and insisted on talking dirty over the phone. He gave instructions on what he wanted her to do with her body so she played along but completely ignored him. He became a ridiculous annoyance with his nauseating phone calls. After one vile call, she felt physically sick and quickly left the station.

* * *

Walking in heavy rain without an umbrella, she slowly climbed the steep California Street hill while people scurried past to escape the torrential downpour. She ascended the steps to Saint Mary's, and the massive wooden door creaked as she entered the empty sanctuary. Soaked, she blankly shuffled over to light a candle to pray in front of an imposing Virgin Mary statue. Kneeling, she stared absently at the serpent beneath her bare feet as her left foot crushed the snake's neck while his nasty long red tongue lashed out in agony. Mary's simple veil and white robes flowed from her extended arms, and her palms faced outward.

A hand touched her shoulder. "Vanessa, is something wrong? I heard someone crying."

"Father, you must hear my confession," she replied with tear-stained cheeks.

Father Gotley nodded, and she followed him into the small wooden stall and knelt as the elderly priest slid open the tiny window and the scarlet red curtain that separated them.

"I hate my husband, Father!" she cried.

"I shall not tolerate such blasphemy in the Lord's holy house!"

"With all my heart and with all my soul, I hate him!" She sobbed.

"You have taken a sacred vow 'to death do us part.' Marriage requires a quite normal period of adjustment for a newlywed such as yourself. Some men have entirely different sex drives than their wives. I advise you to have both patience and understanding with your new husband. Once you are acquainted with his sexual needs, take comfort in them. Your gratifying reward will be children blessed by the Holy Father. An obedient wife should please her husband and honor her hallowed marriage vows."

"Father, I can't stay married!" She wept. "I hate that man!"

"My dear, there is a thin line between love and hate. You must honor your faith and your holy vows. Divorce is not an option for a devout Catholic." He raised his hand for the blessing. "For penance, say the rosary daily to pray for forgiveness. Go now to love and serve the Lord."

* * *

Outside the church, she entered the intense storm raging outside. The rain plunged down the city's steep hills, and the deluge rampaged as her saturated clothes and drenched shoes sloshed beneath her feet. Unaware of the cascading blast of chilly rain that assaulted her entire body, she noticed nothing, and her dull eyes didn't react to the surrounding physical elements. Hours later, she arrived at Tod's mansion by foot and was greeted by their astonished butler, who quickly summoned the staff. She waved them away and retreated to the privacy of the master suite to slowly peel off her permeated clothes in front of the roaring fireplace. Grabbing the comforter, she sank down on the floor and wrapped it around her body. As she watched the flames, she grabbed the phone to tell the news director she was unable to go on the air tonight. Since becoming an anchor, it was the first time she had felt unable to perform.

Trisha's interpretation of what happened in Zermatt was that Vanessa's extreme inexperience made sexual acts seem bizarre that were in fact considered quite normal. Men got a real rush from having sex outdoors, and getting caught in illicit acts added an element of danger. If she had an orgasm that day, she might perceive it as normal instead of strange and unorthodox. Men could be very weird about sex, so she should engage in the offbeat and try to get some enjoyment out of his sexual games. Surely, the worldly Trisha and the holy priest could not be wrong.

* * *

On October 17, 1989, San Francisco experienced a 7.1 earthquake on the Richter Magnitude Scale that took out a fifty-foot section of the Bay Bridge, along with collapsing a 1.5-mile-long stretch of the upper deck of the Nimitz Freeway on Interstate 880 in Oakland. In the Marina District, older buildings fell down as a gas leak fed an all-night fire. It was a grim reminder of the 1906 earthquake, when fire had leveled the city. The awesome tremor hit at 5:01 p.m. as Vanessa prepared for the early newscast, while Tod waited at Candlestick Park for the World Series to begin. Dubbed the Bay Bridge Series, it featured the Oakland Athletics and the San Francisco Giants. When the earthquake struck, the Von Westerkamp family were sitting in their season box as the stadium began to percolate up and down and then sideways. Tod's mother grabbed her son when a horrifying series of terrifying aftershocks rocked "the Stick," San Francisco's nickname for their stadium.

ABC Network lost their broadcast momentarily, but the world had witnessed the earthquake in real time. Larger-than-life players—Will Clark and Kevin Mitchell on one side and Jose Canseco and Mark McGwire on the other—were rattled and confused citizens just like everyone else. As the home pitcher left the clubhouse, the lights blew out. Don Robinson ran into the manager's office and dropped down on the floor. Being a 235-pounder, Robinson later blamed himself for the aftershock. As night fell, officials called the game.

San Francisco Giant Will Clark said, "It sounded like an F-15 overhead, just a big, humongous roar. I looked up, and the stadium was swaying back and forth."

The A's Mark McGwire was doing a hamstring stretch and said, "It felt like I was riding a surfboard. I'm from the South where you deal with hurricanes. If it's coming your way, you get the hell out. When the ground starts shaking, you have nowhere to go. It's a helpless feeling. My brother-in-law, Jason, is a six-foot-five, 270-pound guy from Mississippi, and he yelled down at me on the field, 'I got to get back to Mississippi. The red clay there does not move.'"

The Giants' Mike Krukow said, "Our family was in town and got a suite at the SFO Airport Marriott. The room looked ransacked, the TV on the floor, broken windows, and shattered glass."

A remarkable scene of ballplayers caressing their offspring and wives on the field told the world what had happened. Total darkness blanketed the city, and without power or phone service, the casualties started to mount as the Bay Area entered a state of emergency.

* * *

Temporarily off the air, KPIX's engineers used a portable generator to restore the station's signal. The news team went into high gear and reported live continuously. The station fed the devastation to the CBS Network and its affiliates across the nation. Vanessa worked around the clock and only went home to shower and get more clothes. Tod became increasingly agitated with her devotion to her job.

In the trauma of the quake's aftermath, she focused on being a public servant to her community and filmed a series of Red Cross announcements to instruct how to get needed services like food and shelter. She manned phone banks set up for this purpose.

Vanessa produced one of the most emotionally devastating features ever filmed. When no patients came into the ER at Oakland's Children's Hospital, Doctor James Betts grabbed a medical bag and went to the pancaked Cypress Freeway. Six-year-old Julio Berumen was trapped beneath his dead mother's body in the family car on the collapsed two-decker length of Interstate 880. Climbing two stories on a fireman's ladder, Doctor Betts got inside the crushed car and stretched out belly-down on a backboard to keep his own weight from crushing the boy. Little Julio was breathing on his own, but he was comatose. Betts had to lie on his stomach in the hot, cramped space and cut through one of the two dead women in the front seat using a chainsaw. After starting an IV, Doctor Betts put a tourniquet on the boy's leg and used the First Company firefighters' chainsaw to amputate his right leg to free him. The halogen lights burned the pediatric surgeon's ears as he held the artery that supplies the blood to the lower portion of the leg. Miraculously, Julio survived and was taken to Oakland's Children's Hospital Intensive Care Unit. Later, his father arrived, and Doctor Betts was thrilled that Julio had a family member alive. Vanessa interviewed the brave surgeon who crawled onto the collapsed freeway.

Doctor Betts explained, "I am no hero. This is what I was trained to do."

Hardened reporters watched her segment from the editing booth and cried. After she signed off, tears were in many eyes, including the janitor's.

Surviving on less than three hours of sleep a night for weeks, she was exhausted when the phone rang. "This is not up for negotiation," Tod demanded on the other end. "Get home tonight, or don't bother ever coming home." Maliciously, he slammed the phone down.

* * *

Vanessa knew she had to go home immediately even though she hated to leave her fellow colleagues. The news staff was putting in an insane number of grueling hours so she hesitantly asked Mr. Fellows if she could get some much-needed sleep. Graciously, he told her the weekend anchor would cover for her. Little did he know that sleep was the last thing she would get at home. They hadn't had sex in weeks, which was driving Tod insane.

Tod greeted her with nothing on but his jock strap. She had little patience for his superficiality while people were entombed in their cars on collapsed Interstate 880.

"What a tearjerker story that was, Vanessa!"

"I'm glad it touched you," she said with contempt.

"Like my Halloween costume? I chose it just for you." Deliberately he exposed his penis.

"Like the rest of San Francisco, I forgot it was Halloween night," she answered sarcastically. He was unmoved by the plight of that poor, helpless little boy on the Nimitz.

"We big kids never forget trick-or-treat!"

"This might be a tough town to find a treat in tonight."

"You are my treat! Come here!" he ordered.

"I haven't bathed in two days," she warned.

"I don't care. Get over here right now!"

He had been drinking and failing to comply with his demand would only start a fight. No one would believe from this untouched house that San Francisco had experienced such devastation. Tod plunged his tongue, strongly reeking of alcohol, into her mouth. With extreme aggressiveness, he unzipped her dress and snapped her bra strap off. Brutally, he forced his erect penis inside of her, and she cringed as he pressed forward in a frenzy. With his hands fixed rigidly on her buttocks, he controlled her up and down movements. As she became more tense, he clenched her bottom in a firm clasp, which hurt. His powerful arms held her down as he dictated, "Hold your tush still. It's too soon to come. I might want you from behind."

"Please!" she begged wearily. "I just want to go to sleep."

Ignoring her request, he belligerently clenched each of her buns, and if she moved slightly, he slapped her on the behind. "Don't move your ass," he commanded. "I'm close to the peak, and I'm not ready yet." She closed her eyes and became lifeless as ordered. In her slumber, she heard angry voices. Suddenly awakened by the pain of her nipples being tightly twisted, her heavy eyelids opened, and his provoked face was an inch away. "Wake up! You can sleep at your job but not on my time." His vicious voice scared her awake.

"Tod, please," she pleaded groggily.

"Don't Tod, me! I haven't had sex in two weeks, and I'm not thrilled." He bitterly twisted her nipples. "I'm not hard anymore. Slide down and suck me until I get hard."

"Tod, please," she begged in vain.

"If you're not interested in sucking on me, there's lots of women in this town who are," he said heatedly without letting go of her nipples. "I was under the impression that when you got married, you got it anytime you wanted it."

With the intense resentment in his voice, she knew to delay would make matters worse. She had never seen him get violent before. With all the strength she could muster, she pushed herself up, and he let go of her breasts. A pang in her left breast caused her to look down in anguish at a bluish-colored bruise. Both breasts ached from the abuse.

"Get on all fours so that I can see those boobies hanging down," he instructed. As he put his penis inside her mouth, she became furious but went through the motions. Suddenly, he pinched her nipples again. "Hey baby, watch the teeth. Don't hurt Daddy. We're trying to make a baby here!" Glaring in utter disgust, she kept her lips over her teeth. An eternity passed before he entered her vagina from behind, grabbing her buttocks. On all fours, she watched ships sail by as they passed underneath the bridge. Close to the pinnacle, he stopped and had her go through the entire ordeal again. After an utterly traumatic time against the window glass, he screamed when he climaxed and then leaned over to get his scotch. After a couple of sips, he grabbed ice from a crystal ice bucket and poured another drink. With the cold hand he had submerged in the ice, he petted her clitoris with his frigid fingers. Jolting forward, she tried to wiggle away, but he restrained her, threatening to use an ice cube to give her something to cringe about if she kept jerking. She sat motionless as Tod prolonged his game by twisting her pubic hair and playing with her genitalia until he became distracted by his scotch.

Feeling both physically and emotionally drained, she looked out as a naval ship passed by with men stationed at their posts topside dressed in their white uniforms. She wished that she could summon the American sailors to her side for protection.

CHAPTER NINETEEN

"Merry Christmas, Trisha!"

"I can't believe that you would call me here. Perfect timing though. my parents went to have fruit cake with our neighbors."

"I'm getting brave in my old age. Besides, I have big news!"

"You're divorcing that scum-bag," Trisha guessed.

"I'm not that brave."

"You're having an affair!"

"The last thing I need is another man in my life. I don't even want the one that I have."

"So what gives? You haven't called me at this house in seventeen years, so it's earth-shattering news. My parents went out so I'm all yours. What did the slime ball do now?"

"I'm pregnant," she blurted out. "This has got to be a first, Trisha at a loss for words."

"When did you find out?"

"This morning. I bought an in-home pregnancy test. I've been so distraught that I spaced out when I missed my period. Last night, while I was enduring a marathon Von Westerkamp Christmas Eve dinner, it dawned on me."

"But I thought you had an IUD?"

"I do! My gynecologist told me over the phone that this happens more than women want to believe. It slips down, and it's useless. I can't believe this. I've had unprotected sex exactly twice in my entire life, and I've gotten pregnant both times. It's so unfair!" She broke into tears. "I can't abort this baby. I'm married for God's sake! Plus, I could never handle another abortion."

"Things have changed since 1972. A licensed gynecologist can do it. The Supreme Court says so, at least for now."

"It's not an option. One abortion in a lifetime is enough."

"Since I'm spending another husbandless Christmas, can I at least be the godmother?"

"Sure," Vanessa whimpered as she blew her nose.

"Every woman I know who is headed toward the big four-oh wants a baby, and many are considering a sperm bank. Myself, I prefer the traditional method. At least you know who the father is," she reasoned. "You have the luxury of enjoying your baby. You don't have to work like the rest of the women in this country who have children."

"But I can't stand the sight of him." She sniffled loudly into the receiver.

"My dear Vanessa! Ninety-nine-point-nine percent of the men I've slept with, I couldn't stand the sight of them the next morning after the alcohol wore off. You, at least, had a couple of good engagement months. Besides, your husband has nothing to do but play golf, drink, and have sex. A baby will give him a fourth thing to do with his day. Once you tell him, he will be like all men as proud as a peacock. He'll believe he is the first man in the universe to get somebody pregnant. Have you told him yet?"

"No, you're the first one to know."

"As it should be since the honorable godmother has that reward."

"What should I do about my marriage?"

"What can you do? It might be a tad difficult to go in there and to say, 'Tod, I want a divorce, and oh, I'm two months into the family way. I'm keeping the baby but not you!'"

"You have a lovely way of putting the obvious into perspective," she wept softly.

"Look, Vanessa, the guy is jealous. Hence, the reason for that ludicrous pregnancy contract that he made you sign. You love your job, and he's never had one in his life. As soon as you quit, he'll feel like he's the master again. He will, in all probability, stop trying to control you through sex. He spent his entire life having sex with tons of women. You came along, and he knew how inexperienced you were, but he married you anyway. His sex escapades are way out of your league. It's his way of dominating an independent career woman. You have another whole life besides him, and he doesn't have one. You're it! Hopefully, once you're not working anymore, things will change. Plus, make sure he is in the delivery room when the head comes screeching out. I bet he doesn't look at you the same way again."

"That's a real comforting thought."

"You have nothing to lose. If he continues to be a cad, you can get a job with the snap of your fingers. You can become a working mother like the rest of the mom population. The worst-case scenario is you support your kid doing work that you love. Did I forget to mention that you are immensely gifted? A talent to be reckoned with!"

"Trisha, no matter how upset I am, you always make me laugh." She chuckled.

"Has he done any weird sex stuff lately that I can get off on? It's been quite a while since my last date." Trisha asked half joking, half out of curiosity. "Any hot sexual events lately?"

"You're as bad as he is," she wailed. "You should be married to him, not me!"

"Any hot sexual events lately?"

"Well, not really. Tod left during the November sweeps to play golf. Since his return, he's been quite nice. I think he figured out that he went over the edge. It's just been difficult for me to forgive and to forget what I experienced on Halloween."

"Remember he gave you a baby and forget the rest," her friend cautioned. "It isn't healthy to think of that while a new life is inside of you. It's not good for the mother, and surely it can't be wholesome for the baby. Put it out of your mind. Concentrate on the wonder within you."

"I'm so glad you were home today, Trisha."

"Where else would an old maid be on Christmas Day?"

"I hate it when you talk like that about yourself. You've never wanted to get married, so don't say such stuff. You could never stand the thought of being with the same man, day in and day out, for the rest of your life. You would despise it. It would be worse than death to you!"

"Listen to you, two short years of marriage and you've turned into me," she teased.

"When are you going to break the blessed news to Suzanne?" she asked.

"Tonight at dinner. She will probably get a special bed for me to stay in for nine months."

"I'm dying, positively dying, to hear what their reaction is to the divine event," she cracked. "Hey, tell Tod that the doctor said no sex for nine months."

"You really are worse than he is!"

"Got to go. My parents just drove in. I miss you! Call me!"

* * *

Vanessa looked out the window to see Tod hitting golf balls against a net he had the staff put up on Christmas morning instead of letting them go home. She stared at the whitecaps and the bay was the emptiest that she had ever witnessed. She mustered up enough courage to go downstairs and walked through the garden filled with dazzling winter flowers. Their landscape architect had just won an award for designing the grounds of their estate. He had spectacularly created a dramatic effect by mounding large portions of the lawn, which led to the cliff that cascaded down to the bay. *It would be a marvelous place for a child to play,* she thought as she sat down on a cushioned chair that adorned their Spanish tiled deck.

"Damn, Vanessa, did you let all the staff go home?" Tod yelled out, not realizing that she was six feet away. "Who in the hell is going to pick up all these balls?"

"Maybe your baby can crawl around and get them," she answered softly.

Tod turned around startled. "What? I don't think I caught that."

"There is a good possibility that next August you might have Tod or Todette on your hands. With any luck, you will have a Leo baby if my calculations are correct."

Tod dropped his golf club and ran over to kiss her. He launched into questions and eagerly wanted to know all the details. She had not expected him to be excited and felt quite surprised at his reaction. He grabbed the phone and called his parents to break the news to them. Trisha was right. Tod did think he was the first man ever to get someone pregnant. At his parents' estate that afternoon, they found Suzanne calling to inform everyone she knew on all seven continents. It would have been cheaper to buy thirty seconds of airtime on the CBS Network to inform the Von Westerkamp world. Alexander didn't bother to congratulate his only son and seemed disinterested in the news.

* * *

The Von Westerkamps had generously supported Pacific Hospital as influential benefactors, so the family had their own wing named after them, and Alexander sat on the board. Suzanne instructed her daughter-in-law to have the baby there by the same obstetrician who had delivered Tod some forty-odd years before. Her first question was whether he could still stand up and grab the baby on the way out.

At Suzanne's insistence, Vanessa consented and made an appointment with him. As the head of obstetrics and gynecology, he no longer delivered babies, much to her great relief. She did her own research and found Doctor Joan Wang had the lowest caesarean section rate in the department. After discussing the issue, Joan performed a pelvic exam and gave Vanessa an August 1 due date. Joan strongly recommended amniocentesis because Vanessa was over thirty-five. Happy with her choice, she felt relieved to have a young female obstetrician instead of an ancient male.

* * *

Vanessa went to Mr. Fellows's office to break the news to him. With deeply mixed emotions, he congratulated her on the forthcoming birth. He appreciated her honesty, which made it easier to plan a replacement. She wanted to work right up to her due date, which would take the station through the July ratings.

"It will be extremely difficult to replace you, Vanessa. No one will put in the hours that you have."

* * *

That evening, Tod asked, "Can we have sex, or do I have to be celibate for the first time in my life? Don't get mad," he lied. "I'm only asking because I don't want to hurt the baby."

Annoyed, she answered, "Doctor Wang said it was permissible until the last few weeks."

"You could do nine months of oral sex on me and you practice abstinence. I would really like that. I can't wait until you are out of that job, so we can procreate after golf in the middle of the day. I'm always horny when I get home from a round, and you're never here to fool around with. I really want to fornicate after dinner, too. That was one of my favorites when I was single, and you never show up till one o'clock in the morning. I loved to take my ladies to dinner and then directly to bed. Look at your breasts, baby. They're getting big already. I don't want you to get fat. I don't fuck fat women. I never have, and I never will."

"Tod, have you been drinking?" Vanessa asked with concern.

"So what if I have?"

"It's rather early to be drinking alcohol, isn't it?" Vanessa worried.

Tod knelt and placed one hand on each inner thigh before motioning for her to separate her legs. His tongue slowly licked her clitoris, gently moving back and forth ever so lightly. He had not tried to please her in over a year, so she tried to concentrate. His mouth felt warm and moist as she attempted to focus. It was obviously a special treat, his reward for her pregnancy. Vanessa was not used to having orgasms, so it took a long time. She moaned in pure ecstasy, and Tod sucked hard as she climaxed, which lengthened and made her orgasm even more powerful.

"See what you're missing by working at that damn job. My attorney sent the letter out by registered mail to your boss today. Congratulations, you're all mine now, baby."

* * *

Vanessa felt extremely tired during her first trimester but managed somehow to resume killer work hours for the sweeps. Westinghouse Broadcasting decided that they would not replace their popular female anchor until the fall, fearing a drop in the household and demographic ratings. Corporate wrote her an encouraging letter, stating that she was welcome to stay if the "storks" allowed her to make it through the July rating book. New York made it clear that if she got bored at home, she was welcome back at any time. No questions asked!

* * *

Trisha was still stranded in Birmingham, waiting patiently for Taft Broadcasting to promote her. One of the country's great broadcasting companies, Taft was sold for scrap as the Bass Brothers sold all the assets. She needed to bail out so when Vanessa telephoned about an opening in San Francisco, she jumped on it and called that same day. The general sales manager of KGO-TV, the ABC affiliate, agreed to an interview, so she flew in at her own expense the next day.

She already had an airplane ticket because she was attending Vanessa's surprise baby shower held on the KPIX news set. Everyone from the engineers and cameramen to the on-air talent offered unsolicited advice on video. Hilariously, they used their own baby pictures as they talked on camera. Produced with music and credits at the end for effect, it ran on every television monitor in the studio. Chipping in, the department bought an electric breast pump just in case she wanted to come back to hard news but needed to keep up her milk supply. Highlighted by dual suction cups, the state-of-the-art machine could pump both breasts at once to achieve more milk production. The station's art department created milk cartons with Vanessa's picture on the front with "Vaughn's Dairy" typed in broad letters. It was the most creative party and gift that she and Trisha had ever witnessed. Touched by their effort and generosity, she had mixed emotions. She hated to leave but did want to stay home with her new baby. And Trisha's walking into the news set was Vanessa's biggest surprise and best present.

* * *

As they drove along after the shower, Trisha asked, "How's the old man taking it?"

"Once I gained twenty pounds, he quit touching me physically."

"You mean no sex?" she asked curiously.

"He finds fat women repugnant, and I am now officially in that category."

"That's weird. You're pregnant for God's sake. Every woman gains weight!"

"He won't even touch my stomach to feel the baby move. That's how turned off he is."

"You're kidding! What an ass!"

"He has made three trips to Europe to play golf. Upon his return, he hands me pamphlets from every fat farm in California. The minute the baby comes roaring out, he expects me to go to one. Oh, and I forgot to tell you. My added punishment is that he will not sleep in the master suite with me. I take up all the bed, and he can't sleep because I go to the bathroom too much."

"What a prince!"

"How did your interview go?"

"I think the sales manager was about as thrilled with me as Tod is with you. When you've been in sales as long as I have, you know when you click. The good news is that the general manager came wandering in, and we instantly hit it off. We know a lot of the same people in Washington DC. If he were in charge on this one, I'd be starting tomorrow."

"I could get our general manager to call on your behalf," Vanessa offered.

"No way! Either he wants me, or he doesn't. I'm a big girl, and KGO isn't the only station left in the country. Do you consider Chicago the United States?"

Vanessa ran a yellow light and exclaimed, "Too cold and too far away from me!"

"WGN-TV has an opening, but I'm such a wimpy Southern gal that I don't know if I could take those winters. Imagine how many cars I could wreck in that snow!"

"I'd love for you to live here."

"Me too! This place is like paradise. Hey, maybe I'll even find a man here!"

"You can have mine." She pulled into the gated entrance that opened electronically.

As they drove up to the exclusive estate, Trisha's eyes widened in disbelief. "Look at this joint. How bad could it be to put up with this guy? You can't imagine some of the losers that I have tolerated over the years without money who lived in basements!"

* * *

Trisha didn't get that job, but a month later, KGO's management brought her out at their expense. Their sales staff had been raided by another station, and in their desperation to get salespeople out on the street, Trisha was treated completely differently this time. The sales manager greeted her and cheerfully announced they booked her at the swanky Fairmont Hotel. After a personal guided tour of the station, they took her to the Waterfront Restaurant. Mesmerized by Treasure Island and the Bay Bridge, she thought, *I want this job. I'd pay them!*

The restaurant's cozy little bar was situated to the right of the main dining floor with its snug and homey atmosphere. After a couple of cocktails, the managers started to loosen up, and Trisha reminded herself to go easy on the alcohol. She ordered her favorite dish, crab cakes, and throughout dinner, the two men kept commenting about a couple who were making out in the bar. She didn't bother to turn around when they cracked. "Why don't they get a hotel room? They are about to do it!" With this job on the line, she couldn't get excited about a couple making a spectacle of themselves in public.

* * *

When the general manager asked for the check, she bolted for the bathroom to give them a few minutes alone to discuss her employment. As she approached the bar, she saw Tod was the other part of the couple that the two men had been commenting about all evening. A stunningly beautiful blonde dressed to perfection sat beside him. A miniskirt and high heels exposed shapely legs, and her plunging neckline revealed a large bosom. Obviously, she was some type of high fashion model. Trisha had never seen a woman that foxy and alluring except in magazines. Tod had one hand between her thighs as she kept her legs tightly crossed. A high heel shoe bounced off the end of her toes as she wiggled one foot while his fingers wandered down her neck to touch her breasts. She gurgled with delight as he roamed her upper torso. Trisha stood there frozen. Mortified, she walked right past them to the bathroom as her heart pounded. Wanting to go for Tod's throat, she couldn't create a scene when she was persuading these men to hire her.

In a boiling rage, she approached the bathroom mirror and took a deep breath to calm down her horrible temper. Extremely upset, she emerged from the restroom and stomped straight up to Tod. Only inches separated her body from his when she blurted out, "Don't you think you should be home with your pregnant wife just in case her water breaks?"

Completely unfazed by her presence, Tod made no attempt to take his hands off the woman. "A pleasure to see you again, Trisha. Call next time you're in town."

"Listen up, you pond scum. Get your buns back home to your spouse, who is carrying your child." Her loud voice rose in anger. "She's only a week away from delivery."

He knocked his drink over on purpose, and it fell on Trisha's dress, soaking through to her bra. "Cool off, bitch, and go back under that rock from which you came."

She slapped him across the face. "You're the worst male whore. You will rot in hell."

* * *

Everyone at the Waterfront stared at the scene she had just caused. She knew it meant she would not get the job that she desperately wanted. Sitting down at the table, she quickly used the linen napkin to dry her dress. "So, gentlemen, do I have the job or not?"

Taken aback by her bluntness and the obvious uproar she had just been involved in, the sales manager replied, "We're not prepared to make an offer, at this time."

"When will you be prepared? I've flown out here twice."

"How do you know Tod Von Westerkamp?" the general manager interrupted.

"I was the maiden of honor in his wedding."

"How in the world do you know that family?" he asked.

"Vanessa Vaughn happens to be my oldest and dearest friend. I'd like to take this knife and cut his heart out." She had picked one off the table for effect.

"We should have called you when her last contract was close to expiring. We've tried to get her on our news team for years. Vanessa Vaughn is a phenomenal talent."

"And so am I. You should hire me," she boldly boasted.

"I couldn't agree more. Quit procrastinating on this decision, Bill. You've already interviewed half of the salespeople on the West Coast. Let's give this young lady a shot," he ordered. "What's happening over there?" he asked as his underling's face turned bright red in anger. "You came back a tad wet."

"I just suggested that he might want to go home and practice being a husband since he's a week away from becoming a father. Would you gentlemen mind if I have another vodka tonic?"

"This is not a good town to cross a Von Westerkamp," he observed while ignoring his sulking subordinate across the table.

"I don't care. There is nothing that he can do to me."

"I moved here from ABC Spot Sales in New York, and I have been amazed at the power that family wields in this city. Plus their son has never held a job. His main occupation is women and plenty of them. His lifestyle is the envy of men. Did your friend really think he'd change?"

"Vanessa is extremely naive about men. She focused on her career and completely bypassed the dating game." The waiter placed her mixed drink down.

"Is it true that she plans on staying home with her child?"

"Yes, she wants to become a full-time mother and not miss those precious infant years."

"If she ever wants to come back into the business, we're a great company to work for."

"I know. That's why I have flown out here twice. I want to be at an ABC O and O."

"We would love to have you on our team. Right, Bill?" He slapped him on the back. "It's terrific that you are currently at an ABC affiliate. You are already up to speed on the ABC lineup. This is a major market, and we don't roll over for these media queens. We go for rate and share, getting it on our terms. Listen, I really need to run. The wife gets anxious after I've been out five nights in a row. Bill, I'll leave the financial arrangements up to you to negotiate. It's been a real pleasure, Trisha. Let Miss Vaughn know that we are interested in her anytime. Tell her I am a huge fan and would love to see her on my news staff." He stood up and left.

She turned around and noted that Tod and the blonde were gone. The sales manager was less than cordial after his boss left. "I reiterate that your salary requirements are too high."

"You get what you pay for, and I'm well worth it!"

* * *

After the sales manager bid her good night and was safely out of sight, she went to the public telephone. She left a message at the news desk to tell Vanessa she was on the way and not to leave until she got there. Walking outside, she took a deep breath and inhaled the cool night air. At a very brisk pace, she passed the piers along the city's waterfront until she realized that she had missed Broadway completely and had to double back. The walk was difficult in her high heels until she arrived at the station's lobby.

* * *

She sat down on the sofa to rest her feet as the security guard called upstairs. Glancing up at the television monitor, Vanessa and her male anchor were doing their usual chitchat ending. Music started to play, as the credits rolled by.

Minutes later, Vanessa greeted her. "What in the world are you doing here, Trisha?"

"I have a brainstorm," she gushed enthusiastically. "Come spend the night with me at the Fairmont. I got upgraded to a suite since they were sold out. What do you think?"

"Weird idea. How did the interview go?"

"The general manager forced his sales manager to hire me, which should make for a very unpleasant work situation. But who cares? I get the hell out of Birmingham. I've gone through every available man in that town. It's time to move on and let the West Coast men have a shot!" She followed her friend into her office.

Vanessa plopped down into the chair behind her desk and punched the button to put the call on the speakerphone. Tod's voice echoed throughout the room. "I'm down in San Jose and won't make it back tonight. I didn't want you to wait up."

"OK, sweetie, thanks for calling." Vanessa clicked it off and looked up. "It's a crazy idea, but I do have my suitcase packed for the hospital in the trunk of my car. So why not? We can stay up all night gossiping like the old days. Let's go!"

"Where is Mr. Tod?"

"Down in San Jose playing in a golf tournament."

"Shouldn't he be staying closer to home for the big event?"

"I have mixed emotions about him being in the delivery room since he missed all the Lamaze classes. I spent my time practicing the breathing with the teacher. It's his loss, not mine."

* * *

Trisha knew fate placed her in town to protect Vanessa. At the Fairmont, they got undressed and ordered room service. Her friend had an entire meal, while she only drank cocktails. Staying up all night talking and laughing, she never revealed that Tod was with another woman. They giggled until dawn and finally fell asleep.

In the middle of a terrible nightmare when her wake-up call rang, she was inside the delivery room when a very Black baby with a huge afro came out from between Vanessa's legs. During the bizarre fantasy, all the nurses and doctors gathered around to gawk at the infant with a large head of kinky hair. Moving quietly, she showered and dressed for her KGO-TV appointment. Vanessa was sleeping peacefully as she took a large gulp of her leftover vodka tonic sitting on the nightstand.

* * *

At the elevator, the forcefully difficult image was so real, so graphic, and so frightening. She took a cab to KGO-TV and barely made it through the salary negotiations. Her haunted mind could not let go of this powerful illusion. Afterward, she rushed to the hotel.

* * *

As the entered the suite, Vanessa announced. "Great timing! I ordered two full breakfasts with lots of bacon. It will be here any minute. Sorry, no grits! This is San Francisco room service. How in the world did you get up? I couldn't budge. It was my best night's sleep in nine months."

"Sounds great," she lied. "I'll need a couple of pots of coffee to make it to the airport." They enjoyed each other's company until Trisha caught her flight back East.

* * *

The next night, Vanessa's water broke. Her contractions started out mildly but soon became very painful and intense with five-minute intervals. Staying on her feet throughout the night, she kept a tight grip on the back of a kitchen chair and focused on her breathing. At five o'clock in the morning, she awoke Tod, and he helped her into his brand-new Bentley. She kept a death grip on the door handle as he sped to the emergency room entrance.

* * *

A nice man in a white coat helped her into a wheelchair and pushed her up to the delivery floor. Her private suite had hardwood floors, decorator furniture, and a Jacuzzi tub overlooking the bay. The attending nurse gave her a pelvic exam and said she was six centimeters dilated. The technician hooked her up to an infant heart monitor, which displayed the intensity of the contractions and its effect on the heart rate of the fetus. She stood up during the contractions and held tightly to the machine. Mesmerized by the baby's heart rate, Tod was quite attentive to his wife, who was in excruciating pain. After five hours of unbearable contractions, the nurse told her to push. After pushing for three solid hours, Doctor Wang was paged, and twenty minutes later, she pushed the baby out.

Doctor Wang congratulated Tod as she handed him a tiny little baby boy covered with blood and other substances. The nurses whisked him away for a series of tests before placing him under a heat lamp. Vanessa was in a pool of sweat as Tod muttered, "Good work, ladies." The nurses looked at him with absolute disdain as he got on the phone to call his golfing buddies. Every time he put down the receiver, she reminded him to call Trisha, but he completely ignored his wife. All wrapped up in a beautiful blanket that Suzanne had ordered the staff to use, the infant had a tiny cotton cap on his head and was sound asleep when Vanessa took him into her arms. She studied his minuscule face and tried to decide who he looked like, but he was so tiny, she did not recognize anyone. After glazing at his face for a long time, she gently uncovered his toes and wiggled his big toe. He made a face that scared her, so she quickly put the wrap back. His creamy colored skin had light red patches while his thick black hair was odd for a newborn.

The door swung open, and the nurse told her to try to breast feed. The nurse positioned his mouth on her breast, and he slowly latched on and started to suck.

"Remember," the nurse lectured, "babies do not get the milk simply by taking the nipple into their mouth and sucking. Milk is formed in the glandular tissue, and then it passes through small ducts toward the center of the breast, where it collects in sinuses. These storage spaces are in a circle right behind the areola, the dark area around the nipple. A short duct leads from each sinus through the nipple to the outside. When your little guy is nursing properly, all the areolas should be in his mouth. His gums need to squeeze the sinuses, which forces the milk through your nipple and into his mouth. If your baby takes only the nipple into his mouth, he will get almost no milk. If he starts to chew on the nipple, take your finger and break the suction. If you don't, you will get a blister."

"Thank you," she answered meekly as her mother-in-law burst into the room.

"What in the world are you doing to my grandson?" Suzanne blurted out as she grabbed the newborn, who had an impressive grip on his mother's nipple. Vanessa screamed out in agony as she pulled on him while his mouth kept a firm lock on her tender breast.

"Let go!" She broke the suction by placing her finger in the corner of his mouth as the door swung open, and Tod walked in with his father. Suzanne took the infant into her arms.

Alexander studied his grandson's face. "Brett is pure Von Westerkamp," he announced.

"You really should comb your hair. People will be coming by," Tod ordered.

"Excuse me, where did you get that name?" She was incredulous he hadn't consulted her.

"Listening to the Giants game on the way here, I decided to name him after my favorite."

Vanessa sat straight up. "Name our son after a baseball player? I don't think so, Tod."

"Now, hear me out. You wanted him named after Charleston's Rhett Butler. It's a great opportunity for compromise. Brett is close to Rhett. You get what you want; I get what I want."

"It sounds to me like you get what you want, Tod." She was very annoyed.

"I love it, Tod!" Suzanne sided with her son as always.

"Me too, son," Alexander chimed in, nodding in agreement.

"Well, I guess it's three to one. Surprise, surprise!"

"It's settled. Brett it is! My golfing buddies said breast feeding will make him queer."

"I demand two t's, at least." She ignored his last statement.

"OK, two t's, it is." Tod nodded.

"What is this silliness with breast feeding? My friends tell me it is pure poison."

"Suzanne, we have gone over this before," she argued. "Babies receive immunity to a variety of infections through the colostrum, the fluid that comes in before the real milk."

"You're the only one I know who believes this nonsense."

"The milk is pure," the nurse interrupted. "Your grandson can't catch an intestinal infection from it. Be happy she has chosen to breast feed; it gives Rhett a great advantage."

"What about your figure?" Suzanne ignored the nurse.

"We should let the new mother rest now." The nurse politely ordered them to leave. The Von Westerkamps complied but took little Brett with them as she leaned back and fell asleep.

* * *

After Vanessa's discharge from the hospital, she returned home to be greeted by a new chef, a personal trainer, and a gym. Tod hired them, mirrored the basement, and installed state-of-the-art weight machines and life cycles. She ignored her husband and the trainer. Instead, she put Brett in his stroller and pushed him as far as she could. Since she was breast feeding, all she needed was a supply of diapers to stay gone. Eventually, she was able to push Brett for three miles. As he grew bigger, she breast-fed him against Suzanne's wishes. Tod took little interest in his infant child. He only talked about the day when Brett could hold a golf club in his hands.

To her amazement, she did not miss the television business at all. On rare occasions when she watched her old newscast, she found it to be terribly depressing. Refusing to hire a nanny, she found Tod spending a lot of time away from their mansion. By Christmas, she was back to her prenatal weight and agreed to attend society functions.

Meanwhile, Trisha settled into her job at KGO-TV, and the sales manager who reluctantly hired her thought she was a terrific salesperson. As the only woman on the sales staff, she told Vanessa all the gossip about the current intrigue in the television industry.

* * *

On Brett's first birthday, Suzanne insisted on a huge bash. Absurdly, she invited over two hundred people to the party at her estate. Since the August weather was unpredictable, she had large canopies placed over outdoor tables for a sit-down, eight-course lunch. Live ponies brought in for the children to ride frightened little Brett, as did the four performing clowns and a man in a Superman costume. Brett fell asleep and managed to miss most of the affair.

While he slept, Suzanne proceeded to bring all her friends in to see her new grandson as well as the lavish nursery she had put in at her own mansion. Persevering through another ridiculous and auspicious social function, the two women only agreed upon their undying adoration for the baby.

Tod refused to travel with an infant so he went alone to Europe often. His complete detachment from his son baffled Vanessa, as it seemed he had no paternal instincts. All those years being shipped away to boarding schools appeared to have taken their toll. Ironically, they both had similar childhoods with one exception. No one had loved him while Vanessa had Sister Rosalie's unconditional love. Though she was now very thin, Tod paid no attention to her. She was so wrapped up in the first year of her son's life that she didn't give it much thought.

CHAPTER TWENTY

Eighteen months old, Brett woke up noticeably short of breath and in severe pain. Their chauffeur rushed them to the hospital, where Brett's pediatrician met them in the examining room. The concerned physician ordered a series of tests and instructed Vanessa to head down to the lab. The Von Westerkamp's received royal treatment at this hospital since they were its largest financial benefactors. Two orderlies greeted her with a wheelchair as she held her baby boy tightly on her lap. In the laboratory, the technician took blood from the screaming child as he fought hard to breathe, and his young face turned a pale blue. Gasping for air, he was rushed to pediatrics. Two pediatricians entered and talked in medical lingo that she did not understand. His inordinate amount of pain grieved her as she prayed silently for his recovery.

Doctor North, the chief administrator of the hospital, appeared. He was a close friend of Alexander's, and her father-in-law had donated generously to fund their expansion plans for additional buildings. He attended all their dinner parties and played golf regularly with Alexander. "Don't worry. Little Brett will receive the best medical care in the world here."

"Thank you, Doctor North. Do you have any idea what is wrong?"

"When the lab results are back, I've ordered them to be put on my desk. I will personally be involved in this case. Also, I've taken the liberty of calling Alex, who was about to tee off at the Olympic Club. I was playing too until the board called a last-minute meeting. Where's Tod?"

"Will you have the results soon?"

"Yes. As soon as I know the results, so will you," Dr. North replied. "Where's Tod?"

"At the Silverado Country Club in Napa Valley playing in a tournament."

"I'll give him a call. Now relax. Everything is going to be fine." He left abruptly. For once, she was grateful for the connections of their family name. Ironically, Alexander was the one on the way during this medical crisis. He kept Brett at arm's length. He seemed so disinterested in touching or holding his grandson. Tod mentioned he had been treated the same way. She was relieved that Suzanne had not been called because she would have been hysterical.

She stayed by her son's bedside as he fought the vicious assault that the staff found so mysterious. His curly black hair was wet with sweat and perspiration, and his dark charcoal eyes had an intense look as he gasped for air. A stern-looking nurse took Brett's temperature and his blood pressure and informed Vanessa he had an extremely high fever. Then, she brought in a breathing machine used for childhood asthma, which helped him catch his breath. She remembered Suzanne had said asthma ran in her family, so maybe this was an asthma attack.

* * *

Alexander Von Westerkamp parked his Rolls Royce right next to a huge 'No Parking' sign. Strolling inside, he completely ignored an attendant who told him to move his car and took the elevator to the top floor which opened into a huge suite of plushy-decorated offices. "Hello, Mr. Von Westerkamp. Doctor North is in the lab and wanted me to page him the minute you arrived. May I get you a cup of coffee?" The secretary stood in front of him, but he completely ignored her. "Let me show you into Doctor North's office, where you will be more comfortable." Staying cheerful, she didn't react to his harsh demeanor and opened the massive double doors where an engraved brass name plate read, "Doctor Richard P. North, Chief Administrator." His massive office had a wet bar with tall stools in one corner and a solid oak conference table with ten chairs that faced the city view. Behind his large desk were bookshelves and a credenza with a large sofa to the side. "Are you sure that there isn't something I can get for you, Mr. Von Westerkamp?" He treated all employees with disdain from a lifetime of believing that people like this secretary were beneath him. "Please don't hesitate to let me know,' she said after he repeatedly failed to respond. Before she shut the doors, Alexander went to the wet bar, reached for a crystal decanter filled with one-hundred-year-old scotch, and poured himself a glass. At the window, he glanced down at the traffic caused by his double-parked Rolls Royce. Finishing his drink quickly, he poured another as the enormous doors swung open, and Doctor North appeared. "Better make yourself a double. I have some very disturbing news that cannot be sugarcoated."

"What's up, Doc? I don't take my golf game being interrupted lightly."

"Your grandson is in sickle-cell crisis."

"What the hell, I thought sickle cell was a Negro disease."

"Sickle cell disease, also called sickle cell anemia, is a hereditary blood disease that occurs chiefly among Blacks. Attacks include severe pain, high fever, and damage to body tissues. Your grandson is experiencing a classic sickle cell anemia crisis." His clinical manner stunned Alexander into silence as he started his third glass of scotch. "Sickle cell anemia occurs if both parent's red blood cells contain too many hemoglobin molecules of an abnormal type. Hemoglobin gives the red blood cells their color and carries the oxygen to the body tissues. Too much of the abnormal hemoglobin, called hemoglobin S, causes the cells to sickle. The sickle cell shape clogs blood vessels, interferes with blood flow and deprives the body of oxygen which causes a painful attack called a crisis. That's happening to Brett at this moment."

"Cut to the chase, Rick! Stop the bull crap. Are you saying that my grandson is a nigger?"

"Most anthropologists today reject the idea that human beings can be divided into biologically defined races."

"You are touting yourself as an anthropologist?" Belligerently, he put his scotch down.

"Look, Alex! Children inherit half their genes from their father and half from their mother. Scientists have found that carriers of the sickling gene have a higher resistance to malaria, a dangerous disease transmitted by certain mosquitoes. Sickle cell anemia is a rare disorder, but it occurs more often among populations of western Africa and the Caribbean, most of whom live in areas threatened by malaria. Thus, the sickling gene, despite its negative effects, represents an important advantage for people in these areas."

"Rick, you only use this much double talk at a board meeting when you've spent too much of the hospital's money. Now talk in English that I can understand."

"I have a strong suspicion that Vanessa is an African American. All the scientific proof points to that conclusion," Doctor North said affirmatively.

"What proof?" he asked skeptically.

"An estimated sixty thousand American Blacks suffer from the disease, and another 2.5 million carry the HbS gene. She's Black. I'd bet my medical license on it."

"That's impossible! Tod checked her out through a private investigator. He even saw her parents' death certificates," he lied as the alcohol clouded his memory.

"Both her parents were Black for her to carry this gene. The PI screwed up. He blew it."

"You're saying that the little baby boy is going to grow up to be a big Black buck?"

"Who knows what he's going to look like at twenty, but I guarantee he is half Black!"

"Rick, I always thought you were a quack."

"There is one more issue. Tod must be a gene carrier or has the trait."

"What?"

"If one parent has sickle cell anemia and the other has sickle cell trait, there is a 50 percent risk that their children will have sickle cell anemia."

"I can't believe you are spouting this malarkey. There are no nigger genes in my family."

"It's a blood disease and if I tested Tod's blood, he would have sickle cell trait."

"Impossible!"

"Listen to me, Alex. Two genes for the sickle hemogloblin must be inherited from both parents in order to have the disease. It has proven to be a recessive gene so Tod's gene must be very, very recessive. Large amounts of melanin in the skin help to protect it from sunburn and thus reduce the risk of skin cancer. Dark pigment in the eyes improves vision in bright sunlight. Look at your grandson's coloring, dark eyes, and dark hair. Miss Vanessa has some powerful genes that have rampaged through to your grandson. I never drink during the day, but I think I'll make an exception. Pour me a double on the rocks."

"Just cover this up like you do when Suzanne is admitted to the psychiatric unit?"

"I don't know, Alex. That really would be tough." He took his stiff drink and gulped it.

"Imagine if the press gets wind of this? I'll be ruined in this town. Listen, Rick, old buddy, let me remind you about the time that you operated after too many highballs. I pulled every political string I had to keep that MD behind your name. Not to mention how I highhandedly keep you in this plush job when the board raises their ugly little heads."

"Alex, it won't do any good to cover this up. The next time that kid has a crisis, any two-bit lab tech will figure it out. The machine will flag it as abnormal, and the technician will look at the blood smear under a microscope. The cells are sickled, and it's in the chart."

"I will not be made the laughingstock when some big nigger teenager rides around the city with corn rows in his kinky hair. Make this go away like when Suzanne is locked up in your psych unit. Doc, my son never had the sickle cell gene, understood? It was your medical error."

"Alex, you are not thinking clearly. Listen to yourself!"

"You don't get it, do you? I'm not negotiating here. Just take care of the records. I'll take care of that Black bitch and the little Black bastard she produced. Clear on this? Understand?"

"Alex, you don't understand! Many victims of this disease die in childhood, and few live past the age of forty. The odds are not in Brett's favor."

"And they just have gotten a whole lot worse!"

"What are you saying?"

"Rick, let me worry about that. Just cover your ass, and make sure it looks like this sickle crap never happened. Change the diagnosis, and you'll be fine."

"Alex, I won't be a party to this. Changing a medical record and purging the results is as far as I go. Prison gray does not suit me. Pay her to go away like all the others in Tod's life."

"Who knows about this?" Alexander's mind suddenly became more focused.

"Right now, only the laboratory technician who read the blood smear."

"He needs to disappear," he commanded.

"For God's sake, she's a thirty-year veteran of this hospital."

"Get rid of her. Offer her early retirement."

"Calm down. Let's worry about the record first." Doctor North signed on to his computer while Alexander stood behind him. As a systems administrator, it allowed him file maintenance access privilege to the results database. Using the HEX editor to flip the bites, he changed the results to negative and ordered a printout at the Pediatrics Nursing Station, indicating pneumococcal sepsis. It specified the presence of pathogenic organisms or their toxins in the blood, and no longer showed the sickled cells. All indications now pointed to the intravenous administration of a Claforan antibiotic, plus some liquid Tylenol with codeine for pain.

"So, what did you do?" He slurred his words, now on his fifth scotch.

"I changed the indications to enable them to treat him, so he will not be in pain. There is no reason for this child to suffer. This course of action will give him some relief."

"A correction is in order. You aren't as much of a quack as I thought."

"I used my administrator privilege to change the computer's hard disk. Old records are loaded onto a magnetic tape for storage, so these will become the permanent ones."

"You aren't forgetting anything?" Alex asked impatiently.

"No, I was at the ward's machine when Brett's chart printed out. I ripped it off myself."

"Did anyone see you?"

"No, the nurses were trying to appear busy and efficient. As head of this hospital they wouldn't even dare to look in my direction or remotely question my interest in their printer."

"That's why you're the boss," he quipped sarcastically.

"Alex, think about this rationally when you aren't drinking and making wild statements. You are scaring the hell out of me. Calm down. Proceed with utmost caution. That's his son."

"Tod could care less about the little bastard. He's spending less time with that little brat than I did with him.

"And Miss Vanessa?"

"The honeymoon is over. He's screwing every broad he can get his hands on."

"God, I envy him." Doctor North licked his lips.

"Once Tod finds out that she sold him down the river, that nigger bitch will be headed downstream herself. My son must never know about your quack blood diagnosis, Doc. Never!"

* * *

His secretary knocked, and Tod barged in. "Interrupt my game? I just got a hole-in-one. Can't this hospital handle one little sick kid? Or is this a ploy to get another wing from us?"

"There's a slight problem with your little bride. She's as Black as the ace of spades."

"What is your belly full of scotch saying exactly?" Tod looked perplexed.

"You married a nigger, son," Alexander said angrily. "And you bred one too!"

"Doctor North?" Arrogantly, he ignored his father.

"Tod, Brett is in sickle cell crisis, a genetically inherited disease which afflicts one in four hundred African Americans. Vanessa is a member of the Negroid race," Doctor North explained.

"That's impossible!" He blurted out combatively. "No way, her hair is silkier than mine!"

"Start believing it. You'll have a big Black son running around with Von Westerkamp behind his first name. Face it, son: you screwed up again. It will be hard to bail you out."

"Who knows?" Tod banged his hand on the desk with hostility.

"Through the miracle of modern medicine, no one." Alexander chuckled.

"Doctor North?"

"Don't worry, son. I've taken care of everything," he answered quickly.

"How in the world did you do that? Doesn't this hospital have any operating procedures?"

"Tod, let's just call it a privilege of high office." He sipped his scotch.

"Well, frankly, I'd like a second opinion," Tod quipped.

"Like hell you do! I will not be the laughingstock of this city. Is that clear to you, son?"

"What's the plan, Dad, a one-way ticket back to Mozambique?"

Suddenly, Alexander broke into uncontrollable laughter as Doctor North and Tod both stared, stunned by his behavior. "Son, all the gold-digging broads that you have been with, and you picked the mulatto who is parading around as White. The orphan story was very convenient, I must say. I can't wait to see the photographs that the media produces with all our South Carolina cousins. Buck and Buck, Junior. Poor little orphan Vanessa. No family, my ass! Her relatives will crawl out of the woodwork, waiting to spring the good news on us for money."

"Dad, get a grip! What have you guys done with them?" Tod showed no emotion.

"Nothing. They are in pediatrics right now. Sickle cells tend to clog up capillary blood vessels, impede blood flow, and produce pain in bones, muscles, and the abdomen. Treatment involves pain relievers and antibiotics, which is what your son is getting to pull him through."

"Precisely, how did you pull this off?"

"I used my administrator security clearance to change the record. Now, the diagnosis will tell the pediatrician what to prescribe. Brett will get through this crisis in a few days and should be fine." Doctor North proceeded to answer all of Tod's questions concerning sickle cell crisis, and he no longer had any doubts about Vanessa's true race. "Son," Doctor North offered his opinion, "you will never convince me that she was unaware of her racial heritage. She knew."

"I get the big picture, Doctor North."

"Yeah, well, it's too bad that you did not get the big picture before you got us into this mess," Alex interjected. "I wonder if that Black bitch was screwing some big Black buck, Tod? Maybe the little bastard isn't even yours! Orphan, my ass!"

"You need to get down to pediatrics to see them," Doctor North advised.

"I don't want to see her Black ass." Tod reacted belligerently to the verbal torment.

"Rick's right, son. Get down there, and act like the concerned father that you aren't."

"I can't stomach looking at the whore." Tod blinked his eyes in disgust.

"I'll make sure that you won't look at her much longer. Right now, you need to portray the distraught, concerned father. Understood? We don't want to raise any suspicions."

"Yeah, I'll be the devoted father!" Tod disappeared through the immense double doors.

"Don't do anything illegal. There are worse things than an interracial marriage."

"Easy for you to say; you are not in my position."

"Alex, just pay her off."

"Rick, people disappear all the time."

"My involvement stops here and now." Doctor North knew exactly how ruthless Alex was, mowing down his business rivals with glee, destroying their lives, and bragging about it afterward on the golf course.

"You are up to your neck in this already, Rick. Besides, no one is asking you to kill anyone. You do that all too well on the operating table, legitimately."

"Nobody is going to die, Alex. Pay her to go away, just like that Polynesian woman Tod was involved with years ago that you had vanish."

"Just make sure that there are no leaks inside this hospital. Understood?"

"There won't be. I haven't been practicing medicine for forty years for nothing."

"I'd better go, since there are some people I need to call." Alexander got off the bar stool.

"Go by pediatrics. It looks strange if you leave before seeing your seriously ill grandson."

"Yes, the dutiful grandfather will arrive and put on quite a show. Count on that!"

* * *

When Tod arrived on the pediatrics ward, he winked at the buxom blonde in her much-too-tight nursing uniform. He flung open the door to his son's plush private room. Vanessa was caressing her son's hand, which now had an I.V. Tod went to the crib and studied his son's face. The infant's eyes were shut, but Tod knew that Richard North was right when he referenced racial facial characteristics. His crazy mother claimed that Brett was all Von Westerkamp, but none of his son's features were like his. The toddler's skin was a dark olive color, and his hair had an endless array of tight black curls. There was not one curl on anyone's hair on both sides of his family. Tod stood there, void of any compassion, as he examined the boy's face.

Their pediatrician entered with Alexander. Tod had never met him before since he remained uninvolved and had never bothered to go to his son's check-ups. "Oh, I'm glad you are both here," the pediatrician announced. "I have the lab results back, and little Brett here is going to be fine." As he explained the diagnosis and the necessary therapy involved, Vanessa asked an endless stream of questions that he patiently answered.

Alex chimed in. "Hey, Doc! I want the best medical care for my first-born grandson."

"Don't you worry. Our specialty is pleasing grandparents," the pediatrician answered.

The minute their performance was over, Tod and his father left together. Vanessa thought, *That it was very strange*, since they didn't speak to her. But at least they came by and interrupted their golf games, which was a true sacrifice for them. *In their own distorted way, they must care.*

* * *

Trisha came by after work and stayed until visiting hours were over. Vanessa felt very relieved and looked forward to her visits. As Brett got better, they joked and laughed like the old times. Her marriage was at the point where Tod never spoke to her, and her friend was her only companion in whom she could confide. Looking forward to going home, she was happy to leave such a sterile environment. Tod called and told her to come up to Alexander's Big Sur beach house. It was a very strange request since it was well known that his father had his extramarital trysts there. Plus, she didn't like the idea of Brett going to a house that he did not know. She thought it would be better for him to be in his own bedroom and surrounded by familiar things. But Tod was adamant that she come when Brett was discharged. Against her better judgment, she relented and agreed to go because she was emotionally drained and could not argue with him.

* * *

Doctor North broke into a cold sweat after he learned of Brett's imminent discharge. Knowing this was headed for trouble, he felt powerless to stop Alexander, a cold-blooded and vicious man who was completely immoral and callous. Alexander demanded tyrannical control over his empire that Vanessa had now invaded. He knew she would experience a cruel and brutal fate and shuddered at the thought of what evil would befall her and her infant son.

CHAPTER TWENTY-ONE

Trisha arrived to take her godson home, and an orderly rolled the toddler into the parking lot. The wheelchair zigzagged slightly, and Brett gurgled with delight. Trisha offered to drive them to the Big Sur beach house, so Tod had his brand-new Range Rover delivered to the hospital. He told Vanessa it would be a safer vehicle on the sharp turns and steep cliffs along the Pacific Coast Highway. Playing singing games with Brett, she entered the freeway as the toddler squealed with joy and tried to hum along. Vanessa smiled happily as she watched the silhouette of the brown hills against the darkened sky. Brett was healthy again, and her best friend was here, which meant this would be a fun trip.

"Hey, Vanessa! I bought this. Paul McCartney is singing 'Mary, Mary Had a Lamb.'"

"That was so sweet of you," Vanessa replied as she turned on the inside light to read the label. "Oh, wow, Little Richard doing 'Itsy Bitsy Spider.'"

"It's great, huh, and I had an excuse to buy it." She laughed. "By the way, does Toddy expect me to drive back to San Francisco tonight?"

"Who cares? He should have picked us up from the hospital. You're staying."

"Yeah, another dateless Saturday night. I'm having a string of them lately, the worst run I've had in years," she joked. "I've never been to Big Sur, and I am positively dying to see it."

"The rugged coastline is breathtakingly scenic, but the rocky cliffs cascade straight down to the sea. Drive slowly! This is not a flat South Carolina swamp."

"I am not going to drive like a typical TV time salesperson when my godson is in the car." Trisha snapped her fingers to the music. "Sit back and relax."

Brett's drowsy eyes slowly closed, and he fell asleep in his car seat beside his mother. Vanessa glanced at the clear yet somber February evening as a plane's lights flashed in the sky.

Hours later, they stopped at a small roadside diner. Vanessa got a table while Trisha went across the street to get gas. A pickup truck pulled up next to her at the gas pump. "Hey," the driver yelled out of his filthy vehicle, "I was behind you, and you're leaking oil bad." She felt uncomfortable because the shadowy stranger appeared to come from the tough side of town. "Want me to look? I'm a mechanic." He offered his credentials.

Trisha hesitated and then mumbled, "OK."

She kept pumping gas while he crawled under the car. His actions struck her as being very odd, so she decided to leave immediately. Placing the nozzle back on the pump, she quickly went inside to pay the cashier. The grubby man was still underneath the Range Rover when she returned. "Find anything wrong?" she inquired as she bent down to look.

"Nope, looks fine. Didn't mean to scare you. Live around here?" He pushed himself out.

"No, just passing through," she uttered as she slammed the door shut and locked it. Concerned, her blue eyes watched him in the rearview mirror. Cautiously, she drove around the block instead of going straight to the diner and parked in back.

* * *

"What happened to you?" Vanessa asked as she finally slid into the booth.

"Another male encounter of the weirdo kind. I wish for once when a guy tries to pick me up, he's at least taken a bath and has at least one front tooth! Did you order?

"Yeah, the bacon and eggs sounded great."

"Better to stick to the basics in a place like this." She motioned to the stuffed shark on the wall as Brett ripped open a packet, and sugar soared into the air and layered the tabletop.

* * *

After dinner, Vanessa said, "Gee, it's already after eleven. I'd better call Tod." When she returned, they piled into the car for the last portion of the drive to the exclusive Von Westerkamp beach estate. After Carmel, they entered the steep and winding Pacific Coast Highway. The sheer cliffs and narrow lanes were scary, but Trisha calmly maneuvered the car along this frightening stretch of road. "Don't worry, Brett won't get a chill. I'm turning the heat on full blast so I can open the sunroof for fresh air to help me stay awake. It's been a long week at the station."

Vanessa recognized a landmark indicating Big Sur was ten miles away. "Another five miles. You can't miss it. When you see massive trees, stop. That's where the gated entrance is."

She glanced in the rearview mirror at her exhausted friend, who was soundly asleep, and Brett's head rested peacefully against his car seat. The winding road was mostly deserted as she ejected the children's compact disc and replaced it with the Beatles. While she hummed along with the music, she tried to concentrate on driving along the extremely dangerous curves. She remembered that her father always had cautioned her not to ride the brakes on steep terrain, so she consciously avoided using the brake pedal. When she did hit the brakes, she felt like they slipped but decided that it must be her wild imagination at work on these steep cliffs.

* * *

At the next curve, Trisha slammed her foot on the pedal, and nothing happened. Instead, the car gained momentum. In desperation, she looked down at the gauge, which showed the increasing speed. The speedometer continued to climb as her foot pumped the brakes. Feeling an incredible rush of adrenaline, she grabbed the keys to turn the car off. Ahead, a sign posted a speed limit of twenty-five miles per hour. As they passed it, the car accelerated to sixty. Her heart pounded fiercely against her chest as an oncoming driver blew his horn to signal her to slow down. A "dangerous curve" sign was posted on the next turn and mandated driving fifteen miles per hour. Maintaining her composure, she took up both narrow lanes of the highway as the Range Rover hit seventy. No cars were in sight as her sweaty palms held on tight to the steering wheel, and she hit the next set of spiraling turns. Weaving from side to side on a very steep section, she lost control, and the vehicle flew off the cliff. It sailed forward and then straight down. Her perspiring hands kept a rigid death grip on the wheel. Like an airborne rocket, it soared through the darkness of the night and crash-landed on top of the ocean. She thought she was dead until a wave came rushing across the top of the car, and freezing water poured inside the sunroof, soaking her. The driver's airbag had opened, and she was completely unhurt. Its protection surrounded her as the shocking coldness of the salty water permeated her body.

"Vanessa, are you OK?" Trisha screamed as she unlatched her own seat belt just as the gamy water washed over her face and into her mouth. Spitting it out, she climbed into the back seat and saw Vanessa's bleeding head as the fishy-smelling water surged around them. Her friend was obviously hurt and slightly confused as she hit the button on her seat belt. Helping her dazed friend up onto the roof while spitting the salty water out between her lips, she placed Vanessa's hands on the ski rack and shrieked, "Try and hold on tight!"

"Save my baby," Vanessa whispered through her clenched teeth.

Quickly, Trisha climbed down through the sunroof and into the back seat. Icy water rose briskly inside Brett's car seat as she released the seat belt and yanked it over his head. She pulled the stunned toddler through the sunroof by balancing her feet on the two front seats. With a solid grip on his body, she whisked him onto the top of the car. When she scaled the ceiling, Trisha saw a distant cliff. Taking a deep breath, she jumped from the car's roof into the dark, murky whirlpool of water. A breaker rushed over her just as she surfaced and gulped the nasty saltwater. While gasping for air, she used the side stroke and kept the little boy's head in a lock under her left arm. Trisha swam as fast as she could against the frosty current. It was slack tide. Yet, choppy waves worked against her as she raced to shore. The undrinkable water sucked into her mouth instead of air, and she swallowed it. She came up for a deep breath just as the frigid whitecaps surged over her head. Tasting the salty and foul water in her mouth, she raised her head to gulp the nippy breeze. A glacial chill permeated her body, but she continued to kick as hard as she could while holding Brett's head tightly with her frosty hand. Her body banged against a boulder submerged in the ocean, and it knocked her backward. As the breaker hit the rock again, the rush of water forced her down on to the broken stones below. Her knees collided with sharp gravel as she tried to get up. The swell sent her flying forward into shallow water as she smashed onto the rocks. Her eyes stung so much that she could barely see the rocky beach on which she had landed. As she was dragging herself across the slippery rocks with the choking child in her arms, he threw up all over her. Gently, she placed him onto a patch of sand and kissed his cheek. "Stay here, honey." She looked in the stark darkness for the top of the Range Rover.

Diving back in, she swam past the big rock that she had walloped her body against. Using the breaststroke, she swam as the sheer force of the waves pushed her out to sea. The chrome lining around the roof of the car bobbed in the water with Vanessa's upper body locked around the ski rack. With her feet partially under it, her hands pressed forward in a secure clasp as Trisha spotted her. She yelled just as the salty water rushed into her mouth, and she grabbed on through the opening in the roof. Strong waves smashed against the submerged car as Vanessa swayed up. The car dragged her down. While the wintry water slapped Trisha against the vehicle and with the last strength she could muster, she grabbed Vanessa's waist. "Hold your breath, and breathe when you can." The cold water swirled around them as Trisha knocked her friend over and held her in the "hair carry" position that she had learned in high school. As Vanessa fought to break free, she yanked tightly on her hair and kept swimming. Her arms flailed around and attacked Trisha as she pulled both their bodies through the freezing water. Keeping a firm grip on her friend's hair, she made only slight progress as large waves knocked against them. Panicking, Vanessa hit her, but Trisha stayed focused and kept swimming until they banged into a huge boulder, which threw them both completely underwater. Letting go of her friend for the first time, she felt sharp gravel beneath her feet. As they smashed into the boulder again, a wave crashed over them, and their bodies collided and struck the rock. Pulling herself up, she dragged Vanessa onto the rocky beach. Once they were far enough away from the pounding surf, she went to look for Brett, who was exactly where she had left him.

After picking up the dazed child, she went back to get his mother. Vanessa coughed violently when Trisha slapped her on the back, and a dark vomit erupted from her lips as she continued to throw up until she had dry heaves. Trisha helped her up while holding on to the shivering child. As they moved closer to the cliff, she collapsed on the rocks to catch her breath while Vanessa huddled with her bawling son. Looking around, she wondered how to get off the beach as she stared at the cliff that went straight up to see if there was a way to climb it. The only way out was to scale the steep, vertical bank. "I'm going for help. Don't move, and try to keep Brett warm. Use this dried kelp to huddle under and keep the wind off him."

After struggling to her feet, she wandered around until she noticed an indentation in the bluff. "Move over here so this little cave in the slope can protect you from the cold wind." She nodded as Trisha picked up little Brett to take him over to the tiny alcove. Then, she went back for Vanessa, who clung to her body as she pulled her up. Moving slowly toward the primitive shelter, she helped her onto the rock and grabbed dried kelp to place on top of them. "Hold Brett tight. Your body heat will keep him warm and snug. I'll be back as fast as I can. Hang in there!"

"Remember, a clump of trees," Vanessa whispered weakly.

* * *

Trisha disappeared into the darkness and climbed over the boulders in her way until she saw a light on top of the bluff and decided to ascend the steep bank there. Blood oozed from her mangled feet as she grabbed onto the next rock to pull herself up. With her cut hands and scraped knees, she slowly made her way up the slope. Too afraid to look down, she scaled the cliff, one foot at a time. Bruised and battered, her body banged continuously against the rocky surface while her arms and legs bled unmercifully as she clashed with the cliff of massive stone. She knew the accident was entirely her fault as she inched her way up the mountain. After an exceptionally long, painful climb, she saw the top of the bank within her grasp. Managing to pull her body up one more time, she walloped it against the peak as she crawled on her bloody knees at the summit. Glancing up, she saw a flicker in the distance as she struggled to stand. She wobbled toward the faint light through a clump of trees while the ocean pounded beneath her against the rocks. Dragging herself through the wooded area and toward the illumination, her remaining energy felt restored at the sight of a massive gated entrance.

It was too high to climb over, so she hobbled along by the iron fence and stumbled when pine needles and rocks punctured her bare feet. Hearing voices nearby, Trisha started to trot, and with every step she took, they became louder. After getting closer, she could distinguish they were male voices, but she wasn't sure from where they were coming. Stopping to get her bearings, she realized the voices were coming from people in an outdoor hot tub, less than twenty feet away. As she started to yell out, she heard their distinct male voices quite clearly.

"Son, you won't have to worry about that Black bitch wife of yours. By now, she should be at the bottom of the deep blue sea with that bastard nigger child of hers."

"I hope you're right, father. That Range Rover had an airbag, you know."

"She wasn't driving, son," his father retorted. "My man reported that he disconnected the fitting on the brakes, and her friend was the one who drove away. Besides, if they don't drown, the cold water and sharks should finish them off. Just, be convincing as the grieving widower."

"I will set the standard for mourning!" Tod broke out into laughter as he raised his glass to clink his father's and then took a sip. "A role I was born to play!"

"Son, first it was that Polynesian girl and now this. You're a magnet for Black skin."

* * *

Trisha slowly sank to the dusty ground next to the iron fence and continued to listen to their conversation until they got out of the hot tub and went into their palatial beach house. Stunned, she imagined that she might be dead because this had to be hell! Wavering as she struggled to her feet, she followed the fence until she reached the main highway. Her head throbbing, she felt dizzy as she walked slowly down the paved road until an old truck came by. The cab's dilapidated condition made her almost afraid to stop it. Frantically waving her arms and hands, she put her body in front of the beaten-up vehicle just as it came slowly to a halt. Inside, a weathered-looking Hispanic gardener talked excitedly. Trisha could barely understand the fast-paced Spanish coming from his cracked lips partially hidden beneath his broad straw hat. With her rusty high school Spanish, she managed to ask if she could get into his truck? He shook his head negatively, but she ignored him and opened the door to climb inside. She explained that a car she had driven went over the side of the cliff, and her friend and her baby were still down below. When she mentioned calling the police for assistance, he immediately became agitated and motioned for her to get out. From his violent reaction, she knew he had to be an illegal alien. In desperation, she agreed not to notify the authorities if he would just help to get her friends out. They drove along until they found the exact curve where the car went over the cliff. Then, they looked over the side where the Range Rover had disappeared beneath the surf below. He told Trisha that he did odd jobs along this stretch of Big Sur, and he knew a better way to get to that part of the beach. After driving to a lookout point, they climbed to the beach from there. With some burlap bags and rope that he used for gardening, it was a much easier climb down after what she had just experienced. This entrance had a progression of rocks that acted as a natural staircase.

* * *

When they reached the rocky shoreline, he led the way, as she tried desperately to remember what the beach looked like where she had left them. She yelled their names while they scaled the surrounding boulders. He shouted in Spanish while she screamed in English.

"Over here," Vanessa's weak voice answered from inside the tiny natural cave.

"Thank you, Lord!" Trisha yelled when she saw her trembling friend. Vanessa and Brett were both quivering from the cold as the Hispanic man ran over and covered their shaking bodies with his dry burlap bags. He picked up the toddler and helped Vanessa to her feet. Walking alongside the low tide, they stayed close to the water until they reached the spot where they would begin their climb. The wrinkled old man took Brett right up the side of the mountain without any hesitation as she struggled to hold on to her friend while continuing upward. She pulled Vanessa up after she climbed onto the next rock. He was right. This was a much easier way to get up the bluff since a series of huge boulders created a safer way to scale the steep bank. Trisha begged him to take them to safety when they reached his truck, but he said he had to work and welcomed them to stay inside the cab of his truck. With no alternative, all three huddled together underneath the burlap bags for warmth and soon fell asleep.

* * *

When he returned, he told them he could not take them to the police but would take them to a safe place. Too exhausted to argue with him, she looked at Vanessa as she clung to her child in a mild state of shock.

The gardener drove them to the Mission District of San Francisco. A large Hispanic section of the city, it housed big illegal populations of Mexicans, Central Americans, and South Americans. Poor and crime-ridden, the neighborhood contained some of the city's worst housing projects. Many White San Franciscans, out of fear, never ventured into the Mission. The gardener's family lived above a taqueria on Valencia Street in a one-bedroom flat that housed several families. He took them inside and spoke briefly with his aunt in Spanish. Then, he left to return to what work he could find for that day. Graciously, the old, wrinkled lady offered them dry clothes. The flat was full of children of every age, who stared at them in wonderment with big brown eyes. The elderly woman explained that their family name was Sanchez, and they were originally from Mexico, but they had no papers to be in this country and could not call the police for them. Mrs. Sanchez prepared corn tortillas and offered them the only bed they had. After they ate and drank some water, all three went to sleep in the adjoining room. Trisha closed her eyes and knew that when she awoke, she had to tell Vanessa the truth.

CHAPTER TWENTY-TWO

A frantic call was made to the Monterey County Sheriff Department about the long overdue arrival of Vanessa and Brett Von Westerkamp. Shortly thereafter, two officers met with Alexander and Tod at their opulent beach estate. Alexander immediately demanded that a search be initiated for the missing Range Rover and its occupants. Quickly, they launched a probe of the dangerous curves along the Pacific Coast Highway. Patrol cars were instructed to look for tire tracks in the extensive stretch of roadway cliffs where cars were difficult to maneuver, even under the best of conditions. Days later, skid marks that led off the ridge of the mountain were found.

The Monterey County Search and Rescue divers dove off the coast to locate the vehicle. After an extensive search, the car was found, and well-trained scuba divers performed an investigation inside the car. Two females' purses, belonging to Trisha Bibbs and Vanessa Von Westerkamp, were recovered from a Range Rover registered to Tod Von Westerkamp. Since the scuba divers did not find any bodies in the submerged car, the Coast Guard continued their search for any remains of the three people believed to have been inside the vehicle. After eight days, the Coast Guard called off the search, and the coroner's office ruled on the case. All three were presumed dead. Every newspaper in the state of California made their coverage of the story front page news. The Von Westerkamps demonstrated an enormous outpouring of grief for the electronic media who swarmed over the funeral at Saint Mark's Lutheran Church.

Little Brett's casket was photographed extensively with a huge bouquet of flowers draped over it. The death of one of America's youngest and richest heirs fascinated the public, and the child's picture was shown continuously on television.

* * *

Trisha's sister, Barb, flew in from Texas to take care of her personal effects so she drove to Monterey to speak with the officers who were at the scene of the accident. Dissatisfied with their answers, Barb decided to contact the Homicide Division lieutenant. After she waited for hours, he told his secretary to have her meet with one of his detectives. An angry Barb Bibbs was escorted into Detective Blair Radcliff's office. When she entered his small cubicle, the surfboard leaning against the wall totally infuriated her.

"I can see why it takes so long to get in to see officers around here. The surf must be up!" Irate, she glared at the blond-haired detective and motioned to the surfboard. "Is that your partner?" Standing next to her was a handsome Black man who towered over her. "I can't understand why my sister's case was closed without an investigation. Trisha was an expert swimmer, and that Range Rover had an airbag," Barb rattled on breathlessly.

"Hold on. Calm down! Who are you talking about?" the Black detective asked.

"The Von Westerkamp case! Didn't your lieutenant tell you why I am here?"

"Start from the beginning," the blond detective asked, leaning against his surfboard.

"You are familiar with the Von Westerkamp case, aren't you? It's in your jurisdiction, and why this department thinks it's an open-and-shut case is beyond me. My sister grew up swimming on the treacherous barrier islands of the East Coast. There is no question she could have easily made it to shore. It's a walk in the park for her."

The blond smirked. "Lady, the water out there is fifty degrees, so no one can last long in that freezing water. Trust me! I surf every day in a full body wet suit. The ocean here is bitterly cold, and hypothermia can set in quickly."

"Why was this case closed when no bodies were found? You've got an empty car, so what kind of police work is this? My sister could have gotten them all out of the car and onto the beach. I know it! You have to believe me! She's not dead unless you two produce her body."

"Lady, first, homicide was never even called into this case. And, for one simple reason, there is no case," the blond said sarcastically. "Besides, let's suppose that they got out of the car and reached the beach. Why wouldn't they just go to the nearest phone booth and call home?"

"I don't know why! I thought that's why we paid taxes for police!" Barb argued. "I demand that you launch an investigation immediately."

"No can do, lady! That's up to the lieutenant, not us." The blond got up to escort her out.

"He sent me to you guys. I've read the underwater recovery team report. All the seat belts were unfastened, including the one in the car seat. Doesn't that tell you something? There is no way an eighteen-month-old baby undid his seat belt and climbed out on his own."

"The lieutenant wants to see you both right now," a uniformed officer interrupted them.

"Sorry, Miss Bibbs, the boss man calls." The blond detective motioned her out.

"I'll wait." Barb refused to budge.

"Have it your way." He followed his partner upstairs to their superior's office.

* * *

"Shut the door," their lieutenant ordered. "That woman has been making a lot of waves for you, Radcliff. She's called everyone in the entire state. Both Texas senators called the governor's office. Turns out, the chief went to school with a close friend of her husband's. To satisfy her, he promised we will investigate this matter more thoroughly. Now, go over the report, and make sure nothing was missed. And for God's sake, don't piss off the Von Westerkamps in the process. That's all this department needs are them breathing down our throats. Got it, ladies?"

"Seems like a big waste of time to me."

"Well, girls, that's why we pay you, so we can waste your time," the lieutenant barked. "Get out of my sight and try working for a change. Stay off that damn surfboard!"

* * *

The two detectives went back to their cubicles, where Barb Bibbs was still waiting. The Black detective introduced himself. "My name is Cliff Sillman, and this is Detective Blair Radcliff. We're all yours. Let's start from the beginning." Sitting behind the desk, he took notes while his partner leaned next to his surfboard. Presenting her arguments concerning the disappearance of her sister, she explained that Trisha competed in state swim meets since elementary school and still held many unbreakable records. The detectives promised to review the file and see what might come up. After she left, they confirmed that all the seat belts in the vehicle had been unfastened.

* * *

At the site, they wandered around the beach at low tide. Cliff found a burlap bag used for gardening in an indentation along the cliff. It was folded, which seemed unusual. After talking to people who lived near the site, all of them mentioned a gardener who worked odd jobs along that stretch of the Pacific Coast Highway. After lunch, they spotted an old, dilapidated truck, which fit the description of the gardener's vehicle, and pulled him over.

Cliff spoke fluent Spanish and asked him questions while Blair snooped around the back of his truck. The Hispanic man was extremely nervous, but Cliff figured it was because the laborer was an illegal. Blair came around to the front of the truck with a burlap bag exactly like the one left on the beach. The gardener became fidgety and scared as the detective held the burlap bag in his hands. Anxious, he told them he needed to get back to work and swore that he had seen nothing. After twenty minutes, they decided to let him go, but Cliff decided to drive to San Francisco to speak with Tod Von Westerkamp.

* * *

The next day, Cliff arrived at Tod Von Westerkamp's Seacliff mansion for his scheduled appointment. The butler escorted the detective inside to wait until Tod arrived home from his golf game. While a young maid polished the staircase, Cliff used his fluent command of the Spanish language to flirt with her. Cliff's mother was Puerto Rican, and he had been raised in a bilingual home. The flattered maid smiled as she furnished information about which rooms were Mrs. Von Westerkamp's. Cliff excused himself to go to the bathroom and disappeared down the hall into Vanessa's study. Quietly, he entered the exquisitely decorated room, which was furnished in eighteenth-century antiques. Quickly, Cliff rummaged through the drawers of her desk and came upon an engraved legal-size notebook with a clasp. Curious, he opened the book, but it only held an empty pad of notepaper.

When he started to close it, he felt something under the velvet cover. As he ran his fingers over that section, he discovered a hard object underneath. Cliff searched for a way to get at the firm article and noticed a small hidden zipper under a flap. As he opened the secret compartment, he used his index finger to explore inside, and a small rock fell out and banged on the desktop. Picking it up, he ran the smooth stone through his fingers. As he placed it inside, it hit something that prevented him from sliding it back in. Reaching inside, he retrieved an old black-and-white photograph and glared down at an incredibly young Vanessa Von Westerkamp. Dressed in a prom gown, she stood beside a Black male teenager wearing a tuxedo and a Black nun garbed in a full white habit. The nun stood in the middle with the male's arm around her shoulder, and Vanessa's arm was around her waist. Cliff quickly stuffed the picture into the inner pocket of his coat. Carefully, he put the notebook back in its place and shut the drawer. A bottle of pills in the corner of the desk drew his attention. As he reached for the medicine, an angry Tod Von Westerkamp stormed in just as Cliff slid the bottle into his pocket.

"What is the meaning of this? Who are you?" Tod asked impatiently.

"Detective Cliff Sillman with the MCSD. We had an appointment."

"Is this the latest police procedure, intruding without a search warrant? Rumbling around private possessions without permission? Get the hell out of here. Benjamin, escort him out."

"I profusely apologize, but I got bored waiting all day for you. May I ask a few questions?"

"Very few, now get on with it," Tod snapped.

"Could your wife swim?"

"You didn't drive all the way here to ask a lame question like that. Now, get to the point!"

"Could she?"

"I never saw her go into the pool during our entire marriage."

"Why was your son hospitalized?" Cliff asked.

"Pneumonia. Benjamin, usher Mr. Sillman out. This is a complete waste of my time."

* * *

Cliff got in his car and immediately drove to the Marina District. Barb Bibbs was at her sister's apartment, putting personal effects into boxes. After she buzzed him in, his six-foot-four frame scaled the stairs three at a time, and then he strolled through the open door.

"Detective Sillman, to what do I owe this honor?" Barb looked up from the floor. "I have one hour until I leave for the airport. I could cancel my flight if you need me."

"No, that's not necessary." Cliff plopped his large frame next to her on the carpet and pulled the photograph out of his pocket. "Do you know these people?"

Barb took the old black-and-white photograph into her hands and studied it. "No, but I had a dress exactly like that in high school. That's weird! I'm seven years older so I never met any of her high school friends. Detective, I swear to you, if my sister survived the crash, she got to the shore. She swam every night of the week at the city pools."

"The city pools are a little different than the freezing water and dangerous surf of the Big Sur area. Not to mention the sharks that constantly attack the surfers."

"We grew up swimming in the Atlantic Ocean on a barrier island and were used to the undertow. We knew how to deal with it. I know that you think that I am a crackpot, but until I see a body, I know Trisha made it to the beach. Even as a little kid, she was a swimming phenom."

"What pools did she swim in?"

"Her coworkers said that she went to the Visitation Valley pool every day after work. Check it out. The lifeguards will tell you what kind of swimmer she was."

Cliff got up. "By the way, where did you go to high school?"

"My dad was a career Marine, so I went to high school in three different swamps. You know the Marine Corps, if they find a swamp, they build a base there," Barb answered. "Call me if I can help out. My dad retired at Parris Island, and that's how we got to Charleston."

Cliff disappeared down the stairs and headed to the city pool.

* * *

As he drove up, the pool was surrounded by the most notoriously dangerous housing projects in the entire city. It was a weird place for a White woman to swim. A heavyset Black woman sat behind bulletproof glass. As he produced his badge, the pool's cashier motioned him inside. He wandered through the men's smelly showers, which had a strong disinfectant splashed on the concrete floor. As he entered the pool area, two Black lifeguards sat on top of a platform seat designed for viewing the swimmers. He pulled out his badge. The head lifeguard looked down and asked if he had come about the gangs shooting out their windows. Cliff shook his head and presented a picture of Trisha Bibbs. "Do you know her?"

The head lifeguard nodded. "Yeah, why?"

"What can you tell me about her?"

He looked ahead to the swimmers in the pool. "Nothing, except she swam every night."

"What kind of swimmer was she?"

"Expert."

"What does that mean?"

"She got here when we opened and stayed until we closed. She swam about ten miles a week and kept a good pace," the lifeguard answered but focused his eyes on the lap swimmers.

"Are you aware that she is presumed dead from drowning?"

"Doubtful."

"What do you mean?" Cliff asked curiously.

"Doubtful! That's all."

"Could you please elaborate, sir?"

"Look, man, I don't buy it," the Black lifeguard interjected. "There is no way that woman drowned. No way! Swimmers of her caliber don't drown. The paper said that the airbag opened."

"We don't really have any proof that she was the one driving."

"It's impossible she died from drowning." He looked away from the pool for the first time and focused his eyes on Cliff. "Listen, man, she swam to Alcatraz with the Dolphins, the swim club started in the 1877 to swim in the bay. She swam in the morning in the bay and in the evening with us. That's the type of swimmer she happened to be. That's all I know." His gaze returned to the pool.

* * *

Cliff entered his squad car just when the police radio dispatcher instructed him to return to headquarters. Driving along the highway, he mulled everything over in his mind. Tod's attitude certainly bothered him as he placed the photograph on the dashboard to study it. Cliff was Black. Could Vanessa be Black? Nothing about her even remotely looked like an African American, he reasoned, while scrutinizing her flawless face in the old photograph.

* * *

When Cliff arrived at the Monterey County Sheriff Department, he went straight to his boss's office. "Shut the door, Sillman. You've fucked up big-time. All I wanted you to do was humor that broad, but you go and piss off the Von Westerkamps. The mayor was on my ass all morning, and the chief just gave me a new asshole. What the fuck? Why did you rummage through his house? You didn't have a warrant because there is no crime!"

"I've got some information," Cliff interrupted.

"I don't give a flying fuck if you uncovered Jimmy Hoffa. It's over my head now, and it's coming straight from the top. You've got three weeks' vacation. Take it, and get out of my sight."

"I have something," Cliff argued.

"Get out of my sight, and fuck off. The chief has ordered the file on this case to be closed. You better hope I cool down before you get back, or you will be directing Cannery traffic."

"Please, you should see this," Cliff pleaded.

"Get out. Get out of my office, now!"

Everyone stared as Cliff walked out.

He went to his old desk and sat down to collect his thoughts. The lieutenant's secretary came in. "Cliff, the boss is furious with you. Please leave before he explodes."

* * *

Cliff drove over to his partner's house, a tiny little bungalow near the coast. Like always, he walked right in without knocking. Just back from surfing, his blond hair was still wet.

"Hey, buddy, tell me this isn't happening. What in the hell did you do? The boss is livid."

"Look at this." Sitting down on the worn sofa in the small living room, he pulled the old photograph out of his pocket. Blair plopped down while his wife, Gabrielle, slowly lowered her pregnant body down beside him. Her long blond ponytail came undone as she leaned over to examine the tattered black-and-white photograph.

Gabrielle spoke first. "This photo is vintage sixties, the dress, the tux! See the Spanish moss hanging down from that oak tree. It has to be the Deep South. Nobody back then would go out with a Black man. Look, his class ring is on the nun's shoulder."

"Did you show this to the lieutenant?" Blair asked.

"He wouldn't let me. He threw me out of his office."

"This sure makes this case a whole lot more interesting." Blair looked up as he tossed his wet hair with a towel. "The media would have a field day with this photo."

"There is no case. The lieutenant is closing the file," Cliff interjected.

"Good time to get kicked off a case, Cliff. Who will drive me to the hospital while Blair's surfing?" She kissed Cliff on the cheek. All three studied the picture quietly.

Cliff glanced up. "Blair, go to the lab, and get that ring portion blown up."

"Don't you think we're in enough trouble already? I've got a kid on the way. If you get us kicked off the force, you're going to support my family. I'm on my way." Blair hopped into his old, beat-up Volkswagen and entered the crime lab through the back door.

The technician informed him the enlargement would be ready within the hour if he waited.

Blair went straight home and showed "Bishop England High School, Class of 1968" to his wife and partner. Gabrielle stated the obvious first. "With the nun, at least you know it's a Catholic school. Go ask the Jesuits, who know everything. If they don't, they'll just make it up."

"Good idea, honey. The Jesuits will be more helpful to a woman who is about to deliver."

* * *

All three got in his Volkswagen with the surfboard on top and drove over to the Jesuit Monastery in Monterey. Gabrielle rang the doorbell, and a bald

Jesuit appeared. Innocently, she showed him the old photo. After studying it, the priest lectured, "Young lady, John England graduated from St. Patrick's College in Carlow, Ireland, and became a bishop in 1820. He refused to swear allegiance to the British throne, so Pope Pius XII thought he was in great peril. Pope Pius sent him to the port of Charleston where he became the first bishop of the Carolinas and Georgia, but he had no church. He found a vacant house on Broad and Legare Streets, which is now Charleston's Cathedral. Appalled by slavery, he was outspoken against it. He died in 1842 and is buried in a vault beneath the cathedral. That high school must be in Charleston." Gabrielle thanked him, and he quickly shut the door.

Arriving at the Monterey Public Library minutes before its nine o'clock closing time, they found Bishop England High School listed in the Charleston Yellow Pages. The threesome celebrated their find by going to their favorite burger joint in Monterey.

* * *

The next morning, Cliff called the high school, but there was no Vanessa Vaughn in their academic records. Totally intrigued by the people in the photo, he decided to pursue the case against orders. Using his frequent flyer miles, he flew to the South for the first time in his life. He was operating on pure instinct when he ventured into the part of his country that he had always feared as a Black man.

CHAPTER TWENTY-THREE

Cliff arrived at the Charleston, South Carolina airport and as the electric doors opened, he felt the Carolina humidity on his skin for the first time. Amazed that the weather could be this wickedly hot in early March, he walked outside and felt ill at ease hearing thick Southern accents. Born and raised in mountainous California, he found the terrain unlike anything he had seen before in his life. Inside the rental car, he flipped on the radio, and smiled as he drove into downtown where his rental car bounced off the cobblestone streets. Magnificent antebellum homes stood in preserved grandeur and overlooked a panoramic expanse of South Atlantic waters. But the town was totally flat, not a hill in sight. Antique cannons evoked images of war, and stately oak trees mushroomed above the copper-plated rooftops. The architecture was mesmerizing, and he felt like he had entered another century.

* * *

He located Bishop England High School on Calhoun Street as uniformed teenagers were changing classes. As Cliff entered the hallways, a student directed him to the main office. He presented his badge to the elderly nun behind the front desk. She thought he was here from the Charleston Police Department about the rotten fish put in Saint Mary's statue hands, an impression Cliff found impossible to correct. Although she spent a half hour searching for a record on Vanessa Vaughn, the senile nun could find nothing. She directed him to the library, where another ancient nun showed him the school yearbook section. Pulling out the photograph, he inquired if the fragile nun knew any of these people. She explained that the man in the picture was a young Doctor Hale, a distinguished graduate of the school, who practiced medicine in downtown Charleston.

In the 1968 Bishop England yearbook, he found Barry Hale's senior picture. It was the same man. Searching through every class photograph, he located a sophomore named Vanessa Condon. There she was! Her name was not really Vanessa Vaughn; it was Vanessa Condon. After thanking the nun, he headed for the Charleston County Hall of Records.

* * *

Cliff entered the stately building and went straight to the birth certificate section. Finding no birth certificate for Vanessa Condon, he did find one for Vanessa Vaughn, who happened to be White and born on October 10, 1952. In the bound books containing death certificates, he found a death certificate for Vanessa Vaughn dated February 6, 1953. *Bingo, he thought. I better go pay a visit on Doctor Hale and see what he knows.*

* * *

At Saint Francis Hospital's admitting desk, he asked to see Doctor Hale. The clerk asked which Doctor Hale he wanted to see. One was in surgery, and the other was in his office. Electing to see the one who was available, he listened as the clerk gave him verbal instructions. On the third floor, he just knocked on the office suite's glass. An elderly Black man with solid white hair opened the door. His badge indicated that he was Doctor Hale, Senior.

"May I help you, sir?" he asked politely, with a delightfully sophisticated Southern accent.

"I'm Detective Cliff Sillman from the Monterey, California, Sheriff Department, and I'm investigating a possible homicide," he lied.

"Son, I haven't been in the state of California since I was in the military many, many years ago shipping out to Korea through San Francisco. I doubt I can be of much assistance to you," he answered. "Please have a seat."

"Have you ever known a Vanessa Vaughn?"

"No, Detective. I have not."

"How about a Vanessa Condon?"

Doctor Hale looked incredibly surprised. "Is Vanessa in some kind of trouble?"

Cliff produced the photograph from his pocket and placed it in front of the old surgeon. "Do you know the people in this picture, Doctor Hale?" He took reading glasses out of the pocket of his white coat and put them on. Holding the picture in his hands, he studied it and then put it down. "This is my only son, Barry, Vanessa Condon, and Sister Rosalie, who died some twenty years ago. It's been that long since I've paid my eyes on Vanessa. Is she in trouble?"

"Is Vanessa Black, Doctor Hale?" Cliff asked bluntly.

"That's a mighty strange question, young man. Do you believe that I am Black?"

"I need to speak to your son."

"I implore you not to get him involved in your investigation, Detective. This is a chapter in his life that is best kept closed. As for Vanessa's race, or anyone's race, for that matter, race is now an outdated concept. There has been way too much interbreeding for that idea to survive in today's medical community. Most of the distinctions people make between themselves and others have much more to do with culture than with biology."

"You decline to speculate as to whether she was Black?"

"What does her race have to do with a homicide?" He leaned back with a puzzled look.

"I have this hunch that her husband found out and was none too thrilled. It's a hunch."

"He thought she was Caucasian, you mean?"

"I'm not certain. In this case, nothing seems to be as it appears." Cliff looked over at the pictures on his desk. His son, wife, and grandchild created a twenty-year lapse between the photograph Cliff had. "Thank you for your time, Doctor Hale."

"Detective, my wife, may she rest in peace, also thought Vanessa was Caucasian."

"So did I and all of the San Francisco Bay Area's five million population!"

* * *

Cliff went downstairs to the admitting desk and learned that Barry was performing a nine-hour surgery and would not be free until after seven o'clock. He spent the next couple of hours wandering around on foot and exploring the city's fascinating streets. It was like stepping back into a past century—certainly not a time period he wanted to experience. He got back to the hospital around seven o'clock and sat in the waiting room. The surgical technician had promised that he would have Doctor Hale see him after surgery. It was well after eight o'clock when a tall Black physician in surgical garb appeared. "I'm Doctor Hale. My staff says you needed to speak with me."

Cliff pulled out his sheriff's badge and flashed it. Barry threw his hands up in the air and proclaimed, "Most people wait to see how the patient did before they call the sheriffs in."

"What can you tell me about Vanessa Vaughn?" Cliff asked abruptly. "I mean Vanessa Condon." He took the photograph out of his pocket and gave it to Barry. The surgeon's demeanor changed as he stared blankly at the picture. "Is this the same person?" the detective asked as he produced a current picture of Vanessa Von Westerkamp.

Barry took both snapshots into his hands. "I haven't seen her in over twenty years. She disappeared after Sister Rosalie died."

"Do you know this lady?" Cliff handed Barry a photograph of Trisha Bibbs. "She was with Vanessa when she disappeared."

"I'll be damned, that bitch!" He tossed the photo back at the detective.

"Any place in this city where two brothers can safely go to have a beer together? I'll buy."

"This town is like any other place in this country. Educated, tolerant people exist beside uneducated, intolerant people. The South is no different than the rest of this country. Got it?"

"Got it!" he muttered as he followed the surgeon, who took the steps three at a time just like Cliff always did.

CHAPTER TWENTY-THREE

* * *

A couple of blocks away, they entered a small, dimly lit pub where a platter of spicy Charleston shrimp was placed on the bar. Barry ordered a couple of draft beers and grabbed the cold mugs with one hand and a large plate of shrimp with the other. Cliff followed him over to a corner booth, and they sat down. He stared at Barry in his green surgical pants and top as he sipped his beer. The surgeon explained that Vanessa had disappeared over twenty years ago without a trace, but he knew that she would have stayed connected with her best friend. But Trisha always denied knowing what happened to Vanessa.

After devouring the shrimp, they ordered another round of beer. Barry insisted that Cliff try some Charleston she crab soup, since he had never been to the low country. He loved it and ate three large bowls as he brought Barry up to date on Vanessa's life over the last two decades.

"Why are you here? Do you suspect foul play?"

"Her sister, Barb, thinks it is absolutely impossible that Trisha drowned."

"Gee, I totally forgot she had a sister," he commented. "She was a lot older than we were and was away at college. I never met her. She's right, you know. Trisha was a fish."

"You mean she drank like a fish or swam like a fish?" he asked innocently.

"Both! Those two women, what a deadly combination! Trisha swam on Folly Island. It has the most treacherous undercurrents in the world. Every year, tourists who do not respect the mighty Atlantic Ocean drown. I'd bet my medical license on her making it to the shore!"

The detective pulled the bottle of prescription medicine out of his pocket and handed it to Barry. "Why would an eighteen-month-old baby need this type of drug?"

He read the label. "I'd need to see the chart, but he was obviously in some type of pain. What did the pediatrician say?"

"Pneumonia."

"Pneumonia? Do you have the lab work?"

"No, but my hunch is it's all related to the baby and his hospital stay. The Von Westerkamp family has given millions of dollars to that hospital which built two additional wings. Now that I'm here, I don't like the way this thing smells."

"Could you get me a copy of his blood test? That would tell us a whole lot about the child and what happened in the hospital," Barry interjected.

"Let me ask you a question. What are you doing this weekend?"

"I'm not on call again until Tuesday night, so I'm going fishing this weekend."

"How about going fishing in the San Francisco Bay? I know a fabulous spot."

"Detective, I have never done one impulsive thing in my entire life."

"It's the most beautiful bay in the world," Cliff said enticingly. "If the answer lies inside that hospital, you are the only one who can find it out. I certainly know zero about medicine." Barry started laughing. "I don't get it, Doc. What's so funny?"

"The idea of taking off for the West Coast. It's wild, completely absurd, and totally out of character for me."

"Then, let's go. I'll even spring for your ticket with my frequent flyer miles."

"Hold on a minute! Just a little matter of a child, an ex-wife, and a busy practice."

"That's all? We're out of here! I'm great with wives. Just ask my partner."

"I'll make you a deal!".

"You can get me a weekend pass with the boss lady, I'll go." He reached across the table to shake his hand. "We've been divorced for five years but co-parent."

"Deal!" Cliff shook his hand with a firm grasp.

* * *

Following in his rental car behind Barry, he pulled up in front of a huge home near the Citadel. Spanish moss hung from large oak trees, and massive white columns in the front supported a large porch. Once inside the towering double doors, Cliff glanced around the impeccably furnished home with its grand foyer and massive spiral staircase.

Barry's ex-wife, Michelle, greeted them and was a very gracious hostess. The detective explained the case, while she asked dozens of questions in her thick Bostonian accent. She tried to clarify what help her ex-husband could be to the California Sheriff's Department. Michelle was the chief pathologist in charge of the hospital's laboratory, so she briefed him on lab report results and procedures. As they tried to unravel the mystery surrounding this case, Barry put his son to bed. When he rejoined them, Cliff winked at Barry since Michelle had already agreed to let her ex-husband escort Cliff to the West Coast. Indeed, the single bachelor had charmed another wife because Barry had his son this weekend.

* * *

Their 5:00 a.m. flight landed at San Francisco International Airport at 10:00 a.m. They drove straight to Pacific Hospital and along the bay Cliff pointed out Candlestick Park. "Let me ask you a question, Barry. Was it a choice between Vanessa and Michelle?"

"For my parents, there was no choice. They ran the show. God, she was beautiful! The truth is I never stopped loving her. To this day, she is never far from my thoughts."

"Let's hope she's still alive," Cliff retorted as he turned off the ignition in front of the hospital. "I need to tell you I got thrown off this case. If I go inside with you, I lose my badge."

"Great time to tell me that I have no backup."

"You mean you're not going to punch me out?"

"I hate to break it to you, but my father called your department right after you left his office. He sent a note to me in surgery, specifically telling me not to talk to a renegade officer. You see, we Southerners are not only dumb but a highly suspicious lot." Barry's eyes twinkled. "Besides, you'll just get in my way."

"Take this beeper just in case you get into any trouble. If I don't hear from you, I'll know something has gone wrong. Got it?"

"Got it!" Barry grabbed his white medical coat from the back seat. After he got out, he put it on and walked briskly toward the front entrance.

* * *

As the door opened, the full implications of being inside a San Francisco hospital hit him. To get his bearings, he decided to go to the doctor's lounge. After entering the room, Barry sat down on the sofa and tried to act casual as he picked up a copy of the *New England Journal of Medicine* to thumb through. He felt like someone was staring at him, so he glanced up and met the eyes of a young man, who jumped up.

"Barry! Barry Hale! Do you remember me? I was at Harvard Medical School while you were doing your residency. I was assigned to your group my first year," the red-haired man exclaimed excitedly. He didn't remember him but tried to search his brain for any vague clue or recollection. "Lance Paine. I'm Lance Paine." He shook his hand. It's great to see you. You were my idol. What are you doing here?"

He gained his composure and decided to level with his fellow Harvard alumnus. "I have an old friend, Vanessa Condon. I mean Vanessa Von Westerkamp. Do you know her?" he asked.

"Who doesn't? The case has been covered extensively by the media. Did you know her?"

"We were old classmates," he answered cavalierly. "I was personally very perplexed by her son's illness. What is your position here, Lance?"

"I'm the chief pathologist," he answered proudly.

"It's highly unusual, but is there any way I could look at her son's lab results?"

"Unless you have admitting privileges, you know I can't do that. It's against regulations."

"I know. Forgive me for even suggesting such an impropriety. I deal with death through my medical work. I just thought maybe out of professional courtesy, I could take a peek."

"I don't know; that's highly irregular," Lance insisted.

Deciding to change the subject, Barry talked about the old days at Harvard. They shared information about old colleagues and where they were practicing medicine. They gossiped extensively about the teaching staff and who was still there. Finally, Lance leaned over. "All right, as you say. I will let you peek out of professional courtesy."

"Thank you, Doctor Paine. I know it's silly and illogical, but I just want to look" He lied convincingly. They got up as the door swung open. The chief administrator, Dr. North, entered.

"Hello, Doctor North. This is an old colleague from Harvard, Doctor Barry Hale."

"What brings you to San Francisco?" The two physicians shook hands.

"I'm here to do some fishing," Barry lied. "Nice meeting you. This is a fabulous facility."

"Do you always wear your lab coat to go fishing, Doctor Hale?" Doctor North asked.

"Had to make sure Lance remembered me." He smiled.

After they left, Doctor North thought it was quite odd. Lance and Barry took the stairwell and entered pathology. Lance shut his office door, sat down, and signed on to his computer. Within moments, he pulled up the lab results of the patient, Brett Von Westerkamp. He swiveled the screen around, so Barry could read it. Completely in order and normal. Nothing was unusual.

"This tells me very little. Will there be any difference on the floppy?" He looked up.

"There shouldn't be. Old records are loaded onto magnetic tapes for storage. This has not been stored on a floppy yet," Doctor Paine answered.

"Where do you keep the lab worksheets?" He asked a question Michelle had insisted on.

"We store them in the basement and keep them for two years in boxes by chronological order. If you think I will go down to that God-forsaken basement and look through dozens of boxes with you, you've lost it. That, I will not do!"

"Would you mind if looked for the worksheet? I have taken enough of your precious time. I could do this myself if you don't mind?" Barry said convincingly.

"Doctor Hale, if you are crazy enough to go and look through hundreds of worksheets, be my guest! Just don't expect any help." Lance nodded his head in disbelief.

"Deal!" Barry shook Lance's hand. "Show me the way, and I will get out of your hair."

* * *

Lance's technician, an older Asian lady, escorted Doctor Hale down to the damp basement. Bare light bulbs hung down creating an eerie feeling as she told him she had rarely been down there in all her years at the hospital. She wasn't sure about the correct storage procedure for the worksheets but she mentioned they were required by law to keep the worksheets for two years. She helped Barry get started and then excused herself after a few minutes. The dim lighting made it exceedingly difficult to read the lab sheets, and many days were not in the correct order as he flipped through them. It was a tedious task, but Barry was patient.

Lance came down and Barry promised to call him if he found anything unusual. Lance invited him to lunch the next day so that they could catch up.

* * *

Doctor North was paranoid and couldn't get the Black doctor out of his mind. Why have a physician's coat on when he was here to go fishing? He called down to the lab before going home. "Let me speak to Doctor Paine!" he barked.

"He's left for the day, Doctor North," the technician replied.

"Did Doctor Paine's friend go with him?" he inquired.

"No, sir, he is still in the basement looking through old worksheets," she answered.

He slammed down the phone. "Damn it! I forgot the damn worksheet!" he yelled into his empty office. "The one damn way they can trace it!" Running past his secretary's empty desk, he sprinted to the elevator, and as his heart pounded, he quickly realized the true implications of his screw-up. The original results of the blood smear from the lab would show a cover-up had taken place. As he watched each floor light during the elevator's descent, sweat permeated his clothes.

* * *

"Got it!" Barry said out loud as he read Brett Von Westerkamp's name at the top of the worksheet. Quickly, he read the lab results, indicating that the cells were sickling. "The child was in sickle cell crisis." *Oh my God, she was Black! All those years with Michelle, and Vanessa was Black*, he thought. He stuffed the worksheet into his coat pocket and crammed the rest back into the box. He got on his knees and slid the carton back on the shelf.

Doctor North surprised him from behind. "Find what you were looking for? I assume you must be an old Negro relative," he said maliciously.

"Actually, my parents always thought she was White." Barry got up from the floor. "They were wrong, weren't they, Doctor North?"

"Quite wrong, actually." The tone of his voice was full of venom. "I would venture to say that Vanessa was a full-blooded Negroid just like you."

"Is that so?" Calmly, Barry reached into his pocket and pressed the button on the beeper to alert Cliff. This man was a combination of every racist he had ever encountered.

"Give me the worksheet!" he shouted as he held out his hand.

"Sorry, buddy, no can do." Barry moved just as Richard North lunged at his chest, and the impact sent him flying backward, landing him against the temporary shelves, which came crashing down on top of him. Doctor North kicked him in the stomach until Barry could regain his footing and get up. They struck each other furiously as their battle moved them through the medical equipment storage area. The two men smashed against old hospital beds and gurneys on wheels as they fought. Barry lunged forward and managed to ram Doctor North into a nearby wheelchair. He released the brake, which sent him plunging across the floor. Grabbing an old microscope off the shelf, he pounded Doctor North in the face. His own blood ran down his face and into his eyes, blinding him. Doctor North grabbed the instrument that had struck his forehead and whipped around to tackle Barry and club him with the fixture by striking him on the head. Barry snatched the cord of the overhead light and tried to strangle Doctor North by placing it tightly around his neck. Doctor North reached for the cord with his fingers around his throat and kicked Barry with his feet as he struggled to free himself. Both men bled profusely as they beat each other unmercifully with the old hospital instruments that they managed to snatch off the shelves.

Barry grabbed a heavy metal bedpan and walloped Doctor North in the chest, knocking him to the floor as North thrust his feet forward when Barry approached. They rolled around on the cement floor as their assault on one another moved them closer to old surgical instruments. Doctor North spotted an old metal surgical tray and clutched it in his hand to clobber Barry's head.

As he turned to strike, an old scalpel fell out of the tray and onto the floor. Both men leaped toward the instrument with which they were uniquely familiar. Doctor North grabbed it first and lunged toward Barry. He stabbed him repeatedly in the chest, and Barry fell to the floor in a heap, surrounded by his own blood as Doctor North stumbled to his feet. As Doctor North limped toward the door, Barry grabbed his feet, and he crashed onto the floor. Blinded, Barry relentlessly pounded him with his fists in a violent attack to prevent his escape.

* * *

When the beeper went off, Cliff ran to the laboratory, and the Asian technician told him Doctor Hale was down in the basement. Quickly taking the stairs three at a time, he reached the storage area where the door was wide open. Inside was total chaos with equipment scattered everywhere. Cliff found Barry huddled in a heap with blood everywhere. As the detective took him into his arms, Barry whispered, "Sickle cell crisis. Pocket. And you think we Southerners are slow. You Californians are slower!" His eye lids closed as Cliff reached into Barry's coat to retrieve the lab worksheet. Sliding it into his jacket, he ran and found a nurse on the next floor. She paged, citing a code blue. Cliff stayed with Barry until he was wheeled away, and the nurse instructed him to wait in the lounge area.

Cliff went to a phone booth and called his partner. "Blair, the kid had sickle cell. It's on the lab report."

"Bull's eye! Now get the hell out of there before we get kicked off the force."

"Did you find anything out on that end?"

"Yeah, I've been surfing along that stretch of Highway One, and that same gardener is there every day. He's got to know something."

"Go after him!"

"No can do, buddy. The guy doesn't speak a word of English. I need the Puerto Rican Romeo. Get your buns down here now."

"Meet me at the spot where they went over and have him there." He hung up.

* * *

Arriving later, Cliff drove up next to his partner's beat-up Volkswagen. Blair stood by the side of the road with the Hispanic gardener and his dilapidated truck. The elderly man appeared visibly shaken and extremely nervous. When Cliff interrogated him in fluent Spanish, he maintained that he knew nothing. Agitated and upset about Barry Hale, he threw the older man against his truck and asked for his immigration papers. Begging for mercy, he told the detective that he had nine children and cousins to feed. Shouting in Spanish, Cliff told him to start talking, or he was going to call immigration. He threatened the poor man and told him he would never see his family again. As he physically held tightly on to him, the gardener told them everything. He had fed and housed the three, but the baby got sick, so he took them to Mission Dolores Convent, where they were hiding with the nuns.

Cliff let go of him and yelled, "Let's go! I don't have any gas. Let's take yours." Both detectives jumped into the Volkswagen and headed for the Mission District in San Francisco.

* * *

When they arrived at the Mission Dolores Convent, Sister Superior answered the main door, and Cliff presented his police badge. "Son, your credentials mean nothing in the house of the Lord," the nun said softly as she started to shut the door. He put his foot in the doorway and forced it to stay open. "Listen, Sister. These women are in a lot of trouble. We can help them."

"Shall I call the police, gentlemen?" the nun countered.

"We are Sheriffs," Blair interjected as he tossed his bleached-blond hair back.

"Good day, gentlemen." She slammed the door and threw all her weight behind it.

"I thought you were Catholic?" Blair asked disgustedly. "You sure aren't good at charming the nuns. Now, we have to break into this holy place, and the lieutenant is going freak out. Not to mention the Big Lieutenant in the sky!" He glanced up at the church's bell tower.

"Good idea, beach boy." He went around back with his partner.

After scaling the side of the convent, they climbed in through a window on the second floor. Quietly, they peered into the empty hallway but heard singing from the upper story. He motioned to go right as he took off down the corridor to the left. Each man softly opened every door they passed and looked inside. Each room was stark except for a single twin bed, a crucifix hanging overhead, and a tiny nightstand.

When Blair opened the very last door, a blond lady screamed at the sight of him. He slammed the door shut behind him and told her not to be afraid. He pulled out his badge and flashed it. "Don't be alarmed! I'm here to help you. I'm Blair Radcliff with the Monterey County Sheriff Department."

"You scared the hell out of me," Trisha replied nervously. "You sure don't look like it. You look like a refugee from a beach movie! Do you always work in your bathing suit?"

Cliff heard the scream, ran down the hall, and entered. "Gee, Miss Bibbs, you're not supposed to be alive. The lifeguards were right about your swimming ability."

"I'm a great floater," she cracked. "My thighs are the best flotation devices ever created!"

"Did the others make it?" Cliff pulled his badge out of his pocket to present.

"Were you sent by the Von Westerkamps to finish their botched job?"

"You will be perfectly safe now," Cliff assured her.

"Give me one reason why I should trust you two? You are probably on their payroll."

"We are here to help, and you really don't have many options," Cliff argued. "Now, is Mrs. Von Westerkamp alive or not? Barry Hale wants to know."

"What did you just say?" Trisha asked excitedly. Cliff sat down next on the bed to explain everything. "You left Barry at that hospital? Are you nuts? If he isn't dead, he will be soon. The Von Westerkamps control that hospital. He won't get out of there alive," she blurted out and jumped up. "We've got to get him out of there now!" Cliff knew that she was right and was angry at himself for not anticipating that could happen. Trisha showed them a way out of the convent through a back door. They ran across the courtyard, and all three jumped into Blair's Volkswagen and took off for Pacific Hospital.

* * *

Doctor Lance Paine felt totally responsible for the assault on Doctor Hale. He checked on him as much as possible after surgery for severe chest wounds. The

San Francisco Police Department had no clues as to who had committed the attack. Within minutes, the Volkswagen roared up to the hospital entrance. Trisha and the two detectives ran into the lobby and asked the receptionist for Doctor Hale's room number. Only immediate family members were allowed to see him. Trisha lied and said that Doctor Hale was her husband, so the clerk pointed the way to the elevator. Knowing they were not allowed in, the detectives strolled casually until the clerk turned her back. Then, they ran to the stairs and sprinted all the way to the fourth floor.

When the elevator opened, Trisha ran through the hall, reading the numbers on the doors. Entering the room, she noticed a pair of shiny black shoes exposed beneath the curtain. Pulling it back, she saw the savagely beaten face of Doctor Richard North bending over Barry with a needle in his hand. She instantly recognized him from the wedding and knew he was a close friend of Alexander Von Westerkamp. "What are you doing?" Trisha screamed at the top of her lungs, which startled Doctor North. She lunged forward to get the needle and knocked over the IV stand, which came crashing down on top of Barry's body. She grabbed Doctor North and struggled with him as he took the needle and accidentally plunged it into her arm. Stumbling backward, she fell against the bed onto the floor.

* * *

As the two detectives arrived, Doctor North disappeared down the hall and into an emergency exit. At a full sprint, Cliff and Blair followed in pursuit, past Trisha's collapsed body as the nurse screamed at them to stop. They chased him up the stairwell until he went through another emergency exit. It led to the construction site of the new Von Westerkamp wing being built. The carpenters had finished for the day, and the framing was completely deserted, exposing the city lights in the distance. There were no walls, just the steel I-beam framing for the new addition and the concrete floor. The detectives entered the open construction site.

Doctor North was cowering behind an electric power saw stand and some uncut lumber. The partners motioned to each other to spread out. After a few moments, Blair spotted him and approached from behind. Doctor North turned around with a rigging ax in his right hand and a clawhammer in his left. He swung wildly with both hands as Blair picked up a drill and took a swing at him. He quickly knocked it out of his hands with the rigging ax. Blair nabbed a staple hammer off a nearby work bench and headed back toward the physician.

Doctor North grabbed a portable power saw as Blair picked up a piece of lumber for protection. The doctor sawed the wood he was holding in half as Blair backed up, drew his gun, and told him to drop the saw. Doctor North threw the saw straight at him as the detective fired. The bullet ricocheted off the power saw, which was still running. The doctor threw a bucket at Blair as he tried to knock the gun out of his hand. A shower of nails landed on top of Blair, but he was able to hold onto his gun as Cliff approached from behind. Doctor North turned on the power nail gun in his hand and sprayed nails straight at him as he turned. Blair fired his gun again and hit Doctor North in the arm. He staggered backward with a look of utter horror on his face and crashed through an unfinished structure, screaming as he fell to his death. They went over to the ledge and looked at the body heaped on the surface, six stories below. Hospital security guards arrived at the scene with their guns drawn. The detectives raised their hands in surrender and yelled, "Monterey County Sheriff." After producing their badges, the guards escorted them off the construction site. They learned that Trisha was in critical condition and fighting for her life. Her chances of survival were not good since she had been injected with a highly toxic substance.

* * *

"We got to get to the convent. Step on it. Make this buggy move!" Cliff yelled.

They arrived at the convent and a young novice answered the door, and Blair blatantly flirted with the youthful nun as she giggled in return. Sister Superior had not yet returned from Saint Mary's Hospital, but they could wait if they liked. Instead, they pushed past her and started to go through every room, bathroom, and closet in the building. Vanessa and her baby were not in the building, so they went back to the parking lot and jumped in the Volkswagen.

"Cliff, the Von Westerkamps were scheduled to play at the Pebble Beach Golf Tournament today. This is too good to be true. They are back within our jurisdiction!" Blair exclaimed. He cranked up the volume on the radio as the car jerked forward. "Even money says that by the time we get there, they are on the nineteenth hole."

* * *

At Pebble Beach, the most exclusive private club in the country, Cliff and Blair watched from the sidelines while the golfers made their rounds through the magnificently landscaped course, nestled in the Del Monte Forest. They waited patiently for the Von Westerkamp men to finish. The golf carts were artfully arranged in rows outside the clubhouse, which overlooked the Pacific Ocean. The golf pro told them the Von Westerkamps were in the Tap Room at their usual table next to the memorial wall dedicated to Bing Crosby.

The bar was full as they entered. Men dressed in golfing attire were joking and laughing among themselves. Cliff spotted Tod Von Westerkamp seated at a table with eight gentlemen. Across from him was his father, Alexander. Cliff casually strolled over to their table, which was filled with mixed drinks, and threw his badge down in front of Tod. "You're under arrest for the attempted murder of Vanessa Von Westerkamp, Brett Von Westerkamp, and Trisha Bibbs. You have the right to remain silent," Cliff read them their Miranda rights.

Blair approached Alexander from behind and handcuffed him as he screamed, "Charles, call the police!"

The bartender immediately picked up the phone behind the bar to dial 911.

"Sorry, sweetheart, we are the Sheriffs," Blair retorted as he dragged Alexander outside.

Tod yelled as he ran, "This is a setup! They aren't real cops!" Cliff chased after him and tackled him from behind. Pulling him down to the floor to subdue him, he handcuffed his wrists behind his back. A hush fell over the bar as the detectives pushed the two men outside. The golfers sat in stunned silence as Cliff dragged him over to the Volkswagen and threw him into the back seat with his father. Blair put the car into first gear and drove quietly out of the Pebble Beach Golf Club. As he passed the tree-lined entrance, police cars with their sirens wailing and lights flashing sped past them.

* * *

Cliff and Blair were called into their lieutenant's office. He slammed the door behind them and barked, "You two fuck-ups, let's go over this case that I personally threw you off of two weeks ago. One, I have a dead head of hospital. Two, I have a near-dead Trisha Bibbs. Three, I have a close-to-dead doctor from South Carolina. Lord only knows what he has to do with this! And last, but certainly not least, I have every god damn politician in this state on my ass and the mayor's ass. With one phone call, the Von Westerkamps have put together enough legal muscle to close this department down permanently! We've got a battalion of attorneys on our ass to release them. You know, Radcliff, I always figured you had brain damage from spending too much time on that surfboard of yours. The sun fried your brains, and what you had left, you banged into that blasted board. But, Sillman, you never had a fucking brain to begin with! You're just a big fucking fuck-up! Now, where is Vanessa Von Westerkamp, or did you two fuck-ups manage to kill her off too?"

Blair squirmed in his seat uncomfortably. "We're not sure, sir."

"What the fuck?" the lieutenant roared.

"We're not completely sure, sir." Cliff tried to shield his partner from the wrath that was about to fall on them. "Trisha Bibbs refused to reveal her location."

"Ladies," the lieutenant ranted with absolute fury in his voice. "Get your two asses out there, and don't come back without her. And for God's sake, don't kill her in the process. Now, get the fuck out of my sight!" Cliff and Blair hurried for the door. "Ladies, a barge brought up the car today. Looks like you two fucked-up vaginas got lucky." He deadpanned.

"Someone tampered with the brakes?" Blair asked, wanting a positive confirmation.

"You got lucky, beach boy. That's all! Now get the fuck out of here before we have a lot more dead people filling up the morgue!" he screamed. "Find her and the kid, you two morons."

* * *

Once downstairs, they hopped into Blair's Volkswagen and took off for San Francisco. "Where do you think she is?" Cliff asked, as his partner threw the car into reverse.

"Those nuns must know, so how about this time, I try to use some of my California boy charm on them?" Blair grabbed his sunglasses out of the dashboard.

"You can't do any worse than I did."

"You spent twelve years in Catholic school," Blair cracked. "Let's go!"

"Where?" Cliff asked, puzzled.

"To the only place a mother would be with a baby who has sickle cell," Blair yelled. "God, I'm going to be a great parent," he declared as he quickly drove over to Saint Mary's Hospital.

* * *

They ran inside and went straight to the pediatric ward. They slipped past the nurses' station, pretending to be visiting parents. Wandering from room to room, they looked inside each one and apologized to the parents for intruding on their privacy. Finally, they entered a private room where a nun was rocking a toddler to sleep in her arms.

"Sorry, Sister," Blair apologized as Cliff placed his hand on the doorknob and prevented his partner from shutting it. Not answering, the nun glanced down at the floor to shield her face. Cliff walked inside the room and stood in front of the nun as he peered into the stunningly beautiful face of Vanessa Van Westerkamp. She clutched her son closely to her chest and held him tightly while keeping her eyes fixed on the floor.

Cliff spoke first. "Don't be alarmed, Mrs. Van Westerkamp. We are here to help you. We are detectives with the Monterey County Sheriff Department and have been searching a long time for you. You're safe now and have nothing to be afraid of because you're under our protection."

Vanessa looked at Cliff. She was the most gorgeous woman he had ever seen as he dropped to his knees and placed his hands on the arms of the rocking chair to console her. Neither man tried to speak as she wept silently. When she regained her composure, she asked about Trisha. Both men glanced down, and Blair answered that she was at the hospital with Barry Hale. After a few seconds, Cliff asked if she would like to see them. Vanessa stared at him in disbelief but nodded her head affirmatively. In a consoling voice, Cliff explained that he had gone to Charleston to seek Barry's help and that Barry was now nearby. He asked if the baby needed to stay there, so she explained Brett was fine, but the nuns felt like the Catholic hospital was the best and safest place for them to hide. The toddler was asleep, so she entrusted his care to the pediatric nurses who came into the hospital room.

* * *

They left Saint Mary's and drove over to Pacific Hospital. Silently, they sneaked past the nurses' station and escorted Vanessa into Barry's room. Once behind the curtain, she laid eyes on Barry for the first time in over twenty years. His eyes opened and flickered with recognition as she bent down and buried her face in his chest. Barry moved his arm around her as she sobbed uncontrollably, but he managed a big smile for the two detectives standing behind her.

"Oh, Barry, you never should have come," she cried. "I caused this. It's all my fault."

"I'm fine. In my field, we call this an IV drip nap." He hugged her as his IV dangled.

Vanessa looked up and stared into his face for the first time in two decades. Just inches away, she studied his features. His face was cut and swollen with one eye totally blackened. His cheeks were bruised and bloody. Although he looked a lot older than when she had last seen him, his expression was unchanged, and his appearance was still charmingly handsome. Inside her chest, she felt that pounding that she had always experienced in his presence. Her feelings were as strong now as they had been when she was a teenager. She leaned over and kissed him softly on his battered lips. She ran her hands through his hair and let her fingers linger there. "I still love you. I never stopped loving you," Vanessa whispered into his ear while kissing it.

"Me too," Barry answered so softly that she wasn't sure if he had really said it. "Me too." He stroked her back. "Me too," he said for a third time as his brown eyes squinted.

"You'll have to leave now," a nurse announced in a stern voice.

"She stays, nurse. You're the one that needs to leave," Barry ordered as the detectives shrugged their shoulders at the nurse. "Cliff, why don't you and your buddy take a hike? The show's over, so take the hint, guys." He focused back on Vanessa and pulled her up on the hospital bed with his strong, muscular arms and kissed her passionately. "Vanessa, don't leave me. Don't ever leave me again. I've loved you and no one else since I was a teenager. Now, it's our turn to be together. And I promise you, we will spend the rest of our lives together, so help me God."

Printed in the USA
CPSIA information can be obtained
at www.ICGtesting.com
LVHW012315100824
787895LV00012B/469